TEN TRENDS TO SEDUCE YOUR BESTFRIEND

PENNY REID

WWW.PENNYREID.NINJA/NEWSLETTER/

COPYRIGHT

This book is a work of fiction. Names, characters, places, rants, facts, contrivances, and incidents are either the product of the author's questionable imagination or are used factitiously. Any resemblance to actual persons, living or dead or undead, events, locales is entirely coincidental if not somewhat disturbing/concerning.

Made in the United States of America

Print Edition

ISBN: 978-1-942874-84-3

DEDICATION

For Nora.

CHAPTER 1
WINNIE

"I've said it before and I'll say it again, a spectrophotometer has innumerable uses." The words left my mouth as the unmistakable and unexpected sound of the front door opening met my ears.

I glanced at the clock on my phone while carefully cloaking my confusion. Two voices sounded from the entryway. My roommate, Amelia, home from work way, *way* earlier than usual, had brought someone with her. No big deal. I was almost finished with today's live video. All that remained was the wrap-up.

"For those of you who've tuned in before, you already know Mable." I lifted the spectrophotometer with both hands, showing it to my audience. "I picked Mable up on eBay for a mere twenty-five dollars. She's a Fisher Unico 1000, if any of you want to use the same instrument when you replicate this experiment with your own sports drinks at home." The tan plastic of the spectrophotometer had scratches and dings, but it worked fine. "Mable is an older model, but I find value in doing some things old school, you know? If old school isn't for you, the newer ones are Bluetooth compatible and much smaller. The readouts will sync directly to the app, saving you from having to record your findings with these prehistoric tools." Giving the live audience a wry grin, I lifted my number 2 pencil and college ruled notebook paper.

Most of my videos were done in the kitchen of the one-bedroom apartment Amelia and I shared in First Hill, a neighborhood east of downtown

Seattle. Our center-of-the-old-house-top-floor apartment only had one window (in the bathroom), but it did have several skylights. On sunny days —despite the rumors, Seattle has plenty sunny days from May to September —the kitchen had the best light.

As it was not yet May, today was not a sunny day, but the kitchen still had the best light.

"Win? Are you here?" Amelia's voice carried to me, which meant my viewers could hear her as well.

"That's my lovely roommate, so unless Go Direct wants to sponsor this account and send me a brand new SpectroVis Plus Spectrophotometer— which, for the record, I would name Brad and love with all my heart—I guess that's all for today. I hope you enjoyed today's lesson. Or—" I winked at the camera "—at the very least, you'll think twice before picking up any red sports drinks."

"Fred is here?"

I stiffened, unable to halt or conceal my visceral reaction. Only one person called me "Fred."

What is he doing here? I hadn't seen him in weeks.

The swirling in my stomach demanded I forgo my planned wrap-up spiel in favor of ending the live video as soon as possible. Lifting my thumb to the screen, I rushed to say, "Till next time, this is the Chemistry Maven signing—"

I was too late.

Byron had jogged up behind where I stood, encircled my wrist with one of his big man hands, and pulled it away from my phone. The light, warm scent of his pine and sandalwood aftershave battered my senses. I felt my lashes flutter, but I did stop myself short of sucking in a startled breath as his face came into view next to mine.

On my phone screen.

During my live video.

Byron bent and placed his chin on my shoulder, his clean-shaven but somehow perpetually scruffy cheek sliding along mine, his stomach and chest brushing against my back. He'd randomly started doing this kind of stuff about two years ago—brushing against me, gently pushing my hair off my shoulder, touching my hip as he passed behind—like he knew how much the benign contact flustered me when he was the one doing it. Everywhere he touched scorched my skin, incidental or purposeful, it didn't matter how long it had been since we last saw each other or how little we actually spoke.

I ignored another twist in my stomach, irritated with my body for being entirely predictable.

"What are you doing, Fred?" The question was a rumble. A dark, thick slash of an eyebrow arched over a pale blue-green eye as he inspected the image of us captured by my phone's screen. His hands slid to my hips, and he stared at us for a moment while my mouth opened and closed unproductively, mind blank, chest hot, cheeks pink.

Darn it.

I was a people person! I loved hugs and cuddles, and I was generous with physical affection. If a different person had come in here and placed their chin on my shoulder, I wouldn't have thought twice about it. My friends had labeled me "the touchy feely one" as I freely cried at movies, poignant greeting cards, or excellent commercials. I was good on my feet, good under pressure, good at improvising.

I knew I would spend the rest of this afternoon feeling like a goofus for being so entirely rattled and incapable of forming words the moment Byron had stepped behind me.

Darn it all to heck!

While I wrestled my brain, he squinted, flinching away at the emojis erupting around our faces. "Wait. What is this?"

The thinly veiled disapproval in his tone smacked me out of my daze and I fought against an eye roll—at myself—but I did grit my teeth. "Everyone, say hi to Byron. Byron, say hi to everyone." My statement was met with a plethora of waves, shocked faces, and heart-eyes emojis. I quickly read the torrent of new comments as heat climbed up my neck.

Who is that?

He's soooo hot.

He has the prettiest eyes

Wait. That's Byron Visser. HOLY SHIT!

OMG! Is that Byron Visser??!?!

Is that your boyfriend?

How the hell do you know Byron Visser?

THAT'S BYRON VISSER!

Do you actually know Byron Visser?

I LOVE YOUR BOOKS BYRON!!

Ask him when the third book will come out. I NEEEEED IT!

Only mildly surprised by the deluge of love Byron received for saying exactly nine words, I quietly lamented my inability to obtain ten total comments in thirty minutes from the same audience. My audience. *My* followers.

I was jealous.

Just a little bit. I shouldn't have been. Comparing myself to Byron Visser was like comparing an exceptionally helpful, productive, and positive customer service call to the experience of a hit Broadway show. Both might be awesome once-in-a-lifetime events, but for different reasons.

Yes, these lovely people tuned in to watch my monthly scientific experiments. Some were hobbyists, some were parents learning how to safely perform their own experiments at home with their kids, some were nonscientist science teachers looking for resources for their classroom.

But I hoped most of my audience was comprised of young women who felt curious about engineering, chemistry and physics and biology, mathematics, technology, and their everyday applications, and why science, technology, engineering, and mathematics might be relevant to them. Teenage girls and women of all ages who didn't feel welcomed by traditional STEM academic settings were why I'd started this account in the first place. I was happy to be a resource, no matter who was watching or whatever their reason, and I knew my followers appreciated me.

That said, I doubted they'd recognize me on the street. If they did, I doubted they'd ask for an autograph.

Whereas Byron Visser was not only indisputably and enormously talented and intelligent, he was legit famous. Social media famous thanks to a fan video that had gone viral after his first book was published, and real world famous thanks to his books being instant best sellers. And that movie deal. Plus the rumors of him dating supermodels. Also that hot shirtless photo spread of him in the one—and only one—magazine interview he'd ever done.

So, yeah. Famous.

But I knew the real Byron though. Real Byron was sarcastic and standoffish. He was not a people person. Our friend group since college—which he'd only tangentially been part of during my undergrad and then not the year after I graduated because he eschewed all group gatherings—had labeled him "the reclusive genius one." I wasn't sure he knew any of our names other than Amelia's and Jeff's. By his own admission, he didn't like people in general.

Case in point, instead of saying hi to my live audience—which seemed like the appropriate thing to do, especially given that he'd interrupted my video and the comment feed erupted with praise for him—Byron being Byron, scowled at the screen, grunted, then walked out of view.

I exhaled slowly and silently as he departed, taking the five-o'clock shadow of his jaw and the warmth of his body with him. An explosion of LOLs and heart emojis followed in his wake.

My face heated. "Okay, thank you Byron for your truly fascinating addition to today's conversation. Thank goodness you were here to chime in. What would we do without you?"

Byron leaned against the wall in our tiny dining room, settling in to observe and judge, glaring at me. The right side of his full upper lip always seemed poised to curl. That paired with his dark wing-like eyebrows over his oddly colored eyes gave his face a permanent dissatisfied, disapproving expression, no matter what was happening or where he was.

Ignoring his unnerving presence, I forced a smile for the camera and continued brightly, "And yes, for the record, that is the author Byron Visser, avid recluse, eschewer of shirts, and serial grunter." Perhaps I was riding high on a wave of indignation, or perhaps irritation was an excellent lubricant for my brain because—even though I knew he was watching me—I didn't trip over my words.

Another grunt sounded from Byron's direction followed by a hearty laugh from Amelia. He could grunt all he wanted, nothing I'd said was untrue. I'd known the dude for over six years and he never called me by my real name and barely said anything to me that wasn't critical.

Not allowing myself to be distracted by the tsunami of comments, most of which were related to Byron's hotness and talent and the prettiness of his eyes—and all of which I had to wistfully admit were true—I returned my thumb to the top of my screen, letting it hover over the End Live button, and forced my hand steady.

Since he'd already interrupted the video, and since I was feeling uncharacteristically brave in his presence, I decided to deliver the spiel I'd originally planned. "Tune in next time. We'll be talking about the naming conventions of chemical compounds, but I promise this is super interesting and relevant to the rest of your life. Haven't you ever wondered what those ingredients are in your food and cosmetics? Leave me a comment with an ingredient that freaks you out or sounds weird and scary, we'll be drawing out the compounds so you can see and know what's going on. Knowledge is power, my friends. Be powerful. Oh! Also, leave any and all questions in the comments below and I'll do my best to answer them during the month. Here's your joke for the week: What do you do with a dead chemist? You barium! Ha! Okay, okay. Sorry. That was bad. Anyway, this is the Chemistry Maven signing off."

I ended the video, smile dropping, and gave myself a few seconds to catch my breath. Removing my phone from the stand, I clicked through screens in order to save the lesson to my account, all the while endeavoring to ignore the weight of Byron Visser's gaze and the erratic beating of my heart. It drove me bonkers that he always put me on edge, no matter what mood I'd been in before his arrival.

"Sorry! We just got back from lunch, and I thought you'd be out." Amelia walked past my mess of open sports drink bottles, pipettes, and test tubes scattered all over the kitchen peninsula. After lifting the lid and inspecting the water level, she flicked on the electric tea kettle.

"It's no problem." I waved away her apology, glancing at Byron and then immediately returning my attention to my phone. A burst of heat spread from the base of my spine to my fingertips. Our eyes had connected. I hated it when that happened.

I sensed him push away from the wall, heard his footsteps move further into the apartment. I imagined he was probably scrutinizing my paltry collection of houseplants and found them lacking. Or perhaps he'd slipped on a white glove to test the cleanliness of our shelves.

Why is he here?

I hadn't seen him in ages. Even though he'd always been a good friend of Amelia's—they'd grown up together in Eastern Oregon—he and I never interacted in any meaningful way. I tended to avoid him, and when I couldn't, he was like a menacing thundercloud on an otherwise sunny day.

"Do you want some tea, Win?" The scrape of mugs being moved pulled my gaze to my roommate.

"Yes, please. I picked up some of that Sexy Peppermint from Serena's booth at the farmers' market." I motioned toward the pantry. "But I already put it away."

Amelia and I called it "Sexy Peppermint," but it was actually called Passionate Peppermint. Our friend had started a side-hustle as a tea maker, and she branded her boxes with contemporary bodice-ripper illustrations. I also enjoyed Carnal Chamomile and Lusty Lemon & Ginger.

"Oooh, sounds good. I'll have that too. Byron?"

"What?" His voice rumbled from somewhere behind me. My spine straightened, my stomach tensed, and I grit my teeth at the involuntary reflexes.

Placing a hand on her hip, Amelia sent a look over my shoulder. "Do you want some tea?"

"No. This *Sedum morganianum* needs more sun," he said. "And if you want it to grow down vertically, you need to put it in a hanging planter."

Working my jaw, I almost laughed. Almost. I'd been right, Byron had been scrutinizing my houseplants and he found them lacking.

"That's the sunniest spot in the apartment," Amelia mumbled, closing the cabinet door and then turning for the pantry as she lifted her voice with a teasing lilt, "Not all twenty-somethings can afford to buy a house in Seattle, Byron."

"Or rent an apartment with windows, apparently," he drawled.

Good grief.

Amelia merely chuckled at his comment. How she could stand him, I had *no* idea.

"The mysteries of the universe are vast and plentiful," I muttered.

"What was that?" Amelia asked, placing our Passionate Peppermint tea bags into the mugs.

"What? Oh. Nothing." Finished typing out the caption and saving the video, I placed my phone on the counter and started cleaning up the bottles and beakers littering our beige Formica countertop.

I felt my roommate track my movements as she said, "You look really pretty today. I love your hair like that."

"Oh, thank you." Absentmindedly, I smoothed a hand down my long auburn hair, currently worn in waves over my shoulders. I didn't usually get a chance to do anything with it other than pull it back in a ponytail or braid, but I planned to bleach it blond soon during a live video for my channel. *For science!*

"Hey, how'd your video go?"

"Good. I mean—it went well." I pressed my lips together, reprimanding myself for the use of *good* instead of the grammatically correct *well.* Byron had never corrected my grammar out loud, but I suspected he did so in his big, brilliant, pretty head.

"That's great! I can't wait to watch it later."

"You don't have to . . . watch it." *Ha! Take that! Who has two thumbs and doesn't end her sentences with a preposition? This girl, that's who.*

"I want to see it," she said, and I felt her gaze move over me, assessing.

I smiled tightly. She knew I avoided Byron whenever possible, but we'd never explicitly talked about why. I hadn't wanted to admit how clumsy I felt around him and, really, I knew I was the problem. I *knew* it, but I couldn't seem to do anything about it.

He barely spoke to me and, here I was, putting uncharitable thoughts in his mouth and brain. Why am I this way? I usually thought the best of people. Why did I have to work so hard to think the best of Byron?

"Sorry again for interrupting." Amelia placed a mug in front of me, her eyebrows pulling together. "I didn't know you'd be here. I thought you had something at the school."

"Oh, no. That meeting got canceled." Today was the Friday before the public school's spring break. "They want us to come in tomorrow instead."

"You work weekends?" Byron's usual dust-dry tone held a hint of loftiness and censure.

I breathed in. I breathed out. About this one topic, I actually did know what he was thinking.

In college, I'd witnessed Byron attempt to talk Jeff Choi—Byron's roommate, one of the sweetest guys ever, and a member of our larger friend group—out of becoming a teacher so many times I'd lost count. Byron had said teaching was an underpaid and underappreciated profession. He'd said it drained the life out of people. He'd said the system takes advantage of teachers and sets them up to fail, so why would any intelligent, reasonable person with an aptitude for science or mathematics or engineering ever willingly accept a teacher's salary to do a teacher's job?

Byron didn't like my career choice. He'd made no secret about it any time the subject arose, like now. The fact that I'd chosen teaching despite having to carry a hefty student loan debt probably meant he considered me stupid.

I didn't care what he thought. Or, more precisely, I don't want to care. But since he was indisputably one of the smartest and most successful people I'd ever met who donated a buttload of money to charity every year and seemed to be a walking encyclopedia about literally everything, this was easier said than done.

"Yes, I work weekends," I said finally, answering his question but not adding that every single teacher I knew worked weekends. Of course we did. When else would we get any planning or grading done?

"They pay teachers to work weekends now?"

I'd guessed the question was coming, but it still made my chest tight with embarrassment. "No. They don't pay teachers to work weekends."

"Then you shouldn't," he said, like it was so simple. "You undervalue yourself when you work without payment."

My throat burned to say that there were more considerations than just payment, that I loved teaching. I loved my students, I cared about them and their successes and failures. Deeply. Thoughts of them kept me up at night, plotting how I might help one of them understand a tricky concept better, or what to do about a brilliant student who had a terrible home life, or how I might hint to another kiddo that they had a gift for engineering without making them feel self-conscious in front of their classmates.

A paycheck was necessary to live, obviously, but it wasn't why I was a teacher, it wasn't why I worked so hard at the school and on my social media accounts.

And now my heart hurt, and I was sweaty and sad, and—once again—I hated that I let him make me feel this way.

"You know what?" I wiped my hands on a towel and meticulously folded it, leaving it on the countertop. "I don't think I want any tea. I think I'll go for a run."

Amelia sent me an apologetic smile and I gave my head a little shake, hopefully communicating that it was no big deal. We'd been roommates since college when we'd randomly been assigned to live together in the dorm. Even if I could afford a place of my own, I'd still want to live with Amelia. Living with her had been the first time in my life I'd felt free to be completely myself. She'd been a premed major at the time and my major had been chemistry; like oxygen and hydrogen, we were destined to bond.

I loved her. She was the best. It wasn't her fault I allowed one of her oldest and best friends to make me feel foolish and tongue-tied every time we shared the same space. That was on me.

And so what could I do other than leave?

CHAPTER 2
WINNIE

"Sorry about bringing Byron. He asked if he could come over, and I thought you'd be home much later." Amelia met me at the door as soon as I was inside the apartment, holding out a glass of water. "Anyway, sorry."

Accepting the glass, I shrugged and walked past her. "It's fine." Still out of breath from my run, I paced the short distance between the kitchen peninsula and the couch, needing to cool down. I should've walked around the block again, but the rain had gone from a drizzle to something more aggressive.

"It's not fine. I know he irritates you." She moved to the couch and sat, pulling a fuzzy blanket over her legs. What looked like a new mug of tea and a plate of my ginger cookies sat on the coffee table to her left.

"Only because he doesn't laugh at my witty anecdotes. Him pretending to find me funny would go a long way," I joked . . . kinda not joking.

Then again when had I last tried to tell Byron a joke? It must've been years since I made any kind of effort.

"It's more than that, I know it is." She picked up her mug and blew on the surface. "I need polite Winnie to take a smoke break so I can talk to honest Winnie. You don't like him. Does he make you uncomfortable?"

"He doesn't make me uncomfortable," I denied reflexively despite her permission to be honest, not wanting to upset my friend.

But then I rolled my eyes at this irritating, deep-rooted need within me to avoid conflict and make everyone else happy all the time, something about myself I'd sincerely been trying to change.

"Okay, fine. He isn't my favorite person," I admitted with reluctance. "But he doesn't make me uncomfortable. Besides, it doesn't matter. You two are good friends. Period." *Are we really talking about this now? What's the point?* I drank the entire glass of water and then twisted around to inspect the kitchen. "Is there any tea left?"

"There's still hot water. I wish you would tell me if you don't want me to bring him by." She nodded toward the kettle. "Are you sure he doesn't make you uncomfortable?" Her voice raised an octave with the question. "You grit your teeth and act like you have a hernia whenever he's around."

"Well, he does, kinda." Flustered, I quickly washed out the dirty water glass and placed it on the rack to dry.

I wasn't prepared to have this conversation, yet I knew we should. It felt overdue. Nevertheless, I was determined to measure my words carefully. The last thing I wanted was to cause trouble between Amelia and her childhood friend.

"Byron doesn't. . . make me. . . feel. . . uncomfortable," I said haltingly. "But I feel discomfort around him."

I turned to find that Amelia had scrunched her face. "You feel discomfort around him, but he doesn't make you feel uncomfortable?"

"I know, it doesn't make any sense." I laughed, pouring hot water into a mug while my shoulders shivered in the damp running jacket.

"What can I do to help you feel less discomfort around him?"

"Nothing." Peeling off my outer layer and slinging it over a kitchen chair, I carried my mug to the couch and sat crisscross on the cushion, facing her. "He's so—"

"Quiet?"

"Perfect."

She made a face. "Perfect?"

"Yeah. He's absolutely brilliant, self-made, hugely talented and creative. He donates all that money to charity every year and seems to know everything about everything. I guess I feel like an uninformed child whenever we're in a room together and I don't know how to—you know—not be intimidated. That's on me." This was the conclusion I'd come to years ago.

To borrow the phrase my second-grade teacher often used, being around people "filled my bucket." This seemed to be unilaterally true. Except with Byron Visser.

Even when we first met—before he was this famous wunderkind author, before he'd earned his double PhDs, before he'd bulked out after joining a rugby club a few years ago and people started tripping all over themselves when he walked in a room, back when he was an awkwardly adorable, tall, lanky undergrad with no degrees, wearing all black, whose head seemed too big for his body and he'd hide his face behind thick, wavy black hair that fell past his shoulder blades—something about him set me off-kilter and made my skin buzz. In my entire life, only *he* had this effect on me.

Actually, that's not true. The closest I'd experienced this disconcerting biological anarchy had been during an extremely difficult time two weeks into my freshman year of high school—I won't bore you with a long story involving white shorts, the boys' varsity soccer team, my period, and Instagram—after which I'd felt shaky, hyperaware, and embarrassed for weeks.

Sudden hot flashes, inability to form coherent sentences, tightness in my chest, pounding heart, trembling hands—being around or near Byron had always made me feel this way. The moment our eyes had first met, I'd felt it. I couldn't breathe. It was like being sucker punched in the stomach. I'd worked hard to ignore the inexplicable discomfort. I liked people, and Byron was, after all, just a person.

But during our first meeting, I'd said something about rollerblading over the summer at Alki Beach. I'd pronounced it *Al-key* instead of *Al-kye*. He'd immediately corrected me.

He hadn't done it rudely. It had been very matter-of-fact, lacking in emotion. Even so, I'd withdrawn completely, and his offhanded correction had permanently flipped a switch. No matter what and how I tried, I couldn't seem to unflip it. Almost everything out of his mouth since that moment had struck me as condescending and judgmental, even when I knew objectively that it wasn't.

Therefore, I was the problem and avoided him.

"He makes you feel like a child?" Amelia eyes seemed to widen and narrow at the same time, it was a look of outrage. "What did he say? I've told him—"

"No, no. It's not him. It's me." I covered her hand, trying not to worry too much about what she'd told Byron. I shouldn't care what he thought about me, so why should I be embarrassed if Amelia talked to him about it? I shouldn't be embarrassed. I shouldn't be anything where Byron was concerned. I doubted I even registered on his radar. He probably called me Fred because he didn't know or care to remember my real name. "I guess super smart people make me nervous? But, like I said, that's my problem, not his."

"What are you talking about? You're super smart."

"You know what I mean. There's smart and then there's *smart.*" I didn't feel like this was a controversial statement. Even though Byron had existed only on the fringes of our college friend group, we all marveled at his encyclopedic knowledge during the very few times he'd shown up to a party or get-together. And when his first book had released, it had left us all breathless with effusive admiration. To put it a different way, I was very smart, but I was no Toni Morrison, Albert Einstein, Marie Curie, or Byron Visser.

"And you think Byron is the latter?"

"Come on, Amelia. He graduated early with a degree in physics and holds PhDs in electrical engineering and biomedical engineering. He's written two fiction best sellers and he's been nominated for every major literary award for his debut novel. And he's what, twenty-six? He's amazing."

"Twenty-seven. But that doesn't—I mean—yes. His mother is some kind of genius professor who will probably invent bionic spines and win the Nobel Prize or something, but he's *Byron.* And you've known him forever, before he published those books, before he was anyone."

I didn't know that about his mother, but it made sense. "Right, but we've barely interacted. He's spoken less than one hundred words—total—to me in six years. Probably closer to fifty. Even in undergrad, he never came out with us. And I've always felt weird around him. Perhaps I sensed his brilliance early on. But I don't—don't *dislike* him."

"You don't dislike him?"

I grimaced. "Okay, actually, yes." Even though this was me being honest, a jolt of worry made my heart accelerate.

"Finally! She admits it." Amelia lifted her hand along the back of the couch and then let it fall, teasing, "Your ability to tap dance around the truth or ask for what you want is Olympic-level impressive."

I gave her a wry smile. Amelia knew about my upbringing. I didn't need to explain to her why I was so reluctant to speak uncomfortable truths. "I do dislike him. Happy now?"

"Yes!" She patted my leg. "So happy to learn you dislike my oldest friend. Yay!"

I laughed. "But it's when he brings up how teachers aren't paid enough, or anything at all related to my job. Or when he corrects my terrible pronunciation of common words. Or like today, when he criticized my houseplant. Or when he glares at me, saying nothing."

"So basically every time you see him?"

We both laughed, and I shook my head at myself. *Dislike* wasn't quite the right word. His general simmering disdain reminded me of my uncle. I'd been raised by my aunt and uncle after my mom passed and, suffice it to say, the best part of my childhood had been acting as a second mother to my six cousins.

Comparing Byron to Uncle Jacob likely wasn't fair since they didn't look at all alike, my uncle had been gregarious with everyone but a select few. Whereas Byron was gregarious with no one. And Byron had never screamed at me for making what I considered small mistakes. But they both had a habit of rarely opening their mouths in my presence unless to correct or criticize. They also glared openly, their gazes heavy with judgment.

"So you—who never dislikes anyone—dislike Byron, and you feel discomfort around him, but you think it's you and not him?" Amelia narrowed her eyes. "Again, be honest, does he creep you out?"

"No. Like I said, he makes me nervous because of me and my hang-ups. I'm the problem."

"It's the staring, isn't it? The staring makes you nervous."

"He does stare, doesn't he?" I deflected, even though his staring obviously wasn't the only cause of my discomfort.

Amelia studied me thoughtfully. "He's always stared, you know. He's a big people watcher. He observes rather than interacts. But that's a byproduct of him being a writer. Even when we were kids, he'd stare at people with those creepy green eyes."

"His eyes aren't creepy. They're—"

"What?"

I didn't want to say they were beautiful. I didn't want Amelia to read too much into the comment. His eyes *were* beautiful, a grayish hazel around his pupil, followed by a ring of green and an outer ring of blue at the edge of his iris.

"They're unusual," I said slowly, as though I'd just now given the matter some consideration. "But that doesn't make them creepy."

"But unusual eyes plus staring does make him creepy. I'll have to talk to him about it. I'm like his conscience, his cricket in a top hat, but for social situations."

"Well don't talk to him on my account." I felt a pressing urge to change the subject. "By the way, what are you doing home so early?"

"Oh!" She clapped once and leaned forward, her eyes growing excited. "Actually, I came home to talk to you, hoping you'd be here after your meeting. You know that girls in STEM grant my company applied for? The really big one?"

Amelia had been premed in college but had changed her mind in her fourth year. She ended up dual majoring in biology and marketing with a focus on technical writing. She was set to graduate this May with her master's degree in education and currently worked for a huge, fancy nonprofit that created STEM curricula and related content—like videos, learning games and apps—for schools.

"Yes, I remember." I also leaned forward, on the figurative edge of my seat. If she was about to say what I thought she might be about to say, then—

"Well, we got it!"

I set my tea down so I could reach forward and give her a hug, not caring that I likely smelled like sweat and rain. "You're a rock star! This is so exciting!"

"It is, and that's why I rushed home. They gave everyone the afternoon off, and I wanted to talk to you as soon as possible. They're going to be listing the community manager positions on the website the month after we receive the funds, and I want you to apply."

"Are you kidding?" Anticipation and hope had my head buzzing. "Yes. Absolutely, you know I will."

While the grant had been in the early planning stages, Amelia told me about the community manager positions. They were contract positions that paid influencers who already had STEM-focused social media accounts. The influencers would be expected to target girls and women with their marketing efforts, advertise women in STEM events hosted by Amelia's company, scholarship opportunities, and receive materials and resources for encouraging women to consider careers in STEM.

Other than the advertising and scholarship part, it was a job I already did with my live videos and lessons but didn't receive resources or get paid for. The perfect side-hustle that would help me pay off my student loans, doing what I already loved while not taking up more of my limited free time.

"Good. Excellent." She beamed. "Glad to hear it. But we also need to strategize, beef up your resumé, and work on your numbers. I talked to my boss, and she gave me the metrics and requirements." Amelia paired her last sentence with a grimace, twisting her fingers in front of her.

My heart sank. "How many followers do I need in order to be competitive?"

"The good news is that your followers to following ratio is fine, well within the metrics. But—and don't despair or freak out—you need at a minimum one hundred thousand followers."

"What?!" I gasped as hard as I'd ever gasped in the entirety of my life.

"In order to be truly competitive, a follower count of five hundred thousand or more would be ideal. And an engagement per video or post of at least six percent."

My shoulders drooped. *Darn.* "Well, I have the engagement at least. But where am I going to find seventy-five thousand followers in one month? Never mind four hundred and seventy-five thousand."

"It'll be more than a month. We'll get the funding in six weeks, and we'll post the community manager positions the month after." She said this like the paltry reprieve changed everything.

It changed nothing. I'd been building my social media accounts for years. Ten weeks was a blink of an eye. "Okay, how am I going to get four hundred and seventy-five thousand followers in two and a half months?"

She steepled her hands and tapped her fingertips together, peering at me. "I have some ideas."

My burst of a laugh sounded like a scoff. "Really? You got some college-aged, chemistry-curious women in your trench coat? Are they waiting for us outside in the hall?"

"Have some faith. We can do this. We need to think outside the box." Amelia tapped my knee.

"What box? The box of reality?"

She made a face. "The box of your current content and social media accounts."

I sighed. Loudly. "You want me to spend more time on TikTok."

"Would that be so bad? TikTok is where it's at."

"No. But—" I struggled to define my objections, finally settling on, "—I feel like my content, the videos I do, don't translate well to bite-sized clips. I'm a long format person, not a thirty-second or three-minute engineering and technology person."

"But you could be. You made that list last year of thirty-second STEM facts, and those have done well on TikTok. I still think that list has great potential. And if anyone can make these concepts entertaining and engaging in thirty seconds, it's you."

"Okay." I sighed again. "Okay, I'll resurrect it."

"And there's something else."

I peeked at her, bracing myself. "What?"

She also seemed to be bracing herself. "You should branch out."

"Meaning?"

"Don't say no until you hear me out."

"Okay . . ."

"You should expand the kind of content you're offering on TikTok and elsewhere, switch things up, do some popular challenges that aren't necessarily related to STEM."

I waited a beat, searching my brain for a clue as to what she meant, and finally asked, "Like what?"

"Like makeup, fashion, and romance challenges."

I reared back. "You want me to do what?"

"Do the girly and romantic TikTok challenges." She'd lifted her fingers and made air quotes around the word *girly*.

"What?" I shot up from the couch. "Makeup and fashion? Romance challenges? With who?" Before she could answer, I lifted my hand to cut her off. "And besides, I thought the influencers, the community manager accounts, were supposed to be STEM focused?"

"Yes—obviously, they should have a STEM focus—and no. They shouldn't be *just* STEM videos. At least I don't think they should. Think about it, you need to connect with your audience, make them see you as a real person they can relate to. Everyone who knows you loves you. That's what you need to leverage."

"By doing makeup and fashion TikTok challenges?" For some reason, the idea filled me with a heavy, deep sense of disappointment.

"And romance challenges! You're cute, friendly, engaging. I'd watch you kiss someone." Amelia nodded at her own assertion, picking up her tea and taking a sip.

I waited for her to either expand on her statement further or bust out with a *Just kidding*! She did neither.

So I moved my finger in a circle in front of my face. "You see this? This is my confused face because I am confused."

"Look, lots of women—in college and older, girls in high school, and even younger—are interested in how to apply makeup. Obviously, not all women. I'm just saying, you are a makeup applying master. I didn't know the first thing about eye shadow until you taught me."

"Yes, but—"

"And many women—not all, but many—love romance and romantic stories. It's not a mystery that if someone wants to build their following faster, they do so by posting live videos as well as challenges that are trending and sticking in the algorithms, and a lot of those sticky trends are fashion or romance-related challenges."

"But. . . I'm a scientist. I'm a teacher."

"So?" She shrugged, picking up a ginger cookie. "What part of being a scientist or a teacher says you can't also enjoy makeup, fashion, and love stories?"

"Who is going to listen to me talk about magnetic fields if I'm making googly eyes at some random person in the very next video? Which, again, is still a problem."

"What's a problem?"

"Who would I do these so-called romantic challenges with? You? And what would Elijah say about it?"

"Tempting, but no. Besides, it would be best if you paired off with someone already on TikTok, someone who has a following."

"Then who? You know I don't date, I don't have the time." I'd gone on so many dates during the first two years after I'd broken up with my high school boyfriend, I'd lost track of the number. A few had made it to date three, but I hadn't liked anyone enough to continue past date three.

Amelia, Serena, and I had made a pact our senior year to take twelve months off from dating. Now Serena was engaged to a great guy, Amelia had a super cool boyfriend named Elijah, and I was happily—and perpetually—single, not missing the emotional roller coaster of romance one bit. But even if I wanted to date, I didn't have the time. Being a full-time teacher and managing my social media accounts and lessons, I barely had time to hang out with my friends unless it was virtually.

"Okay, first and foremost," Amelia set down her ginger cookie and dusted her fingers of crumbs, "your audience will listen with rapt interest to your magnetic field videos because magnetic fields are fascinating, but you have to get the audience there in the first place. So pick someone. You have a ton of guy friends, many of whom you know would jump at the chance to —oh! Wait!" Eyes widening abruptly, she leaned forward and gave the coffee table three quick pats. "What about Jeff?"

I opened my mouth to protest the insanity of her suggestion, but as soon as Jeff's name crossed her lips, my brain stalled.

. . . *Oh.*

Jeff.

Jeff Choi.

I'd met Jeff the second month of my sophomore year. Like me, Jeff had decided to be a high school STEM teacher and spend his life kindling the fire of curiosity in young people for the very same reason I had, because a STEM teacher had kindled that same kind of curiosity in him. We loved the same movies and books and art and artists and music and basically everything. He was kind and smart and so darn cute. From his thick, unruly brown hair to his smiling brown eyes to his square jaw to his corny jokes, I adored him.

But—and I swear—I'd never let myself actually think about being with Jeff because of one very huge issue. The fire of curiosity hadn't been the only thing kindled during his freshman year of high school. Up until recently, Jeff had been with the same person—with a few on-again, off-again breakups in between—for over eleven years.

They'd gone to different colleges for undergrad, and she'd finished law school last year on the East Coast while he'd stayed in Seattle to teach. I'd only met her a few times as she'd rarely traveled to see him, and when she did visit, she never seemed interested in getting to know his friends.

However, two months ago, just six months after she'd returned from the East Coast and they'd been making plans to finally move in together, they'd broken up. He'd been in a bad mood—well, bad mood for Jeff—ever since. I'd been waiting for him to start acting more like himself before contemplating the possibility that maybe, perhaps, this time he and I might make a connection.

To be clear, I hadn't been contemplating it yet. Every time the thought entered my brain, I shut it down.

"Lucy was the one to break up with Jeff." Amelia cut into my thoughts, reminding me of Jeff's singlehood even though she definitely didn't need to.

"I know that. I was there when Serena told us." I suddenly felt fidgety and too hot.

Amelia was the only one among our friends who knew I sometimes struggled where Jeff was concerned, but even she didn't know that my feelings had been growing roots for six long years. I wasn't in love with him or obsessed or anything like that. Our friendship had always been excessively platonic. And whenever I'd found myself thinking about Jeff a little too often, I'd avoid him for a few weeks, until I had a better handle on my inconvenient thoughts.

But now he was single.

And so was I.

Scrutinizing me, Amelia wagged her eyebrows. "Oh yeah, do it with Jeff. That's perfect. Tell him it's for a job—which it technically is—but then you are bound to get closer if you're kissing each other for a few TikTok challenges."

I scratched my neck, my heart doing erratic things. "I don't know . . ."

"What don't you know?"

"He's rebounding. He and Lucy were together for years. And this feels sneaky."

"Sneaky how?" She leaned back, her right eyebrow rising a scant millimeter. "Lucy broke up with him. We've met her—briefly—two times in six years, and she was standoffish both times. It's been two months. Now it's your chance. I know you like him. And I know for a fact he's into you."

I did like him. But even assuming he was at all interested in me, did I want to be the first person he was with after an eleven-year relationship? And did I want my first potentially serious relationship as an adult to be with Jeff Choi? And would he care that I was a twenty-six-year-old virgin? And what if—

STAAAAHP! You are getting so far ahead of yourself, you're practically at the edge of the solar system. Chill.

"Forget it." I waved away the idea. "There's no use talking about this. I'm not asking Jeff for help with the romantic challenges because I'm not doing them. Nor am I doing makeup tutorials or fashion challenges because having those kinds of things on my account would undermine my credibility as a scientist."

"But that's my point! It wouldn't—or shouldn't." Amelia leaned forward again, her eyes moving between mine as her voice adopted an earnest tone. "Yes, not all teenage girls and college-aged women care about fashion and romance. Fine. But many do, and there is absolutely nothing wrong with that. They have crushes, they want to fall in love, they want to have healthy and satisfying sex. Connect with them as a person who wants those same things, has their same fears, while also doing chemistry experiments, going to science centers, visiting NASA, doing badass STEM shit."

"I don't know. I don't want—"

"What?"

To be rejected. To be laughed at. "I don't want to get in trouble with my school. You know that, as a teacher, I have to be super careful about what I post on social media." I didn't use my real name for any of my social media handles, but I did show my face. If students wanted to track me down, they could. "Nor do I want to undermine what I've built."

"I'm not suggesting you post porn, Winnie. How would making fun videos about eye shadow application or romantic challenges undermine you or get you in trouble with your school?"

"Come on, Amelia. You were premed. Bio had more women than chemistry, but it still wasn't anywhere near fifty-fifty. If you want to be taken seriously in STEM, you have to be emotionless. You have to . . ."

"What?"

"Act like a guy," I blurted unthinkingly and then cringed, regretting the words. "Wait. That's not—"

"Act like a guy? What does that even mean? You think guys don't have crushes? You think guys don't want to fall in love and have satisfying sex or care about what they look like? Just as many men marry women as women marry men. Have you seen Harry Styles in a dress? I hate to break it to you, but somatic nuclear transfer is a relatively new method for human procreation. Prior to—oh—twenty or thirty years ago, penis insertion into a—"

"Ha ha ha. Stop. You know what I'm talking about. As a woman, and maybe even as a man, you can't be taken seriously in the scientific community if you express any interest in—in—"

"Compassion? Romance? Emotion? Beauty and fashion as a form of expression? Interpersonal dynamics and relationships? All the things many women—again, not all, but many—seem to intrinsically value and find interesting?"

"Fine." I surrendered. "Yes, that."

"But don't you think that's part of the problem for girls and anyone else with these interests?" Now her tone was beseeching. "Don't you think that's part of the barrier women consider as an entry into STEM fields? It's like science, engineering, mathematics, and technology careers have been roped off from them. It's not even an option because they've been told they can't be themselves and be a scientist. They've been told their interests are frivolous. You can't adore pop music and be taken seriously. You can't openly read romance novels for enjoyment and have articles published in a major peer review publication. You can't wear clothes you enjoy and not get side-eyed. That's a problem! Why should anyone have to bury who they are, what they look like, what they want, what they value, what they enjoy in order to get a seat at the table? They shouldn't—girls and women shouldn't. And you could show them that they don't have to."

I huffed loudly because she had a really, really great point. *Darn it.*

Amelia must've sensed her near victory because she went in for the kill. "Be yourself as a fully realized, three-dimensional woman, do the things I know you enjoy and also be a scientist. It doesn't have to be fashion and makeup, it can be video games and running, or dancing challenges and DIY projects. You can be a person and a woman and a scientist, you can show all sides. And in doing so, you can reach an audience that never would've considered the fact that being both—being yourself and being a scientist—is actually possible."

She was so good at persuasive arguments. *Again, darn it.*

"Okay. Fine." I threw my hands up, sitting back down. "You win. You are one hundred percent right. I will do smoky-eye tutorials and everything else."

She turned her head as though to look at me from a new angle. "And do the romance challenges?"

"They can't be at all risqué. They have to be completely wholesome otherwise I might get in trouble with my school. But yes. Fine. I'll—"

"Goooood, gooood." She dropped her voice an octave and added a creepy British accent. "Yesss . . . Embrace your destiny."

"Stop it. I hate it when you do your Palpatine impression."

"Prefer Yoda, you do?" She wasn't as good at Yoda and instead sounded like Kermit the Frog.

"Why are you this way?"

She snickered, snatching her tea from the table again and taking a big sip before asking, "When will you ask him?"

"Who?"

"Jeff-rey," she sing-songed.

"Oh." My heart squeezed.

"Ask. Him." Amelia pointed at me. "He's already on TikTok. He's adorable. Your follower count will go through the roof, and that's what you need."

"I'd be using him."

She shrugged. "I don't think he'd mind."

"Let me—let me think about it."

"Hmm. . ." She continued to inspect me, and I could see her mind working. Which was why the next words out of her mouth struck me as suspicious. "Hey, so, are we playing *Stardew Valley* this week?"

Stardew Valley was an awesome throwback farming game reminiscent of 1990s RPGs in the tradition of *The Legend of Zelda: A Link to the Past.* With its pixelated, rudimentary 2-D graphics and wide-open gameplay, it had become a refuge for my soul during the last few years when I could've easily been crushed by my lingering student debt and the overwhelming nature of being a new teacher.

"Uh, yeah. I still play every Friday, so we'll be playing tonight. But next week we're not playing because of the camping trip. They're leaving Wednesday." I wished I could've gotten together with my friends, met somewhere face-to-face to see them in person, enjoy their company. But everyone was so busy these days with life changes and new relationships, or wedding planning and baby showers, or business trips and career advancement.

We used to be such a tight-knit group, but now we were drifting apart. I was determined to be the touchstone for everyone, the organizer of quarterly in-person events so that we didn't drift too far. Likewise, I'd arranged the shared game server for anyone available on Fridays.

If an hour or two on Fridays was all they could fit into their busy schedules—even if some could only join our group chat for a half hour once a month or so—then it was better than nothing.

"Oh yeah, that's right. Byron mentioned that. Jeff and them are going camping for spring break." Amelia looked thoughtful.

"Yeah, they are. And by the way, your farm is a mess." Initially, almost everyone would play together on Fridays. But after a few months, most people couldn't make it consistently and it ended up being me, Jeff, and Laura (another friend from college, computer science major who currently worked for "The Zon.") Others would stop by randomly and play, and that was always great.

Amelia's mouth fell open. "You haven't been clearing away the debris? Watering my plants?"

"No. You haven't played since last month. That's like, two years in Stardew Valley time. Your fields are fallow, like the effs you do not give about them."

She made a grunting sound. "Fine. I'm joining tonight."

"Good. Looking forward to it." My heart gave a little leap of happiness. It would be good to have her there.

Amelia narrowed her eyes, chewing on another cookie while openly inspecting me. "Will you help me plow and water my land? Fertilize my soil?"

"You supply the seeds and fertilizer, and I'll need ten percent of your crop yield, but sure."

Her mouth opened in a display of outrage. "That's highway robbery."

"I'll throw in an iridium sprinkler."

Giving me a hard stare, she held out her hand. "Fine. Deal."

We shook on it. Little did she know I had a glut of iridium.

But at least that was settled. Now all I had to do was figure out literally everything else about my life, starting with whether or not I would ask Jeff to be my PG TikTok romantic challenge partner, and how to do so without becoming his rebound lady.

CHAPTER 3
WINNIE

Just before sitting down to join the *Stardew Valley* game, armed with my mug of hot chocolate and plate of Swiss cheese slices, I made the mistake of checking the stats on the sports drink lab video I'd recorded earlier in the day. To my complete shock and abject fascination, it had been viewed over one hundred thousand times and counting. And I'd gained over three thousand new followers. But then I discovered that 80 percent of the comments were about Byron Visser and the other 20 percent were about him and I having "great chemistry."

How could we have great chemistry? We'd shared the screen for exactly ten seconds.

"Why does your face look like that? You're blushing." Amelia sat across from me at our small oval kitchen table; she'd procured herself another cup of peppermint tea and three more ginger cookies on a white plate. Her addiction to my gluten-free ginger cookies was likely why she hadn't abandoned me yet for a place of her own. Thank God for her willingness to share expenses, the cost of rent in Seattle was insane. Without a roommate, there was no way I'd be able to afford any place near the school where I taught. Plus, I loved her, and I would miss her desperately if—when—she moved out.

I turned off my phone and set it next to my laptop. "I'm reading comments on my video from earlier. Are you logged in yet?"

"Yep. So is Laura, but Jeff texted that he's running late. I watched your video, it was really good." Amelia picked up her phone, lifting an eyebrow at whatever she read there, then quickly typed out a response with her thumbs.

"Did you read the comments?" I asked, trying not to feel despondent, tearing a slice of cheese in half as I waited for the game platform to load.

"No, why?" Her eyes were still on her phone.

"Most of them were about Byron," I muttered.

I wasn't jealous this time, I swear. Of course his readers and fans would be excited to see him, and I didn't begrudge him or them that excitement. But I couldn't help feeling disappointed. I took a lot of pride in my STEM videos and the experiments I pulled together. I worked really hard, and I guess it felt demoralizing on some level to have my video and the comments hijacked, the conversation steered away from STEM.

If you do these romance challenges and the other videos, then you'll be diluting your STEM-focused message all the time. Is that okay with you?

Amelia's gaze flicked up, held mine for a few seconds, then returned to her phone screen. "Well, Byron has no social media accounts, won't do interviews anymore, won't go to any events or cons, doesn't respond to fan mail, won't sign books—not even for charity auctions—so I imagine seeing him pop up in your video was quite a thrill for fans of his books."

"Why is he like that?" I clicked on the Join Co-op button at the prompt. "Why can't he engage more with his readers?"

This also confused me about Byron. He had—literally—millions of loyal fans, hungry for his next book or a scrap of information about his personal life, and he never gave status updates or interviews. It seemed so strange to me.

Amelia didn't respond, so I glanced up from the loading screen to look at her. Her lips were curved in a sneaky-looking smile.

"Who are you texting?" I asked.

"Jeff."

My frown was immediate. "What are you two texting about?"

She tried and failed to quell a smile. "Nothing."

Alarm shot through me. "Amelia!"

Giving into her grin, she typed out another message. "Give me a sec . . ."

"Do not—"

"He said yes!" She let her phone fall to the table with a *clack* and lifted both her arms, fist-pumping the air.

I stared at her, horrified, worried, curious, and horrified again. "What did you do?"

She picked up the cell and held it out to me, a series of text messages on the screen. "Jeff agreed to do the romantic challenges with you for TikTok."

My jaw dropped as I committed fully to being horrified, a rush of hot anxiety rolling through me. With shaking hands, I took her phone and scrolled through the messages.

Amelia: Here's a hint, Winnie needs a favor and she doesn't want to ask you because she feels like she'd be using you

Jeff: Are you logged into SDV yet? I'm running late. What's the favor

Amelia: You know that community manager job? She needs to gain more followers on social media, so I think she should do romantic challenges with someone and I think that someone should be you

Jeff: What kind of romantic challenges

Amelia: You've seen the Sit on your best guy friend's lap one? Or Kiss your crush one? She has a list of ten we're working on

Jeff: Fuck yeah! But would Win want to do that stuff with me?

Amelia: Come on

Jeff: What? Really?

Amelia: Talk to her

Jeff: Srsly?

"YOU TOLD HIM!" I screeched, staring at my *former* friend, the shock pouring from every cell of my body. "How could you do that?"

"Winnie, please." She rolled her eyes. "As I told you earlier today, he's into you."

"What? No, he's not."

"Yes. He is." She picked up her tea, giving me a flat look over the rim of the cup. "He asked if I thought you'd go out with him. Did you scroll all the way up to earlier today?"

The ground beneath my feet felt unsteady as I shifted my attention back to the phone. I scrolled up to the messages from this afternoon.

Jeff: Is Winnie still not dating anyone

Amelia: Depends. Why

Jeff: Do you think she'd go on a date with me if I asked

Amelia: You should ask and find out

Jeff: Any hints? Tell me if I have a chance. Help a guy out

Amelia: Here's a hint, Winnie needs a favor and she doesn't want to ask you because she feels like she'd be using you

I gasped, covering my mouth, then I returned my eyes to Amelia. Her grin had morphed into a smirky smile.

"I *told* you. Ask him to help you with the romantic challenges. He'd be perfect for so many reasons. You're both teachers, you both have a STEM-focused social media following already. Just think, you two can document your love story in real time."

Legs unsteady, I sat in my chair, rereading the text messages again because I couldn't believe it. My heart expanded in my chest and I felt a squee bubbling up from the well of excited happiness inside me, but before I could give voice to it, Amelia's phone rang.

I jerked upright, staring at Jeff's face on her screen. "It's Jeff!"

"Ooo-kay." Amelia lifted an eyebrow.

"What should I do?"

"You can either give it to me or you can—"

"I'm going to answer it," I said, sliding the bar at the bottom and bringing it to my ear. "Hello?"

"Uh, Amelia?"

"No." I grimaced, second-guessing my impulsive decision to answer my friend's phone. "No, it's Winnie. But I can put her on."

"No, no. I'm glad you answered." Jeff chuckled, it carried an edge of nervousness. "I guess she showed you our text messages?"

"Maaaybe." I grinned like an idiot, certain I now floated on a cloud.

"If you want me to help you with those TikTok challenges, I'm happy to. You wouldn't be using me."

I released a silent sigh because he was just so . . . so . . .

"He's so cute." Amelia chuckled, her eyes on her laptop screen.

"But I have to be up-front with you, Win," he continued. "I just broke up with Lucy—or she broke up with me. It was time, and it's been two months, but it's still fresh, you know?"

The reminder of his ex-girlfriend sobered me from my internal squeeing rainbow of happiness cloud vibes. I nodded. "I understand. And I appreciate your honesty about it. So I feel like I should tell you, I've had a—a—" I gulped. "Well, I've liked you for a while. And so you should know that before you agree to help me with TikTok." I felt Amelia's attention on me, and I looked at her. She was staring at me with wide eyes, clearly surprised by my sudden emotional bravery.

She knew the household where I'd grown up had punished honesty. Asking for what I needed—let alone what I wanted—would be punished by withholding whatever I'd asked for, and then I would be further punished for being greedy. If I needed something, if I wanted something, I had to figure out how to make my uncle think it had been his idea.

Since leaving for college, I'd been working really, really hard to change the ingrained habits that had become instincts, but the path had been rocky. Even with Amelia, who I trusted more than anyone else, I still felt reticent about admitting the truth of my feelings.

But if Jeff could be honest and brave, then so could I. See? *I knew we'd be perfect for each other.*

"Are you serious?" His laugh this time sounded disbelieving.

"Yes." I studied the thigh pocket on the side of my green cargo pants, shoving away the panic threatening to choke me. *He likes you, he wanted to ask you out, stop being a nincompoop.* "But I would never have said anything if you were still with Lucy."

He sighed, chuckling some more. "Life is so weird. I can't believe this."

"Do you still want to do the challenges? No pressure if—"

"No, no. I want to do it. We're—well, we've been friends for a long time." I heard him shift, like he'd gone from standing to sitting. "I would love to do them with you, and maybe we can, I don't know, have fun together?"

"I'd like that." I worked to keep my grin under control, but it wouldn't be curtailed, it took over my face and my cheeks hurt. *Ah! Best day ever!*

"Okay. Good." He sounded like he was smiling as well. "Hey, send me over the list of challenges, okay?"

"Yeah. Sure. I'll do that tonight." I turned back to my computer, pulling up the list Amelia and I had been working on this afternoon.

"When can we get started?" he asked. "Tomorrow?"

Now I laughed because he sounded so eager, and heck if that didn't send my heart soaring. "I can't tomorrow or Sunday, but how about Monday?" It was spring break for both of us. I'd planned to spend the week prepping all my assignments for the remainder of the year and getting a jump on the thirty-second videos for TikTok, but spending Monday strategizing romantic challenge videos with Jeff sounded so much better.

"I leave for the camping trip on Wednesday, but I'll be back Saturday. We can do more when I get back."

"That works."

Amelia reached over and wiggled the screen of my laptop. "Ask him if we can shoot it at Byron's house. He and Byron have much better light than we do."

I nodded. I was in such a good mood, not even the thought of seeing Byron again could dampen it. "Hey, can we shoot it at your place? Amelia can hold the camera. We've been working on a script for the first one."

"A script?"

"Yes, we want to script each one so we can get it right with minimal takes and tell a story. Let me put you on speaker phone." I put him on speaker and placed her cell on the table so Amelia could join in on our planning conversation.

"Hey Jeff," she said, grinning at me.

"Hey Amelia, old buddy, old pal."

Ah! He is SO CUTE!

"Ha ha. So, listen. We want to do this right. Each TikTok challenge will build on the last and tell a story, okay?" Amelia was all business. "We want people to tune in and check back frequently on her account to see if a new romantic challenge has been posted. We're going for viral here, a viral romance, got it?"

"Uh, I think so. Yeah."

"So that means the first few videos will be you two as friends, creating tension—will they, won't they—and then the later videos will be you two as . . ." Amelia glanced at me, seeming to search my face for permission to finish her thought. I nodded, and she continued, "Well, they'd be like you two are dating, even if you're not dating. We can film them this week and next, and then release them over the next ten weeks. You might have to do some acting. Is that okay?"

"Totally fine! I'm happy to help, and it all sounds good to me."

I exhaled a relieved breath, nibbling my bottom lip before adding quickly, "It might be a good idea for us to record as many as possible on Monday, to get them out of the way. What do you think?"

"Yeah, yeah, sure. Sounds good. What time are you coming over?" He sounded like he was genuinely looking forward to it.

I looked to Amelia, and she shrugged. "I can get off at five at the earliest, so five thirty? Six? Then we'll do as many as we can."

"Okay, see you guys then."

Amelia plucked her phone from the table, turned off the speaker function, and lifted it to her ear. "We'll see you then. And Jeff? You owe me."

I thought I heard him laugh on the other side. His happy sound plus how Amelia was wagging her eyebrows in my direction made me feel lightheaded and giddy.

I couldn't believe it. This was happening. After six years of not allowing myself to think about the possibility of being with Jeff Choi, this was finally, finally happening.

* * *

This couldn't be happening.

"That one was pretty great." Jeff grinned at Amelia.

The look she gave him could only be described as pained. I tried to muster a smile, but it felt tight and weird on my face. *This is a disaster.*

Everything had been perfect at first. When we'd initially walked into Byron's house in the fancy section of Capitol Hill, I'd been on cloud nine. Jeff had taken our coats, offered us a drink, made us laugh, told a few jokes—like he always did. He'd then handed me my water and sat next to me on their couch in the front room—a.k.a. the salon—putting his arm behind me, his thigh brushing mine. Both actions had felt like giant and positive steps over the platonic-friendship line.

But then Byron had sauntered down the stairs in his signature black pants and black long-sleeved shirt and strolled into the salon. My stomach had tensed and my heart had taken off at a gallop. He'd given Amelia a quick chin lift as a hello. His eyes then drifted over to me, narrowing on Jeff's arm placement. They'd seemed to narrow further as they slid to where our legs touched. He'd halted midstride.

"You two, this is happening?" he'd asked, looking between us, tone flat.

My neck heated. The way Byron had looked at me—chin angled down, that right side of his lip barely curling, the blue-green intensity of his eyes darkening—I felt like I'd been caught, like my hope of something with Jeff made me foolish.

It's all in your head, Winnie. Byron barely knows who you are, he's not thinking about you, he doesn't care about you and Jeff getting together, he doesn't care about you at all. Ignore him.

Jeff had laughed and squeezed my shoulder. "Come on, man. I'm helping Winnie with those videos. I told you they were coming over."

Byron had leaned his back against the wall and folded his arms such that the black Henley he wore stretched over his broad shoulders. His eyes had seemed to darken further as they'd locked with mine. "Oh yeah. Mind if I watch?"

My heart had gone from a gallop to warp speed.

Mind if I watch?

I'd fought a shiver.

If I'd felt comfortable being honest, I would have said, *Yes, I mind.* But that's not how I'd been raised. I'd been taught that admitting to being bothered by a person—especially when I was a guest in their house—was rude, because it was rude.

So I'd choked out "Of course not" while my insides twisted and tightened.

After that, everything had gone horribly wrong.

We'd moved from the salon to the family room to get the best light. Byron's house had one of those glass accordion patio doors running along the entire back wall off the combo kitchen and family room area, leading out onto an amazing deck with a built-in firepit and Jacuzzi.

The plan Amelia and I had worked out for the scene was as follows: Jeff would sit on the family room couch, pretending to play *Super Mario Bros.*; I'd step into the camera frame and lift a finger to my lips and grin mischievously, as though telling the audience to be quiet (Amelia said this would make them feel like they were part of the video, in the room with us); I would then crawl on the couch over to Jeff on my hands and knees; he'd do a double take, ask me what I was doing, I'd sit on his lap and tell him I wanted to sit there; he'd be surprised but pleased; and then the video would end with me laying my head on his chest and smiling softly at the camera. End scene. Very PG. Very sweet. Solid challenge video.

That's not what happened.

"No, it wasn't great, Jeffrey." Byron's full upper lip that always seemed on the precipice of curling with disgust actually did. Arms still crossed, he stepped away from the wall. "You've been acting like a dick for two months. Can't you stop thinking about yourself for ten minutes?"

Yikes. That was harsh.

Amelia lifted her hand in a placating gesture. "Byron—"

"He's feeling sorry for himself," he cut her off, not quite shouting, "and none of this helps Fred."

Confused as to why Byron was taking this so personally, I said weakly, "It was fine."

But it wasn't really fine. I couldn't post that video, or any of the other five we'd filmed. I knew Jeff was trying to help by being spontaneous and goofy, and I adored him for it, but I wished he'd just follow the script.

Making matters worse, Byron had been present for each and every disastrous take: the one where Jeff had broken out into a fit of giggles; the one where Jeff had elbowed me off the couch; the one where he'd whacked me playfully on the butt with the game controller; the two where he'd licked my face and cracked up after; and this last one where he'd shoved his tongue down my throat in a truly ridiculous stage kiss.

Byron hadn't said a word—just quietly seethed in the corner, the right side of his lip inching higher, his eyes narrowing into blade-like slits—until the last video. And now it seemed he was primed to unleash his ire.

"But you need better than fine, don't you?" Byron swung his glare to me. When I hesitated, he repeated, "Don't you?"

Flustered by his directness and confrontational tone, I turned to Amelia for help. She looked tired and exhausted. The sun had set, we hadn't eaten, and she'd been at work all day. Guilt plucked at my heart. *We should go.*

"Here." Flicking his wrist, Byron motioned that Jeff should move out of the way. "Let me show you. Go stand over there, out of the frame."

"You're going to show me how to kiss Winnie?" Jeff looked between us.

"No. You shouldn't have kissed her," Byron ground out, his jaw working. "Or licked her face."

"Why not? If given the chance, I'm pretty sure you'd lick her face." Jeff joked, dutifully leaning against the wall where Byron had stood earlier.

"I could tell you weren't playing a video game, that part looked obviously fake." Byron ignored Jeff's statement, casting his frown around the room, his tone distracted. "And that was a terrible kiss."

Jeff put a hand on his chest, like Byron had injured him with his words, but his mouth quirked with a small smile. "Bro—"

"You're wasting everyone's time." Byron was not smiling. He pushed his fingers through his longish hair, visibly agitated. "Do it right or not at all."

The conversation continued around me as I tried not to be disappointed in Jeff. He said he'd help, but it seemed like he was more interested in being the center of attention than being part of a team. Maybe I could just do the makeup tutorials, dance challenges, fashion trends, thirty-second STEM, throw in some video game duets, and forget about the romantic challenges.

"Win, was that a bad kiss?" Jeff's question had me looking at him. His eyes sparkled like this was all good fun. The two men could not have been more different, and not for the first time I wondered how they'd managed to be roommates for so long.

"If any of those are posted, you would ruin the story arc, deflate the tension before it had any momentum." Byron glared at Jeff, his tone quiet and accusatory. "The entire narrative lost, boring."

"And there is no greater sin than a boring narrative," Amelia said with a small, tired smile.

"Exactly." Byron sat in the spot Jeff had occupied, picking up the game controller. "Okay, watch this. Fred!"

I stiffened. I'd only been half listening, trying to figure out how to leave without being rude. Amelia needed to eat, and I needed to rethink this whole romantic challenge thing.

"Do the"—without looking at me, Byron flicked his fingers in my direction, motioning that I should come over—"do the thing."

In my confusion, I looked at Jeff and then at Byron. "The thing?"

"Crawl over and sit on my lap, like you did with Jeffrey. I'll show him what to do."

CHAPTER 4
WINNIE

Unable to believe my ears, I tripped over my words, "You—you want me to—you want me to sit on—on your—"

Byron patted the couch at his side. "I'm going to show Jeff how to do it right, without destroying the plot of the story you and Amelia mapped out."

My stomach swirled and I chased my breath. "Uh—" I looked at Amelia and found her eyes on me.

My friend shrugged, giving her chin a slight lift toward the surly writer. "I agree with Byron. That kiss was terrible—sorry Jeff—and we can't use the other ones. If you posted any one of those, no one would tune in to find out what happens next between you two."

"Fine, fine." Jeff chuckled, finally looking remorseful. "Sorry. Go ahead, Win. Let's see how I should do this."

Byron stared straight ahead at the television, navigating through the Mario Brothers game prompts until he started a saved session. He began playing a board, his attention wholly focused on the screen.

I scratched my neck as the momentum of the moment caught up with me. *What the heck?* They wanted me to crawl over and straddle Byron Visser's lap? That's what they wanted me to do? The swirls in my stomach morphed into a hurricane.

I couldn't do that.

Sucking in a deep breath, I turned to Byron, planning to tell him that it was okay, we'd go with what we already filmed, but before I could, he said,

"You don't want to touch me?" His sharp gaze sliced to mine, gave me a perfunctory examination, and then cut away. All the while he wore a supremely bored expression.

"No." I stood straighter. "I just—"

"It'll take one minute," he said, sighing as though to punctuate and underline his boredom. "I want to help."

"You don't have to if you don't want to, Win," Amelia piped in softly, lowering my phone. "We'll figure something else out."

I looked at her, at the compassion and concern in her gaze, and I realized how silly I was acting. I had no doubt in my mind that whatever Byron was planning, it would be exactly right for what we needed. I'd read his books. They were just as amazing and impressive as he was. If there was one thing Byron seemed to understand intrinsically, it was how to tell a great story, and ultimately wasn't that what we were trying to do?

Then Jeff could reenact the scene and we'd be finished. Amelia was doing everything in her power to assist me in obtaining that community manager position, giving up her Monday night, helping me strategize, lending her expertise and support. The least I could do was sit on Byron's lap so he could act out the scene for Jeff.

Finally, I managed a somewhat convincing "It's really okay, no big deal" and gave my friend a smile.

Her gaze hinted at concern, but she lifted the phone back into position. "Give me a second, let me start a new video. I think—here. Okay, on the count of three, go. One, two, three."

Squaring my shoulders, I stepped into the frame and looked at the camera for a beat, raising my finger to my lips just as I'd done before while also attempting to calm the storm in my stomach. *This is fine. This is no big deal. Do your part.*

Ignoring all the warning bells, alarms, and fire horns blaring between my ears telling me this was a bad idea, I forced the same grin I'd worn earlier. Or I tried to force a smile. I had a feeling this one carried an undercurrent of uncertainty.

Wiping my damp hands on my yoga pants, I strolled forward. Just like before, I placed a knee on the couch. Byron continued to play the game—actually play it—as I crawled over to him. When I reached his side, I stared at the sharp lines of his handsome profile and paused, gulping, my heart bouncing around my ribcage. Hints of warm, woodsy aftershave and clean soap teased my nose.

He smells really good.

Byron glanced at me and then performed a perfect and totally believable double take. "Uh, hi," he said, sounding and looking confused. "Can I help you with something?"

I rolled my lips between my teeth and held my breath. And then I did it. I placed a hand on his shoulder, lifted to my knees, and climbed on.

I sat on Byron Visser's lap. Straddling his narrow hips, our stomachs and chests scant inches apart. I exhaled as my palms slid from his shoulders to twine my arms around his neck. My face even with his. Our breath mingled. Our eyes locked. And I felt like I was going to swallow my tongue.

Oh God.

Breathe.

Breathe!

Peripherally, I was aware of Amelia taking a step or two toward us, getting a closer shot of our faces as Byron's gorgeous and unusual eyes—now wide with mock surprise—moved between mine, searching.

"What are you doing?" he asked, his voice rough, like he had trouble getting the sentence out.

"I wanted to sit here." I said my line, the words breathless.

He blinked several times, his lips parting. "Okay," he croaked before swallowing thickly. A flicker of something hot and needy passed behind his eyes and—I swear to God—I forgot what I was supposed to do next.

His thighs were so solid beneath me, his body warm and firm. His presence seemed to surround me, draw me closer even though we didn't touch anywhere except where I touched him. Unlike Jeff in his calamitous multiple takes, Byron hadn't placed his hands on my thighs or butt. He'd kept them up and away from my body at first, and then placed them on the couch on either side of my legs.

But his eyes—his truly magnificent eyes with their rings of hazel and green and blue—told me my touch wasn't unwelcomed. He craved it. He'd been *thinking* about it. A lot. And being caught in the snare of his brilliant stare was absolutely intoxicating.

I leaned a millimeter closer. His gaze seemed to flare and heat a split second before it dropped to my mouth. And I—

Oh no.

Oh no. No. No. No, Winnie. This is Byron Visser.

He's acting. He. Is. Acting.

This is an act. He calls you Fred because he doesn't remember your name. He doesn't like you. He never opens his mouth except to criticize.

This. Is. An. Act!

I felt the rising and sobering flush of embarrassment a moment before the heat climbed over my cheeks and I yanked away, tearing my eyes from his captivating face.

"Sorry, sorry. This was a dumb idea. Sorry." Instead of placing my head on his shoulder and smiling at the camera as we'd planned, I untwined my arms from around his neck and pushed off him.

Byron's hand closed over mine. "Wait—"

"Forget about it." Sitting on the couch briefly to get my bearings, I wrenched my hand from his grip, then launched myself up and walked quickly away, heading blindly for somewhere else, anywhere not in the same room as Byron Visser. *What the hell, Win?*

"Winnie. Win, wait—" Byron called, the sound of his voice drowned out by the rushing of blood between my ears and the music from the TV announcing that one of the Mario Brothers had perished.

"Holy shit, that was great!" Jeff jumped in front of me like a clown from a jack-in-the-box, sending my heart straight to my throat. Not seeming to notice that I was startled, he placed his hands on my shoulders and beamed down at me. "So much better than what I did. And I see now what you wanted me to do, how you want it to play out. I'm on the edge of my seat now, wondering what's going to happen next."

My mouth opened and closed as I wrestled with distress. Was it not obvious that I'd spaced out and forgotten Byron and I were being filmed?

"I agree, that was great," Amelia said from the other side of the room. I turned, my eyes instinctively searching for Byron and finding him some distance behind Amelia, facing away from the family room and leaning both hands against the quartz countertop of the kitchen island.

Amelia crossed to me, holding my phone up, her gaze encouraging. "I recorded the whole thing. We can play it back and Jeff can try to mimic what Byron did. I really liked how you changed it up though. Leaving the room, that was a good addition. People will be squealing at their screens. Much better than ending the scene with you still on his lap. Oh, thanks Byron!"

Byron had pushed away and straightened from the counter. He walked toward the salon. Not sparing any of us a glance, he lifted a hand and gave a vague wave before exiting. A moment later, his unhurried steps sounded on the front stairs leading to the second floor.

I stared at the doorway for several seconds while Jeff and Amelia discussed and picked apart the scene, and I thought I might be losing it.

What just happened?

Was I losing it? Had he been merely acting? The way he'd looked at me, that flicker of heat, he'd been so entirely convincing. Or was that—did he—was Byron—gah!

"Here, let me play it back. You can see what he does with his hands. He doesn't touch her, and it was very effective. It made the moment deliciously tense." Amelia typed in the password for my cell.

But before she could navigate to the video, Jeff's phone chimed and he pulled it out, frowning at the screen and then suddenly flinching back.

"I have to go." Now he sounded breathless, and not at all the jokester he'd been all evening.

Amelia lowered my phone. "Anything wrong?"

"It's Lucy." Jeff's voice cracked on the last syllable of his ex-girlfriend's name and his eyes shifted to mine, an apology carved on his features. "I'm sorry, Win. She wants me to meet her. I haven't heard from her in months. Maybe we could—maybe you could come back later? Or we could figure out—"

"Don't worry about it." I sent him a soft smile to cover my pang of disappointment. "We should be heading out anyway."

Jeff wrapped his fingers around my hand—the same hand Byron had grabbed earlier—and squeezed. "Thanks. I'll—I'll call you when I get back from camping. We'll—uh—hang out."

Nodding, I forced a smile and walked to the front door, my heart sinking even as my stomach continued to spin and swirl with the aftereffects of Byron's acting. I pulled on my coat, unsure what bothered me more: Jeff dropping me the second his ex-girlfriend messaged him or that Byron Visser's short and impromptu performance had been so entirely convincing that I'd almost fallen for it.

* * *

If I could help it, I never worked at our apartment when Amelia wasn't there. I'd discovered during undergrad that my productivity increased when I worked in a public place or adjacent to someone else. Something about the noise and motion, the ebb and flow of another person, helped me concentrate.

We lived within walking distance of approximately fifty thousand coffee shops (or it felt that way) where I could've camped out and sipped on a cold brew while hogging a table for hours. But—and don't judge me too harshly—I didn't drink caffeine.

That's right. I lived in the coffee capital of the United States, and I didn't drink coffee. Even small doses of caffeine made me feel wonky and jittery. I was one of those white chocolate eating, kombucha brewing, herbal tea drinking people. My caffeine aversion plus my wheat allergy plus my unwillingness to pay four dollars for a cup of tea meant I rarely entered a coffee shop.

So why live in Seattle? If the rent and cost of living were so high and I didn't work in tech and I didn't partake in coffee culture?

Several reasons: proximity to world-class hiking, boating, snowboarding, and skiing; proximity to Amelia and Serena and my other awesome college buds; public transportation and the Washington State Ferries system; the rain, I loved the rain; bountiful fresh fish any time of year at the market; and the Seattle Public Library.

You haven't truly lived until you've spent a day exploring the downtown Seattle Public Library. It was magical. With its diamond-shaped windows and geometric lines, the exterior looked like a giant glass sculpture in the middle of a bustling downtown.

But the inside—especially on gray, rainy days—was akin to what I imagined being within a cloud filled with books, floating on a sky island might feel like. And it was my work location of choice any time I had a full planning day. My second location of choice was the Seattle to Bremerton Island ferry, and only if I had thirty bucks burning a hole in my pocket and two hours of work to finish, which rarely happened.

My point was, no one gave me dirty looks for buying the cheapest thing on the menu and then hogging a table for four hours at the library. And, *come on*, sitting in a book-filled cloud on a sky island? What could be better than that?

I'd been working at my favorite table for a while, not noticing or keeping track of the time, when a person slid into the chair across from me and closed my laptop. I flinched, taken aback by the audacity of this interloper until my eyes connected with Amelia's, her fingers lingering on my computer.

"What are you doing here?" I whispered, frowning at her wet rain jacket. She had the hood up.

My roommate leaned forward, clasping her hands in front of her on the table, her gaze serious business. "First and foremost, you need to remember that we have years of friendship under our belt. We're basically soul mates."

Confused by her sudden appearance and her cryptic words, I woke up my phone and checked the time. "It's just after eleven. Are you here to grab lunch?"

She waved away my question, her eyes rimmed with something between worry and panic. "And you're not allowed to hate your soul mate. It's against soul mate law."

I squinted at her. "What are you talking about?"

"Similar to bird law, soul mate law disallows hating your—"

"I heard you the first time. Why do you think I would hate you? And why are you stalking me in the middle of the day?" To be sure, I quickly turned over my shoulder to inspect the clock on the wall above the door. *11:03 a.m.*

"Because I . . ." she wore a grimace and croaked, "I made a mistake."

Cocking my head to the side, I glanced left and right to ascertain whether we were causing a disturbance. No one seemed to care. This was another great thing about living in Seattle. As long as you didn't try to actively befriend anyone or get to know them, you could literally dance naked in the street and people wouldn't give you a second glance.

Ask for directions? Folks would fall all over themselves trying to be helpful.

Drop your wallet? They'd track you down ten blocks to return it (ask me how I know).

Try to make chitchat or a friend connection? No. Nope. Nopity nope nope nope. *I say good day, sir.*

"What kind of mistake?" I asked, deciding my lesson plans could wait.

"I pressed the wrong button," she whined quietly, threading, unthreading, and then rethreading her fingers.

I smiled at her nervousness. It was kinda cute. "What does that mean?"

Amelia let her hands drop. "That means you have to promise we're okay, no matter what, and you won't hate me."

"Hate you for what?"

"Promise first," she demanded.

"Fine, I promise." That was easy, I couldn't fathom a reality where I hated Amelia.

Earlier today, she'd made me breakfast and then proceeded to trash-talk Jeff, ranting about his shoddy treatment of me the night before. I hadn't felt like discussing it—or anything else that had occurred—when we'd arrived home last night from Byron's palatial house. But with tea and eggs this morning, she'd helped me feel better, telling me how awesome I was, that I deserved better than being overlooked and undervalued by Jeff Choi. I think I'd needed to hear those words.

After she'd left for work this morning, I'd played sad music and took a bath, coming to the conclusion that what happened with Jeff—him getting my hopes up and then ditching me for Lucy after a single text—had been a good thing.

Jeff had been the only man I'd met since high school that I really liked, could really see myself with past a few dates, and could actually see myself being intimate with. Maybe he was the good guy I thought he was. But he hadn't been a good guy to me yesterday, and wasn't that all that mattered?

I needed to let the idea of him go because that's what he was. An idea. A sweet, funny, gregarious idea. But now it was time for me to shake off that idea. If or when I wanted a relationship, I needed to find a real human person, with real human feelings who reciprocated mine. Not an idea.

And that was another thing!

Maybe I didn't need a relationship, ever. Maybe I was destined to never have a romantic partner. Or maybe five or ten years from now, once my student loans were paid, when I had a little bit of free time, I should focus on having fun rather than searching for a long-term anything. Maybe I needed to stop being so serious, stop with the preconceived notions of what direction my life should take and take things as they came—starting with whatever presently had Amelia taking a monumentally deep breath, her expression stamped with anxiety.

"Okay. You promised," she said, pulling out her phone. Navigating through a few screens, she held it out to me. "Remember your promise when I show you this."

I shifted my focus from my friend to her phone, studying the video playing there. It was Byron, sitting on the couch, playing *Super Mario Bros*.

"This is the video from yesterday." My stomach did a weird thing at the sight of him, and the sight of me crawling on all fours toward him, and what came after. I blinked away from the replay, before the part where I'd forgotten we were being filmed. "Why would I be mad at you about this? I knew you were filming."

"Look harder."

My forehead wrinkled, giving my attention back to her phone. I didn't know what she wanted me to see, but now the video was repeating and—

"OH MY GOD!" I grabbed the phone. "This—this is—"

"Shh! Yes." Now Amelia looked around, presumably to make certain none of the Seattleites surrounding us felt a disturbance in the politeness force. "Yes. I recorded it live. I'm so, so, so sorry."

I leaned forward. "So that means it's been—"

"Posted since last night. That's right." She covered her face again, groaning. "I'm so sorry."

My eyes caught on the number of views, and I stood from the table, my chair scraping noisily on the linoleum. "ONE MILLION VIEWS?"

"Sorry!" she whispered loudly to someone at a nearby table. "We'll just—we're leaving." Amelia grabbed my laptop and notebook and tilted her head toward the exit. "Time to go, and it was one point three the last time I checked. Now get your bag."

Numbly, I lowered her phone and grabbed for my backpack and coat, fumbling with the strap. My fingers didn't seem to work. She walked around the table and placed a hand on my back, helping to usher me out of the quiet area and waiting until we were standing in the hall to say, "I'm so sorry. It was an accident."

"I can't . . ." I couldn't do anything. I couldn't think, I couldn't move, I couldn't speak. *One point three million views. What must Byron think?* "Oh crap," I whispered, my gaze swinging around the interior of the library, unable to settle. "What about Byron? Does he know? How is he going to feel about this?"

"I don't know if he knows. I've been trying to call him all morning. He won't pick up his phone, and I'm frankly a little scared to leave a voice mail. Since he's not on social media, he might not know." Stuffing my laptop and notebook into my backpack, Amelia put the strap on my shoulder and took her cell phone from where I still gripped it.

I immediately covered my face like I could hide from this. My cheeks were hot. As much time as I'd spent this morning coming to terms with Jeff's decisions last night, I'd spent ZERO seconds thinking about my ridiculous reaction to Byron's performance. I wouldn't allow myself to think about it. What was the point? He'd been pretending, acting, playing a part, and—as per usual—I'd left the interaction feeling like a fool.

"We have to delete it," I rasped, my mouth dry, my brain on fire. "Before he sees it and finds out, we have to delete it."

"No! No. Don't do that." She pressed the phone to her chest.

"What? Why not?"

"Think for a second." She pushed me toward the elevator. "If you delete it, it might become a whole thing. He's a famous guy who millions of people are starving to know more about. He has no social media and suddenly he's on TikTok with you? And this isn't like your lab video from Friday, this is you two *together,* acting like you're close friends crushing on each other. We need to call him—together—and tell him. But first we need him to answer his damn phone." Amelia nodded at her own assertion while stabbing the elevator call button with her index finger.

"Call him? You want to call him together?" *Oh God.* I didn't want to call him. I never wanted to talk to him again. "You don't think he'll want us to take it down ASAP? Like you said, millions of people want to know about him. Don't you think he'll view this as an invasion of privacy?"

"Maybe."

"Maybe?" I flinched back. "I think you mean, *most certainly yes*."

"No." She pulled me by the arm into the elevator and pressed all the right buttons. "We should call him, leave a voice mail together where we tell him exactly what happened, and ask what he wants to do about it. If you take it down, it might create more difficulty for him than if you left it up and let it run its course."

I covered my face again, leaning against the wall for support. "I can't believe this is happening."

"Hey, on the bright side, you have over ten thousand new followers. That's . . . something."

I groaned. I would've given up every single one of my new followers if it would've somehow undone the posting of that video. What a nightmare.

CHAPTER 5
WINNIE

We debated what to do on the way back to our apartment, opting to walk in the rain instead of taking the light rail. I still wanted to delete the video. I thought that's what Byron would want, and the longer it was up, the more people would see it.

Amelia remained adamant that we call Byron first, that deleting it might bring it more attention than leaving it up. In the end, she convinced me not to delete it yet, mostly because nothing could ever truly be deleted from the internet, and to leave a voice mail on his cell. Byron was likely to hear about it—from his publicist, publisher, or agent—soon. Better for us to tell him, so we could apologize profusely.

"I'll call him again." Amelia tossed her keys into the basket by the front door as we entered and then draped her rain jacket on a kitchen chair. "I'll call him and tell him it was my fault, then you ask him to call back when he can, and that'll be it."

I trailed after her, dumping my belongings on the table, and peeled off my coat. "What can we do to make this better? Should I make him cupcakes? What does he like?"

"He likes darkness, rain, and silence," she replied, then laughed. "Actually, like you, he likes See's candy. *Dark* chocolate. But don't buy him any, my apology should suffice. Hopefully." She chewed on her thumbnail. "Okay, let's do this and wait for him to call us back. That's all we can do."

I didn't want to wait. The longer we waited, the more eyes would see that video. "How mad do you think he'll be? On the Muppet Scale?"

Our junior year of college, we binged *The Muppet Show* and often used the Muppet Scale to describe how angry we or others were in any particular situation. It's difficult to stay angry when discussing the Muppets, with Sam the Eagle at the low end and Miss Piggy finding Kermit canoodling with another pig on the high end.

"Maybe Kermit being kept in the dark about the banana sketch?" Amelia made a considering face, darting into the kitchen and flipping on the tea kettle.

"That mad?" I tucked my hands under my chin to warm my fingers.

She set her phone on the counter between us, blowing out a breath that made her cheeks puff as the phone rang on speaker. "Okay, here goes nothing."

He answered after one ring. "Amelia."

"Byron!" She stared at me over our kitchen counter, her expression pained and panicky and likely a mirror image of mine. "You answered."

"Yeah." The sound of his deep voice made my stomach swirl and tense. *Oh God. This is going to be bad.* "What's up?"

"Uh . . . Heeey," she said weakly, licking her lips. "How ya doing, Byron?"

"What's wrong?"

Amelia grimaced. "What makes you think anything is—"

"You've called me ten times and haven't left any messages. You okay? What happened?"

"I'm fine. But—" Amelia placed both hands flat on the countertop and lowered her head, looking defeated. "Okay, okay. Here's the deal, I'm going to get straight to the point."

"Please don't. You know I adore playing your little guessing games."

"Holster the sarcasm for five minutes and listen. So—" she gathered a deep breath "—I made a mistake."

"Okay . . .?"

I unfurled my fingers to cup my neck on either side, my hands still freezing. This was it. She'd tell him and he'd lose his fracking mind. I just knew it.

In what I considered a huge overreaction, Byron had taken down all his social media accounts after a fan shared a recording of him at Comic-Con. He'd been comforting a crying reader who'd become overwhelmed with emotion upon meeting him. His arm around her shoulders, he consoled her, letting her cry against his chest while the whole of the internet swooned at his display of compassion. Even I—who avoided him at all costs—thought the whole thing had been sweet. Astonishing, but sweet.

Meanwhile, he'd been so angry about being filmed without his consent, Byron had deleted all his profiles the week after it had gone viral.

I'd never discussed the matter with him or asked why he'd taken such drastic action after such a benign recording. Nor had I been privy to his wrath at the time. However—given his reaction to a video that made him look like a saint—I felt certain he'd reach at least that level of angry now.

"And, well, here's what happened"—Amelia scrunched her eyes shut—"I accidentally live-streamed that video of you and Winnie yesterday, it uploaded and posted. But I swear, I thought I'd saved it in drafts. And I didn't realize what had happened until this morning."

I tucked my fists under my chin again, shifting my weight from foot to foot, staring at the phone on the counter and half expecting it to explode, or at least start smoking like in a cartoon.

But it didn't. Byron said nothing.

Several seconds ticked by, then several more.

Amelia opened one eyelid and then the other. "Byron? Did you hear me?"

"I did."

We looked at each other. I could see his serene tenor did nothing to ease her anxiety.

She soldiered on. "And now it's been viewed, uh, almost two million times."

"Huh." Sounds from his side told us that he'd stood or moved in some way. "Well that explains all the other calls this morning."

"From whom?"

"Publisher, agent, publicist."

"What did they say?" Amelia asked while we traded another stare, and I knew she was thinking what I was thinking.

He sounded too calm. Granted, I'd never witnessed an angry Byron. With me, he was all robotic monotone and boredom. The closest I'd ever seen him to approaching truly angry had been yesterday when Jeff messed up all our takes. And even then, he'd been mostly chill.

But I assumed, since he and Amelia had been friends forever, she'd seen him angry before.

"I didn't answer the calls," Byron said, his tone still unruffled.

"Right, of course you didn't." Amelia sent the ceiling a beseeching look. "But listen, it's not Winnie's fault. She had no idea."

Complete silence on his end. Then, "Does she know?"

"I told her before I called you. We were going to leave you a message together."

Another pause, the sound of something rolling over hardwood—maybe an office chair? "Is she there?"

"Yes, she's right here, and you're on speaker. But this is my mistake so I'm the one telling you."

Byron cleared his throat. "What does she want to do?"

"I don't know. But she thought you would want to delete it. I figured we should check with you first."

"Why delete it?" he asked, like the very idea was preposterous, maybe the worst idea ever. "If it's been viewed almost two million times, that's good, right? She has new followers?"

"Yes, but—" Amelia glanced at me, looking for help.

I sighed, yanked up my proverbial big-girl pants despite feeling slightly nauseous, and stepped up to explain my reasoning. "Hey, Byron."

"Fred."

I slid my teeth to the side but powered through the spike of irritation at his use of "Fred." He'd used my real name yesterday—a fact I hadn't allowed myself to think about—so now I knew he did, indeed, know my real name. Which meant he called me Fred as a nickname. On purpose. *Why would he do that?*

"Listen," I croaked unevenly, swallowing the unsteadiness before forging on, "I suggested we remove the video because it felt like an invasion of privacy, but Amelia asked me not to delete it and to check with you first. Say the word and it's gone."

"Yours or mine?"

"Pardon?" I asked, not understanding.

"Do you consider the video an invasion of your privacy? Or mine?"

The spelled-out question surprised me, sent hot, flustery flutters twisting in my stomach. *Did he know I'd lost my head during the filming yesterday?*

I had to work to infuse my words with false confidence. "Your privacy, of course. You agreed to help show Jeff what to do, not to do the challenge with me and have it posted publicly. I'm sorry this happened."

"Don't apologize. It's not your fault."

"Even so, it's up on my account. I will delete it now if you want." My stomach continued to riot and twist. I placed my hand over it.

He didn't seem angry, and that was good. And if he'd realized my foolishness yesterday, so what? It's not like I would see him again anytime soon. Hopefully, by the time our paths crossed again in the distant future, he'd forget all about it.

But then he asked "What do you want to do? Do you want to delete it?" and my brain froze.

Why is he asking me?!

Now I looked to Amelia for help. She stared at me wide-eyed, then shrugged.

"Win?" he prompted, his voice low and oddly soft. "Do you want to delete it?"

"I don't really feel like it's up to me," I answered.

"Let's say I was okay with leaving the video. What do you want?"

I continued staring at Amelia across the kitchen peninsula, silently imploring her to answer for me or give me some hint as to what he wanted me to say. This felt like a trap.

Frowning, Amelia mouthed, "Don't look at me."

I sighed, frustrated and flustered. "Well, it doesn't make much sense having it up since the rest of the challenges will be done with Jeff."

As soon as the words left my mouth, I remembered how Jeff had dropped me last night the second he heard from Lucy. *So, no. No challenges will be done with Jeff.*

"Or someone else," I amended, cringing.

Amelia sent me a sympathetic look. I waved away her pity, waiting for Byron to respond. He didn't say anything.

"Byron?" I strained my ears. "Are you there?"

"I'm coming over." A door opened and closed on his side of the call, followed by the sound of jingling keys.

"What?" My eyes widened as they locked with Amelia's. She looked just as surprised as me.

"I'll be there in . . . ten minutes. Unless you want pastries. Do you want pastries?"

I stared open-mouthed at nothing, unsure how to respond to his bizarre question. Was he serious?

"Bakery Nuevo or Macrina?" Amelia piped in immediately. "Either is fine. But if you're going to Macrina, pick me up some of their everything bagels."

I reached over the counter and smacked Amelia on the shoulder, sending her a severe frown.

She glared at me in return, whispering, "What? I'm hungry. I haven't had lunch."

"I'll be there in twenty. *Don't* delete the video." Without offering a goodbye or even a small hint as to what he was thinking, Byron ended the call.

* * *

Twenty minutes later, my stomach in knots, I sat on the couch as Amelia jogged the short distance to our apartment door. Then I stood, thinking maybe that would be better. Then I sat again, rubbing my forehead and giving myself another stern talking-to.

Stop it! You have nothing to be nervous about. He probably didn't notice or care about you spacing out while sitting on his lap yesterday. He's probably used to women getting lost in the hypnotic rings of his gorgeous eyes. Just act normal.

Problem was, acting normal in front of Byron usually meant ignoring him, or saying as little as possible so as not to be criticized. I couldn't ignore him today, which meant this meeting would likely end with me feeling like a buffoon.

Voices filtered to me from the entryway, and I heard the sound of paper bags exchanging hands followed by Amelia's exclamation, "Bagels *and* scones? I love you. You know I love you, right? Well, I do. So much."

"I know," he said, the deep cadence sending a shiver up and then down my spine. I shot to my feet, deciding that standing was best. *Or maybe I should sit?*

Amelia strolled into the room, her nose stuck in one of the bags. Byron followed right behind her, his eyes colliding with mine. Rather than lower my gaze as per usual, this time I held his and lifted my chin for good measure. I was both used to and unused to his stare. Used to it because he stared all the time. Like Amelia had pointed out on Friday, Byron stared at people. He observed and watched. He just did. But *I* was unused to meeting his eyes, as I did now, and as I'd done yesterday when I'd sat on his lap.

I couldn't be certain, but his expression struck me as bracing. Had he been anyone else, I would assume this meant he was here to deliver bad news and had brought the scones and bagels as a peace offering, or as a way to soften a blow.

"Fred." He gave me a stiff nod as he pulled off his jacket, his gaze as watchful as ever.

I twisted my lips to the side and returned his nod. I couldn't ignore him, true. But I could say as little as possible.

"The scones are from Nuflours and they're gluten-free." Byron placed his coat over the back of a chair.

My attention shifted momentarily to where Amelia moved around the kitchen. She'd already withdrawn three plates from the cabinet.

"Thank you. That was really nice of you," I said, not hiding my confusion. *How does he know I'm celiac?*

Amelia only knew because we lived together. My allergy made me feel like death, but it wasn't anaphylactic in nature. I'd never explicitly told anyone in college, never brought it up or asked for a gluten-free option in restaurants. As a general rule, I avoided restaurants. My uncle used to enjoy berating the servers, and I'd never had a relaxing restaurant dining experience until college.

Unfortunately, in my experience, nine times out of ten the server would forget I was gluten-free and I'd end up being that weirdo who ate nothing on their plate. On the rare occasions I went to a restaurant these days, I only ordered whatever was certain to be wheat-free, least likely to have cross contamination, and was cheapest. Over the years, I'd developed the habit of carrying gluten-free protein bars and snacks with me.

It's not that I wanted to hide my allergy, it was more that, as I grew up, peoples' reactions varied, and I found it easier to say nothing. I never knew if I was going to get a side-eye of disbelief or an avalanche of sympathy and questions like, *Then what on earth do you eat?*

I was surprised Byron knew.

"I'm making more tea. What kind does everyone want?" Amelia asked, placing a scone on one plate and bagels on the others.

Byron, his hand braced on the same chair that held his jacket, shook his head. "Nothing for me."

"Not even a bagel?" Amelia sent him a perplexed look.

"I already ate." His attention returned to me, scrutinizing, watchful.

I crossed my arms, they felt weird hanging next to my sides, and got right to the point. "I can delete the video."

His jaw ticked. "Jeff and Lucy are getting back together," he said, then also crossed his arms. The intensity of his watchful scrutinizing seeming to increase tenfold.

"We figured." Amelia saved me from having to respond, carrying two plates over to the kitchen table. "Lucy texted him last night right after you left. He said he had to go meet her, then we left."

Something like surprise flickered behind his gaze, and he nodded, but still watched me. "I doubt Lucy will let him do the videos—the TikTok challenges."

I crept over to the table, standing next to Amelia and inspecting the scones. *Blueberry. My favorite.*

Meanwhile, Amelia snorted. "Yeah. You're right. We'll have to find someone—"

"I'll do it," he said.

"What?" Amelia reared back.

"I—you—you what?" I tried to speak around my malfunctioning tongue. He couldn't have possibly said what I thought he'd said.

"I'll do it." Byron moved his focus to Amelia. "I'll do the videos. With her."

"You will?" Amelia's eyebrows sprinted to her hairline. We were in a similar state of shock.

"Yes. But I have stipulations. And I want something in return." He shoved his hands into his pockets and addressed Amelia exclusively, like I wasn't in the room and this wasn't my project.

Ire replaced surprise, and I lifted a finger to object. I hadn't asked him for help. And if he offered to help, I wasn't sure I wanted his help. I knew he looked down on me, my choices, my career. So how would doing romantic challenges with Byron even work?

Before I could pair my raised finger with an objection, Amelia grabbed my hand and removed it from the scene of our debate, stepping slightly in front of me. "Sure. Yes. Anything you want."

"What?" I snapped.

She shushed me, stepping more completely between us. "What are your stipulations?"

"I don't want an audience." His eyes, hooded and remote, slid over Amelia's shoulder to tangle with mine. "If or when we do the videos, it's just me and Fred."

I frowned, but I wasn't all that surprised by this stipulation. Byron didn't like crowds. I suspected that anything more than two people felt like a crowd to him. Even so, this stipulation would exponentially increase the logistical difficulty of the project.

Twisting my objecting finger out of Amelia's grip, I moved to stand at her shoulder. "Then who will hold the camera? Filming without a third person holding the camera will only increase the likelihood of a sloppily framed recording. Having a camera person ensures we'd both stay in the shot and only have to do it once or twice."

"How do most people do these things?" Byron pointed his question at Amelia. "Is there usually a third person in the room filming?"

"I don't think so." She picked up her bagel and tore off a piece. "Usually, the person doing the challenge sets up the camera facing themselves and hits record, checking every so often that both people are still in the shot and letting it film whatever happens. I actually think your stipulation is a good one. It'll make the videos feel more authentic, real."

Since Byron addressed his questions to Amelia, I decided to address my objections to her as well. "But, again, if we have someone filming, we can reduce the chances of having to record the same video multiple times in order to get it right. Like the Toxic Dance Challenge. We'll be moving around a lot."

Amelia was right of course. Setting up my phone to record it myself would be more authentic, so I didn't really understand why I continued to push the issue. *Except* . . . The idea of doing some of these challenges with Byron, the two of us in a room and no one else, it felt too intimate. *Am I really thinking about doing this with him?*

On the one hand, two million views and counting on a single live video spoke for itself. At this rate, I would have no issue reaching the needed number of followers in two months.

And yet, on the other hand, I only ever thought of Byron as Amelia's friend and Jeff's roommate and a guy who intimidated the heck out of me. He and I had never been alone together, not once that I could recall, and now we were going to be touching, kissing, capturing everything on video, intending to share the moments with (ideally) hundreds of thousands of people, if not millions?

"Wait—wait a minute." I lifted my hands and gave my head a quick shake. "I don't know if this is a good idea. It made sense with Jeff because—"

"You wouldn't be pretending with Jeff," Byron finished my sentence, his eyes dropping to his shoes while an acrimonious-looking smirk tugged at the corner of his mouth.

"Yes," I ground out, batting away the embarrassment at my admission. "But since—it's just—with you, I don't—"

"You don't like me." His gaze lifted abruptly and he gave me the inclement burden of his attention. "Say it. Be honest."

I swallowed convulsively, my chest hot and tight. I didn't say things like that. I didn't say things to hurt people, or that were hurtful, even if they held a kernel of truth. "Byron—"

"But, if we do this," he continued, his tone a shade mocking to my ears, "if you pretend with *me*, you will amass enough followers to get your job as a brand manager for Amelia's company."

"Community manager," I grit out, correcting him. He made it all sound so sordid and underhanded, like I would be twirling my thin, waxed mustache while duping young women into considering a career in STEM.

I crossed my arms again, wishing I could put a wall between me and the unsettling, hypercritical intensity of his focus. Instead, I pointed out the obvious, "Clearly, you don't much care for me either. Neither of us would enjoy this. I don't understand why you'd agree to it, or what you'd get out of it, or why you'd consider it in the first place."

"I'm not casting aspersions on your character, Fred." He mimicked my posture. "I'm stating fact. And since you'd be pretending with me in order to achieve a goal—increasing your body count on Instatok so you can get the job—then you might as well commit to it fully."

Instatok? Body count? *Rude!*

I tilted my head to the side, narrowing my eyes on him. "Commit to it fully? What does that mean?"

"You want people to respond to you? Follow you? Well, people respond to authenticity. The videos should look and feel as authentic as possible, right?"

Reluctantly, I eventually conceded. "Right."

"Thus, my stipulation stands. If you want me to do this, then no third person holding the camera, no one else in the room." He'd placed his hands on the back of the kitchen chair and leaned slightly over it, adding with a whisper of a smirk, like the words were a dare, "Just you and me."

CHAPTER 6
WINNIE

It was on the tip of my tongue to remind Byron that I wasn't sure I wanted to do this with him at all, but his gaze felt like too much, too heavy. My brain went clumsy with the weight of it, and I snapped my mouth shut, not trusting myself to form coherent sentences.

After a disorienting stretch of uncomfortable silence, during which Byron and I glared at each other and I refused to speak, Amelia—mercifully—was the one to break it. "This all makes sense. The more realistic it looks, the better. Okay, Byron. Other stipulations?"

Releasing me from the bear trap of his gaze, Byron's features seemed to relax a smidge, his focus resettling on Amelia. "I've seen the list, so I know what's on there."

Amelia tapped her chin thoughtfully. "The list is tamer than I'd like, but Winnie is a teacher and can't do anything to risk her position."

"So nice that her employer gets the ultimate say in what she posts to her personal accounts." He flung his sarcasm around like a Frisbee. "That doesn't sound like *1984* at all."

I swear to Newton, if he criticizes my profession one more time . . . I was not a violent person, but I found myself wondering what the air speed velocity of my fist would be if I punched him in the face.

"We're not changing the list," I said, seething. "And we're not talking about my job, or my employer, or my career choices. Ever."

Other than the slight curl of his upper lip, he continued as though I hadn't spoken, "The list is fine. But I don't want to know when she's going to do the videos."

"You don't want to know when she's filming? You want her to surprise you?" Amelia's gaze darted to me, then back to him. "You want Winnie to film them whenever and wherever?"

"Exactly."

An involuntary sound emerged from my chest. "We should do them all at once, knock them out in one day."

He shook his head, still not looking at me. "Not if you two want it to look authentic. One challenge a month."

"What? No! Twice a week at least," I countered. "I only have ten weeks to get this done."

"It needs to look real, not rehearsed." He said this so calmly, so reasonably, like I was being ridiculous with my demands. "You have ten weeks, ten videos," he continued. "Once a week. I don't want to know when you're filming. That's my final offer."

Byron's infamous bluntness must've been rubbing off on me because I said, "If you're coming over here, or we're somewhere else and it's only the two of us, then obviously I'll be filming a video. It's not going to be a surprise, Byron. Why else would we be spending time together?"

His jaw worked, his lashes flickered, but he said nothing.

For some reason, his nonanswer death stare irked me more than usual. "Fine. Do I have to hide the phone too? And pick all the red M&M's out of your candy bag? What's next, No Eye Contact Tuesdays? Green towels only?"

"No." Byron pronounced the word slowly and carefully, his eyes—pointed at a spot on the wall behind and above my head—glittered like icicles. "I don't care if you put the phone in my face, Fred. I don't want to practice anything ahead of time. I don't want to stage it or be given lines to recite. None of that shit."

"Then how will you know what to do?" I asked, pressing the issue.

His glare cut back to me, burrowed into and held mine for several sluggish beats of my heart before he said, "I think I'll be able to figure it out."

"You might have to film it twice. Or maybe three times," Amelia warned.

He shrugged.

"There will be kissing involved." I felt compelled to spell it out. "The Kiss Your Crush or Secret Crush Challenge is nonnegotiable. None of the list is negotiable. We're doing every single one of those challenges, even the Toxic Dance Challenge."

He shrugged again, looking less irritated but positively disinterested by the prospect, and suddenly tired of the subject.

"Fine," Amelia said to Byron, then turned to look at me. "Fine?"

I grunted, figuring I was entitled to at least one grunt since he used them so frequently. Let them interpret that as they would.

"So . . ." My roommate lifted her fingers to tick off his stipulations. "You two will be alone when the videos are made. You don't care if she's holding the camera while she films and don't care if it's all up in your face, but you don't want to practice your reaction ahead of time or talk it through. And you don't care if you have to film the same challenge several times if there's a camera issue or one of you are out of the frame. Anything else?"

Amelia's summary gave me a moment to stew, to think. I had to admit, when taken together, his stipulations weren't so bad. Being alone when we recorded and not talking through or discussing the videos beforehand—how either of us would react or what we'd say—should reduce the awkwardness and make the whole ordeal feel less disingenuous.

But it would still be disingenuous, wouldn't it? Less disingenuous is still disingenuous.

Before I could give that thought the consideration it deserved, Byron said, "I need a date."

"You need a what?" Amelia and I asked in unison.

"A date. To a thing." Now he looked at neither of us, his eyes drifting to the kitchen, his expression and tone weary.

"What sort of thing?" I didn't care that my voice sounded heavy with suspicion.

"An awards thing, and some other stuff," he said, then cleared his throat.

"Oh!" Amelia snapped and then pointed at him. "You mean the Jupiter Awards?"

"Yes."

Amelia and I shared another look and I asked, "And you want me to go as your date?"

"Yeah." He continued his bored examination of the kitchen, like this was the most tedious conversation he'd ever been forced to endure.

Amelia and I swapped another look, and I shrugged. "I guess—I mean, sure. I'll go. But you could ask anyone and—"

"No. I need . . ." His gaze flickered over me. "I need someone like you."

I placed my fingertips on the center of my chest, gesturing to myself. "Someone like me?"

"Yes," he said matter-of-factly, then added with a sardonic lilt, "You're good at peopling."

You're good at peopling. Was that a compliment?

"He's right, you're a good choice. You can carry a conversation with almost anyone, no matter who they are or their background." Amelia nudged my shoulder. "It's fancy dress. You'll have to get something gorgeous."

"Oh no. Please. Don't make me." I may have kept my social media STEM focused until now, but my love for getting dressed up was no secret among my friends. Give me any reason at all to wear sequins and false eyelashes and I'd be wearing sequins and false eyelashes and four-inch heels and the reddest lipstick I could find.

"Good." He nodded, pulling out his rickety old flip phone and glancing at the monochrome screen.

"That's it? That's all you want?" I squinted at him, certain I was missing something. Why would the notoriously reclusive Byron Visser agree to suffer through ten TikTok romantic challenges, posted publicly, for one measly date?

"There might be other things," he mumbled, eyes on his phone.

"Other things?" Amelia made a short sound of impatience. "Byron, you'll have to be more specific. Winnie isn't going to agree to something as vague as 'other things.'"

"There will be other events," he grit out. "Or there might be. And a trip to New York. I need a . . . person. Like her."

"Oh. I see." Amelia nodded as though she truly did see. "This is about the contract?"

"What am I missing?" I inspected my roommate. She didn't look concerned, but I needed more information—especially if I would be going to New York—before I agreed to his request.

Byron looked at Amelia, communicating something to my friend using his hoarfrost glare.

She then turned to me, presumably to translate the outcome of their staring contest. "Byron's original contract was only for one book and included availability for interviews, book signings, publicity tours, all of that. But when the first title did so well and they started negotiating for the other two books in the trilogy, his agent was able to get rid of almost all the publicity requirements."

I was not surprised that Byron had negotiated his way out of publicity, interviews, and book signings. He barely spoke to anyone, he never showed up for the quarterly get-togethers I organized for our college friend group—which, I guess, he'd never wanted to be a part of anyway—though I always made sure to invite him. I'd also invited him to our *Stardew Valley* Friday night games. He'd never come, not once.

So of course he would leverage the popularity of his first book to get out of having to interact with people.

"But now that the book is nominated for all these awards," Amelia continued, "the nominations triggered a clause in the contract, which means he does have to do some—not a lot, a few—events. He has to go to the Jupiter Awards ceremony and to New York for some publicity, a few interviews."

I looked him over, trying to understand what my role in this would be. "You want me to be there for the publicity stuff? The events?"

"I was told I could bring someone," he said, voice tight, not looking at me in a way that felt pointed.

"That means he wants you to be his buffer," Amelia translated. "His agent will be there, but he wants you to pose as his date and carry the conversation for him should he be forced to engage in chitchat with strangers. Run interference with fervent fans, give him an excuse to leave if things get weird, that kind of thing."

"Oh." I nodded, looking between them. "That's easy. I can be a buffer."

"Good." Amelia looked relieved and thankful, like this favor was actually for her. "I was going to go with him, but now that we got the grant, the timeline of the trips doesn't work out. But, Byron, you have to buy her the dress for the Jupiter Awards." With this last part, Amelia pointed at him, her statement surprising me.

As did his immediate "No problem."

I opened my mouth to say it wasn't necessary, I'd figure something out, but Amelia wasn't finished. "And the shoes. And a purse or whatever else she needs."

"Fine." Again, his acquiescence was immediate, but this time it was followed by an abrupt "I have to go." He grabbed his jacket, pulling it on.

I stiffened at his sudden announcement, but Amelia didn't seem at all surprised. "I also have to get back to work, but we're decided? You two are doing this? TikTok celebrity and a new dress in exchange for a date to the Jupiter Awards, paid trip to New York, and Byron's stipulations?" Amelia turned toward the door of our apartment, glancing over her shoulder to peer at him.

I hadn't quite caught up with the conversation, still wordlessly processing the fact that my friend had negotiated a new fancy dress for me when Byron was the one doing *me* a favor.

"Yep," he said, shoving his phone back in his pocket, grabbing his jacket, and turning toward Amelia, presumably to follow her out.

"Wait." Unthinkingly, I trailed after him and reached for his arm, tugging until he turned. Things didn't feel quite settled . . . *were they?*

His stare fastened to where my hand held his forearm.

"So, listen. I—thank you. Thank you for doing this. I know you don't have to, but thank you. I appreciate it. Thank y—"

"Stop thanking me," he snapped.

Rearing back, feeling like I'd been verbally slapped, I released his arm and slid my fingers into the back pockets of my jeans, heat rising to my cheeks. I struggled to put the lid back on the box of my long-dormant childhood memories, of being snapped at for no reason, and measured my breathing. *How am I ever going to get through this with him?*

"Okay. I won't thank you." Like when dealing with my uncle or irate parents of students, I maintained a calm exterior. "But just so we're clear, this means you have to answer your phone when I call or call me back when you can. Since we're only doing this once a week, if I need to shoot a video for my account, I have to be able to reach you."

"I always answer when you call." The look he gave me could only be described as hard.

Actually, no. It could also be described as irritated, or frustrated, or something akin to impatient. Only angrier.

Surprisingly, his anger didn't fluster me this time. "Byron, I've called you maybe twice in six years. This is serious."

"Do I not look serious?" he asked, sounding like a monotone robot and glancing at the door as though he couldn't wait to leave.

"You look like someone who is infamous for never answering his phone. Promise me you'll be reachable when I need you."

He lifted his chin, settling that unnerving, hooded gaze on me once more. "I promise, if you want or need me, I'll be there," he said, his voice just above a whisper.

Something about it made the hair on my nape prickle. Was I being unreasonable? Or was he mocking me? "I'm not saying you have to answer if you're busy. It's not like I'll bother you more than once a week. Does that work?"

"Yes."

"I'm just saying—"

"I know what you're saying, I get it," he ground out, turning and walking past Amelia as he opened the door. "When you call, I'll answer."

* * *

The watch count for the video continued to grow, as did my number of followers. Over the two and a half weeks since the bargain I'd struck with Byron, many of those new followers had also gone back to my older posts across my social media accounts and engaged with my STEM-focused videos.

Viewership numbers were up on all my content, as were comments and likes. More people tuned in for my latest live STEM video—more engagement, more comments and questions about naming conventions for chemical compounds—than for any lesson prior. The video had lasted an hour and I'd drawn the chemical structure for over twenty compounds, answering a plethora of great questions from the audience.

This should've made me happy.

Hadn't I wanted more engagement? More questions? More viewers with an active interest in STEM? Hadn't I wanted to be a meaningful resource? Yes. I did. And I definitely wanted that community manager position. Any movement closer to the 500k follower goal should've made me ecstatic.

Yet, I wasn't.

I wasn't happy. Which explained why, on the Thursday night of a three-day weekend, I found myself wandering through the aisles of Phoenix Comics & Games on Broadway, looking to spend my savings for the month by splurging on a new board game.

Instead, I came face-to-face with Jeff Choi.

DARN IT!

Ducking behind the aisle I'd just exited, I turned and gauged the distance to the door. I was average height. Maybe he hadn't seen—

"Winnie?" Jeff's voice a precursor to his head poking around the corner, a small smile spread over his face as our eyes met. "I thought that was you."

"Oh, hi Jeff." I smiled, waved, and ignored the heavy weight in my chest.

"How are you? I haven't seen you in a while." Peering down at me with his soft eyes, he sounded and seemed truly interested in how I'd been.

Not only had we not seen each other or spoken since his text from Lucy, we'd stopped playing *Stardew Valley* together. This wasn't due to a concerted effort on my part to stop playing with him, but once he and Lucy reconciled, Amelia received a text informing her that Lucy didn't want him joining the co-op on Fridays anymore.

Amelia, Serena, and I had started a new co-op and named it No Boys Allowed Farms.

"Good. I'm good." I nodded, allowing my gaze to sweep over the store. In the back, a few people had clustered together to play Magic: The Gathering.

"Are you here to play?" He tossed a thumb over his shoulder.

"Nah. I'm more of a Pokémon Go person."

His smile widened and his velvet gaze seemed to warm. "Yes, I know."

We stared at each other for several moments, the heaviness in my chest increasing with every beat of my heart. This was awful. I needed to go. Now.

And so I said, "Well, I should—"

As he said, "I wanted to—"

We both laughed.

I gestured that he should continue. "Go ahead, what did you want to say?"

"I wanted to say I'm really sorry about what happened that day you came over with Amelia. I can't stop thinking about it." He shuffled a few inches closer, his gaze earnest and kind. Really kind. *Too* kind. Making me suspect his kindness was a cover for pity.

My heart sank. The last thing I wanted from anyone was pity, especially from Jeff. "You don't need to explain." I lifted my hands between us, perhaps an unconscious movement to ward off his sympathy, and gained a step back. "I'm happy for you."

That was the truth. I was happy for Jeff. Being with Lucy obviously made him happy. He only seemed miserable whenever she broke up with him.

"Thank you, Winnie. That means a lot," he said, but then his eyes narrowed, like he had a sudden thought. "Hey, why don't you and Amelia come over tomorrow? Lucy and I are having a small get-together at the house."

"What house?"

He grinned. "Byron's house."

"You are?" I couldn't imagine Byron sanctioning a dinner party at his house. With people.

I hadn't seen or talked to or texted Byron since he'd shown up at our apartment with scones and bagels over two weeks ago. At first, I hadn't called because of his once-a-week stipulation on recording the videos. But when the waiting period had ended, I'd made excuses to Amelia (and myself) about being too busy. I told her (and myself) I'd call him the next day. Tuesday became Wednesday, Wednesday became Sunday, Sunday became today. I still couldn't bring myself to call.

Aside from not wanting to be around Byron in general, and not wanting to pretend Byron and I were good friends, the more I thought about the idea of using his fame and elusiveness to grow my social media accounts, the ickier I felt. Add to this a difficult week at work during which half my students had failed a pop quiz and seemed to be struggling with our latest chapter on force and velocity, my inability—due to lack of time—to pull together a new lesson for my social media accounts, and my conflicted feelings about Jeff, and I wasn't quite myself these days.

I admit it, I'd been in a funk. I'd purchased two tickets to funky town, and I didn't know how to leave.

"Yeah. A party—a dinner party, I guess. Are we old enough to have dinner parties?" He laughed, making a cute face.

"We're in our midtwenties, we can do whatever we want. Dinner parties, yacht parties, political parties. But, uh, is Byron out of town?"

"No. Byron will be there."

I scratched my neck, squinting my disbelief. "At the party? Really?"

"Well, he'll be at the house. Lucy invited him and got his blessing to use the house, but whether or not he makes it downstairs is a different matter entirely." Jeff gave his eyes a quasi-half-roll, and I huffed a laugh. We traded a commiserating stare and I felt something in me ease; a worry I'd been carrying around for over two weeks dissipated.

It was nice to see Jeff. And it was nice to see him looking so carefree and happy. He hadn't been in a good place after Lucy had broken up with him, but now he seemed so much better. And seeing one of my friends happy made me happy.

"Okay, well. I should . . ." My mood lifted, I tilted my head toward the door.

Before I could turn fully toward the exit, Jeff caught my hand. "Hey, Win. Wait."

"Yes?" I asked, giving him my full attention, and feeling gratitude for the chance meeting. This short discussion had saved me fifty dollars in retail therapy. My savings account would be pleased.

His eyes moved between mine like he was looking for something, but all he said was, "I'm glad we're still friends."

I squeezed his hand and then slipped my fingers from his grip, stuffing them into my coat pocket. "Me too, Jeff. And I really am happy for you."

"Thank you," he said, his tone thoughtful. "We'll see you tomorrow?"

Not giving myself a moment to think about it, I said, "Yeah, sure. We'll be there."

Even as I left the game shop after we said our goodbyes, the decision felt right. Seeing Jeff with Lucy, seeing how happy he was and working to dispel the lingering awkwardness between us seemed like the answer. Who knows, maybe Lucy and I would become friends, maybe she liked *Stardew Valley* and would play with us on Fridays.

If this quick conversation was any indication, the dinner party should be exactly the thing to help me secure two tickets *out* of funky town.

CHAPTER 7
WINNIE

"Why do you feel guilty? You have nothing to feel guilty about." Amelia pulled her coat tighter around her neck as we stepped off the bus. Byron's house was three blocks from the bus stop.

"I wish I'd never told Jeff that I'd liked him, and I most especially wish that I'd never told him I'd liked him for a while. That was a big mistake."

Amelia heaved a noisy sigh. "I don't think it was a mistake. It was brave and emotionally mature." She switched the wine bottle bag to her other hand and hooked our arms together as we set off across the street. "As long as I've known you, Jeff is the only guy you've ever liked or lusted after."

"I've never *lusted* after him." Jeff was cute and handsome and kind, but I'd never fantasized about him or objectified him. First, it would be inappropriate since he'd almost always had a girlfriend. And second, in the past, when I thought about Jeff, I thought about how much I respected and related to his love of teaching and enjoyed his company. I loved that he was always so friendly, polite, kind, and patient. I'd never heard him raise his voice, not once. My feelings for him had been based on admiration, not lust.

"But you said once—though you were totally drunk—that you wouldn't mind losing your V-card to him. That's big."

I huffed. "Can we not talk about that?" I hated that being a virgin at twenty-six was considered weird by society when it felt perfectly natural to me. It wasn't my fault I'd never met a person I wanted to have sex with who also wanted to have sex with me. I wasn't saving myself for marriage or for the perfect guy. I wanted to have sex! But I didn't want to have sex just to have sex. "My point is, there's a time for bravery and then there's a time for caution and wisdom. It *was* a mistake to tell Jeff the truth."

"Win—"

"No. I should've waited until I knew for sure he and Lucy were over, when I was one hundred percent certain of his feelings. That would've been wise. Now I've gone and made things awkward between us, possibly forever."

"And you feel guilty about it?"

"I feel something like guilt." I steered us around a puddle. "But not quite guilt."

Embarrassment, maybe? Regret? Whatever it was, I wanted it to stop. I hated confrontation. I wanted to be friends with Jeff again, and I wanted to feel like myself again.

"You shouldn't feel anything like guilt. Think about it this way: Lucy has never made any effort to befriend Jeff's friends, and she broke things off with Jeff for two months. And Jeff made the first move with you three weeks ago. You did absolutely nothing wrong."

"But I almost sorta kinda went on a date with someone else's current boyfriend." I looked both ways before crossing the next street.

Cars in Seattle were pretty good about stopping for pedestrians but, interestingly, bicyclists were not. Especially not the MAMILs (Middle Aged Men In Lycra) and especially not in this neighborhood, where the MAMILs were plentiful but not varied.

"He was single at the time!" She groaned. "You are so stubborn about this kind of stuff. I've never met anyone with more rigid ideas about right and wrong—apart from maybe Byron. Except you are too hard on yourself and he's too hard on everyone else."

She was missing the point. "Jeff and I have been friends for years, and he's been dating Lucy the whole time, except for those two months. It was irresponsible of me—"

"They've broken up several times before, this wasn't the first."

"Even so, I feel like I've broken the sacred tenets of both woman and friend code." I hiked the strap of my purse higher on my shoulder as we approached a hill that ran the entire length of the block. "My instinct since they got back together is to avoid him. I haven't wanted to see or talk to Jeff at all."

"So then why are we going to this dinner party?"

"Because every time prior to yesterday when I thought about our lost chance, I felt a pang of restlessness and sadness. I don't want to feel that way anymore." As much as I hated confrontation, I hated it when things were unsettled and uncomfortable even more. It reminded me of walking on eggshells around my uncle, never knowing when he was about to explode. "I don't want to feel awkward around him. Our chance meeting yesterday helped me dispel some of the bad feelings and I'm hopeful that if we go tonight, then maybe we can befriend Lucy."

Amelia seemed to huff, although the heavy breath could've been caused by the sharpness of the incline. "Let me guess, the sadness only makes you feel worse because you're mourning the loss of a chance with someone who has a girlfriend, and then you feel something like guilt for these *very natural* thoughts and feelings."

"Exactly. And then it makes me feel gross about myself. He ditched me the first time she texted. Like, where is my pride?" Bah! *Feelings. They are the worst.* "I want to see them together, all reconciled and in love. I want to be happy for my friend. I need to get over the *idea* of Jeff. And it's frustrating because it's not like I have this burning desire to be in a relationship with anyone. I don't even want a boyfriend. I don't even have time for a pet rock. I have too much going on."

"Okay, I get it." She nodded, huffing and puffing as we crested the hill. "And I have your back. We'll go in, eat the free food, circulate around the room, eat the free food, do our best to make Lucy like us, eat the free food, and then leave—maybe with doggie bags."

I snorted as we trudged up the stairs at the front of the property. Amelia would travel all the way to Spokane for free food.

Byron's front yard was less of a traditional yard and more of a winding path with two flights of stairs around four ancient cedar trees and all manner of ferns and bushes. You could barely see the house from the road even though it—like the cedars—was massive. The dude owned a one-hundred-year-old legit mansion.

Likewise, when you made it to the front porch (which was huge, by the way) and looked out toward the road, you didn't see the road as the house was so high up. You saw the trunks of ancient cedar trees, all manner of ferns and bushes, sky, and on a clear day, the Cascades. It must've felt like living in the middle of Seattle while also being in the middle of a forest.

When we finally trekked all the way to the porch, I lowered the hood of my coat as Amelia caught her breath, then stepped forward and rang the doorbell.

"I didn't text Byron that we were coming. Maybe I should—"

Before Amelia could finish her thought, the door swung open, revealing Lucy's smiling face, which morphed precipitously into a not smiling face. "Oh. Hello."

"Hi Lucy," I said brightly. "I'm Winnie, this is Amelia."

Her stony stare moved between us. "I know who you are."

"Uh. Okay. Well, thank you for having us."

"Excuse me?" She reared back slightly, her frown severe.

"Uhh. . ." I glanced at Amelia.

My roommate stood frozen, like she didn't know what to do. Or maybe she hoped by not moving Lucy wouldn't notice her next to me.

"Oh! You're here." Jeff burst forward, circumventing his openly hostile-looking girlfriend and bent to give me and then Amelia a kiss on the cheek. "Thanks for coming, come on in."

But when he stepped back, Lucy still blocked entry with her body, her gaze incendiary. "You invited them?"

"Yeah. The more the merrier." He shrugged, seemingly unconcerned by her obvious displeasure.

Amelia and I swapped a quick glance, communicating the entirety of our shared thoughts in a single second.

"We don't—we can leave." Amelia pointed behind us. I didn't miss how she gripped the wine to her side protectively.

"No. Don't be silly. Thanks for coming," Jeff repeated, beaming.

"Yeah. Thanks for showing up," Lucy ground out. "We'll need to add a few more plates, but I'm sure I can find some paper ones for the kitchen table. The dining room is already full."

"Lucy!" He sounded shocked but also amused.

"Well, I'm sorry, Jeff. But you didn't tell me you'd invited anyone. And I've been planning this for a week."

Yikes.

I backed up a step, holding my hands out. "We don't have to stay—"

"No, no." Lucy finally relinquished her defensive position, motioning that we should come in, and heaved a harassed sigh. "It's not your fault. Sorry, I'm being rude. I wish he'd told me."

"I didn't think it would be a big deal." Jeff put his arm around her waist and nuzzled her neck. "Come on, baby. Let them stay."

"I already said it's fine." She removed his hands from her body and shot him a hard look as Amelia and I reluctantly stepped inside.

"We brought wine," Amelia said, handing over the bag to Lucy.

Lucy immediately passed the bag to Jeff. "I'm allergic to phosphates. I don't drink wine."

"Do you mean sulfites?" Amelia asked. "Wine doesn't have phosphates."

"Anything unnatural, it makes me sick," Lucy snapped, her eyes slicing to me, like maybe *I* was full of sulfites and made her sick.

"Ooo-kay. Well, maybe Jeff and Byron can use it for spaghetti sauce then," Amelia said using her most chipper of voices, adding, "It also has medicinal uses, like numbing pain."

Uncertain if we should stay or go, I removed my coat in slow motion, casting a glance at Amelia to gauge her thoughts. She'd already shucked her rain jacket and walked to the front closet. Retrieving two hangers, she motioned me over.

"Uh, excuse us." I hurried to my friend's side.

"Sure thing," Lucy said flatly, clearly still irritated, not that I blamed her.

"Trouble in paradise," Amelia whispered, nudging my shoulder. "But then they're always like this, aren't they?"

"I don't blame her for being irritated. She obviously planned this dinner, and he didn't tell her we were coming." I snuck a glance over my shoulder, jolting when I spotted Lucy glaring at me—at me, not Amelia—like I'd strangled her pet snake. Hastily, I hung up my coat. "Maybe we should leave before dinner. I'll fake a leg cramp."

"No! I was promised free food. We're staying for the whole thing." Amelia also looked over her shoulder, whispering, "Plus, Jeff should be allowed to invite his friends if he wants. . . Hey. Why is she staring at you like that?"

I shrugged, not needing or wanting to look again. "I don't know."

"Oh no," Amelia said on a breath and turning back to me. "You don't think Jeff told Lucy about the two of you?"

"What would he tell? Nothing happened."

Her frown turned anxious. "He kissed you and licked your face."

"Not in a sexy way!"

"Shh!" She grabbed my hand and we weaved through the twenty or so people already gathered—none of whom we recognized—and further into Byron's house. Huddling close to each other near the fireplace, we gave our backs to where Lucy and Jeff were standing.

"All I know is I should've kept the bottle of wine." Amelia braced a hand on the mantel, inspecting the pictures there even though several were of her and Byron, and she'd been responsible for having most of them printed and framed. "That wine cost me twenty-four dollars."

"Whoa. Big spender."

"Well, I thought—you know—I'd bring something nice. Next time he's getting a two-buck chuck."

Unable to help myself, I let my gaze wander back to where Lucy and Jeff were standing earlier. Sure enough, they still stood at the door, arguing. She wasn't glaring at me anymore, but she did sweep her hand in my direction, making no attempt to disguise her unhappiness in front of their guests. And though she was visibly upset, he still seemed unconcerned.

Actually . . . no. He seemed really happy, smiling his charming smile like he enjoyed coaxing her into a better mood.

Huh. Was Amelia right? Had they always been like this? I'd rarely seen them together, but since Amelia spent so much time with Byron, and Byron and Jeff had been roommates since college, it was likely she'd also spent a significant amount of time with Jeff and Lucy.

"Where is Byron?" Amelia cut into my thoughts, fitting our hands together.

"You didn't actually expect him to be down here, did you? There's . . . people. And the room is well-lit." I didn't expect to see him at all.

"Did you two connect yet? About the next video?"

"Not yet," I hedged.

"How many people did she invite? There must be twenty or more people here, not including our hosts. And where are we all going to sit?" Amelia craned her neck, presumably counting everyone in the living room—where we stood—and all the people visible across the entryway in the parlor. Beyond the parlor and to the right was the dining room, which housed a huge antique mahogany table. But she was right, it only sat sixteen people maximum.

I shrugged, my eye caught by two guys across the room next to the liquor cabinet. Dressed in khakis and button-down shirts, they were checking us out, and I wasn't quite sure how to feel about that.

Both relatively tall and fit, they had a pallor that told me they worked out in a gym and not outside. One had auburn hair close to my color, just a little darker, with pretty brown eyes and a smirky-looking smile. The other had blond hair, blue eyes, and a sandy-colored, close-cropped beard.

As a rule, I didn't usually mind being checked out regardless of who was doing the checking. I'd spent a good amount of time getting ready for tonight, flat ironing my hair, applying dinner-party-appropriate makeup, and this was one of my favorite dresses. A black wraparound with three-quarter sleeves, the deep V neck did quality things for my boobs.

But these guys were probably Lucy's friends and worked with her at the law firm. After the unpleasantness at the door and how distasteful she found our presence, I didn't particularly want to upset her further.

* * *

Free, tasty food made the awkwardness of the evening and missing our Friday game of *Stardew Valley* almost worth it. Almost.

Lucy had been pointedly unpleasant whenever we interacted, and I began to suspect Jeff must've told her something misleading about me and our blip of an afternoon together before they'd reconciled. Maybe not an outright lie —I didn't think he'd do that—but perhaps a variation of the truth? Something to make my presence here tonight upsetting for her. All of this reinforced that staying single forever was likely my best option for a happy, fulfilling life.

Thankfully, Lucy had been called away each time we bumped into each other to deal with seating arrangements or some related subject, sparing me her glares and Jeff's fumbling attempts to unruffle her feathers while also working overtime to be nice to me *in front of his girlfriend!* What was wrong with him?

Instead of sitting at the dining room table together, the guests were instructed to take turns and eat in shifts. That part was weird at first, but in the end, it all worked out.

Amelia and I spent most of the evening hanging out with two lovely women. Danielle Hardy Socier was in her last year of medical school and Olivia Canelli was a hugely successful yoga fitness guru who also practiced non-contact therapeutic touch, or NCTT.

We made a cheerful foursome and exchanged numbers when it was our turn to sit at the dining room table, splitting Amelia's twenty-four-dollar bottle of wine between the four of us and making a toast each time we drank. We took turns regaling each other with best-of and worst-of camping trip stories.

"Hey, I'll be right back," I whispered to Amelia during a pause in our merry conversation.

"Where are you going?" She caught my hand, holding me in place.

I turned to Olivia and Danielle. "Anyone else need to use the ladies' room?" The wine plus three glasses of water plus all those vegan dishes had finally caught up with me.

Our new friends shook their heads and Danielle said, "I'll save you a piece of the apple crisp. I've had it before and it's so good."

Amelia, still holding my hand, looked pointedly over my shoulder and then back to me. "Use the bathroom on the second level. It's on the right at the top of the stairs. There's probably a line for the one down here, so *avoid* it."

I surreptitiously glanced over my shoulder. *Ah!* So Jeff and Lucy were blocking the path to the bathroom on this level and Amelia wanted to spare me a run-in.

"Thank you," I said, squeezing her hand before we both let go.

Keeping my back to where Lucy and Jeff hovered, I strolled to the back stairs. The house had two staircases—a grand, front stairway with a huge, carved newel post adorned by a bronze and marble art deco sculpture lamp, and a servants' stairway adorned by nothing but a serviceable banister and lit by a single wall sconce. I'd never used either of the stairways, as I'd never been to the second level, but I knew where they were located.

The door behind me closed, muffling the chatter of the party, and I climbed the narrow, carpeted flight, unable to stop myself from wondering about the oddness of the evening.

I couldn't help but wonder why Jeff would say anything about me to Lucy. Nothing had happened between us. And if he had said something to Lucy that upset her, why ask me and Amelia to dinner tonight? And why not tell his girlfriend he'd asked us? Why surprise her? Especially when she'd worked so hard on making the dinner party nice.

The whole thing was confusing and weird and distracting, which is why I think I can be excused for following Amelia's directions, opening the first door on the right I encountered, and startling myself upon seeing a shirtless, underwear-clad Byron Visser. Gasping. And then slamming the door shut in my own face.

CHAPTER 8
WINNIE

"Oh God! Sorry. Sorry!" I yelled through the now closed door. Backing up and spinning in a circle, I blinked furiously against the image of a mostly naked Byron branded on my brain.

Black underwear. He wore black underwear. Not boxers. Not boxer briefs. Black underwear with a gray waistband. File that under things I never wanted or needed to know.

And those thighs . . .

Chest full of heat, agitation, and shards of embarrassment-tinted glass, I pushed away the image of his muscular thighs and rushed forward, opening another random door on the right. The interior of the room looked like an office, but the lights were off. I couldn't be certain. Regardless, it definitely wasn't a bathroom.

"Darn it," I whispered, spinning again and counting the doors off the landing. *Where is the godforsaken bathroom?!* There were seven doors and what looked like two hallways leading to more doors. Every single one of them was closed.

That is, they were all closed until door number one—the door I'd tried first—opened and Byron stepped out. His hands hovered at his waist as though he'd just finished pulling up the dark gray pajama pants he now wore. No shirt was in sight.

GREAT.

"Sorry," I said by way of greeting and averted my eyes from his sculpted chest, a renewed and fiercer wave of heat pressing down on me. My cheeks had to be as red as my lipstick by now.

Obviously, I've seen naked male chests before, lots of them, and all shapes, colors, and sizes. I've been to the beach. I watch movies and teen dramas. I'd even seen Byron's naked male chest before—when he did the shirtless interview that one time for the magazine.

But I'd never seen Byron's naked chest live. Never close. Never in person. Never . . . *there.* Within touching distance.

Not that there will be any touching. I stared at the tufted carpet beneath my shoes and brought my hand to my forehead. *Why am I even thinking of touching? There will be no touching!*

"Hello." His deep, rumbly voice held a suggestion of amusement. "Lost?"

"Sorry. I'm looking for the bathroom. Amelia said it was on the right. Sorry." I gestured vaguely to the doors on the right side of the landing.

"There's a bathroom off my room."

I peeked at him, found his eyes fastened to my face, his expression enigmatic but not quite neutral. My stomach twisted. "Sorry, but the only bathroom on this level is off your room?"

"No. There are seven on this level." He lifted his chin toward several doors in turn. "Each bedroom has an en suite bathroom. Amelia must've meant that one over there." He pointed to a door on the left, nearest the grand staircase. "It's the only one accessible from the landing."

"Oh." I straightened. "I thought it was on the right. Sorry."

"Depends on which stairs you take." His eyes remained hooked on mine, held, suspending the air in my lungs. "She probably thought you were taking the front stairs."

"I see. Thanks. Sorry." Irritated by how breathless that came out, I gave him a forced smile and darted for the door he'd indicated, needing to free myself from the hypnotic sight of his abdominal muscles.

But before I'd made it to the bathroom, he called to my back, "You apologize too much."

His words brought me up short and I half turned, frowning at him over my shoulder. "Pardon me?"

Byron had shoved his hands into the pockets of his pajama pants. "You apologize when you have nothing to be sorry for." Tone even, like we were discussing the weather rather than a critique of my verbal habits, his tongue darted out to lick his lips. "You shouldn't do that."

I gave my head a quick, incredulous shake and continued to the bathroom, saying nothing but feeling like an absolute dolt, certain my cheeks were flaming red. Why did he have to do that to me? Why—on the rare occasion we shared the same space—was he always telling me what I should and shouldn't say? And why did I let it bother me so much?

Anxious to escape, I closed the door behind me before I'd bothered to flick on the light. I was flustered and required a moment or two to find the switch, during which I mumbled to myself about rude people and dinner parties and houses with too many doors.

Once the switch finally clicked on, I did my business while still wearing my mighty scowl, making myself a promise that I would never apologize to Byron again. And I would never come to this house again. I had no reason to come to this house *ever again.*

There. It was decided.

I'd just finished washing my hands when I made myself another promise, namely that I wouldn't be doing the romance challenges. Not with anyone, and definitely not with Byron Visser.

"I don't need him. I'll do the Toxic Dance Challenge by myself. And I'll do my review of lip stains and see how many new followers I get." I reached for the door. "Maybe I'll even go over the science and technology behind lip stains and why they—AH!"

"There was no graceful way to do that," Byron said, hovering outside the bathroom.

I glanced behind me. Was he talking about me going pee? "No graceful way to do what?"

"Wait for you."

"You're waiting for me?" I turned my head to the side, peering at him through the corner of my eye. "Did I use the bathroom wrong?"

The side of his mouth tugged the merest scant millimeter upward. "New York. The Jupiter Awards. We need to discuss logistics."

I stared at him, my brain sluggishly reminding me that I had indeed agreed to accompany this shirtless manifestation of supreme irritation and intimidation to the Jupiter Awards and on a trip to New York. I sighed, exhaling despair. As we'd once again proven during the last five minutes, we couldn't spend any length of time in the same space without me becoming flustered by his mere presence.

But I'd promised. So . . .

"Okay. You're right." Resigned to my fate, I sighed again. "Go ahead. Discuss."

Gaze narrowing, the slight curve of his mouth flattened. "You changed your mind? About our agreement?"

Usually at this point I'd try to pacify the person, sacrificing my own comfort in the long or short term in order to avoid confrontation. But I was no longer in the mood to be polite tonight, so I said, "I don't know."

Byron lifted his chin, absorbing this information. "That's why you didn't call me or follow up on the deal."

I stared at him, caught.

"To be clear, you didn't call me, right?"

"No, I didn't."

"I thought there was something wrong with my phone," he muttered, looking distracted.

"If you thought there was something wrong with your phone, you could've called me and checked."

"No." Byron stepped away from the door and turned, giving me a view of his muscular back as he rolled his broad shoulders and strolled across the landing.

"What? Why not?" I trailed after him, swallowing an inexplicable excess of saliva as my gaze dropped to his very round backside and he strolled through the door to his bedroom.

Byron walked the length of the big room and stopped at a green laundry hamper next to the bed. "That's not part of our agreement."

"What does that mean?" Without consciously meaning to do so, I noticed and documented the cozy furnishings of his bedroom—two barrister bookcases in the corner filled with ancient-looking tomes, a big, cushy brown leather sofa nearby facing a leaded glass window that likely had an excellent view of the Cascades during daylight, a substantial tiger oak craftsman-style full- or queen-sized bedframe with a plain white feather duvet on top, two navy pillows, the bed unmade. On either side of the sturdy frame were matching tiger oak craftsman nightstands, just as substantial. The left side was cluttered with books, a lamp, a tissue box, and the right nightstand was completely bare.

The walls were plain white, but the picture rails, trim, and baseboards had never been painted, the original mahogany favored by Seattle homebuilders in the early nineteen hundreds. But he did have art on his walls, original-looking oil paintings and signed prints, all hanging from the picture rails. One in particular snagged my notice. It was of a woman at rest, reading a book, and—

"I'm not calling you." Byon's flat statement punctured my snoopy stupor.

I tore my attention from the painting, requiring a second to search my brain for the thread of our conversation before responding. "Byron, you can call me."

"Can I?" He bent at the waist and plucked a black T-shirt from the top of a pile of black clothes.

Against my will, my eyes took a quick second to devour the sight of his bare torso, the deliciously precise angles and curves of his musculature, and the smooth skin of his abs in profile. *Goodness*. He really was perfect.

I gulped another rush of inappropriate saliva, rasping, "We're friends."

"Are we?" A dry laugh escaped him as he pulled on his shirt. "Last I heard, you don't like me."

I hesitated, then backtracked. "We've known each other for six years. That means you can call me."

"Knowing someone for years doesn't mean they're okay with phone calls. Even I know that." His vivid glare cut to mine as his head emerged from the neck of the shirt, his longish hair disheveled. Byron shoved the black strands away from his eyes and forehead, the muscle at his jaw ticking like he dared me to contradict him.

"True. . ." I said, adding nothing else. The inane word echoed between us while Byron stared at me—not quite a glare but with no hint of warmth or friendliness either—and I stared at him, hovering without purpose at the entrance to his bedroom.

I should've left. But my feet didn't—wouldn't—move. I felt lost. I'd come here tonight with high hopes, looking forward to shutting the book on my crush and ideas about Jeff and me, and anticipating a future of friendship with both Lucy and Jeff. Instead, Lucy seemed to hate my guts, Jeff was being weird, and Byron was . . .

Well. Byron was being Byron.

"I think—"

"Have you decided to back out of the deal? Or when are we going to do another video?" he demanded.

If he'd sounded bored or disinterested, I wouldn't have hesitated calling it off then and there. But he didn't. He sounded uncharacteristically invested and interested, and dare I say *upset?*

I stalled. "I thought you didn't want to know when we're doing the videos."

"You said once a week. It's been almost three." He lifted his chin as he spoke, his eyes releasing mine to skim down the front of my dress.

"I don't know. I—"

"Say it, you changed your mind."

"No," I said, forcing myself to stop twisting my fingers as his gaze—having reached my shoes—traveled upward again.

Byron tilted his head to the side, his attention somewhere between my waist and my neck. "No?"

"Fine. Maybe."

His eyes cut back to mine, narrowed. "Why?"

I shrugged, my bravery failing me. Or perhaps good manners finally kicked in.

This was the longest conversation we'd ever had, just the two of us, and the first time I'd answered his pointed—borderline rude—questions honestly rather than endeavoring to steer the conversation into more courteous waters. For some reason, in the present moment, I didn't feel nearly as irritated with him as usual. But that might've been because I'd already expended my quota of Byron-related frustration earlier in the bathroom. I'd also felt irritated with almost everything and everyone all night. I was tired.

However, my simmering, directionless discontent didn't mean I was ready to mimic his rudeness.

"Why?" he asked again, the line of his mouth insolent. "If you're going to renege on our deal, the least you can do is tell me why—and the truth."

A disbelieving smile quirked my lips. "You think I'm going to lie to you?"

"Yes."

I reared back. "You think I'm a liar?"

"Yes."

I huffed a laugh to cover the abrupt spike of anger. "Oh yeah? When have I ever lied?"

"Every time you allow someone to treat you like shit and, instead of calling them on it, you change the subject, or tell a joke, or try to make them feel better for being a pathetic, sheep-biting footlicker."

My mouth fell open and I gaped, not knowing which part of his statement to process first.

Sheep-biting footlicker. What the—? Who says that kind of thing? What did it even mean? And what did it say about me that I found it charming and wanted to laugh?

But also, *Every time you allow someone to treat you like—*

"Excuse you!" I planted my fists on my hips. "I do not allow people to treat me like shit. Being a kind person makes me a liar? Well then, I guess you're the most honest person I know."

The slight curve at the corner of his mouth returned. "That's the most truthful thing I've ever heard you say."

"Oh? Really?"

He shrugged. "Other than when you said you didn't like me."

"I see." Giving him my most sarcastic, caustic series of head nods, I took another step into the room, then another. "Then how about this? You're a grumpy, snobby, pretentious a-hole. Is that enough *honesty* for you?"

He pressed his lips together as though he were fighting a laugh. "A-hole? I assume that stands for asshole?"

"Then you'd assume wrong, Doctor Apathy Hole." I pivoted my head back and forth on my neck to punctuate my insult.

Byron's slashing eyebrows ticked up and he strolled closer. "Doctor? Not Mister?"

"You have two PhDs. I didn't want to be rude."

"Ah. Yes. Heaven forbid." His deep voice was barely above a whisper, and he mostly lost his battle with the smile he'd been trying to suppress. It tugged forcefully at his full lips, yet he refused to cede even the smallest flash of teeth. That said, those unusual eyes of his were definitely sparkling with amusement.

And while we're on the subject, *how dare he!*

How dare he unleash an eye sparkle at this moment after I'd been taunted into lowering myself to his level. How dare he walk around his own house in nothing but snug-fitting pajamas that highlighted the magnificence of his body. How dare he saunter onto the landing with no shirt on and reprimand me for apologizing too much. I did apologize too much, true. But who the heck was he to reprimand me for it?

Also, how *DARE* he wear black underwear. *And those thighs . . .*

I glowered at him, unsmiling, confused, my neck hot. On the one hand, I was frustrated for being oddly charmed by our exchange. On the other, I was upset that I'd been baited into name-calling and acting like the childish moron he clearly thought I was. Meanwhile, he continued staring at me, his lips relaxing into a pleased-looking curve while a moment filled with spiky tension passed between us.

Eventually, Byron took another step toward me, his gaze more relaxed than usual. "Feel better?" he asked, that pleased curve lingering on his full lips. "Now that you've called me Dr. Apathy Hole."

"I don't like being mean and calling people names, even if they're true," I answered, allowing the glower to fall from my features. "So, no. I don't feel better."

His smile waned. "You can be honest without calling people names."

"But *you* can't seem to be honest without being mean," I said, and immediately wondered if I should regret the words.

Again, he lifted his chin, absorbing my statement, his gaze turning contemplative. "I see."

"What do you see?"

"That's why you want to renege on the deal."

Exhausted, I rubbed my forehead. I needed to get back to Amelia. This was the strangest conversation I'd ever had, especially considering I'd known this particular person for six years. "That's not the reason."

"Really?" The single word positively dripped with scorn. "If being honest and setting boundaries makes me mean, I'm fine with you thinking I'm mean, Fred. But not taking advantage of an opportunity that will make a huge difference in your quality of life, help you pay off those loans, simply because you don't like me, or I'm *mean* is—"

"I said you being mean isn't the reason. I'm telling the truth."

"Then what other reason could there be? I'm handing you an opportunity here, asking very little in exchange." Now his tone took on a frustrated, pleading edge. "Fine. You don't want to come to New York or the Jupiter Awards? Don't. That's fine. You're off the hook."

"Byron—"

"Let me help." He lifted his hands like he might grab mine but then seemed to stop himself at the last minute, instead shoving stiff fingers into his hair, dropping his eyes to the carpet. Breathing out, he leveled me with a direct stare that felt beseeching and hit me like a hot, lead weight between my ribs. "Let me do this one thing. You don't have to like me in order to let me help you."

"It feels disingenuous, okay?" I blurted, compelled by the unexpected softness behind his eyes. "It feels wrong to get followers this way."

Byron paused, his gaze turning introspective. "How so?"

"We'd be lying, and I'd be kitesurfing on your fame." I gestured to him. "They're not tuning in for me, they're tuning in for you, and I want to earn my audience. I'd want them to be there for me, for my STEM videos, not your fame. And if I couldn't have that, then at the very least—the very least—I don't want to lie to get followers."

"I disagree."

I tried for a breezy laugh. "Oh yeah? With what?"

"All of it."

"You think they'd be tuning in for me?"

"No. They wouldn't be tuning in for me, or for you. They'd be tuning in for *us,* this story you and Amelia pulled together, the tension of unrequited feelings, one type of relationship growing into something different. But even if you were kitesurfing on my fame, I don't mind. I don't care. Neither should you."

"But I do care." I exhaled a mighty breath. "At least with Jeff, I had a crush on him."

Byron's lip suddenly curled, his sneer making its first appearance, his eyes losing their softness and shuttering closed like a slammed window. "You still have a thing for him?"

"No. No, no, no." I paired the denial with a laugh and a dismissive hand wave. "Tonight cured me of that. But—what I'm saying is—the story we wrote at the time was at least partially true. But with you?" I shrugged. "I thought I could do this, but it doesn't feel right."

Tracking me as I backed toward the door, he looked pained. And determined. And frustrated.

So I added, "Listen, I will go with you to New York and the awards ceremony, no matter what I decide about the challenges. I said I would, so I will. I will be your buffer. I'm not going to leave you hanging, I promise."

"Wait." Strolling forward, he thrust his fingers into his hair again, his attention moving up and to the right, fastening on the wall behind me. "Wait, don't—what if—" His jaw set, he let his hand drop to his side. "What if it weren't disingenuous?"

My face didn't know whether to smile or frown. "What? Tell a different story? Two long-term acquaintances who can't stand each other, suffering through romantic trends and challenges together?"

"No," he drawled, like he didn't find any part of what I'd said funny.

I almost rolled my eyes—almost—but managed to refrain, if only because I'd already behaved like a child earlier when I called him Dr. Apathy Hole. But I was convinced his inability or unwillingness to find humor in the ridiculous was why we'd never be friends. We'd never get along. We'd never like each other. And that was that.

These were the thoughts running through my mind as Byron's jaw worked for a protracted moment before he lowered his glare from the wall, ensnared mine, and said, "I like you."

CHAPTER 9
BYRON

"You—what?"

"I like you," I said, surrendering the truth, uncovering it for her to see. My heart thundered, the organ supplying an unwelcomed, frenzied percussion over which my thoughts skipped and raced. I hadn't expected that. Nor had I expected the rope-like heat cinching my throat.

But if I was going to do this, I was just going to fucking do it. "I have a . . . thing for you," I explained with outward calm, no reason to be otherwise. "If you want to call it that."

Winnie's brown eyes, so much the color of cinnamon, bounced between mine. She looked horrified. I managed a swallow as the rope cinched tighter. I hadn't anticipated that she might be horrified.

Surprised? Yes. Flattered? Maybe. Amused? Perhaps.

Horrified? No.

"You can't, there's no way," the words pure air, a wheeze squeezed out of her. "Are you having a stroke? Do I need to call an ambulance?"

Wrestling a grimace, I tried not to swallow my tongue. *Well. This sucks.* "Fred."

"I'm sorry, that wasn't—I—I. . ." She lifted a hand as though to ward me off. "Are you joking?"

"No."

"You—"

"Yes. I like you. I have a crush on you. I have a thing for you." The statements followed no map. I had no plan.

Correction: I did have a plan. The plan had been to never tell her. Why the hell would I ever tell her? Spontaneously communicating my irrelevant feelings hadn't worked well for me in the past. This—the inadvisable habit of volunteering information to insouciant parties—was a lesson I obviously hadn't quite learned.

Work on that, Byron. Fix that about yourself. Edit it out of your repertoire and then move on.

Breathing in through my nose, I held the air in my lungs for the count of three, liberating it carefully. The seizing tightness lessened.

"But—but when? And how?" She stumbled a step forward, her mouth opening and closing, her bright brown stare beneath thick, inky lashes scanning my face. This might've been the longest she'd ever held my eyes. "And . . . why?"

It occurred to me that Winnie, being Winnie, might be overreacting. She felt deeply, took people and their tragedies inside her heart when it would be better to filter out the noise, learn from the precautionary tales of other peoples' lives, and move on. Mucking about with a helper complex was her way, infuriating as it was to watch.

I sought to calm her. "It's not a big deal."

She flinched, blinking once. "Oh?"

"No." My feelings, as inconvenient as they were for me, had nothing to do with her. She'd done nothing to encourage them, nothing purposeful to inspire them. I expected nothing. I wanted nothing—*except* to help her, as we'd previously agreed and as she'd promised.

"Ah. Okay." Relief permeated her words. "So you a little bit like me."

"No." Never one to accept inaccuracy, though the tips of my ears burned, I corrected, "I *a lot* like you. But it's not a big deal."

"Not a big deal?" she croaked.

"No."

"Because . . .?" Winnie shook her head, her long hair sliding over her shoulders, once again making no attempt to conceal her horror.

And this—her lovely, lively, expressive face contorting with dismay at the mere suggestion of my hidden affection, as though I was a burdensome, geriatric dog who worshipped her, and now she found herself in the unenviable position of being beholden to me—almost made me laugh.

I should have found another way.

"It isn't a big deal." I was not one of her charity cases. My like for her—

my admiration—was as irrelevant as her feelings of dislike toward me. "And now that you know, we can move on from it."

"What does that mean?"

"We can do the challenges, and they won't be disingenuous."

Her coloring had gone pale, greenish. "Because you like me. A lot."

"Correct." A laugh did escape me now. She was panicking. What did Winnie think? That I would trouble her with my inconvenient attraction? "You don't need to worry, Fred. My feelings aren't your problem."

She looked no less dismayed. "Seriously, are you joking?"

I glared at her. "No."

"Am I . . ."

"What?"

She shifted her weight back and forth between her feet, her voice pitching higher. "Am I allowed to ask questions about this?"

I stiffened. *Questions?* No. No follow-up questions. What could she possibly want to—

"Winnie? Are you still up here?"

We both looked in the direction of Amelia's voice a moment before she emerged from the main stairs.

"Yes. I'm here." Winnie cleared her throat, darting a frantic glance at me, like I was a bomb set to explode. "I'm—uh—"

"Byron. Hey." Amelia walked into my room. "Everything okay?"

"Fine," I said, scratching my hot and itchy neck.

"Good." Amelia glanced between us. "Glad I found you together. Did you schedule a time to do a video? It's been weeks."

Winnie swayed. Perhaps the question made her dizzy. "No, we—"

"Yeah." I nodded once. "We're on it."

Winnie's eyes widened, visibly confused and wary. I gave her a quick, tight smile. I'd told her the truth so that she might consent to allowing my help, to assuage her fears of being disingenuous. That's all she was getting from me.

"Oh yeah?" Amelia folded her arms. "When?"

"I'll be over tomorrow for the three-day weekend." I cleared my throat of all lingering misery. "We'll film two as we've missed a few weeks."

"Oh. Good." Amelia nodded at me approvingly. "Glad to hear it. Now can we go?" She turned to Winnie, grabbing her hand. "Our new friends left, and I can't handle another conversation about tort reform."

"Yeah. Yes," Winnie said weakly. "We can go."

"Thanks, Byron." Amelia winked at me while pulling Winnie from my bedroom. "And get some sleep. You look tired, man."

Sensing Winnie's attention swing toward me, I lowered my eyes to avoid hers. They remained glued to the carpet as the two women departed. I waited for the sounds of their footsteps to completely fade along with the barbed ache in my lungs.

You shouldn't have said anything. That was a mistake.

I shut the door. I would not think about it. I would not waste time or energy or thought on an unalterable situation. I'd told her. It was done. No eradicating the words now.

I decided to write.

Rubbing my chest, the air of my bedroom oddly heavy and stagnant, I walked to my office and was inexplicably reminded of my first and only car accident at seventeen years old: the release of adrenaline, the way time paused, fast forwarded, stalled, and skipped, the air heavy and stagnant. Briefly, I wondered if anyone had ever experienced PTSD as a result of confessing unreciprocated feelings.

Thirty minutes of irrational agitation, lack of focus, and no words later, I decided to go on a run.

Standing from my desk, I left my office and paced to the laundry basket next to my bed. I'd just pulled off my shirt when my phone buzzed.

Winnie: Were you joking?

The cinching rope around my neck returned and my stomach tensed, compressing itself into a tight ball. I wasn't a liar, but I briefly debated whether a lie in this instance might've been the right course. A kindness for the both of us. On the rare occasions when I'd fantasized about telling Winnie the truth or pondered what she might actually say, her reaction had never been this big, this . . . tumultuous.

In my fantasies, she'd behaved fantastically.

But in my ponderings, when I'd endeavored to imagine what real Winnie might say or do, she'd expressed mild surprise, gently shared her inability to return such sentiments, and we'd laughed together at the futility of my feelings. She'd never been angry, or as violently disbelieving, or as aggressively aghast as she'd been this evening.

Perhaps her overreaction had been rooted in causes unknown to me, but now I could see that while my intent had been to ease her concerns about being disingenuous in the challenge videos, I'd instead made her upset and uncomfortable.

Still, I wasn't a liar. Not even to spare someone discomfort, and especially not to spare me discomfort. If I started lying to myself, I would never stop. Thus, I replied,

Byron: No. Not joking.

The drum of my heart lodged itself in my throat, and I squeezed my eyes shut. *Discomfort is temporary, lies are forever.*

The phone buzzed again.

Winnie: I'm not sure what I'm supposed to say

Byron: Say nothing. If it made you uncomfortable, it shouldn't. I don't want or need anything from you

Winnie: I am very confused

My eyebrows inched upward at the second *very* in all caps, that she'd taken the time to capitalize such a prosaic word instead of opting for a synonym—excessively, extraordinarily, extremely—any of which would've been more effective than a double *very*.

While still contemplating her peculiar vernacular choice, Winnie's number lit up my screen and my stomach tightened further. For the first time in our acquaintance, I considered not answering my phone when Winnifred Gobaldi called. Prior to now, she'd called me exactly six times in six years. This made seven.

Yet I'd promised I'd pick up the phone if she wanted or needed me. With a sigh to steady the renewed rapid percussion of my pulse, I finally did.

"Fred."

"Byron, you can't—you can't tell me you like me and then act like it's nothing. You can't do that."

I lifted my eyes to the ceiling. "Okay."

"What do you mean 'okay'?"

"Okay, I won't tell you I like you."

"But you do."

"Correct."

She inhaled sharply, making a noise of pure exasperation on her exhale. "You don't like me! You can't stand me. You treat me like I'm an idiot—"

"I've never done that."

"Oh? Really? 'It's pronounced Al-*kie* Beach, not Al-*key.*'" She'd dropped her voice as though she were quoting a book or a movie.

"What are you talking about?"

"Those were your first words to me."

My attention fell from the ceiling, and I stared at nothing, her words a riddle I could not solve, so I focused on a single piece of her puzzling statement. "Wait. You remember my first words to you?"

"That's not the point! The point is, you never say anything to me unless it's to correct something I've said or to criticize something I've done. How can you possibly say you like me? You don't. You're messing with me."

If her goal had been to anger me, this call had been a raging success. "I'm not messing with you, Fred. Believe me, I wish I were."

"What does that mean? And why are *you* mad? I'm the one who should be mad."

"It means I like you, but I don't particularly want to," I bit out, perilously close to yelling.

"Why not? I'm nice, aren't I? I don't go around correcting other people's grammar, do I? I don't get my black underwear in a twist when someone says Roman Empire when they really mean Byzantium Empire, do I?"

"I've never corrected anyone's grammar." *Out loud.*

"No! Just their pronunciation of places and the minutia of trivial things."

"Is it your wish for me to encourage you to espouse falsehoods and mispronounce the names of public places? Would you prefer I be *nice* and allow you to stumble around like an infant, appearing uninformed and uneducated?"

"No, Dr. Sarcastico Apathy Hole!" she yelled, and I winced at her volume, necessitating that I hold the phone away from my ear. "I'd like the first words from a stranger to be something other than a critique and—you know what? Forget it. Forget I called. I don't even know why I called. I can't talk to you! Even when you tell me you like me, it pisses me off."

"Fine," I said, careful to exude as much calm as possible. "I'll see you tomorrow."

"What? No."

"Yes. I'll be over tomorrow for the video."

She huffed.

"I'll be there at ten. I'll bring scones. And since every word out of my mouth is so entirely offensive to you, I won't say anything."

Now she growled.

"And, since I *do* like you—whether you believe it or not—nothing about this is disingenuous, so you can't use that as an excuse anymore."

"I wasn't using it as an—"

"Bye, Fred."

I hung up, stopping myself before I threw the phone across the room. But then it vibrated. Grinding my teeth, I glared at the screen and the messages arriving in quick succession.

Winnie: I still don't believe you like me or have a thing for me or whatever

Winnie: You don't. And I'm REALLY ANGRY that you're messing with me like this

Winnie: They better be gluten-free blueberry scones or your not getting in the door

Winnie: YOU'RE! Not your. You're. You are

Winnie: Goodnight

CHAPTER 10
WINNIE

Amelia knew something was wrong. She filled the silence on our way back to First Hill without asking me any questions, seeming to intrinsically understand I needed space.

But the next morning after breakfast, after I'd tossed and turned and punched my pillow wishing it were Byron's beautiful, perpetually aloof face, she gave me a hug and whispered softly, "Jeff isn't worth your time. I'm so sorry I ever tried to encourage the two of you." Squeezing me, she added, "I wanted to be a good wingwoman."

"You're the best wingwoman." I leaned into the hug. "And I don't care about Jeff. He's always been a nice guy, and I hope—whatever happens—we'll eventually be friends again. But he and Lucy can have each other."

I hadn't spared one single second thinking about Jeff since leaving the dinner party. Thinking about Jeff and his perplexing behavior hadn't even entered my mind. Whereas Byron's strange confession—how, in a strange bending of my expectations, he'd kept his cool the entire time while I'd been the one to lose my temper—had occupied the whole of my brain for going on twelve hours now. Including my dreams, fitful as they were. He'd popped up in the background over and over again.

I'd dreamt of grocery shopping, he'd been the butcher judging my choice of tenderloin cuts. I'd dreamt of giving a presentation at a Parent-Teacher Organization meeting, he'd been the AV specialist, judging the quality of my

PowerPoint graphics. I'd dreamt of going to my doctor's for a checkup, he'd been the visiting gynecologist.

That one got weird real fast.

No one should be having sexy dreams involving specula and stirrups, especially when their orgasm is judged on the Wong-Baker Faces Pain Scale afterward. Worse, I'd woken up feeling both turned on and distressed, self-conscious and horny. Explain the science behind that.

And don't even get me started as to why—in the name of all that is hot and unholy—I would be having sex dreams about Byron Visser now.

You know why.

I swallowed around the stone of truth: I had big like for Byron. Or, more precisely, my body had BIG SEXY LIKE for him, and this feeling was nothing like I'd felt for Jeff, or any of my ex-boyfriends, or anyone else I'd ever met. What I experienced whenever Byron entered my radius felt more akin to the intense embarrassment I'd experienced during those first two weeks of high school, when the soccer team had messed with me, than what I generally thought of and experienced as attraction.

What I needed to do was read up on the chemistry of pheromones. Something about his biology made mine go berserk, and if I could figure it out, maybe I could stop it. *Oh! This would make a good STEM lesson for Instagram.*

"Winnie?" Amelia leaned away from our hug and tried to capture my eyes. "Are you sure you're okay?"

I chewed on the inside of my lip, debating whether to ask her opinion about Byron.

If he was messing with me, if he'd somehow figured out that my mitochondria carried a torch for him and he was playing pituitary gland games (a.k.a. mind games), I didn't want Amelia to be angry on my behalf. I didn't want to insert myself into their relationship, even indirectly.

And if he wasn't messing with me, if he was telling the truth and he had a thing for me, I wasn't sure I wanted Amelia to know that either. Amelia never shied away from confrontation.

In the end, I simply nodded and shrugged, not allowing myself to make my problem her problem. I made a mental note to make Instant Pot chicken tikka masala tonight. She and Elijah were going snowshoeing this afternoon and I wanted them to come home to spicy, savory food.

As soon as she left for Elijah's, I rushed to the bathroom, took a long, hot shower, and unsuccessfully fought the urge to touch myself while imagining Byron giving me quietly spoken, hypercritical feedback on my masturbation technique, and then fantasy me shut him up by pushing him to his knees, twisting my fingers into his black hair, and bringing his mouth to my body. Fantasy Byron seemed more than happy to oblige.

I came in the shower harder than I had a right to, given the bizarre nature of my imagination, awash in steam and confusion. Was criticism my kink? Did some part of me yearn to be reprimanded and judged and mistreated? If so, what the heck was wrong with me?

Whatever it was, I needed to pull myself together before he showed up at 10:00 a.m. with scones. As I toweled off and dressed, bits and pieces of our conversations from the night before danced around in my head, taunting me.

"So you a little bit like me."

"No. I a lot *like you."*

My skin felt too tight at the memory, the heated look in his hooded eyes, the gravelly texture of his voice. But then I recalled that he'd followed it up with,

"It's not a big deal."

"I don't want or need anything from you."

"I like you, but I don't particularly want to."

A jolt of anger cooled my body's ardor while sending my blood pressure spiking. By the time I was dressed and drying my hair, I felt like I could've breathed fire.

Only Byron. Only Byron could make someone feel foolish while confessing feelings for them. Maybe in his own twisted, apathetic kind of way he did like me. Or maybe he didn't like me. Or maybe I would never know. But—I reflected as I applied my moisturizer and mascara—did it matter?

No!

It didn't matter. He had no intention of ever actually doing anything about his alleged feelings, otherwise he wouldn't have called them "no big deal."

Likewise, I couldn't imagine a reality or a universe where I ever acted on my body's preoccupation with him. Byron Visser was the human manifestation of caution tape holding a red flag and a flare while setting off a smoke alarm.

What mattered was that he was adamant about doing these challenges with me. While trying to thoughtfully consider everything, I uncapped my lip gloss and applied it. He wanted to do the videos? We'd do them. I'd amass enough followers to be competitive for the community manager position, then I'd be able to pay back my student loans while also teaching and (hopefully) making a difference in the world.

I really hope I can make a difference in the world. I really hope something wonderful comes out of this. I really hope this isn't all pointless—

A knock sounded from the front door, interrupting my existential debate and rage application of lip gloss. Closing my eyes and leaning against the bathroom sink, I gave myself three seconds to calm down. If he yelled at me today, if he screamed at me or raised his voice or nitpicked my pronunciation of a word or anything else, I was ending the agreement. I simply would not put up with that. Capping the makeup, I set it lightly in my tray and strolled unhurriedly to the door.

I couldn't decide if he was messing with me, but I was determined to be cool and reserved, calm and collected.

"Who is it?" I asked, even though it was 10:00 a.m. on the dot.

Beyond the door, I heard Byron clear his throat, remaining silent for a long stretch, then eventually saying, "The scones are both gluten-free and blueberry."

A shiver started behind my ears and raced down my spine at the sound of his rumbly voice. I clamped down on the feeling, strangling it.

"How many?" I asked, unlatching the top lock, willing my fingers to remain steady.

"Four."

Flipping the dead bolt, I opened the door, swallowing around a knot as his broody, unsmiling, perfect face came into view.

"Hi," I said, struggling to not launch a hundred questions at him, like when did he start having a thing for me, and why, and how come he hadn't ever said anything, and how could he possibly like someone he also clearly didn't actually like?

He held up the bag in his hand. "The ransom."

Pressing my lips together to stem a wry smile at his sarcasm, I backed up, giving him space. As he moved forward, I turned, trying frantically to grab hold of my indifference again. "Thank you for the scones, and for coming over. I appreciate your time. If you don't mind, please put the scones on the kitchen table. I'll be back in a sec."

I walked to my bedroom, grabbed my phone and my daily journal, took several deep breaths, then returned to the kitchen. The bag of scones had been placed on the table and, without looking, I sensed Byron leaning against the wall in the small dining area—his preferred spot to hover and pass judgment—his arms crossed. In my peripheral vision, I saw his jacket had been folded over the chair closest to the front door.

"We're doing the Best Friend Check-In / Opposites Attract today," I said, all business. "Technically, it should've been the first video we posted, but it should be okay that numbers one and two got flipped." Setting the journal on the table facing him, I opened it to the original handwritten list of trends for the challenge videos.

He didn't move. He remained silent. I steeled my expression and glanced at him. Byron stared at me as though waiting for . . . something.

Refusing to think about his words last night or allow them to further rattle me, I straightened from the table and crossed my arms, mimicking his stance while maintaining my professional tone. "I have a ton of work to do this weekend and I'm sure you do too, so we can make this quick. I don't want to waste your time. If you want to choose your own caption or help me brainstorm ideas for the both of us, feel free to speak up. But I know you said you didn't want to rehearse or talk about the videos ahead of time. I can grab the footage of you real fast, we'll dance around in our little circle holding hands, and then you don't need to stay."

Byron regarded me thoughtfully, which was both better and worse than his typical contemptuous glares. Better because I wasn't feeling immediately frustrated by his mere presence, but worse because his lack of outward arrogance meant I noticed how breathtakingly handsome he looked this morning.

His hair was either damp or artfully styled, pushed back and away from his features in a sweeping wave. His jaw was freshly shaven, leaving his face smooth of its usual dark shadow. I'd bet a million dollars he smelled fantastic. He wore a gun metal gray button-down shirt and black wool dress pants instead of his usual black T and jeans. I wondered if he'd had a fancy business meeting this morning, some important event he'd needed to dress to impress for, prior to coming over.

"Remind me, what's the Best Friend Check-In?" Byron pushed away from the wall, the movement shifting my attention from his clothes to his face.

A tightness in my chest eased. He'd dialed down the belligerence today and at least appeared willing to pitch in, even if it did mean we'd be bending one of his rules by discussing the video before filming it.

"It's the Opposites Attract Challenge. We don't speak at all. The background music we're supposed to use is already loaded on the app. Basically, we show a quick video of you being yourself, whatever you want to do that's reflective of the caption we pick. Then we show a quick video of me doing something that's reflective of my caption. Then we place the phone on the ground, filming upward, and hold hands above the phone while swinging our arms." I pointed to the description in my journal. "We dance quickly in a circle with the word 'bestfriends' flashing in the middle. That's it."

He frowned at my written notes. "'Best friends' is an open compound word, it shouldn't be connected like that."

Ah. There he is.

I smiled tightly, working really hard to keep irritation from my voice. "I know that, Byron. But sometimes for this challenge, and for other best friend challenges on social media, the young people of today write it as one word, not two. We can write 'best friend' as two words or one. Either should be fine."

His eyelids didn't do their usual droop-of-disdain thing as I spoke. Instead, he lifted his chin slightly, still inspecting me thoughtfully, and then nodded. "You would know better than I."

My lips parted at his statement, said simply and without a drop of sarcasm. He'd admitted that I might know more about something than he did. He didn't press the issue, he didn't call me an idiot, he hadn't raised his voice. He'd just . . . acquiesced.

"Uh. . ." I gaped, then remembered myself and blinked my attention away, opting to focus on my day journal. "We should, uh, maybe figure out the captions first."

"They have to be opposites, right?" Ambling the short distance to the table, he placed his hands on the back of a chair, his long fingers relaxed. *He has nice hands.*

Something low in my abdomen twisted.

"More or less," I said, ignoring my stomach. "The captions and associated actions should show how different we are." I picked up the bag of scones and peeked inside to distract myself from his hands. I wasn't hungry, but the scones smelled heavenly. "It can be anything, as long as we highlight our differences. Some people have done tall friend, short friend. Others have shown one person as a party animal and the other person being straightlaced or a nondrinker. I saw another video where one friend was super into fashion and the best friend wasn't at all. That kind of thing."

"What are you thinking? For our captions."

Twisting my lips to the side, I returned the bag of scones to the table and tilted my head to read what I'd listed in the journal weeks ago. "Let's see. I made a list here of ways people can be opposite. We could pick one of these."

"Wouldn't it be better to pick something authentic? Unique to us?"

I glanced at him, bracing myself for whatever he was thinking, my palms suddenly sweaty. "Like what?"

His eyelids did that drooping thing. But instead of looking disdainful, he appeared mildly amused. "You like people. I don't."

I felt one side of my mouth give a tug. "I doubt your publicist would like that caption."

He shrugged, the barest hint of a smile hovering over his lips. "So what?"

"I don't want to make anyone's job harder."

Byron opened his mouth as though to argue the point, so I—not wanting to argue at all—cut him off. "But that should be something we can work with. The general idea is good. How about, I have a ton of social media accounts and you have none?"

His thoughtful expression returned, and he pressed the tip of an index finger against his lower lip. "That's a good one."

I straightened, cautiously pleased by his praise. "Thank . . . you . . .?"

"Was that a question?"

"No . . .?" Realizing how that sounded, I hastily amended, "Wait. No. That wasn't a question. It was a statement. Thank you. Thank. You."

His attention suddenly felt somehow heavier, more intense. "You shouldn't thank me."

Here we go.

My brain went on high alert, my whole body tensed, and I hated it. I hated that, with one sentence, our benign conversation had turned into another round of Byron critiquing Winnie, which—even if he never yelled at me—would lead to me gritting my teeth and ignoring Byron and wishing he would leave. I didn't want that, not if we had eight more videos to record after this one.

But I couldn't help feeling a flicker of hope. He'd acquiesced so quickly when I'd explained the alternate acceptable spelling of "bestfriend," and maybe, like with some of my students' parents, if I took a minute to explain the issue, he'd listen.

Almost every instinct demanded that I call off our agreement once and for all, but the Winnie that was tired of avoiding confrontation refused to tense up, and I refused to shut down, so I appealed to him with openness and honesty. "Can we—can we not? Please. Can we just not." Something had to give between us.

"Not what?"

"Not argue. Can I say thank you when you compliment me without you telling me not to? Can I speak without you telling me how what I say is wrong, or inaccurate, or unnecessary? Is that possible?"

Eyes still locked on mine, Byron pulled his bottom lip between his teeth and chewed on it, his gaze losing none of its weight or intensity, but he was processing my request, internal wheels turning. His fingers flexed on the back of the chair as his dark, wing-like eyebrows pulled together.

At this point, I was girding my loins for another critique, an explanation from him as to why he'd said what he said—my feelings didn't matter, he was right, and I was the one who required additional enlightenment—and how I should be thankful for his brilliant elucidation of the facts and the world according to Byron.

But then, apropos of nothing, he blurted, "You are extraordinary."

CHAPTER 11
WINNIE

I squinted at him and his unfinished thought. "I'm extraordinarily what?"

His tongue darted out to quickly wet his lips. "No. You *are* extraordinary. You are exceptional. And watching, hearing you undervalue yourself is . . . difficult."

I held still, heartbeat accelerating, certain I'd heard him wrong.

"You shouldn't feel like you need to thank people for saying something truthful," he continued, tone cautious. "I wasn't being kind or generous. I was telling the truth. It was a good idea. You have good ideas. That's not a compliment, it's a fact."

I worked to dispel his tangle of proclamations paired with the softness of his voice—that he believed I was extraordinary, that I have good ideas—knowing I'd be obsessing about all of it later. But right now, while neither of us were losing our tempers, while we were doing our utmost to be careful, trying not to aggravate each other, I wanted to stay focused on my point, *the* point.

I'd tried ignoring him. I'd tried being polite. I'd tried running away, yelling, name-calling. I'd tried being businesslike and detached. Maybe it was time for me to try being myself. It's not like I would be sacrificing a great friendship by being difficult, we barely knew each other. And if he thought I was a buffoon and stopped liking me against his will, so be it.

Here goes nothing.

"Byron, I'm allowed to say thank you if I want to say thank you without you policing my expression, appropriateness, or rate of gratitude. I'm allowed to say sorry, or excuse me, or yeehaw, or I've got a lovely bunch of coconuts, or whatever I want, as often as I want, without you or anyone tracking, commenting on, or critiquing me."

He opened his mouth, and I could see another excessively logical argument was on the tip of his tongue, so I tried for a Hail Mary pass, a last-ditch effort to make him see and understand my perspective. "At the very least, can you see how someone doing that to you would be frustrating and hurtful? How it might have a negative impact on self-confidence? Especially when that person is someone as talented and accomplished as you are, and every word out of their genius mouth is a correction, like I *am* the infant you accused me of being yesterday. Like I am a weak-minded child in need of constant fixing."

"I—you think I'm—" Byron's mouth snapped shut, his gaze falling to the table as an entire five-act opera's worth of emotions played over his face. Eventually, he released a tight huff. "I do not believe you are a weak-minded child, and it has never been my intention to make you feel that way." The words arrived gruff but still without sarcasm.

I sighed and lifted my fingers to my forehead, rubbing at the tension headache gathering there. "Listen, I . . . I respect you, a lot. I admire you. You're amazing."

The side of his mouth surrendered to a reluctant curve. "You think I'm amazing?"

My eyes lifted to the ceiling before I could stop them, and I ignored the press of heat around my neck. "It's impossible not to think you're amazing. I would be in an extremely small minority if I didn't think you were amazing. But I don't know how to talk to you without worrying you'll judge me, like every conversation is a final exam with right and wrong answers. A lot of that is my own hang-ups, but I think—at least part of it—is how you feel entitled to comment on and correct almost every word out of my mouth."

His throat worked with a swallow, his severe frown returning, but he said nothing.

"For whatever reason, you really want to do these videos with me, you really want to help me. I so appreciate your willingness to help. Thank you. But, until right this moment, even after years of us being acquainted, I've felt like I can't relax or be myself around you. But all of that said, I also don't want *you* to feel like you can't be yourself around me."

This statement had Byron abruptly lifting his eyes to mine. His forehead cleared like I'd just said the magic words.

I extended the peace offering of an encouraging smile, something I'd perfected with the kids in my class when they felt regret—for not turning in homework, for acting up or talking back in class, for making silly mistakes—but were either too proud to apologize or didn't know how.

"Can we start over?" I edged around the table, slowly moving to his side, allowing hope to bleed through my voice.

His weight shifted backward at my approach, his arms lifting to fold over his chest again, and he turned to face me. "Start over."

"We're about to pretend to be best friends for an audience of strangers, millions of them. Can't we also pretend everything that's happened before now doesn't exist? Can't we start fresh?"

He took a retreating step. "No. We can't start over."

My shoulders slumped, the tension headache pulsing between my temples.

But before I could feel too crestfallen by his unwillingness to at least *try*, Byron unfolded his arms and placed a hand on the kitchen chair to his right, shuffling forward a half step, and said, "*I* will stop."

I held very still. "Stop? Stop what?"

His lips firmed, his eyes hardening, and it took me a split second to recognize it was determination, not arrogance, behind his gaze. "I will stop offering unsolicited advice and commentary," he said finally, softly, using his cautious voice. "I'm sorry, Winnie."

We stared at each other, the sound of my name—my *real* name—echoing between us, and I couldn't help it. I smiled.

"But I have some stipulations."

My eyes closed even as my smile widened. "I should have known." I spoke the words to myself more than to him.

Taking a deep breath, I opened my eyes and gestured for him to continue. "Go ahead. What are your stipulations?"

"Until after the New York trip this summer, I can call you. And text you."

"Okay." As far as I was concerned, he'd always been able and allowed to call and text me. This changed nothing.

"And you won't ask me again if I was having a stroke, or was joking or messing with you, about—" He turned his head, his eyes dropping to his hand where it rested on the chair. "About what I said yesterday," he finally finished.

"All right," I said quietly, studying his granite profile while clamping down on my body's swirling, hot, shivery reaction to his presence. Byron's face was all sharp angles and dramatic lines, truly spectacular. I still wasn't at all convinced this beautiful, brilliant, broody genius had a thing for me, but if he didn't want me to ask about it, I wouldn't. "Anything else?"

His eyes moved, cutting to mine. "You still don't believe me, do you?"

"I thought you said I wasn't allowed to talk about it."

His expression seemed to flatten. "Maybe we should do the video."

I reached over and picked up my phone, not exactly flustered, but something close. "Sure."

He wanted to do the video? Fine. But it felt a little ridiculous, like we were ignoring the elephant in the room. And why tell me about the elephant if he didn't want to discuss the elephant? He made no sense.

"Where do you want me?" he asked, words monotone.

In the shower—

"Uh—" I gave myself a quick shake, hastily pushing away the errant thought "—let's see. How about if we film you in my room at my desk, like you're writing? I can set up my laptop. Or do you use notebooks?"

"I'll sit here." As he spoke, he pulled out the chair next to him and sat, crossing his arms. "Go ahead."

"I—you want me to—"

"Start recording."

"Uh, okay."

I opened my camera app and selected Video, lowering the phone to situate him in the frame at a natural angle. His eyes were forward, frank and impassive. He seemed to be waiting, so I hit the red button and nodded my head to let him know I was recording, and he . . . did nothing. Just stared at the camera, looking like a grumpy statue engaging in a staring contest.

I huffed a laugh. "That's all you're going to do? Stare at the camera? Are you trying to hypnotize people with those sexy eyes? Because, if so, it's definitely working."

His cold façade cracked at my words, his eyebrows drawing together quickly. But then a slow smile—beginning on the right side and then sliding to the left—spread over his mouth. He even showed a little bit of teeth.

"Sexy eyes?" The eyes in question gradually lifted to mine above the phone and he leaned back, lifting his chin. Our gazes locked. My heart tripped.

"Oh, come on," I said, inconveniently breathless. "You know what I mean."

"No. Tell me." And something about his expression felt very familiar.

Almost at once, I placed where I'd seen it before. He looked at me now as he'd gazed at me weeks ago when I'd straddled his lap at his house, like he'd been thinking about me. A lot. That same hot and needy flicker passed behind his features, and a heady blush rose up and over my cheeks, threaded heat around the back of my neck and behind my ears. My blood pumped sluggishly, my stomach twisting low again, and my shower fantasy from earlier this morning chose that moment to replay in my memory.

His smile waned. His lips parted. His chest rose and fell. He blinked.

"All right. I think that's fine." Irritatingly, I squeaked the words more than said them, and I turned away before stopping the video. My hands were shaking, and I didn't want him to see me fumble with the phone.

I couldn't think. What were we talking about?

Oh yeah.

My body had the big sexy hots for Byron, and apparently my body's big sexy hots felt exactly like extreme embarrassment.

Pacing to the living room situated ten feet away, I pressed my palm to my chest and struggled to focus on what we were doing, why he was here. *The video. For TikTok. The Best Friend Check-In.*

"I'll do selfie mode for mine, no need for you to film me. That should work." I waved a hand in the air. "Or maybe Amelia can do it later. Let's see . . ."

Glancing around the room, I desperately tried to remember what we needed to do next. "Ah! That's right. I'll place this here." I switched my camera to video selfie mode and placed it on the ground. I then half turned, lifting my hand out for Byron. "Now it's the time on Sprockets where we dance." I tried for light and carefree, uncaring if the *Saturday Night Live* reference was too obscure. My brain was on goofy autopilot now.

Self-preservation.

"Sprockets?" Byron had followed me into the living room and slid his hand into mine, the touch sending an electric shiver up my arm. He must've felt my hand quake. His eyes darted to mine and widened slightly with question.

"Sorry. It's cold in here. Anyway." Grabbing his other hand, I pulled him around until we were facing each other directly above my phone, telling myself not to notice how lovely my hands felt in his. "Let me—" I briefly released his fingers to bend and tap the Record button, then straightened and recaptured his hands. "So we move our arms back and forth like this." I demonstrated almost frantically, bringing our joined hands together and then swinging them apart. "But we also move in a circle, like this." Still swinging our arms, I stepped to the side, tugging him along with me, and watching the screen of my phone to make sure we were both still in the shot.

We were. Which meant all I needed to do was stop avoiding his eyes and record us doing our little dance for about ten seconds, then we'd be done.

"This is ridiculous," he said, tone flat, drawing my attention. His grumpy expression made me laugh, and that was a first.

"What? Don't you like to dance?" I teased. "If I remember correctly, we have the Toxic Dance Challenge coming up next. And I want us to be in perfect sync."

"Are you telling me we have to practice?"

I had no expectation that Byron would actually do the dance challenge with me. Heck, I hadn't even expected Jeff to do it when I'd first made the list with him in mind.

"The moves are legitimately challenging and require practice, yes. But since you stipulated that you didn't want to practice, I figured I'd do it on my own and you'd, I don't know, sorta be next to me." At this point, we likely had enough footage of us moving in a tight circle while swinging our arms, but neither of us seemed inclined to stop the recording. "I saw one that was cool where the guy dipped the girl at the end, and that's all he did. He stood there through the whole thing while she did *amazing* on the choreography of the original dance. Then BAM! Dip. Like a boss—"

Abruptly, Byron tugged me forward. I would've face-planted into his chest except he caught me by the arm, expertly spun me around, and the next thing I knew, he'd dipped me. Low.

I'd sucked in a startled breath when he'd initially yanked on my hands, and I still held that breath now as he leaned over me, our faces inches apart, one strong arm wrapped tightly around my waist, fully supporting my weight, while the fingers of his other hand splayed against my lower back.

He was so close, his eyes and his sharp features filling my vision, our breath mingling, just like that day I'd straddled his lap. Except this time, he was touching me, and we were alone. But like before, I could smell him and —oh God—he smelled so, so, so good.

Quick! Smell him. Document his smell. Write it down for your pheromone investigations later.

Yes, he wore his usual pine and sandalwood aftershave. But underneath, he smelled warm and cozy and clean and spicy. My gaze drifted lower as I frantically tried to parse everything I smelled, and how it made me feel and how my body reacted—from the curling of my toes to the lightness in my head.

"This okay?" His lips formed the words and I found them mesmerizing.

"What aftershave do you use?" I asked, staring at the right side of his upper lip, the spot that curled when he was disgusted with someone or something. I wanted to lick it. *Document that: desire to lick the part of his lip that curls when he sneers.*

"My aftershave?" His arm tightened, drawing me closer. "Why?"

"Um . . ." I debated how to answer, quickly settling on one version of the truth. "I was thinking about a STEM thing I want to do for an Instagram video."

His head drew back, and I lifted my gaze from his mouth to find his searching my face, a deep V between his eyebrows. Meanwhile, my eyes moved between his beautiful irises, memorizing the rings of hazel, green, and blue. *Sexy eyes.*

Gently, he straightened us. I hadn't realized the palms of my hands were on his chest until we were completely upright and he released me, removing himself, and my hands touched air instead of the warm, solid wall of his body.

Mouth clamped shut, Byron bent down, picked up my phone, pressed the End Record button, and held it out to me.

"Here," he said, dropping the phone in my hand and brusquely moving past me for the chair where he'd left his coat. I didn't have a chance to fully process his intent as he walked to the door and called over his shoulder, "See you next week."

* * *

"How'd it go? How many videos did you do? Did you post any yet? Are they still uploading? I haven't seen anything new come through."

I leaned to the side at the sound of the front door closing and Amelia's rapid-fire questions, peeking out of my room and waving to Amelia and Elijah as they came into view.

"How was the snowshoeing?"

"Fun. Hey, I smell something amazing." Elijah—peeling off layers—followed his nose into the kitchen. "Did you make us dinner? Is this . . . is this what I think it is?"

"I'm telling you, this is exactly why I can never move in with you." Amelia winked at me. "We will lose access to Winnie's cooking and then who will make me weekly deliciousness?"

Elijah held his hands up. "I see your point. But what if Winnie taught me how to make your favorite food? Then you could come home to me *and* weekly deliciousness."

My stomach sank and I ducked back into my bedroom, giving both them and myself some privacy. I knew Elijah and Amelia had been talking about moving in together. They'd been dating for over a year and were perfect for each other. I was so happy for my friend.

But at the same time, I was panicking. Just a little. Or a lot.

It'll be fine. You'll be fine. You'll get a new roommate. No big deal. Amelia's happiness is what matters.

Squinting at my laptop screen, at the grades I'd been entering into the online system, I wondered if it was too late to go on a run. I hadn't stepped outside the apartment yet today. I should've gone to the library. Or I should've gone to Pike Place Market and helped Serena at her booth sell her sexy tea to tourists.

I should've done anything other than what I'd done, which was sit alone, in the quiet, and grade assignments all day after Byron left.

But tomorrow would be spent assembling lab material boxes for the last month of school. I had two experiments a week planned, and materials needed to be separated and boxed together. Today had been my only day to catch up on grading, entering the data, and pulling together special study packets for the few students who were falling behind while also pulling together different special packets for the students who needed more challenging material.

"Sooo?" Amelia meandered into my room, the fabric of her snow pants making a swishing sound with each step. "What happened? Did Byron come over? Did you do the video?"

I gestured to my laptop. "I'm still editing it." I didn't typically use TikTok to edit my videos, I used a free program for the PC. My laptop was much newer than my phone and therefore much faster at processing the edits. But for live videos, my phone was fine.

"Can I see?" She rubbed her hands together, pulling the chair by my bed over to the desk.

"Uh, sure." I navigated to the video editing program and made it full screen. Then I hit play. Then I sat back, biting my thumbnail, my internal organs behaving erratically the moment Byron's face appeared.

"Oh. There's Byron." Amelia smiled and read the caption I'd added under his face. "'BYRON: shares no updates, makes no posts, has no social media, and is a sneaky dipper' . . .?" She turned and looked at me. "Dipper? Byron doesn't dip."

"Watch the video."

She made a face. "He's never even smoked a cigarette. He'd never do dip."

"Watch."

I'd cut out the footage of him smiling after I'd inadvertently told him his eyes were sexy. Perhaps I was being a weirdo, but I didn't want to share that part of the recording with anyone.

Also, additional evidence for my Winnie-is-a-weirdo argument, I did keep the footage of his smile for myself and had saved it in three different places including a thumb drive and the cloud. I'd also watched it maybe one hundred times, getting hot and flustered and shivery each and every time, evidence that my body's reaction to Byron couldn't be entirely the fault of pheromones. Even absent his physical presence, my biology responded.

The recording switched to a selfie video of me pretending to be checking status updates on Amelia's old iPad, my laptop, and my Kindle Fire—all of which I'd spread around the kitchen. The caption read "WINNIE: constantly making videos, tutorials, and posting updates, has an account everywhere, even on Myspace (I believe in you, Myspace!) Doesn't know her BFF dips."

Amelia smiled and wrinkled her nose after she read the words. The video switched to the floor shot of us moving in the circle above, swinging our arms, with the "Bestfriends" caption flashing in the center of the screen. And then, just as suddenly as it had happened in real life, I was yanked forward and dipped above the phone as the caption changed in a flash to "NO ONE EVER EXPECTS THE SPANISH INQUISITION OR A BESTIE DIP!"

Amelia laughed, clapping once and leaning back. "Oh my gosh, that was awesome. You two did so great. Now I get it, he *dips*." Turning her smile to me, she asked, "Did you know he was going to dip you?"

"No. I had no idea."

She pushed my shoulder with her fingertips. "See? That was smart of Byron, suggesting that you don't practice or stage it. Your surprise looked real because it was real."

"Ah, Byron. More than just a pretty face."

That made her laugh again. "I guess all his ballroom dancing classes finally paid off."

I snorted, casting a *yeah right* side-eye in her direction.

She stood, stretching. "Why haven't you posted it? It's great."

"Uh . . ." I shut my laptop, also standing. "I thought I should send it to Byron first, make sure he's okay with it."

I felt like Byron and I had taken ten giant steps forward this afternoon prior to filming the video and then at least seven steps backward when he abruptly left. So, yes. Part of the reason I hadn't posted it yet was that I wanted to send it to him first and obtain his sign-off. He'd deleted his social media accounts for a reason, one I didn't fully understand, and I felt an extra level of precaution here was warranted.

But the other reasons why I hadn't posted anything yet had everything to do with me, and my biology, and his whiplash declaration yesterday at his house, and a confusing sense of dread whenever I thought about sharing the video publicly.

"Come on, let's eat. I'm starving." Yawning, Amelia strolled out of my room. "I say if he didn't care about the lap one going live without his permission, he's not going to have a problem with that one. You should post it."

"All the same." My gaze flicked to the thumb drive on my desk, one of the three places I'd saved the extra footage of Byron, and a fissure of something hot and anxious banded around my lungs. "Better to be safe than sorry."

CHAPTER 12
BYRON

Even when I owned a smartphone capable of downloading and running social media apps, and I had accounts on those apps, I'd never conducted a surveillance of my accounts' engagement and activity—comments, likes, subscribes, etc. Nor had I repeatedly checked the status of other accounts and their content. Such behaviors fell into the category of what I'd long ago labeled "active waiting." Waiting of any kind never appealed to me.

And yet I'd spent almost every waking hour of every day since leaving Winnie's apartment last Saturday in a state of perpetual, paralyzed, active waiting. I'd been so consumed, I'd actually ventured to the home feed of the app, mindlessly scrolling through videos, some of which made me laugh. Others, specifically a challenge labeled something like Pin Your Girl Against the Wall, inspired ideas I'd never be able to act upon with Winnie.

Still, the ideas were nice.

Refreshing the screen for the third time today, I frowned as the icons and video previews of her profile arranged themselves. An exact replica of what had existed before I refreshed the page greeted me. Winnie still hadn't posted our new video.

Between those three weeks I'd spent actively waiting for her to call or text so that we could record the challenges on her list and these last few days of purgatory, I was tired of waiting. I wanted to know.

I hunted for my phone and texted her.

Byron: Do we need to redo the video?

I stared at the seven words, so easily typed, the only ones I'd been capable of writing in the last two hours. Leaning forward in my chair, resting my elbows on my knees, I pushed my hair out of my eyes. She'd called my eyes sexy last week and I'd indulged myself replaying the moment far too often, wondering if she'd meant the sentiment or if she'd spoken it merely to solicit a reaction on camera.

The instant her response arrived, I read it.

Winnie: No. It turned out well. Also, hi. How are you?

Byron: Why haven't you posted it

Byron: Fine

Byron: You?

I stared at these new seven words I'd written—that made fourteen. My phone vibrated a moment later, Winnie's number flashing on the screen.

"Hello?" I answered, telling myself not to grip the cheap flip phone so tight.

"Hey, so, I didn't post the video for two reasons."

"Okay."

"First, you left so abruptly. I was a little worried you were angry with me. Did I do something wrong?"

"No. Not at all." She'd done everything right. Too right. And that was the issue.

"Are you sure?"

"Yep." I cleared my throat as I endeavored to erase from my mind the tactile memory of touching her, holding her in my arms. "Don't read anything into it. What's the other reason?"

"Before you say anything, and you're probably going to think I'm being a fruitcake, I still can't stop thinking this—the videos—are disingenuous."

That her unwillingness to believe me remained a source of hesitation was both a relief and an irritant. I'd been worried she'd definitively decided to nix our agreement. Winnie feeling hesitation was far preferable to ending our interactions completely. "We already settled this."

"We didn't settle it. You forbade me from discussing it."

"That is not at all accurate. I didn't forbid you from discussing it. I *requested* that you not question it or accuse me of having a stroke."

"You stipulated that I—" She made a grumbly sound. "You know what, it doesn't matter. At this point, it's not about whether I like you or you like me, I've come to terms with that part."

"You have?" I sat upright.

"Hold on and let me get this out, okay?"

"Okay."

"It's about my content. Maybe you were right. Maybe I am duping young women into considering a career in STEM."

I searched my memory. "When have I ever said that?"

"You didn't say exactly that, but when you first offered to help, that's the impression I got from you."

"Then in the interest of precision, allow me to correct that misimpression. I do not think you are duping young women into considering a career in STEM. You are trying to—and will—inspire them."

She made a short sound I couldn't interpret. "Thank you for that. But maybe this plan Amelia and I concocted—the whole plan, all the extra, non-STEM material, the makeup tutorials, the other challenges, my videos with you—is the wrong way to go about gaining new followers. Maybe the whole plan is disingenuous. And bad. And wrong."

"I disagree." The words were stated automatically, necessitating that I clamp my mouth shut.

I didn't know if I disagreed—truly disagreed—with her concerns. Perhaps her concerns were valid; perhaps diversifying the content offered on her account fell into the category of duplicitous rather than innocuous. I'd never been an end-justifies-the-means type of person. Thus, I understood and appreciated her concerns.

And yet I wanted to do those videos with her.

"Why do you disagree?" she asked, and I heard something like a *snap* over the phone.

I frowned at the odd sound. "What are you doing?"

"Assembling lab kits for the rest of the month. I ran out of the right size boxes on Sunday. I'm using some Tupperware I found at Goodwill. It stacks really well."

"Where? Where are you?"

"In my classroom at the school."

"Why the hell are you—" I cut myself off as I'd been about to ask, *Why the hell are you working on a Thursday at 7:00 p.m.?*

"What?"

"Never mind." The rush of indignation on her behalf tasted sharp and acidic. She'd asked me to stop offering unsolicited opinions. I would stop. Even if the woman worked harder than anyone I'd ever met, possessed an incredible aptitude for science, engineering, technology, and mathematics, managed both her time and other people impressively, juggled multiple demands and priorities with genuine cheerfulness, identified and anticipated potential problems before they manifested into actual problems, and allowed herself to be treated like an indentured servant.

She could've been a CEO, a successful entrepreneur, a patent lawyer, a freaking astronaut—anything. But she wanted to be an underappreciated, overworked, and underpaid teacher. And there wasn't one goddamn thing I could do about it.

"Byron? Are you still there?"

"I am."

"So, tell me"—another snapping sound from her side of the call—"why do you disagree?"

"Why do I disagree? With unpaid labor?"

"Noooo," she drawled, her voice descending an octave. I felt certain she'd rolled her eyes at me. "Why do you disagree with me about the new content on my social media accounts not being disingenuous? Explain it to me. I need someone to help me think through this and everyone I've asked—Serena, Elijah, John, Jason, Amelia, Lauren—they all say I'm overthinking it, but they can't tell me why it's not wrong. I still feel uncomfortable, uneasy, and I can't ignore that. Tell me why, Byron."

"You want my opinion?"

"Yes. If there's anyone on the planet I trust to tell me the hard truth and not care about my feelings, it's you."

The fuck? "I care about your feelings."

"That's not—sorry, that came out wrong. I meant you have logical, objective reasons for your opinions. You do your research. You know more than Wikipedia. You're truthful, even when the truth is hard to hear, and I respect that. That's what I need."

"Oh." *Shit.* "Okay." Pure, unadulterated panic nearly strangled me. How ironic. The one time I possessed only selfish motives for my advocacy of a cause was the one time Winnie desired my advice.

This was precisely why I never lied or gave interviews. More than three seconds are required to consider all available data, facts, and viewpoints prior to arriving at a defensible position.

Resting my shoulders on the back of the chair, I transferred my focus to the ceiling, frantically searching for a valid explanation—from my perspective—other than the inelegant truth.

Other reasons existed which I imagined closely mirrored her friends' justifications, such as: you need this income in order to pay back your student loans; I have no doubt you're the best person for this job and, therefore, you deserve it regardless of your follower count; the wider your audience, the more impact you'll make; once people are exposed to your brilliance, you will undoubtedly inspire them to consider careers in STEM.

Each of those arguments resonated similarly to *the end justifies the means.* And that, I suspected, was fundamentally the cause of her discomfort. Winnie wasn't an end-justifies-the-means person either.

"Well?" She huffed. "Give it to me straight."

We should do the videos as I look forward to seeing you and I want to kiss you. "Uh, so . . ." I stalled, suspecting the truth wouldn't convince her of anything except perhaps that I might be suffering from a stroke. Again. "To be clear, this is solicited advice, then?"

"As I said, yes. Correct. This is solicited advice. Please advise me, Byron-Wan Kenobi."

"Okay." I cleared my throat, more stalling, but it wasn't enough. I couldn't think. I was better on paper. If she'd asked me for a whitepaper and gave me a week, I wouldn't have any problem. I needed time.

"Hey—so . . ." *What will buy me time?* "You should come over."

FUUUUCK! Not that!

"What?"

I glanced down at the sweatpants I'd worn yesterday to rugby, slept in, and still currently wore. I hadn't shaved. I stank.

"Come over." I choked on my own stupidity. "And then we can talk it through."

"Oh. Uh, today?"

"Or tomorrow—" I spoke over her. Tomorrow would be excellent. Even better, next week. I could shower, shave, do a load of laundry, clean the house, rake the leaves, dress properly to receive her, and write down an argument, consider it from all angles, counterarguments, edit, revise, edit, add, delete, finalize.

"I have *Stardew Valley* tomorrow, and I don't like to miss it. But I can come over today. I'm finishing up here. Have you eaten? Do you want me to bring dinner?"

I'd consumed two bowls of cereal, three tablespoons of peanut butter, a can of tuna, and two bananas while standing over the kitchen sink approximately an hour ago. "I'll order delivery."

"Don't order anything. Restaurant food always makes me sick due to cross contamination. I need to stop by the store anyway. And you're the one doing me a favor. I'll bring dinner."

"I am not doing you a favor." *I'm a bad man. A bad, dirty, smelly man.* "Fred, don't bring dinner."

"I'm bringing dinner. See you in a few. Bye!"

She hung up.

CHAPTER 13
BYRON

I showered, styled my hair back—away from my eyes—and shaved. Since I rushed, I cut myself on the side of my neck, necessitating that I tear off a piece of toilet paper and press it to the small wound.

"Dammit."

I dug through the hamper next to my bed, swearing to myself I'd be better at putting clothes in drawers and hanging them in closets rather than amassing a laundry pile of nebulous cleanliness.

"Idiot."

I ran to and down the back stairs while trying to text Winnie and then slipped. I grabbed the banister at the very last second, which caused my phone to leap from my grip and fly to the bottom step. There it landed with a clatter and crash, destroyed. I froze.

"Hmm."

Abandoning the device, I ran back up the stairs two at a time, tore a piece of paper from an old notebook and ripped off an inch of tape. I scrawled *Fred—door is unlocked, come in, leave your groceries outside* in Sharpie and, taking the front stairs this time, hurried to tape the message to the front door's exterior.

"Okay. Good."

Out of breath when there existed no logical reason to be, I jogged to the kitchen and rinsed the dishes in the sink, debating what to make for dinner.

Not pasta, obviously. Not tacos, I only had flour tortillas. Additional ideas were quickly dismissed for similar reasons. What the hell did she eat?

Taking a break from the dishes, I opened the fridge with dripping hands and examined the possibilities. One minute later, exasperated, I grabbed anything from the fridge certain to be wheat-free—cheese, tenderloin steaks, mushrooms, green onions, lettuce, grapes, eggs, potatoes—and spread them out on the counter.

Pinching my bottom lip between my thumb and forefinger, I stared at my options until a meal made itself obvious: steaks, fried mushrooms, and baked potatoes.

Returning the unneeded items to the fridge, I placed the potatoes in the oven, finished the dishes, started the dishwasher, and painstakingly wiped down the counters three times, not wanting to inadvertently poison her with cereal remains or breadcrumbs.

I'd just completed preheating the range's gas grill and seasoning the steaks when I heard a tentative, "Hello? Byron?"

"Fuck. Shit. Fuck." Spinning, I forked the steaks onto the grill and called back, "In the kitchen," while digging in a drawer for tin foil. She appeared as I finished tucking the malleable metal sheet around the steaks and turned to grab a cutting board.

"Hi." I rocked backward, smothering the spark kindling beneath my ribs as I inspected her. Bright eyes, pink cheeks, red lips. Winnie was beautiful, unfairly so. She still wore her coat, scarf, hat, and gloves. "You look cold."

"I am cold." Her thumb pointed toward the front door. "Why'd you want me to leave my groceries outside? And what's that smell?"

"Dinner." I drew a knife from the wooden block, still struggling to suffocate that spark.

She leaned to the side, as though to peek around me. "You're making us dinner?"

"Correct."

"Do you know how to cook?"

"Yes."

"You're not going to feed me chicken nuggets, are you?"

"No. I only serve items I've either grown, foraged, or hunted and butchered myself."

"Are you serious?"

I laughed at her expression. "No, I'm not. That was a joke."

"I can never tell with you."

"Is that a bad thing?"

"It's certainly a thing." Giving me both a side-eye and a smile, Winnie tugged off her gloves and stuffed them in her jacket pocket. "Thank you for dinner."

The smile, though small, rendered me momentarily incapable of forming a response. I didn't want to do or say anything that might jeopardize her overt friendliness. Thus, I unnecessarily wiped my hands on a towel while watching her peel off her jacket, hat, and scarf, hanging all three on the back of a stool.

But despite my silence, her smile did wane, and her eyes narrowed, flicking to mine, then away several times. "What?"

I set down the towel. "What?"

"Do I have something on my face?" She wiped at her nose.

"No." Tugging the mushrooms over to the sink, I rinsed them, rubbing any residual dirt with my thumbs. "If you did, I would tell you."

"Because all imperfections must be immediately rectified?"

I couldn't discern if the question were a rhetorical one meant as a joke or a serious one meant to be answered. Studying her for a moment, I decided it was both. "If I had something on my face, I'd want to be told."

"Even if it's embarrassing?"

"The truth is often embarrassing. I'd prefer to be embarrassed with a truth than coddled with a lie."

"Huh. Interesting." She nodded slowly, her gaze losing its focus and turning inward.

Apparently, I'd revealed a fascinating secret about myself, and this reveal required a considerable amount of deliberation.

I turned off the faucet, thankful for the rudimentary task before me, and set the mushrooms on the cutting board, stealing glances at Winnie as she stared unseeingly forward. She swayed on her feet.

I wanted to ask what she was thinking, if she were okay.

Instead, I said, "Sit."

Her head gave a mighty shake and she blinked, her eyes focusing on me once more. "What?"

"I have wine. If you want some." Gesturing to the stool where she'd draped her cold weather attire, I repeated, "Sit," softer this time.

"No wine, thank you. Not tonight, anyway." As she claimed her seat, Winnie lifted a hand to rub her upper back just beneath her neck, tilting her head to the right. "I'm already so tired."

I studied the circles beneath her eyes, how she pressed her fingers between her shoulder blades. "Does your back hurt?"

"A little. I've been standing all day." She yawned, moving her hand to cover her mouth. "It's fine though."

"Do you . . ." I wanted to offer her a massage.

And yet I also didn't want to offer her a massage.

Touching Winnie while she filmed the videos, while we each played our part in this "best friends" fiction, had been explicitly defined as part of our agreement. The tidy rules and time limits—from the moment she hit record until the moment the recording ended—created essential boundaries. I knew what was allowed and expected of me while we recorded. Unlike right now.

Her gaze skated over me when I didn't finish my thought. "What?"

"Nothing."

"*O-kaaay.*" Winnie's fingers fell to her lap, her attention on my hands and the mushrooms I chopped. "Then tell me your thoughts. Give it to me straight."

"About the videos." I reminded myself to be careful with the knife.

"Yes. The videos. The challenges. All of it."

I'd had very little time to mentally draft my defense of the videos, a scant few moments in the shower. Ultimately, I'd decided to treat her dilemma as though it were my own and follow the stream of logic to whatever its ultimate destination might be—which would be entirely up to Winnie.

Clearing my throat, I paused slicing the mushrooms, setting the knife down. "It's not a simple question. You are right to think the matter over and give it as much consideration as you have. Doing so demonstrates that you care about your integrity. Likewise, you care deeply for people you don't know, people you'll never meet. We'll call these people your 'potential audience' for the purposes of this conversation." The words arrived much clumsier than I would've liked, but the overall intent remained correct.

As I spoke, Winnie placed her elbow on the countertop and her cheek in her palm, gazing up at me.

"The real question with which I believe you're grappling is whether the end justifies the means. In most if not all circumstances, excepting a few extreme cases, I do not believe the ends can justify the means. All arguments, for and against, related to the good that will be accomplished in due course by amassing additional followers—getting the job, paying back your student loans, inspiring people, helping people—are, in my opinion, irrelevant."

Her expression seemed to turn hazy, a soft-looking smile slowly gracing her lips. Picking up the knife again, I lifted an eyebrow, splitting my attention between her and the mushrooms. I'd never witnessed this expression on her face before. It was . . . distracting.

"Which—uh—brings me to arguments against the new content."

"You're going to tell me why the new content is a bad idea?" she asked.

"Correct. I find the best way to plot a path forward, free of self-doubt, is to first consider why I might be wrong in my present course and all the arguments against it. Sometimes my present course is wrong, and I must make adjustments. Sometimes it isn't, and I continue as planned. And sometimes there is no right answer, and I must simply proceed along the path that is the least harmful, given all alternatives."

"That makes sense." She nodded.

"Doing so also has the byproduct of identifying whether I'm—as you suggested—overthinking an issue. If the arguments against my proposed course are nonissues, frivolous, imaginary, without impact, then I need not trouble myself justifying my plans. I simply move forward."

She blinked slowly, her eyes meandering to my mouth, then neck. Her smile grew and her head tilted about an inch to the side. "I like how you think."

I stiffened. "Winnie. What are you doing?"

"What?" Her soft smile persisted, as did the unidentified yet intoxicating look in her eyes.

My movements ceased. My eyes narrowed. "Why are you looking at me like that?"

"Like what?"

I licked my lips, unable to offer a description that didn't betray my hopes. "You're staring like you're . . . sleepy. And happy." A clumsy description, but valid nonetheless.

"Oh!" She straightened, then laughed. A becoming blush bloomed along the apples of her cheeks. "Sorry. I'm—it's just—" She laughed again, her fingers lifting to her forehead. "I've never heard you talk so much and so freely. You're"—Winnie peeked at me—"really interesting to listen to. Er, to which to listen."

"Oh." She'd complimented my brain, but it hit lower than expected. "Thank you." *She thinks I'm interesting . . .?* I felt myself stand up straighter, taller.

"Don't thank me," she teased. "It's not a compliment when it's the truth."

"Ah, yes. Right." I'm certain the involuntary smile I now wore ruined my attempt at a glare. Turning my back to her, I unnecessarily checked on the internal temperature of the steaks. As expected, they still required another ten minutes. *What was I saying?*

"Do you believe the arguments against me doing the videos are frivolous?"

Ah, yes! "I—no. That is, I don't know. It's not up to me, it's up to you. The arguments against as I see them can be summarized as follows: recording and uploading videos unrelated to the focus of your accounts—specifically in an attempt to gain new followers—is disingenuous, regardless of what topics these additional content videos cover."

"Yes. Exactly. I agree. That's exactly the issue." Her words were punctuated by the sound of her hand smacking the top of the counter. "I feel I haven't been able to articulate it correctly. No one else has understood my perspective when I've tried to explain it."

I tucked the foil tighter around the steaks, taking my time. Stalling. She thought I was interesting. I needed to keep being interesting. "We'll call the original focus of your accounts your 'creator's vision' for the purposes of this discussion, and I'll explain why in a moment."

"Okay, sounds good," she said, her cadence yielding and cheerful, causing an unexpected and immediate response in my body. I loved her voice.

I kept my back to her. Thinking and speaking were simpler tasks when she didn't cloud my vision. "As a creator of anything—whether it be STEM videos, books, movies, paintings—there's always going to be this tension for the creator between what we think our audience wants, what the audience believes it wants, and our original creator's vision."

Walking to the refrigerator, I retrieved the butter. "I'm of the belief that, above all else, the creator's vision must be given the most weight when making decisions. We are all ruled by both conscious and unconscious desires. Your current and potential audience might claim they want one thing when in reality their subconscious wants another. They might espouse a desire for a happy ending, but what they really crave is a tragic story, or vice versa, and are dissatisfied when you attempt to deliver what they've claimed to want."

"So what you're saying is, people don't know what they want." Her dry tone pulled a smile from me.

"Not quite," I said, amused by the generalization and her manner of delivering it. "People *sometimes* know what they want. And even when they do, even when their conscious and subconscious are in sync, what they want and what they need might not be aligned."

"I see . . ."

"Therefore, if you try to make people happy, or if you try to deliver what you think they want, or what they think they want, or what you think they need, you're never going to succeed. The only impossible goal for a creative person is to please their entire audience. Thus, it's better to stay true to your vision first and foremost and always."

"So, you're saying I shouldn't post the additional content and I should stick to my original creator's vision," Winnie said, audibly dismayed.

"No. Don't sound so despondent, I'm not finished yet. As I said, this is not a simple issue."

"Oh my God, Byron. Put me out of my misery already and tell me what to do! No wonder your head is so big. And I thought I was an overthinker."

I laughed, shaking my head at her. She was—in a word—cute. Unthinkingly, I glanced over my shoulder. I shouldn't have.

Elbow still on the counter, cheek still resting in her palm, Winnie's cinnamon eyes were wide and bright, amplifying the teasing grin adorning her mouth. My breath caught. She was so beautiful, and her beauty pierced me.

"What?" Her eyes narrowed slightly as her grin widened. "What's wrong?"

"Uh . . ." I averted my eyes and discovered I'd been unwrapping a stick of butter. *Why do I have butter?* Nothing about butter was interesting. *Be interesting.*

"Do you want me to finish cutting the mushrooms?" she asked.

The mushrooms.

"S—sure." I bent to retrieve a frying pan, grinding my teeth at my ineptness. There was a reason I was a writer, not an orator. It was the same reason why I observed real people and engaged only with fictional ones.

A stool scraped against the floor. A moment later, I sensed her walk around the kitchen island and stand behind me. "I shouldn't focus on trying to make my audience—prospective or current—happy, but I should remain true to my original creative vision," she said, and I was grateful for her summary.

"Correct." Twisting the burner knob of the stove, I waited until the igniter clicked before turning it to high, the gas catching. "And furthermore, I maintain that your audience will find you. And you will make them the happiest by remaining true to yourself."

"Do you want these mushrooms thinly sliced?"

"No. Roughly chopped is fine." Taking a deep breath, I focused for a moment on gauging the correct temperature to melt the butter without browning it.

"My original vision was to do STEM videos for anyone interested in the subjects I covered, to be a resource, to be helpful. But I'd also hoped I could show girls and women that being interested in STEM is not—as Amelia puts it—roped off to them."

"An admirable vision." I stirred the butter with a wooden spoon, grasping on to my final—and the most important—thought. "That being said, I would ask this: Does posting the additional content detract from your original vision? Is the nature of your vision so rigid that the new content will dilute its intention, rendering it less effective or completely ineffective? Or does the new content enhance and contribute to your creator's vision?"

Bracing for the sight of her, I peered over my shoulder. Her back was to me, and she appeared singularly focused on cutting mushrooms. Hoping this long-winded exploration of logic and reason had helped—and had remained interesting—I gave her a moment of quiet contemplation while I melted the entirety of the butter, rewinding and playing back every moment since she'd appeared.

"No. It doesn't," she said eventually, hauling me out of my reminiscence as she positioned herself at my elbow, holding the cutting board covered in roughly chopped mushrooms.

She'd invaded my space. I pulled in a breath, held it, but didn't move.

"You were right to disagree with me when we spoke earlier on the phone, and I see your point. The additional videos do not detract from my STEM videos because Amelia's original argument still stands. Having interests outside of STEM does not make me less of a scientist, or an engineer, it just makes me more human. More real. Relatable. And that does fulfill my original creator's vision of showing women that STEM subjects and careers are accessible to them, that they don't need to hide or change who they are in order to be taken seriously in those fields."

Without asking, she slid the mushrooms off the board and into the waiting frying pan, lifting her chin to catch my stare once the task was accomplished, and condemning me to helplessness with one of her blinding smiles.

"Thank you for helping me, Byron."

Her words soft and sincere, that spark I'd been fastidiously laboring to suppress hit low and hard beneath my ribs, the flame gathering oxygen, swarming to surround and invade my lungs. She was so fucking awesome.

No one deserved this woman and her goodness, her ambition, intelligence, and integrity. Not a single soul.

"I didn't do anything," I said, my voice gruff around my tightening throat, and tore my eyes from hers.

"Ha! He says he didn't do anything." She removed herself a step and leaned her hip against the counter, the weight of her attention inescapable. "Meanwhile, this is the first time—the very first moment—I've felt completely certain of this plan since Amelia and I wrote it all out. I feel like, yes, I am doing the right thing. Even if it doesn't work, at least I know I'm doing the right thing." Winnie gave my shoulder a gentle shove. "Seriously, thank you. I feel so much better. And I don't think I realized how much my indecision about this was stressing me out."

Using the wooden spoon to distribute the butter, I shrugged off her praise, not liking how much I enjoyed it.

The sizzling and smell of frying mushrooms grew pungent during a long moment of blessed wordlessness. Talking to her had been nice. Cooking with her had also been nice. But there existed one excellent reason I rarely sought out Winnie's company: every moment spent in her presence—especially moments free of pretense or necessity, like now—made me dread the impending moments spent outside of it.

I turned off the stove and checked the clock over the oven. Dinner would be done in four minutes, we would finish eating in a half hour, she'd leave approximately twenty minutes after that. I only had one more hour of—

She shifted closer, her proximity drawing my attention.

"Hey, so, you know earlier?" she asked, her voice barely above a whisper. "When you said if you had something on your face you'd want to know?"

I lifted a hand to my chin, rubbed at the corners of my mouth. "I have something on my face?"

"No, just, something right here."

Winnie's fingers returned to my shoulder. They remained, gripping to hold me in place, the heat of her palm reaching the skin beneath my shirt. I turned toward her as her other hand came to my neck, her eyes and her thumb on a spot below my jaw.

"You have a bit of tissue right here." As she situated herself in the tight space between me and the range, she sucked in a breath between her teeth. "Oh. Did you cut yourself shaving? Lift your chin up."

"I did." I still held the wooden spoon in one hand, frozen in place by her nearness and touch. "Is it still bleeding?"

"Just a wee, little bit. Shoot. I should've left the tissue there. Do you have any antibiotic ointment?"

Feet and legs useless, I leaned back to peer down at her, the spark flaring anew. She was close.

"It'll be fine."

Her hand lingered on my neck as her eyes lifted to mine. "I know, but—" Winnie inhaled deeply, her lashes fluttering "—cheesus, Byron. What the heck kind of aftershave do you use? Effortless Subjugation by Kevin Klein?"

"Calvin Klein?" My hand not holding the spoon must've found its way to her hip at some point. That's where I discovered it now resided, tugging her closer.

"Isn't that what I said?"

"No," I whispered, rushing to memorize every detail of her face. She'd never been this close, not without filming one of the videos. "You said 'Kevin Klein.'"

"Oh. Then it should be called Brain Malfunction by Calvin Klein," she whispered, lifting her chin a scant inch, but it was everything. Absolutely everything. A pulse of fierce hope jabbed and sliced at me. My eyes went wide as hers lowered to my mouth, and holy fuck, was she—

"Whoa! Hey—sorry!" Jeff's voice, nails on the chalkboard of creation and existence, invaded the moment, annexing hope and giving rise to misery.

"Jeffrey." I expelled his name, rancor commensurate to the surge of resentment within me permeated each syllable. Shutting my eyes, needing a moment, I wished I'd installed a trapdoor beneath wherever he presently stood, leading to a dungeon complete with giant bloodthirsty crocodiles. Perhaps donning laser beams atop their heads.

"Sorry. We're sorry." He sounded sorry, which meant he hadn't spotted Winnie yet.

My fingers at her hip held her tighter even as I felt her shift on her feet. Perhaps if he didn't see her, he'd leave, and we could pretend he'd never interrupted. We could transport back to our moment.

"We didn't know you had someone—wait . . ."

I held my breath. *No, no, no.*

"Winnie?"

Sheep-biting footlicker.

CHAPTER 14
WINNIE

"Are you guys filming right now?" Jeff sounded so confused, and his confusion—nay, his mere presence—was akin to being doused with a bucket of reality-flavored ice water.

Peeking around Byron's shoulder with wide eyes, I caught sight of Lucy standing next to Jeff, who was currently twisting his neck from side to side. He scanned the room, presumably searching for my phone or a recording device.

I wished the ground would open and swallow me whole.

Had I been flirting with Byron seconds ago? Had I been about to make a complete idiot of myself and attempt to *kiss* Byron? Had that been me? And was this the same Byron who'd told me he liked me, but it wasn't a big deal, he didn't want or need anything from me, and he didn't particularly want to like me? That Byron?

Thank God we'd been interrupted.

A thunderbolt of embarrassed awareness had me snatching my hands from Byron's shoulders, balling them into fists as I tried to put distance between us. Except I couldn't put any distance between us. The stove was directly behind me and Byron's towering body stood directly in front of me. I'd put myself in this position—on purpose—mere moments ago. It had seemed like such a perfectly natural thing to do at the time.

What the Fahrenheit, Winnie? . . . BYRON?!

Byron who, until recently, criticized and corrected me all the damn time and couldn't keep his snarky thoughts about my job to himself. My hormones failed to realize that one evening of extremely enjoyable conversation didn't negate six years of his glares and nitpicking. I'd grown up in a household where I'd been judged constantly, one would think my body wouldn't betray me in this way.

"Did we interrupt a video? Or . . . ?" Jeff had lowered his voice to a whisper, still searching the room for whatever we must've been using to film, because why else would we be embracing?

"No," Byron drawled, not looking at me but instead staring at a spot over my head. Slowly, he turned to face Jeff and Lucy while I struggled against the urge to cover my face.

Now standing next to me, he still held the spoon he'd used to stir the mushrooms in one hand while his other remained on my body, sliding a bit lower and further around my torso. Byron's arm slung along my back and the heat of his palm did mysterious things to my stomach, his long fingers curling at my waist.

Jeff, meanwhile, zeroed in on my hip, apparently analyzing and contemplating our closeness. Plagued by flaming cheeks, I opened my mouth to explain, maybe to say something like, *This isn't what it looks like.*

Except, it was exactly what it looked like. My brain had no idea how to explain what they'd walked in on without lying or admitting too much. And what had my brain been thinking? *You weren't thinking with your brain, Winnie. You were thinking with your biology.*

Jeff's inspection moved between us, and I tried not to squirm under his comically perplexed frown or Lucy's amused smirk.

He stepped forward, a hardness gathering behind his typically affable expression. "Then what are you—"

"Come on, J." Lucy cut in, grabbing his arm and tugging him toward the salon. "Let's give your friends some privacy."

He didn't budge, his frown intensifying as he shook off her hand. Jeff's expression morphed from confused to concerned as his gaze settled on mine. "Do you want us to leave, Winnie?"

Byron's fingers flexed, but he said nothing. However, I could feel the intensity of Byron's glare, pointed at his longtime roommate. It reminded me of the heat emanating from a bonfire.

Did I want them to leave? *Yes.* Yes, I did. As quickly as possible.

But how to communicate this desire without sounding rude would require me to gather a deep, calming breath and step out of Byron's hold so I could think—both of which I did.

Pasting on a friendly smile, I gained another step away from the tall, dark, and handsome man behind me and stood at the kitchen island. I picked up the cutting board, needing to do something with my hands.

"You guys can stay or leave, whatever you want." To my incalculable relief, my voice sounded mostly normal. For good measure, I shrugged, glancing between them as I flipped on the sink faucet to rinse the cutting board. "We're just about to eat. Have you eaten?"

While I spoke, Jeff took another step forward, coming to stand at the edge of the kitchen island directly in front of me, the sink and expanse of countertop between us. His eyes moved between mine, concern still stamped on his forehead. "We can stay—"

"There's not enough for them," came Byron's curt addition to my attempt at politeness and normalcy. "I'm sure they have other plans. *Not* here."

I rolled my lips between my teeth, closing my eyes briefly to regather my wits, and did my best to squash my ingrained, negative reaction to Byron's rudeness. *Why can't he just be nice?*

When I opened my eyes, they connected with Lucy's. She seemed to be fighting a laugh. We swapped a quick, commiserating stare. Apparently, Lucy and Byron weren't strangers, and thankfully she didn't seem to find his behavior offensive.

"Let's go." Her gaze still on me, a soft smile curving her lips, she placed a hand on her boyfriend's back and pushed him toward the front room. "We'll grab something on the way to my place."

Jeff dragged his feet, his attention shifting to someplace behind me and becoming a scowl. I surmised he and the big guy were trading them. A flare of annoyance eclipsed my flustered embarrassment and, giving Lucy a short, grateful nod as they departed, I washed the cutting board with vigor.

What the heck was wrong with Jeff, anyway? So what if he'd walked in on us canoodling? What business was that of his?

"Are you . . . okay?"

I grunted. I didn't want to lie, and I didn't want to discuss my thoughts or feelings about the last few moments, or my foolishness prior to that. *Maybe that's why Byron grunts. To avoid both lies and truth.*

I sensed him hovering behind me, and the weight of his stare, while I continued to unnecessarily clean the cutting board. Renewed embarrassment clouded my vision, and I wondered if I ought to apologize.

I'd been the one who'd invaded his space, stepping between him and the range, touching him, lifting my chin for a freaking kiss. I had no excuse other than to blame my body's nonsensical and unwelcomed biological response. But what could I say?

Sorry. I don't know why I did that. I shouldn't want to touch you, but for some reason my hands do. And I shouldn't want to kiss you, but for some reason my lips do. Admitting any or all of this felt like it would give him too much power.

I'd made the mistake of telling Jeff about my feelings and look where that got me.

"Win—"

"Is dinner ready?" I flipped off the faucet, using the back of a wet hand to rub my forehead. "I'm starved."

A short pause followed by the sound of Byron clearing his throat. "Yeah. I think so."

"Just show me where the plates and utensils are. I'll set the table." Setting the cutting board down on the counter, I picked up a dishcloth and wiped up the dribbles of water around the sink. "And do you have a towel? I'll dry this."

* * *

I set the table while Byron loaded our plates with food. We met and ate in his cavernous dining room, me at the head of the table and him to my right. It felt a little like that scene from Disney's *Beauty and the Beast*, except the flatware didn't dance and none of the plates sang.

He drank red wine and I had water. I commented on how nicely the steaks were seasoned and he said something about how perfectly chopped the mushrooms were. We shared small smiles, and I hoped the innocent exchange meant all earlier awkwardness caused by my weird behavior had been forgotten.

But then, after a brief silence where I ate and he pushed the food around on his plate, Byron said, "Why do you even like that guy?"

"*That guy*?" I made a face, teasing. "You mean Jeff? Your roommate for the last six years?"

"Yeah. You've liked him for a while."

My fork halted midair, and an errant mushroom fell to my plate. "He told you that?"

This. This was why it was never a good idea to confess anything to anyone until one was absolutely certain of the person and the reciprocal nature of their feelings. I couldn't believe Jeff.

"No. He didn't say anything. But it seemed obvious to me."

"Really?" My heart pinged with guilt, and I shoveled the forkful of mushrooms into my mouth. After chewing and swallowing, I added, "I didn't think I was being obvious."

"You weren't." He seemed to inspect me for a moment. "And you didn't do anything wrong."

I gave him a quizzical look. "It's not wrong to like someone who's in a committed long-term relationship?"

"Nope."

"You sound so certain." I speared several mushrooms with my fork instead of scooping them this time.

"Did you do anything to undermine their relationship?"

"No."

"Then, there you go."

I set my utensil down. "But I—"

"Why are you so determined to think poorly of yourself?"

The question made me sit up straighter, examine him closer. He looked frustrated.

"What? No, I'm not."

"Yeah, you are. It's why you accept less than you deserve."

I grunted—deciding to fully embrace the elusive art of the grunt—and flicked my hand through the air, his questions making me hot and flustered. "I don't want to talk about this."

"Fine, then tell me why you've had a thing for Jeff for so long, other than the obvious."

Cutting into my steak, I avoided his steady gaze. "What's the obvious?"

"He's always been really good-looking and fit."

Eating a bite of steak, which was delicious, I contemplated how best to answer his question and realized Byron hadn't yet eaten any of his food. "I guess he is good-looking and fit."

He sent me one of his hooded looks, this one I recognized as his disbelieving face.

So I asked, "What?"

"You say that like his body and face—his physical attractiveness—never played a part in you liking him."

"I suppose it must have. I'm sure I noticed at some point that he's handsome, has a nice smile, but it wasn't why I liked him so much, or why my like of him persisted for so long. Why? Are you telling me you're only ever attracted to really good-looking women?"

"Yes."

A surprised laugh burst out of me, and I shoved his shoulder lightly. He dropped his eyes and a reluctant—or shy?—smile curved his lips.

"Byron Visser, are you saying you're shallow?"

"Yes." He sipped his wine, licked his lips, then drank more heavily from the glass.

"Come on. You have to be attracted to more than just the physical."

His eyes lifted, quickly moved over my face, then fell to his plate. He cleared his throat. "Obviously. But the face—and the body, the voice, how she speaks, how she moves, how she laughs—is definitely a big part of it."

I was about to point out that voice, movement, and laughter were not necessarily external attributes, but before I could, he asked again, "So what is it? What has you so enraptured with *Jeffrey*?" He took another gulp of his wine.

I ignored the hint of mockery in his tone and stalled by taking another bite of steak, washing it down with water, then placing my fork on my plate and leaning back in my chair.

"It's difficult to explain?"

"No, he's . . ."

"What?"

"Really kind. Loyal." I nodded at my reasoning.

"And?"

"He's funny. He makes me laugh." I wasn't sure what Byron had been expecting, but my like of Jeff had always seemed normal and natural to me. Of course I would like Jeff. Everyone liked Jeff. Jeff was likable.

"He is funny," Byron said, as though conceding a point, but then added with a grumble, "Sometimes."

"And we have a ton of stuff in common."

"Like what?"

"Like—and you're not allowed to comment on this—our jobs. And why we decided to be teachers, and our enthusiasm for it. We have the same taste in movies and music, the same sense of humor. We both enjoy the same activities, love camping, hiking, fishing. We both—"

"Don't you think that would get boring?" The right side of his lip curled.

"Boring?"

"Being with someone who likes everything you like? Who never challenges you to think about things in a different way? Try something new?"

I couldn't help it, I leveled him with a flat stare. "Says you—who by your own admission—doesn't like people."

"I like people." He poked at his mushrooms, moving them around his plate.

I snorted. "Fictional people."

"They're still people."

"People *you* control."

Now the right side of his mouth curved, and he gave me back his eyes. "I like control."

I blinked, startled, my ability to form coherent thought momentarily suspended by a burst of heat erupting low in my stomach.

Something about those three words paired with the low tenor of his voice and his piercing stare made the fine hairs on my nape stand at attention and my mouth go completely dry. Either it was my imagination—which had abruptly been besieged by completely inappropriate interpretations of what he might mean by *control*—or Byron Visser's statement had been extremely suggestive and a purposeful double entendre. Worse, my imagination and body seemed completely on board with discovering his precise meaning, whether that be via the scientific method or a haphazard, frenzied exploration on this very table.

Byron said nothing. Just simply looked at me. Admittedly, nothing about this look felt simple. It felt both inscrutable and demanding, mercenary and aloof, and my breathing grew shallower the longer I held it.

And yet, despite the anarchy of my body, and whatever voodoo his unique biology inflicted on my hormones and glands and olfactory systems, I couldn't shake the sense that Byron Visser—famous antisocial genius—was playing with me. To what end, I had no idea.

Tearing my eyes from his, I ignored the swirling heat threatening to consume my good sense and reached for my glass of water. I took a large swallow as I considered what to do next. For maybe the millionth time, his words from weeks ago chanted in my brain.

I like you.

My heart squeezed at the memory, a buzz of electric sensation running up my neck. He was so darn confusing.

It's not a big deal.

Fine. He liked me, but it wasn't a big deal. I needed to not make it a big deal.

I don't want or need anything from you.

I wasn't going to make a polite excuse and leave like I would've done in the past when faced with discomfort in his presence. I would pull on my big-girl safety goggles and find another way.

So I asked myself: if it had been anyone other than Byron making a suggestive statement, what would I do?

Tell a joke. Diffuse tension with humor.

Sucking in a measured breath, I returned my water glass to the table and flipped through my internal joke database, searching for something about control and seizing the first one that occurred to me.

"So, uh, have you heard the one about the scientist couple who had twins?" Picking up my fork and knife, I began to cut off another bite of steak, my attention focused on the progress of the knife. I wasn't quite ready to engage with his stunning gaze yet.

Byron remained silent while I finished cutting my food, brought the bite to my mouth, chewed, swallowed, and took another sip of water. I fiddled with the napkin on my lap and decided to take his lack of prompting as implicit interest in the punch line.

My stare still fastened to my food, I sent him a quick, tight smile and said, "They named one James Lind and the other Control Group."

I heard him breathe out—not a laugh, just an audible exhale. In my peripheral vision, I saw him lean back in his chair.

"I've always been amazed by the number of jokes you know."

Chancing a peek, a rush of relief swept through me when I found very little of his earlier enigmatic look remaining. It had been replaced by a wry tilt to his lips and a slightly raised single eyebrow.

"I have one or two for every occasion." Flicking my hair off my shoulders with my fingertips in a look-how-impressive-I-am movement, I grinned. "They come in handy in the classroom when I'm trying to refocus the kids' attention back to the lesson."

"Is that what you're doing now? Refocusing my attention?"

A fissure of both unease and excitement—an odd emotional compound if there ever was one—shivered down my back, but I was able to find my wits before he could scatter them again. "It just seems ironic to me."

"What's that?" Byron leaned forward, placing his elbows on the arms of his chair and clasping his hands over his lap.

I gestured to him. "It's ironic how you can sit there and suggest that *I* should eschew the comfortable when you barely leave your house. When you have no social media accounts and refuse to interact with the outside world."

The muscle at his temple ticked. "That is correct."

Hoping to disarm the tension further, I tried to poke fun. "Have you—oh, I don't know—ever thought about taking your own advice?"

"You think I should find someone who challenges me and forces me to try new things?"

"That is correct." I mimicked his earlier words as well as his tone, which made the wry tilt of his lips spread into a smile.

"For example?" he asked, reaching forward, his long fingers twisting the stem of his now empty wineglass. "Perhaps something like recording social media challenges?"

My heart shuddered and skipped.

Self-preservation had me circumventing *that* minefield with a subject change. "Uh, well, anyway. Back to your original question. I always thought the person I'd eventually end up with would be someone who was, fundamentally, like me."

"Wait, what was my original question?"

"Why I liked Jeff. I guess I don't know." I shrugged. "Jeff and I just always clicked. He felt like the right fit."

Byron frowned at his wineglass. "Felt? As in past tense?"

"Yes."

He seemed to struggle for a second before asking, "What changed?"

"Well." I scratched the side of my cheek, finally feeling like I'd regained my footing and the conversation had returned to benign, solid ground. "Seeing him with Lucy at the dinner party, how weird their dynamic is together."

His eyes narrowed but remained fastened to his empty glass. "Weird how?"

"She seemed angry the whole time and he seemed to, I don't know, enjoy the fact that she was angry. It was bizarre." My gaze lost focus and turned inward as I recalled their interactions.

"They're always like that."

"But it wasn't just the dinner party." I found myself musing aloud. "He wasn't at all helpful with the videos. You were right, he was making it about himself. Amelia hadn't eaten after work. It was thoughtless and self-centered of him to drag it out like that. Plus how he left me the second Lucy texted him after promising to help. I . . ." Sighing, I shook my head, feeling grumpier and grumpier about Jeff.

"What?"

I glanced at Byron. He seemed to be enthralled, on the edge of his seat waiting for my thoughts, his features free of judgment.

So I replied honestly, "I didn't like how he treated me."

"Why?"

"What do you mean, *why?* I deserve better than that."

His typically stern features visibly relaxed, seemed to soften, a whisper of a smile dancing around his lips. "Yes, you do, Fred. You deserve a lot better than that." He sounded as though he approved of me, my logic, and my feelings.

Pleasure unfurled in my chest, it felt like opening a window on a warm and sunny morning. To counteract the sensation, not wanting to betray how much I enjoyed his approval, I mock-glared at him. "What? Why are you looking at me like that?"

"Like what?"

Debating for a moment, I decided to use his description from earlier. "Like you're sleepy. And happy."

Byron laughed.

Caught completely off guard, air trapped itself in my lungs, and my ability to form coherent thought was once again suspended. Unwittingly, my brain decided I needed to dedicate my life to encouraging Byron to laugh. The sound and sight of it made every nerve and cell in my body buzz with something that felt radiant and absolutely wonderful.

Dopamine. You've just experienced a huge hit of dopamine. This man has direct access to your neurotransmitters. He's hijacked your vascular, endocrine, and neurological systems! WARNING!

Standing abruptly—feeling certain it was absolutely essential to put some distance between me and the addictive substance of Byron's uninhibited smile and laughter—I grabbed my plate and spun for the kitchen.

"Wait—Winnie. Where are you going?" I heard his chair scrape against the floor, and I quickened my steps.

Without turning, I raised my voice. "Uh, I'll do the dishes. I should do the dishes. You made dinner."

"Are you finished?"

Rounding the kitchen island, I hunted for his compost bin. "So full. Couldn't eat another bite."

Opening the cabinets beneath his sink, I found the compost, but then hesitated before dumping the remainder of this truly delicious dinner. *Shoot.* I hated wasting food.

"What's wrong? Is the bag full?" He came to stand next to me.

I shut the cabinet. "Uh, no. I was just thinking, it's a lot of food. Do you have a container or something? I can eat it tomorrow."

"I do," he said, but didn't move to retrieve it.

Glancing at him, I found his attention focused on the wall behind me, his index finger pressed against his bottom lip. I twisted at the waist and followed his line of sight. He seemed to be staring at the oven clock.

"Do you have—should I go?"

"No," he said, the word sharp and sudden. He followed it up with a scowl. "That is, no problem if you need to leave. But since you're here, and we're behind on your videos, perhaps we should film one."

"Oh." I nodded, light-headed as I mentally scanned the remaining challenges we'd yet to record. The next video on the list required me to lay my head in his lap.

In. His. LAP.

"We don't have to." Byron shoved his hands into his pockets, surveying me warily.

"No, it's good. I'll be right back. Pull up a movie." Cringing because my voice sounded high and strange, I walked around him, through the butler's pantry, and back to the dining room. I needed to retrieve my glass and any remaining dishes, but I also hoped movement would allow me to outrun the compound feelings of unease and excitement pulsing through me.

It's fine. I'm fine. I made the list. Nothing on the list is outside my comfort zone. It's fine. It'll be fine.

I breathed in, I breathed out, detecting just a trace of his aftershave lingering in the air as I walked slowly around the table looking for fallen crumbs. I told myself I wasn't stalling, but I was. I needed to think things through before I filmed myself using Byron's lap as a pillow. I needed to get my biology under control. And I had to wonder at the probability of things between Byron and I continuing to be so fraught.

It's not a big deal. . .

At least, from my perspective, they were fraught. Maybe I was the only weirdo here, the only one struggling.

Except . . . *It means I like you, but I don't particularly want to.*

I halted at the sideboard, thinking back to those moments in Byron's room weeks ago, and a thought occurred to me. Maybe—

"Fred? Are you coming?"

I turned at the sound of his voice and blurted my thoughts before I could stop myself. "Did you agree to do the videos with me because you don't want to like me?"

CHAPTER 15
WINNIE

Byron stared at me, wide-eyed and unmoving. "Excuse me?"

"It makes sense. It makes *a lot* of sense. At some point, spending time with someone you're inconveniently attracted to has to get easier. Theoretically, with repeated exposure, the involuntary feelings will eventually disappear."

His gaze turned watchful. "That is a theory. Why? Are you thinking of applying it to Jeff? Spending more time with him?"

"What? No." I scrunched my face. "I don't like *Jeff*. But hear me out." I walked around the table, allowing my stream of consciousness to carry me forward. "If, currently, person A's presence—their smiles, laughter, face, hands, smell, whatever—causes a dump of dopamine in person B's brain, and person A's pheromones radically impact the olfactory systems of person B, I have to believe increased exposure will dull those effects, don't you think?"

Byron blinked, like my words were spoken in a language foreign to him. Or he thought I'd lost my mind somewhere in the butler's pantry, between the kitchen and the dining room.

I soldiered on, deciding to use an analogy. "Like any substance working on neuroreceptors. Prescription drugs as an example. Wouldn't we require more frequent consumption and stronger doses in order to experience the same chemical response each time? Therefore, theoretically, just hanging out should cure person A of their body's biological response to person B."

Clasping my hands together, I felt more and more certain of my hastily compiled plan.

Slowly, he pushed his hands into his pockets, his gaze flickering over me, considering. "You think I want to *cure* myself of liking you?"

"If liking someone is involuntary, then wouldn't a cure be a mercy? I think so." I hedged, not wanting to reveal this theory was more about me than him. However, he raised a good point. Spending time together would help us both rid ourselves of this unwanted attraction.

Byron gave me a single, stunned blink, his mouth opening—probably to argue—so I cut him off. "We should do the video." I walked past him, back through the butler's pantry and kitchen, into the family room, piecing together the specific aims and methods of my experiment as I went. "If this is going to work, moving forward we should try to control the rate and time of exposure, the activities we engage in, how often we touch, etcetera. Then, over time, the effects of exposure will diminish until they fade completely."

Yes. YES! This will work. Take that, *ingrained biological responses!*

Pulling my phone from my coat pocket, I contemplated the arrangement of his family room. Byron had already turned on the television and paused whatever movie he'd selected.

"I do not think your theory is valid."

I glanced over my shoulder. He stood just inside the doorway, his hands still in his pockets, his features free of the loftiness I used to think was hard coded in his DNA. Or maybe, now that we'd spent some time together, it didn't look like loftiness anymore. It just looked like Byron.

Handsome as Hades and twice as brooding, for the first time in our acquaintance, I gave myself permission to simply admire how absolutely magnificent he was—from the thickness of his thighs to the sleek, raven black of his hair, the slight curling of his upper lip to the stunning beauty of his eyes. My stomach gave a weak flutter, my heart squeezing in response, and—you know what?—that was perfectly fine.

I had a plan to wean the Byron-biological warfare from my system, a solid working theory. Soon, no amount of brooding Byron sexiness would affect me at all.

Science for the Win! *That's me. I'm the Win.*

"Why don't you think my theory is valid?" I turned back to the family room, my chest all achy with the aftereffects of my blatant admiring. I decided to place my phone just under the TV. Ensuring the screen faced the couch so I could confirm we both stayed in the shot for the duration of the recording, I woke the phone, navigated to the video, and set it to selfie mode.

"Explain relationships that last fifty years. If repeated or prolonged exposure between two people dulled the effects of love, why would anyone stay together for a half century?"

"I'm not claiming that love isn't lasting. My theory has nothing to do with enduring love, or love at all." Arranging the phone until I was happy with the angle, I walked backward to the couch and sat, inspecting the shot. It looked fine. "I'm talking about *liking* someone. A crush. Ask any couple who's been together for a while. They all claim the initial rush of involuntary feelings fades within the first few months or—worst-case scenario—years, data that supports my theory. Now, come over here. I think we're ready to go."

I stood and walked the short distance to the phone, hitting the Record button as Byron strolled into the frame behind me and claimed a seat, a frown darkening his features. Walking backward again, I sat next to Byron when my legs met the sofa, deciding at the last minute I needed to sit *right* next to him in order for us to be framed correctly.

Checking the shot alignment, I folded my legs beneath me and angled my body toward his. Last thing, I looped my arm around his arm and curled my hand over his bicep. And then I breathed out slowly, needing a second. Byron had an extremely well-formed arm and touching it, being this close to him, did a few twisty things to my internal organs.

But all would be well. Eventually. *Repeated, controlled exposure. That's the answer.*

"There. That's good." My fingers gave his upper arm a little squeeze and stroke, necessitating that I press my knees together. It was a miracle when my voice sounded almost normal as I said, "You can hit play whenever."

"Should I—" He cleared his throat. "Would it be better if I put my arm around you?"

"Whatever feels most natural. What movie are we using?"

Byron didn't put his arm around me. He picked up the remote and pressed play. The Focus Features logo came up on the screen just before music I knew by heart sounded from the speakers.

"*Shaun of the Dead*!" I may have squealed a little, turning to face Byron. "It's one of my favorites."

"I know." He didn't look at me, and his profile appeared impassive, but his voice held a smile.

I quickly calculated how much sleep I'd get if I stayed for the whole movie, my stomach sinking slightly at the realization that it wouldn't be enough. *But tomorrow is Friday and you can sleep in on Saturday, so . . .*

"Is it okay if I stay?" I whispered, my eyes now peeled to the opening scenes.

"Of course."

"I mean, after we're done with the challenge, for the whole movie."

"I figured." Byron shifted, tugging on his arm.

With reluctance, I let it go, already mourning the loss of his closeness and his muscles beneath my hands. But then his arm came around me, and his hand came to my arm, and he guided my head to his shoulder. His other hand reached for mine, bringing my palm to his chest where he cupped it, and my whole body seemed to tense and sigh and rejoice and freeze.

This feels . . . sooo gooooood.

"Is this okay?" he whispered.

No. It wasn't okay. It was great.

"Yes." I snuggled closer, fitting the top of my head under his chin and inhaling because, why not? It was like a dream, and I was so dichotomously comfortable and uneasy. The conflicting sensations made me a little dizzy.

We watched the movie. We laughed at the same parts. And I knew what I needed to do next, but I couldn't seem to bring myself to move. I knew I couldn't keep recording, I didn't have unlimited storage on my phone and the video was already seven minutes long.

You have to, Winnie. You have to move.

But then it would end. We'd have no reason to keep snuggling on the couch after the video was over.

DO IT! This isn't real. Nothing about this is real, and the longer you indulge in the fantasy, the more difficult it will be to reenter reality.

With a mournful, silent sigh, I pushed slightly away from his chest. He let me go, his head swinging in my direction as I straightened. Wordlessly, I gave him a small smile and shifted my butt on the couch. Then, bracing a hand on his truly magnificent thigh—*do not stroke it, DO NOT*—I gently placed my head in his lap, my hands immediately jealous of my cheek.

"What—" he rasped, then cleared his throat. He didn't finish his sentence.

I turned my head, gazing up at him. "This okay?"

He stared at me, seemed to be considering, doing a great job of pretending like his thoughts were in turmoil.

He cleared his throat again. "Let me get you a pillow."

I turned my attention back to the movie. "You don't want me to lay my head on your lap?"

He was already sliding his hands under my head and gently adding a throw pillow. "You'll be more comfortable this way."

I allowed him to add the pillow while protesting, "But I like your lap." Because we were filming and I doubted I'd get another chance, I placed a hand on his thigh, just above the knee, and gave it a squeeze. *That's some good, high-quality thigh right there.*

"And my lap likes you, which is why you should use a pillow."

It took a few seconds for his words to sink in—probably because I remained distracted by his thigh—but when the statement did permeate my brain, my mouth dropped open and my eyes bugged out. I turned my head, staring up at him. Not helping matters, he peered down at me with one of his wry smiles that didn't look at all apologetic.

I smacked his thigh and sat up. He laughed, trying to catch my hands, but he was too late. I picked up the pillow from his lap and delivered a soft whack to his face. Byron easily wrenched the pillow away and bound my wrists with his long fingers, yanking me forward, bringing our faces within inches of each other.

For some reason, we were both breathing hard. I wore a smile, he did not.

"Pillow or no lap," he said.

I lifted an eyebrow, tilting my head. "I have an idea."

His eyes narrowed, heavy with suspicion, but he let my wrists go when I twisted them. Untucking my legs from beneath me, I placed my feet on the floor, and I faced the TV again. I felt his gaze track my movements, and when I patted my own lap, I glanced at him.

"Come on, lay it on me."

He reared back a half inch, visibly surprised.

I was also surprised at my boldness and playfulness. But at the same time, this plan I'd concocted of repeated exposure to Byron had given me bravery in his company where before I'd felt only the instinct to avoid and escape.

I needed to confront these feelings so that they'd dim, diminish, and disappear. If I kept avoiding them and him, they'd never lessen or go away. That was the theory, I felt certainty in my hypothesis, and I was committed to seeing this experiment through.

"Come on, give me your head." I patted my lap again, adding in a whisper, "It'll be a great way to end the video, a good twist."

Understanding and something else solidified in his eyes. He lifted his chin.

Then, Byron Visser, shunner of humans, scooched his butt back, braced his hand on my thigh, and placed his head in my lap. I smiled, impulsively deciding to thread my fingers through his lovely hair. He stiffened, but then a moment later he sighed, and I felt the tension leave his neck as I played with the longish locks.

"I love your hair," I said unthinkingly. But I did love his hair, so whatever.

He placed a hand on my knee, similar to what I'd done to his leg earlier. "You can have it."

I chuckled, feeling . . . oddly happy. Content. *How strange.*

We sat like that for at least a full minute, during which I'm sure I grinned the whole time, feeling myself relax into the couch and the moment, enjoying the feel of his head resting on my lap and the silken strands of his hair being combed between my fingers.

Instead of watching my favorite movie, I found my mind drifting to our evening together and how much I'd enjoyed listening to him talk, how grateful I felt for his help, how conflicted I'd felt after almost kissing him, and wondering if it would have been the worst thing in the world if I had kissed him.

He'd been so thoughtful, making me dinner. It had been so kind. Had I even said thank you? Or had I been too in-my-own-head to return his kindness with basic politeness?

Jeez. Maybe I just needed to chill out with him. I was a pro at chilling out with everyone else, why couldn't I relax and live in the moment with Byron? Why did I allow past misconceptions to continue—

Byron abruptly sat upright, pushed from the couch, walked over to my phone, and picked it up. I stared at him dumbly, and it was on the tip of my tongue to ask what was wrong.

But then he turned and tossed my cell to me, marching past. "Here. That should be enough. Stay as long as you want. I left your food on the counter. See you next week." His features as dispassionate as his tone, I watched his departure until he disappeared through the doorway to the salon, my face awash in mortified heat, my mouth parting in surprise.

Though I shouldn't have been surprised.

Once again, I'd forgotten we were filming.

And once again, obviously, he had not.

CHAPTER 16
WINNIE

I didn't talk to Byron on Friday. I called him twice. He didn't pick up. I left a voice message the first time, but not the second, worried I'd done something wrong. Maybe he didn't want to talk to me?

He was . . . confusing. I couldn't figure him out or predict his behavior from one moment to the next. It felt like every time I allowed myself to open the door to the possibility of a real friendship—or something more than friendship—he slammed it shut.

I needed help, I needed to talk through my confusion with someone I could trust, someone with significantly more dating experience than me, but my go-to advisor wasn't an option. Amelia would easily guess that the guy I wanted to discuss was Byron just as soon as I described his taciturn tendencies.

Serena, however, would not. She didn't know Byron except in passing. She'd been in at least three serious relationships and had dated a lot in college until our pact during senior year. And, as luck would have it, I'd offered to help her with her booth at the market Saturday mornings during the last week of May and the first two weeks of June. Huzzah!

The booth hopped nonstop. We sold out of Passionate Peppermint by midmorning and almost everything else was gone by 4:00 p.m. when we packed up and hauled the remaining merchandise back to her apartment in Belltown.

It wasn't until we were standing in her kitchen, about to chow down on her famous homemade gluten-free chicken soup that I finally worked up enough bravery to broach the topic.

"Hey, so I want to talk to you about something." I spoke to her back as she reheated the soup, stirring it with a wooden spoon. I waited until she looked at me before adding, "I need your advice."

Looking surprised—pleased but surprised—she placed the spoon next to the stove and turned to face me completely. "Okay, what is it?"

"Uh." I scratched my chin. "So, there's this guy I . . . like." I wasn't sure *like* was the correct word, but the English language lacked the right word or phrase to succinctly describe what I felt about Byron. Or maybe the word existed, and I just didn't know it.

Serena's eyes grew huge. "Really?"

"Why do you sound so shocked?"

"No, it's good. It's just, you never like anybody."

"I've liked people." I couldn't help but sound a little defensive.

"What I mean is, you never talk about it." She waved a hand between us, then bent to retrieve two bowls from under the counter. "Ignore me. Forget I said anything. What can I do to help? Or are we planning an attack here? A seduction?"

"No, it's not like that. I'm not sure I should like him."

She froze, not quite having straightened completely from the cabinet, visibly perplexed. "O-kaaay."

"I have this idea for how to stop liking him, but I need to talk to somebody about it, make sure my methods are sound."

Serena looked like she wanted to ask a thousand questions, but eventually settled on, "What's your idea?"

Getting comfortable on the barstool, I told Serena a shortened version of my theory about repeated exposures controlled over time to reduce biological response, my hope being that eventually my body would stop reacting to Byron like he was sustenance and shelter and everything necessary in order to survive. I called him "Jake" and said we worked together so she wouldn't suspect his real identity.

She frowned at intervals as she listened, putting spoons and napkins on the countertop where we'd eat. She also wrinkled her nose once or twice and served us both heaping helpings of soup, letting me explain everything before asking her second question, "So he's married?"

"What? No. He's not married." I picked up my spoon and stirred the steamy broth, enjoying the burst of heat enveloping my cool cheeks. It might've been Memorial Day weekend, but the high today had been forty-eight degrees Fahrenheit. Unusual weather for so late in the spring, but not unheard of.

"But he's dating someone?"

"No. He's single." I blew on a spoonful of broth. "As far as I know, he's not with anyone."

"Then can I ask, why do you want to stop liking him?"

I struggled with how to answer her question and decided the truth was best. "I shouldn't like him because nothing will ever happen between us, and I don't like how I feel when we're together. And I can't stop thinking about him."

"You don't like how you feel when you're together? How do you feel?"

"Hot. And shaky. Uncomfortable, light-headed. Sometimes I get tunnel vision, where all I see is him and everything else goes hazy. He distracts me, makes me nervous. It feels like . . ."

"What?" Serena grinned at me, her elbow on top of the counter and her hand tucked under her chin, apparently fully engrossed in my description.

"Like being really embarrassed all the time."

She sighed dreamily. "I love that feeling."

"Do you? It hasn't been pleasant for me."

"Are you sure he doesn't feel anything for you?" She sounded hopeful.

"I—"

"You're underestimating yourself." She took a bite of soup, then another. "He might reciprocate your feelings if you give him a chance."

I released my spoon and covered my face with both hands. "Actually, he said he likes me."

"What?"

Rubbing my forehead, I grimaced. "But he doesn't want to like me and said it was no big deal and that he doesn't want or need anything from me."

Serena leaned back in her stool. "Hold up, he said *what?*"

Rolling my eyes, I gave her a shortened account of my conversation with Byron from weeks ago while we ate. She listened patiently, her expression growing more and more horrified.

"So let me see if I have this right." She wiped her hands with a napkin. "He tells you he likes you, then says it's no big deal. But when you tried to give him an out—saying he likes you just a little—he says no, he likes you *a lot*, and he doesn't want or need anything from you. *And then*"— she speared the air with her index finger, all indignation and disgust—"when you ask him if he's messing with you, he has the audacity to say that he likes you against his will. Do I have that right?"

"That's the gist of it."

She made a scoffing sound, turning back to her bowl and shoveling soup into her mouth with a vengeance. "No wonder you don't want to like him. He's a jerk."

"No. He's not." I rubbed the center of my chest where an ache had settled for unknown reasons. "I used to think he was kind of a jerk, but the more time we spend together and I get to know him, the less jerk-like he seems." *Except when he leaves abruptly and when you ask him about it, he either says, "Don't read anything into it," or won't answer your calls. Except then.*

She shook her head. "Okay, well, we'll have to agree to disagree."

"Like on Thursday, he invited me over for dinner and—"

"He invited you over for dinner? For a date?"

"No. It wasn't like that. We were doing work stuff. Anyway, he invited me over for dinner. His roommate and his roommate's girlfriend stopped by, and I politely suggested they join us for dinner. But then Jake said there wasn't enough food. But it wasn't just that, he was actually kind of rude about it. So the roommate and girlfriend left."

"Okay?"

"But come to find out, there was more than enough food for all of us. I didn't know it at the time, didn't realize it until I got home and opened the doggie bag he'd put together for me. He'd made *five* steaks and he sent me home with all the leftovers."

"Huh."

I'd been so shocked when I opened the bag upon arriving home and finding three more steaks, the remainder of the mushrooms, and three baked potatoes in addition to my leftovers.

She rubbed her chin. "Steak is expensive."

"I know." The food would last me the better part of a week. I'd had to put most of my perishable groceries in the freezer or cook them and freeze them as whole meals.

"Clearly, he didn't want to share your company with the roommate and girlfriend."

I didn't contradict her assumption or suggest alternative reasoning, which was that Byron was antisocial, and maybe he just didn't want to be around more people. I didn't want to volunteer any information that might make Serena suspect Jake was actually Byron.

"Sorry." Her expression turned suddenly bracing and sympathetic. "I don't think your plan is going to work. It'll backfire."

"What do you mean?"

"Well, if you're just physically attracted to someone and then you start spending time with them, and they're like shallow or you're not compatible, you have no chemistry, then your plan would work. Exposure would cure you of your attraction if there's no chemistry or nothing to like about the person. The feelings would just go away, because once you get to know someone, your feelings of attraction either shrivel and die, or increase."

"But there is chemistry. There's too much chemistry, and that's what I'm trying to fix."

"And that's why your plan won't work. If you're attracted to someone, like *super* attracted, and then you start spending time with them and get to know them better and discover nothing about that person is repulsive or a turnoff, then the feelings will just grow and grow. It just gets worse and worse."

"But at some point they have to fade."

"No. No, no, no. People aren't drugs, they're so much more addictive and dangerous. You don't need more and more exposure to get the same feelings of a high. Even small snippets will sustain you. Just thinking about him is enough. But I do have another question—if you claim he isn't a jerk—why did Jake tell you he liked you if he didn't want or need anything from you? That, to me, seems like a jerk move."

Twisting my fingers, I tried to think of how I could explain without revealing that Jake was Byron. "It's a long story, but he had a good reason. It makes sense in context."

"If you say so."

"I do."

"Then I'm confused. If he likes you, and you like him, why don't y'all try dating each other? Seems like that would make sense. If he's not a jerk and your feelings are reciprocated, why don't you ask him out?"

My heart quickened. "Do you think I should?"

Serena nibbled her bottom lip, her gaze losing focus. "I don't know. You say his confession about liking you makes sense in context, but then for him to say that other shit? I don't know if you should tell him how you feel when he claims that liking you isn't a big deal." She blinked, her gaze sharpening again. "You are . . ." My friend sucked in a deep breath as she studied me, her soup forgotten. "You aren't very experienced, and that's not a criticism at all. You've always seemed to be a bit more tenderhearted than the rest of us." She winced at her own words. "Do you know what I mean? Or am I fucking this up?"

"I know what you mean." I gave her a reassuring smile. Serena was aware that I'd never slept with anyone before. "But it's not on purpose. It's not like I'm saving myself for marriage, or my forever person. It's just, I don't want to have sex just to have sex."

"I get it, I do. I felt that way too. Yet at the same time, you claim you've liked other people before now, but you've kept it to yourself. So I'm thinking you must *really* like this guy."

"Even though I haven't talked about it, I have *really* liked people in the past, and I've obviously been attracted to people before now. But when I would think about those people, I felt warm admiration and appreciation for who they are as a person. This is different."

"How is it different?"

"With B-Jake, it's like the physical attraction is first and foremost, clouding everything. I've never felt this kind of visceral, uncontrollable response."

"Hmm."

"So should I ask him out? Or—"

"How long have you known him?"

"A few years." I'd been a teacher for a few years at the same school, so this seemed plausible.

"How many partners has he had? Like, is he just recently single?"

I thought about the question and realized I'd never seen Byron date anybody, but there had been plenty of rumors online and in magazines of him dating actresses and supermodels after his first book hit all the best seller lists. "There's been rumors of him dating, but nothing concrete. I've never seen him with a date, or a girlfriend, or anything like that, and he has no pictures of anyone—like past girlfriends—at his house."

"But since you two work together, you have to interact with him. You can't avoid him?"

My stomach flopped. "You think I should avoid him?"

"I'm sorry, Win. I honestly don't know." Serena scratched her neck. "Is it possible he thinks you have a boyfriend? And that's why he doesn't want to like you?"

"No."

"Maybe he thinks you're not interested in dating? In general?"

"I don't think that's it."

She seemed to be at a loss. "If that's the case, you say he's not a jerk, but he says jerk-like things. He asks you over for dinner and sends his roommate away, so obviously he wants to spend time with only you, but it's not a date? And he doesn't ask you out?"

"No, he hasn't asked me out."

"Has he maybe hinted that he wants to ask you out?"

"Not at all."

Serena made a grumbly sound, grabbing my hands and holding them in hers. "If he's brave enough to tell you he likes you, then one would think he'd be brave enough to ask you out. I guess"—she gave her head a little shake— "if you were anyone else, and if you didn't have to see him at work, I'd tell you to call him out on his mixed messages. But I feel like maybe he's playing mind games with you. And you being you, and given your history, don't have a lot of experience with those kinds of guys."

"You mean I'm naïve."

"No." She squeezed my hands. "No. That's not what I mean. I'm just saying, intense attraction can be blinding. Nice guys don't say things like, 'I like you, but I don't particularly want to.' Or claim that liking you isn't a big deal. Liking you *is* a big deal because you are a big deal."

For some reason, a lump formed in my throat. "I wish I'd just slept with someone in college."

"Don't say that. You have to do what's right for you. We all have happy memories and regrets, your experience isn't any less or more valid than anyone else's."

"But then at least I would have *some* experience. Now I just feel lost. And stupid. And naïve."

Serena gave my hands another squeeze, making a *tsking* sound before reaching for my shoulders, pulling me off the stool, and wrapping her arms around me. "I'm sorry."

"Why are you sorry?" I clung to her, swallowing reflexively around the building emotion.

"I wish your first experience with this kind of extreme attraction had been with someone worthwhile, not with some skeeveball who's obviously messing with you."

Shutting my eyes tight, I shook my head, but said nothing. I didn't think Byron was messing with me, at least not on purpose.

Her hand moved up and down my back in a soothing motion. "I do want to say just one more thing, a warning of sorts."

"Okay?"

"You can't control how you feel about someone. If you're attracted to him, then so be it. But you can control your actions, what you do with those feelings, whether or not you act upon them." Pulling back, Serena waited until I opened my eyes to continue. "Give yourself permission to feel what you feel without beating yourself up about it. So you're attracted to him. So what? You don't have to do anything with him. I know you work with him, but you can decide to interact with him as little as possible."

I nodded even as every cell in my body rejected her suggestion. I didn't want to ignore Byron, not anymore. Being around him was confusing, and often uncomfortable, but it also felt so incredibly good in indescribable ways. *He's addictive.*

I couldn't help the little burst of a laugh that bubbled out of me at the thought. If my past self could see me now, she never would've believed a reality existed where I actually enjoyed Byron Visser's company.

Seeing my laugh, a soft smile claimed Serena's features. "Have you thought about maybe going on a date with someone else?"

"Uh—" I straightened at her unexpected suggestion, momentarily at a loss for words.

"It might help. Try signing up for an app. You used to have Tinder in college. Reactivate it. I'll help you filter out the jerks, show you what to look out for. Even if you don't meet someone, even if it's just for a few months, even if you're just going through the motions and going on a few dates and they're all duds, focusing that kind of energy on other people—people with actual potential for something more—might make being around Jake at work less difficult."

"I hadn't thought of that." Prior to now, right this minute, I wouldn't have entertained the suggestion. I'd told Amelia the truth a few weeks ago when I'd said I didn't feel a pressing need to be in a relationship. I still didn't.

But Serena's point was a good one, and I'd experienced firsthand how focusing all my romantic energy on just one person was unhealthy. I'd done that with Jeff. I'd stopped going on dates, allowing myself to be content with an unrequited crush. Maybe if I'd kept dating people, I wouldn't have been stuck liking Jeff for so long.

"Just . . ." Serena's forehead wrinkled with what looked like concern. "Be careful around this guy."

"Careful?"

"Guys who play mind games like the chase. He might leave you alone when you stop interacting, or he might redouble his efforts and make your life uncomfortable."

"No." I didn't for one second believe Byron would do anything malicious. "He wouldn't—he's not like that."

"Good. That's good. I hope he's not." She folded her arms. "But you should also be careful when you have to spend time with him, as you're getting to know him better. Be friendly, but not too friendly. And be on your guard."

"On my guard? Against what?"

"Against accidentally falling in love with him." Her expression turned bleakly sober, like she was recalling an unpleasant memory. "Because if you do, you're screwed."

* * *

"Winnie! Are you here?"

"I'm in here. Dinner is almost ready." The salad was nearly made, the spaghetti squash roasted, and two jars of my homemade tomato sauce had been defrosted and reheated.

"It smells wonderful!" She grabbed my shoulders from behind me and placed a kiss on my cheek. "I'll finish setting the table. Do we want wine? I have wine."

I checked the clock. It was a Thursday, but it was also only 6:15 p.m. "I'll have a glass."

"Good. It was on sale, and I've been wanting to try this one for a while. Let me open it up. How was your day?"

"Not bad." I pushed the tomatoes I'd just sliced into the waiting salad bowl. "I'm a little worried about raising enough money to do the science fair next year, but my third period is finally understanding the concept of force constants."

"You're teaching eighth graders force constants?"

"They're capable of it. And it's important to understand."

"I feel like you expect a lot out of thirteen-year-olds. What if they're bad at it?"

"I refuse to accept that." Choosing the ripest of the cucumbers, I cut off each end. "Our world can no longer afford people to be 'bad at science' or 'bad at math.'"

She chuckled, bumping my shoulder with hers as she passed. "You know what I mean."

We shared a small smile even as I kept my thoughts to myself.

I knew what she meant, but as a teacher, I felt like people didn't expect *enough* out of thirteen-year-olds—or twenty-year-olds, or thirty-year-olds, or sixty-year-olds—when it came to grasping scientific concepts. My uncle used to tell his kids they were simply bad at it, and it drove me crazy. How could we expect individuals to accept the fundamental laws of science and not consider magnets as magical or weather patterns as unexplainable voodoo if we didn't push them in the classroom as kids?

There was no such thing as a kid (or an adult) who was bad at science. Science always made sense, that was the beauty of it. Granted, science might be explained or taught in a way that made it difficult for kids to understand, but that wasn't science's fault. Nor was it the kids' fault. Because of this, I had a poster above my smartboard at school that read, "All ye who enter here are scientists."

I also had one that read, "Curiosity may or may not have killed Schrodinger's cat" and it made me laugh every single time.

"Hey, so, I saw Byron today."

My heart spasmed and I almost sliced my thumb instead of the cucumber, but I managed to sound perfectly normal as I said, "Oh? Did you?"

"Yeah. I asked him how the videos were going."

I held my breath for unknown reasons and contemplated the cucumber on my cutting board. *I will not ask what he said. I will not ask what he said. I will not ask—*

"What did he say?"

. . . *Weakling.*

"He said they're going well, which is Byron-speak for exceptionally excellent. I told him about you surpassing one hundred thousand followers on Tuesday and he seemed pleased." The wine cork made a muted pop as she pulled it from the bottle. "And on that note, aren't you two due to record another one? It's been a week, hasn't it?"

Careful to arrange my fingers out of the path of the knife, I sliced the cucumber. Slowly. "I think he's irritated with me."

The sound of Amelia pouring wine into glasses paused. "What? No. Why?"

I added the cucumber to the salad and dusted my hands off on the towel apron around my waist. "He won't answer my calls."

"Oh. No. That's not it." She sounded relieved. "He's not irritated with you. His phone broke."

"His phone broke?"

And crap.

I'd spent all week thinking he was ignoring me, and now I didn't know what to feel.

"Yeah." Amelia twirled out of the kitchen with our wine and pranced over to the table. Sometimes she did this, danced around the apartment like it was a ballroom floor. "He said he dropped it last week on the stairs and it broke. I left work early today to get him a new one, but the service isn't set up yet with his old number. I have his temporary number if you want it."

I examined my friend. "Why did *you* get him a new phone?"

"His agent sent me two thousand dollars and asked me to do it."

"What?"

"Yeah. It was a super cheap flip phone. He's broken so many of those because, it's like, you look at it sideways and it breaks. I guess Byron was dragging his feet this time and suggested he transfer his number to Google Voice to be rid of the cell."

"He's so . . ."

"Stubborn?"

"Difficult," I blurted before I could catch the half-baked thought, and then immediately regretted it. "I'm sorry. I—"

"No, no. It's okay. I can see why people think that. Byron has no desire to go out of his way to make other people's lives easier, especially when those people work for him and make money off him. He's definitely not what anyone would call accommodating, but then he doesn't expect other people to accommodate him either." Amelia seemed to consider the issue for another moment while she placed napkins next to our plates. "He would probably argue that he's not being difficult, he's being consistent with his defined personal boundaries in a world where personal boundaries are often disregarded, which—I've heard him say—encourages selfishness and laziness."

"Him having a cell phone that he consistently answers means that he's encouraging other people to be lazy?" I carried our salad over to the table.

Amelia laughed. "He would argue that it does."

"I would call it being considerate," I grumbled, not sure if I was grumpy because I'd just discovered Byron hadn't been ignoring my calls while I'd twisted myself into knots about it all week or because he could've easily solved his unreliable cell phone issue by buying a high-quality smartphone and putting a case on it.

"Anyway." She walked past me as I mixed the salad and stewed in my thoughts. I could tell she wanted to drop the subject.

But by the time she returned with the bowl of spaghetti squash, more argument fuel had been added to my resentment fire. "You say he doesn't expect other people to accommodate him, but you just spent your afternoon buying him a new phone."

"He didn't ask, his agent did. And I made a thousand dollars off Byron's agent for my troubles. And I didn't mind."

"But he's the one who benefited."

"Uh, no. His agent, publicist, and manager benefit if Byron has a cell phone and is more reachable." Amelia snorted. "Byron was so pissed when I showed up with a new phone. He called me an accomplice."

"Ungrateful."

"Hardly," she said sharply, placing a hand on the back of her chair and leveling me with a piercing look. "What has gotten into you? Are you mad at him about something?"

A flood of too many thoughts and emotions and questions clogged my throat. I didn't have his email, but he could have asked Amelia for mine if his phone didn't work. He could've given me a heads-up! It had been a week. I'd left him messages, several of them, and he could easily check voice mail without a working cell phone.

Was he purposefully playing mind games with me as Serena had suggested on Saturday? The more I thought about it, the more likely it seemed. He was hot then cold then freezing then tepid then freezing again. *And the steak! What is the deal with all that steak?*

While I struggled, Amelia crossed her arms and frowned, inspecting me closely. "He's doing those videos with you, isn't he? And he's doing a great job. The best friends one was a huge hit, as was the most recent one you posted Monday where he put his head on your lap. Your follower count passed a hundred thousand earlier this week, and as far as I can see, his help is the reason. So what is the deal, Win? What do you want from him?"

My heart spasmed again.

What do you want from him? That was the problem. That was why I was all turned around and messed up. I wanted something from Byron.

"You're right," I croaked out, feeling guilty and ungrateful and foolish. "You're right. He's helping me. I should be grateful for his help instead of trying to psychoanalyze him and judge him."

"Yeah. You should be grateful. He's doing you a huge favor."

"And I shouldn't want anything from him, he owes me nothing." My lungs deflated. That was the crux of it.

He wasn't playing mind games with me. I was playing mind games with myself. *Why am I torturing myself?* If he'd liked me enough to ask me out, he would have. And despite my biology—and my heart, if I was being honest with myself—that was the end of our story, and I needed to move the eff on.

Amelia exhaled loudly, pulling me out of my reflections. Her features had softened. "Look, I didn't mean to be harsh, but I've known him forever, and he's important to me. I'm protective of him. I understand that his—" she moved her hand around as though searching for the right word "—his *inflexibility* about certain things can rub people the wrong way, I do. But I know the reasons for why he is the way he is, and he has good ones, okay?"

I nodded, feeling properly chastised. "Okay. I'm sorry."

"Don't apologize, it's fine. I know he can be aggressively blunt and too honest when there's no call to be. If he's being too honest or blunt, let me know and I'll talk to him."

"No." I waved away her offer. "He's not. He's been fine." He'd been rude, but I didn't think he'd been purposefully mean. He didn't want anything from me, and it hadn't occurred to him to let me know his phone wasn't working. I'd get over it.

Her expression told me she didn't 100 percent believe my assurances, but—after a long look—she released my gaze and studied the table. "I'll get the sauce, then we'll eat?"

Amelia walked past me for the kitchen again and I reprimanded myself while serving us both a helping of salad.

But then, abruptly exasperated with my habit of worrying and apologizing and beating myself up, I decided it was time for me to stop tripping all over my good intentions and instead take a page out of Byron's book. What I needed were boundaries.

I wouldn't want anything from Byron; I wouldn't expect anything from Byron other than what we'd already agreed to with the videos; and, as he'd said, his feelings weren't my problem.

Just like my feelings weren't his problem either.

CHAPTER 17
WINNIE

Sunday midmorning, armed with Byron's temporary phone number, and after much typing and deleting, I sent him a text message certain to be respectful of his boundaries and mine.

Winnie: This is Winnie. I got your new number from Amelia, I hope you don't mind. Do you have time for a video today? Should take ten minutes. No problem either way

That done, I opened my fundraising plan for next year's science fair materials and stared at the screen of my laptop, telling myself not to keep sneaking glances at my phone. I mostly succeeded. But I'd been concentrating so determinedly on trying to concentrate, I jumped when my phone buzzed, announcing his reply.

Byron: Yes. When? Where? What can I bring?

My stomach fluttered. I thought his response was cute.

So I reminded my stomach of how not cute it was when he'd jumped up from the sofa last week, tossed my phone at me, and left the room. And how not cute it was when he'd dipped me after the Opposites Attract Challenge and then abruptly walked out. None of that had been cute.

With the word *boundaries* a mantra in my brain, I responded.

Winnie: Whenever you're free today, but text me when you're ten minutes away. Here is fine. No need to bring anything. Door will be unlocked, just walk in

He must've been anticipating my message because my phone buzzed again almost immediately.

Byron: Leaving now. I'm ten minutes away unless you want scones?

My stomach tried to fill with butterflies, but I punched those butterflies in their thorax.

Boundaries. Boundaries. Boundaries.

Winnie: No, thank you

There. See? I didn't need or want anything from him, not even delicious, delicious scones.

Giving myself a mental high five at how well I'd done, I continued my mental pep talk while prepping for his arrival. Even though the Toxic Dance Challenge was the next one on the list, I decided to skip over it and do the Asleep Challenge instead.

During this challenge, person 1 pretended to sleep while recording the room. Ideally, person 2 (best friend or friend or mom or partner or whatever) would stumble upon person 1 and the camera would record what they did. Some people made loud noises, some people just left, and others would be sweet, turning off the lights and leaving quietly.

The point was to *see* what person 2 would do when faced with a sleeping person 1.

Bonus, the Asleep Challenge required me to say nothing to him when he arrived, and hopefully very little once we finished recording. If our previous videos were any indication, he'd leave immediately after, and that was perfectly fine. I was ready to be left.

My phone positioned in the preordained spot to capture all the action, primed and ready to record as soon as I heard his footsteps on the stairs, I situated myself on the couch. Tucking one of our throw pillows under my cheek, I sighed and I waited, checking the clock over the TV more than a few times. Seconds moved by like hours. I swung my ankle back and forth over the edge of the couch, pushing everything related to wants and hopes and wishes down, down, down.

I want to get this over with. I want to be done with these videos and seeing him and being confused all the damn time. I want—

And then suddenly I heard steps on the stairway, the moment I'd been anticipating and dreading was upon me. Sucking in a breath, I frantically sat up, woke my phone, and pressed the Record button. I then flopped back, hoping my position looked natural and believable, like I'd fallen asleep on the couch waiting for him. Meanwhile, my heart tap-danced in my chest.

Worried my flickering eyelids would give me away, I tossed an arm over my forehead just as I heard the door open.

"Fred?"

Breathe in. Breathe out. Relax. You are asleep. Asleep. Asleep. Asleep.

Straining my ears, I heard his footsteps approach from the door, growing a bit louder, and then halting.

"Winnie?" He must've spotted me because he lowered his voice to a whisper.

I didn't move, hoping that at least part of his body was within the frame. I didn't want to rerecord this. Several seconds ticked by, during which I tried to breathe like a person deep in slumber. And then Byron was on the move, his steps noticeably lighter even though he was substantively closer.

In case you're wondering, it's difficult to feign sleep when someone you have odd feelings for moves around your apartment.

What is he doing? Is he—did he walk into my bedroom? Is he snooping? And if he is, what do I do? Do I jump up and catch him red-handed?

I heard him return a split second before I felt a blanket on my legs, stomach, and eventually my chest. Then I sensed him move close, very close, his hands still on the blanket, his knuckles brushing under my chin as he tucked me in. I also smelled him and that lethal aftershave of his, having to struggle not to swallow as a rush of saliva filled my mouth. If it was the last thing I did, I would find out what aftershave he used.

He must've been kneeling next to me. Or maybe he sat on his haunches. Point was, he hovered inches away. Without warning, the barest brush of something warm and soft—his fingertips—skimmed up my forearm before fingers wrapped around my wrist and moved my arm away from my eyes, gently placing it over my chest.

He blew out a quiet breath and his fingertips returned, brushing strands of hair from my forehead.

"Sleeping beauty," he mumbled softly, making my heart swell so suddenly that I must've flinched or twitched or something.

DARN.

A heavy pause, during which he made absolutely no sound, and then, "Fred." His voice was as flat as a pancake.

I fought a smile and lost. He'd figured it out. He had the list, after all. It was time to give up the ruse.

Breathing out deeply but silently, I waited until I felt him pull away—either stand up or move back—and made an overexaggerated snoring sound, whistling on the exhale.

He laughed lightly. "You sound like Popeye the Sailor Man."

I repeated the ridiculous snore, cracking one eye open to find him still squatting next to me, his elbows on his knees, his eyes hooded but clearly amused.

Closing my eye, I snuffed, chuffed, and snored again.

"Why are you pretending to be asleep, Fred?"

"What? What? Where am I?" I made a big show of blinking, acting like my eyes were too heavy to open.

"I said—" his hands came to my sides over the blanket, the only warning I got before he proceeded to tickle me "—why were you pretending to be asleep?"

My body jerked as I laughed, tucking my arms against my chest, trying to wiggle away. "Ah! Stop! Stop!"

He did. He stopped tickling me immediately. But in his quest to punish me for my ruse, he'd also climbed on top and grabbed my hands, bringing them over my head, his knees on either side of my hips.

Byron smiled down at me—with teeth!—his eyes bright, his features relaxed and happy. The sight was truly something to behold, and I knew I was smiling too as I took a mental snapshot of him just as my brain reminded me that this was fake.

This was all fake.

He'd seen the list. He knew we were recording. His smiles weren't for me, they were for the audience he'd helped me build. And the only thing I should be feeling was gratitude for his help, not dazzled by his smile.

"Get off, please," I said.

His eyebrows pulled together, his grin waning as he stared.

I returned his stare with only one thought in my mind. *Boundaries.*

Fully frowning now, his eyes never leaving mine, he climbed off the couch and stood.

"All done. I got what I needed. Thank you." I jumped up, grabbed my phone, and ended the recording. I then lifted my chin along with my eyes, gazing at him through my new boundaries but also doing my best to be my normal, cheerful self.

Byron blinked one of his stunned blinks, his lips parting. "You —we're—"

"All finished. Thanks. I'll message you next week. It was good seeing you." Sending him a friendly smile, I turned and walked the short distance to my bedroom.

Once there, I closed the door behind me and leaned against it.

A second later, I was fighting inexplicable tears and swallowing convulsively.

A second after that, I slid to the floor, folded my arms over my knees and cried, not understanding myself at all. I had no idea if Byron had left yet and my tears didn't seem to care. I'd done exactly what Byron had done to me several times, and I'd tried to be as kind and gentle as possible while doing it.

But now, in retrospect, I felt like dirt. Mean dirt. Full of worms. I didn't want to be a mean person. Mean people were the worst!

Boundaries were healthy. Boundaries were supposed to help me feel less confused, feel less unsettled, feel less sad. Basically, they were supposed to help me feel *less*.

So why the heck did they hurt so much?

* * *

The Asleep Challenge was a huge hit. *HUGE!*

My follower count more than doubled everywhere and the video went insanely viral, covered in magazines and newspapers around the world. Images of Byron Visser, genius literary darling, sweetly tucking in his bestie adorned gossip pages and celebrity news outlets. People debated our relationship status, certain we were faking our friendship and were deeply, deeply in love.

You know what? I felt mostly *meh* about all of it. I couldn't even find the energy to get excited about new engagement on my STEM-focused videos. For whatever reason, motivation to interact and create for my audience—and potential audience—completely eluded me.

And another thing to be filed under totally bizarre, a popular pop culture website did a breakdown of the video with screenshots, GIFs, arrows, and a time-lapse analysis showing how his eyes had gentled the longer he looked at me. They claimed they'd never seen anything so soft. Byron was adored and I was . . .

Well. I was simply called "Friend." *Novelist Byron Visser and Friend.*

It was an odd experience to be featured without a name, like I was an inanimate object or appendage, à la *Novelist Byron Visser and Lamp Post,* or *Novelist Byron Visser and Right Elbow.*

But my inboxes were flooded with direct messages from fashion houses asking if I needed a wedding dress and to keep them in mind, and that was kind of exciting. Not that marrying Byron was in the realm of possibility within any dimension. But—come on—a haute couture dress? Made just for me? A girl could dream.

Several publications reached out to Byron's agent, asking if I'd be interested in a feature article to discuss Byron. And maybe—if there was time—what about me made Byron interested in befriending me. All because someone brilliant, famous, and handsome had done an amazing job convincing the internet I was important to him. *What a world.*

"Is Byron coming over tonight? And are we playing *Stardew Valley*?" Amelia jogged into my bedroom holding a rubber spatula, the smell of vanilla and nutmeg following in her wake. Tonight we'd be having breakfast foods for dinner, Amelia's specialty. "If we're playing *Stardew Valley*, Serena wants to come over and do it in person, but I doubt Byron will come over or stay very long if she's here."

Leaning back in my desk chair, I gave her my undivided attention. "Why would Byron come over?"

"I thought you invited him."

"No."

"Really?" She placed a hand on her hip. "He texted me earlier that he'd be stopping by, and I assumed you two had a video planned."

Fiddling with the edge of my shirt, I was careful to keep the torrent of emotions off my face. "Nope. I haven't talked to him at all since Sunday."

Amelia lifted an eyebrow at this. "Are you serious? You haven't talked to him about the brouhaha and all those nasty people online? Does he even know about it?"

Amelia had been the conduit through which Byron's agent had contacted me about the magazine feature offers. It was highly probable—given Byron's avoidance of social media and how he chose to insulate himself—that he currently possessed no knowledge of our last video going viral.

"I have no idea and—Amelia—I don't want you telling him. Promise me."

She made a sound of disgust.

"Promise me. He hasn't called me, and I've been busy, and I just want to forget about it." I had been busy. The school and the Parent-Teacher Organization had decided on Monday that there was no room for my science fair fundraiser this year, and if I wanted to fund it, I'd have to find the money via a grant or charitable foundation. I understood their reasoning. The school needed to focus on raising money for new computers. The technology in the tech lab was woefully out-of-date.

So, no, I hadn't been spending the entire week clicking around the internet, reading analysis of the video, and me, and whether I was ugly or short or tall or too pale or too dark or my nose was too big. Nor had I filmed or had time to plan a single STEM video for any of my accounts.

Granted, I'd doom-scrolled the stories about Byron and me for a few hours yesterday. The whole thing had been completely bananas. But after encountering more haters, that was it. After seeing two articles addressing my hot-or-not status and how much of my "quirkiness" was for show, I knew no good could come from continued media consumption on the subject.

Instead, I'd been buried in grant applications, writing emails to educational foundations, hoping there existed funding somewhere for the science fair while also handling my end-of-year course load, grading, planning, holding after-school help sessions, meeting with parents, answering parent emails, and everything else.

Thank God I'd assembled all those lab kits last month. If I hadn't, I'd be completely overwhelmed right now.

"Fine. I won't tell him about those fuckers online, but . . ." Amelia's nose wrinkled with confusion. "That is so weird. He even asked if you were home just now when he called."

I refused to allow that information to impact me in the slightest, chanting *boundaries, boundaries, boundaries* in my head, and returned my attention to the spreadsheet I'd made of possible grants. "Sadly, I don't have time tonight to play *Stardew Valley*. I have to get at least ten of these out by Sunday."

Now that I knew there existed a chance Byron might show up tonight, I briefly considered packing up my stuff and heading to the downtown library to avoid him. But then I told myself I was being silly. I was the only one who felt mournful about placing boundaries between us. Maybe he liked me or maybe he'd been playing mind games, it didn't matter. I wasn't letting him anywhere near my olfactory senses or neurotransmitters ever again, not that he'd made any overtures or attempts.

"Okay. Well, Serena may come over." Still looking thoughtful, Amelia backed out of my room. "Do you want me to bring your dinner in here?"

"I can come out and get it. But could you close the door?"

"Sure." She placed her hand on the doorknob. "We'll be quiet."

"No need." Smiling and winking, I picked up my noise-canceling headphones and covered my ears.

As soon as the door closed, I selected my favorite music playlist for concentration and opened a new tab in my browser, searching for tips on completing grant applications for the Garbor Foundation. *Do I know anyone who works there?* It was possible. The central offices were located in South Lake Union, not three miles from where I lived and worked. I made a mental note to check with the school secretaries in the front office about parents who might be employed by the foundation.

Pulling a blue sticky note from the top of the pad, I wrote myself a quick note, stood, walked over to my corkboard, and pinned it under the Reminders heading right under a yellow sticky that read, "Don't forget to call Adam's mom about STEM camps."

I then turned and stopped dead in my tracks. A heat bomb detonated under my ribs and sent shock waves to the tips of each nerve ending. Byron, looking like all my dopamine neurotransmitters' dreams come true, stood in the doorway to my bedroom, his hand resting lightly on the doorknob, his features wide open and so achingly handsome I'm fairly certain the sight of him changed the cellular structure of my lung tissue.

Because they *hurt*.

He lifted his chin. "What's that?"

I glanced over my shoulder, following his line of sight. "You mean my corkboard?"

"What are all those notes?"

Unable to think, I could only mindlessly respond to his prompts. "Some are tasks, some are ideas, and some are reminders."

"What do the colors mean?" He stepped further into my bedroom, shutting the door behind him.

A spark of electricity seemed to zing up the back of my legs, sending restlessness through my entire body. "Oh, well, yellow is for my students, blue is for special projects, green is lesson planning and continuing education, orange is for my social media accounts, and pink is—uh—personal stuff." I tucked my hair behind my ears, wondering why I was telling him this.

And why was he here?

And what did he want?

I wasn't good at boundaries where he was concerned, I didn't like how it felt to enforce them with Byron. He'd caught me unawares, and I didn't know what to do.

"So what does—"

"What do you want?" I asked, deeply agitated by the massive involuntary response coursing through my body. I didn't want this. I didn't want to feel this way. I didn't want to push him away, but I hated this discomfort I always felt in his presence.

"We need to talk." He stuffed his hands in his pockets, his voice growing rough.

I strolled over to my reading chair and stood behind it. If I couldn't erect mental barriers, a corporeal one would have to suffice. "Okay."

He stared at me, his mouth opening, closing, and opening again. "I—I'm sorry I left after we finished filming the first few videos. I believe—though it was not my intention—I behaved rudely. I was unkind. I am sorry."

. . . *What?*

The last thing, the very last thing I'd expected him to do was apologize.

But as I stared at him and reflected on the situation, maybe I shouldn't have been so surprised. During the Opposites Attract Challenge, when I'd been forthright about my feelings, he'd apologized, hadn't he?

And yet . . . when he'd left me after the Opposites Attract Challenge and we'd spoken on the phone after, and I'd asked him if I'd done anything wrong, he'd dismissed my worries.

"It wasn't your intention," I parroted, feeling torn and stuck on the word *intention.*

"No."

If being rude and unkind hadn't been his intention, then he must've had an intention. "Then what was your intention?"

"I find it's best to . . . leave a situation when I might do or say something I'll regret later." Hands still in his pockets, he shrugged.

I repeated his statement in my head, then I dug through it, searching for its true meaning. "Something you might regret? Did I do something wrong? Did I say—"

"No. Not at all." He took a step toward me, his eyes wide and earnest. "You are perfect."

"Did I make you mad?"

"No."

"But you were worried you'd do or say something you'd regret?"

"Yes."

What the—?

I racked my brain. If I hadn't done something wrong, or said anything to make him angry, then why had he left? "Like what?"

He blinked several times, his steady gaze growing unsteady as it dropped to the carpet. "Like . . ."

I waited. And waited.

His throat worked with a swallow and eventually he exhaled. "It's not your problem. It's mine. But you didn't do, and haven't done, anything wrong. This is entirely my fault. And if you're still willing to do the remainder of the videos with me, I have a plan for how to deal with similar circumstances in the future."

"Oh really? Tell me this plan."

"If it happens again, I'll excuse myself for a few minutes. And then, when I'm ready, I'll come back."

Understanding dawned, and with it all the tension left my body. Of course! *How could I have missed this? Why didn't I see it before?*

He had a sensory processing disorder.

I felt a small, compassionate smile tug at my lips, another heat bomb detonating beneath my ribs, but this time it felt warm and friendly instead of agitated and hostile. Goodness, if I'd known this about him earlier, how much torture would I have saved myself? All this worrying and wringing of hands, second-guessing every interaction. I felt so silly. He hadn't been rude or playing mind games. Not at all.

Stepping out from behind the chair, my arms dropped to my sides. "What if you need more than a few minutes? Should we have a safe word?"

Byron's frown was swift, his eyes flickering over me. "A safe word?" he croaked.

Maybe he thought I was making fun of him. I wasn't—not at all—so I closed the gulf between us. I wanted him to see I wasn't mocking him.

"I'm serious. If you need a safe word to pull out of a situation that's too stimulating, that's totally fine. I completely get it."

Still appearing uncertain, he straightened to his full height and squinted at me, his gaze in turmoil, and asked breathlessly, "You do?"

"Yes. I have kids with all sorts of sensory processing disorders in my class."

He flinched, blinked, then his features darkened swiftly.

I grabbed hold of his arm to keep him from retreating. "Wait, listen. I'm not saying you're a kid, and I'm not saying you have a sensory processing disorder, it's none of my business if you do. All I'm saying is that people—being people—have different tolerances and limits. If you need to make a quick escape, if a situation or stimulus becomes too much for you, that's fine with me. You do what you need to do for your mental health. I'll know it's not because of me."

His eyes seemed to widen and narrow at the same time. "Not because of you?"

"Yep. I can't be sensitive to or accommodate each and every kids' sensory needs. As an example, sometimes in class I have to make a loud noise as a byproduct of the lesson. Those kids who can't handle it can go out into the hallway and sit in one of the desks there, take a few minutes, and then come back when they feel ready. Some kids have undersensitivity and need louder noises, brighter colors, they might need hugs or to hold hands, more stimulus. It's not about fault—theirs or mine—and I never take it personally."

Byron held super still, his stare achingly conflicted. He cleared his throat, hesitated, then said, "I appreciate the offer, Fred. But I don't have sensory problems. The last thing I want from you is for you to make excuses for me when I'm unkind, or selfish."

"I don't think you're selfish." Gah! *Sweet man.* "Not at all."

"Oh, *I am.*" He nodded several times, his voice deepening. "I'm sure many people do struggle with, uh, stimuli, but that's not why I—rather, uh, it would be both inaccurate and disingenuous of me to imply, or for you to infer, that the reason for my—my—"

I slid my hand from his arm to his palm, threading our fingers together and taking another step closer. His eyes flared, his attention, clearly distracted by the movement, dropped to where we touched.

"Hey. It's no big deal," I said as his attention returned to my face. "We can use any word you want. How about canyon? Or canal? Or crevice?"

"Not crevice," he said, the words arriving weakly.

"Channel? Cove?"

"Please stop."

"Sorry, I have geography terms on the brain. We're doing a section on natural land formations and we're on the C-words. The important thing is now I know. You pick any word you want."

His gaze grew more hooded, more withdrawn the longer I held it. The rate of his breathing increased. "Listen to me, Fred. I do not have sensory issues. Okay?"

"Okay," I said lightly, hoping he knew I didn't feel sorry for him and he had nothing to be embarrassed about. There was no reason to feel pity or sympathy. This was about understanding. I'd witnessed how difficult these kinds of obstacles could be for my students, some of the coolest, most amazing kids I know. They simply experienced the world differently. Oftentimes, these differences helped fuel creative decision-making.

But now so many things about Byron made complete sense. *No wonder he avoids people and has all those boundaries.* The relief I felt was immeasurable.

He, meanwhile, closed his eyes, exhaled softly, and said, "I need to leave."

"Or—" I moved closer, and his eyes flew open. "Hear me out, we could—"

"Canyon, canal, crevice!"

CHAPTER 18
BYRON

After leaving Winnie's apartment, I immediately called my manager.

She agreed to help me schedule an appointment with a reputable occupational therapist, or whatever medical specialty diagnosed sensory processing disorders, and promised she could pull a few strings to ensure I'd be seen as quickly, and privately, as possible.

Then, trusting the matter to her capable hands, I went on a long run through Interlaken Park, needing the feel of wet, cold, beech tree cellulose fabric clinging to my skin, the sound of raindrops on trees, the pounding of my feet on dirt, helping me focus on this problem, and how to solve it.

Ostensibly, Winnie refused to believe I did not have sensory issues. Furthermore, she believed these imaginary sensory issues were responsible for overwhelming me, causing me to respond to situations in ways that were interpreted falsely as selfish.

She was both right and wrong. I had been overwhelmed. I was also extremely selfish.

I thought about us fucking, and what it would be like, and what we would do, and how much I'd make certain she enjoyed it, no less than five hundred times daily. Considering over eighty-six thousand seconds spanned a twenty-four-hour period, I reassured myself with the fact that the ratio could've been significantly worse. Though the reticent might consider the nature of my imaginings depraved, I did not. I'd chosen celibacy, not repression. And by my standards of substance and self-worth, in all facets of life, quality mattered materially more than quantity.

Each incidence of me leaving abruptly after recording a video had been preceded by an overwhelming desire to touch her, taste her, slide fingers under her shirt and in her pants and fill my hands with her body and heat and skin. To be inside her. To—

I squeezed my eyes shut and slowed to a stop, lifting my face to the silken droplets of rain, letting them pour over me and cool my skin.

Fucking hell, how I wanted her.

I couldn't tell her, not after Winnie's horrified response to my mere *like*. If she knew, if I gave voice to the words, all the progress we'd made during these last several weeks would be for naught, and I doubted she'd wish to see me again. And I wouldn't blame her.

Even so, her assertion needed to be proven wrong. I didn't want her offering excuses for me. I wanted her to continue to tell me when I'd said or done something upsetting, and I suspected a doctor's official report was necessary to convince her that I, at times, actively chose to be an asshole. She shouldn't be expected to anticipate or endure my "Dr. Apathy Hole" persona, and I didn't want her to cease confronting me when I adopted it.

If she rationalized every dick move with some bullshit label or diagnosis, then she'd never see me as fully human, capable, being worthy of—

Friendship.

Shaking my head, I glanced left, then right, and continued on the trail, running until I sprinted.

Solely friendship.

I ran for hours. My body required relief, and no amount of taking matters in hand seemed to make a difference anymore. Just the thought of her filled my veins with fire.

That night, I barely managed to climb the stairs to my room and remove my soaked clothes before passing out. Fortunately and unfortunately, I dreamt of her on Saturday and Sunday, necessitating that I change the sheets while I seethed and chastised myself. I didn't feel shame, but the inconvenient, unsatisfying, and disruptive nighttime fantasies needed to stop. I was twenty-seven fucking years old for Christ's sake.

Early Monday morning, carrying determination like a shield, I entered the belly of the medical center, checked myself in and claimed the most isolated chair available in the harshly lit waiting room. It would all be worth it once I had the doctor's report in hand.

However, to my absolute disgust, after two brutal and frustrating days of tests and assessments, being forced to engage in chitchat with a parade of irritating people asking inane questions in rooms that were too bright, Winnie was the one proven right.

They suspected I had a whole host of sensory-related issues I refused to remember, read about, or research, and wanted me to come back in for more testing. Additionally, the report they sent had been denoted as "preliminary."

"What else did it say?" Amelia, thank God, didn't sound worried. She sounded curious.

She'd randomly called just after the report arrived. Catching me in an uninhibited moment, I'd answered the phone and divulged details I wouldn't usually share. Not even with her. But now I found myself grateful for her pragmatic presence.

I glanced at the smartphone she'd bought me last week, currently residing on my desk. Her voice carried over the speaker as I did not enjoy the feel of the device in my hand. I missed my old phone, the texture of it, the way it moved and curved in an interesting shape instead of merely existing as an inert, boring, flat rectangle.

"I have no idea what the report said. I stopped reading after the first sentence." I'd wanted to shred the document as soon as it appeared, but it arrived via their secure online system. In order to shred it, I'd have to print it.

"You should read the entire report, Byron." After my unintended disclosure and a half hour of mindless ranting, she finally sounded impatient.

I smiled.

Among Amelia's many stellar qualities, she treated me as though I weren't different or odd or irrational. Nor had she ever coddled me.

Growing up in a small town in Eastern Oregon, I'd filled the role of the weird kid with no mother and a father everyone both adored and pitied, a martyr with a broken heart and a broken son. I'd asked too many questions and couldn't be compelled to speak when spoken to. Amelia, however, had considered my indiscriminate intolerance for others perfectly understandable and justified given how my dad lapped up sympathy like a cat does cream.

"What's the point of reading it?" I asked. "There's nothing that can be done."

Crowds, certain voices, loud noises, and particular fabrics had always set my teeth on edge, made thinking a chore. Florescent lights hurt my brain. I loved the feel of tight, soft fabric, especially when wet. But so what? Didn't everyone deal with some level of discomfort or preference in sensation when interacting with the world? Why must my type of discomfort and desire require the application of labels?

I wasn't a jam jar needing to be sorted based on preference and taste. Nor was I a bottle of medicine requiring warning and usage information. *Fuck labels.*

"What are you going to do?"

I checked my printer. It had plenty of paper. Perhaps I would print out the report and shred it. "What do you mean?"

"Is there a medicine you can take? It might help."

"They offered to teach me how to *cope*." I couldn't dissociate myself from my disdain.

They'd wanted me to consider coping strategies as though I hadn't lived my whole life thinking of myself as normal but not average. And now I was supposed to . . . what? Try to *fix* myself? Blend in? Assimilate?

"They're not saying you're broken, Bry. These people are professionals, not your family. Learning how to cope might be good. It might make your life easier."

"No." I shook my head.

"Because you're perfect as you are," she said, her tone joking.

I wasn't perfect. No one was perfect. I had room for improvement. There were things I wanted to change about myself, but didn't everyone?

But fundamentally, I *liked* me. I liked who I was. And I resisted being told I needed to "work on myself" by people who didn't matter and didn't know me.

"I already know how to cope. I've been myself in this world for twenty-seven years, and I've done just fine."

She chuckled. It was without humor. "You mean sequestering yourself from anything or anyone who might irritate you?"

"Correct." And what was so wrong with that? Seriously. What was wrong with avoiding people I disliked?

"Oh, Byron." She sighed, sounding tired. "Are you going to tell me what prompted you to go to the doctor in the first place? If you didn't plan to read the report, why go?"

I grunted.

"You're not going to tell me?"

I grunted again.

"Fine. Whatever, sassy pants. Send me the report, I'd like to read it."

"I'll think about it."

"That means no." She laughed, this time with humor. "If you want to talk about it, I'm here for you."

"I won't."

"Okay. Anyway. So, listen, I'm actually calling about Winnie."

I stiffened, steadying myself against racing thoughts and bracing for the coming conversation. I'd expected Amelia to broach this topic weeks ago. *Why now?*

Had Winnie finally assigned our mutual friend the task of letting me down gently, once and for all? Now that she suspected I had sensory issues? I grimaced.

As much as I would gladly accept any relationship Winnie offered, it had to be free of sympathy and allowances. My childhood had been spent surrounded by people making *allowances.* If Winnie believed my eccentricity wasn't a choice, she would never see me as anything but aberrant.

"You can't tell Winnie about this."

"What?" The single word rang with outrage. "Byron, I would never. How could you think I would?"

"Then I apologize." I licked my suddenly dry lips. "Why are you calling about Winnie? What did she tell you?"

"About what?"

"About me. And her."

"About you and her?" she asked, her voice laced with an arc of confusion. "What about you and her? You mean the videos? She hasn't really said anything, but she seems content with them. She's approaching two hundred and fifty thousand followers on Instagram. She should be ecstatic."

"Huh." I stood from my chair, rubbing the back of my neck, and paced. Could it be that Amelia had decided to feign ignorance? Pretend as though Winnie hadn't told her everything? That seemed unlikely. Amelia didn't spare my—or anyone's—feelings.

"What I want to discuss is that trip to New York coming up in July. As her broker of the deal and personal shopper, I need to know what the budget is for her dress, shoes, purse, and whatnot."

I continued to pace. "Uh, I don't care."

"I'll take that to mean no budget."

"Correct."

"I can get her that Burberry bag for five thousand dollars and you'd be okay with it?"

"Fine." I flicked my hand at the wrist.

"Heh. That's excellent. Okay. Good. How are we doing this? Are you giving me your credit card or will you reimburse me?"

"You can—you can use my credit card."

"Great. Glad that's settled. Now when are we going out to lunch next? It's my treat this time since you got last time, no arguing."

I ceased pacing. "That's it?"

She said nothing for a moment, then, "That's what?"

"Is there anything else about Winnie you'd like to discuss?"

"Uh, why? Do you want her to come to lunch?" Her question sounded genuine.

"She hasn't told you," I said as I realized the truth, and uncertainty soared, fjords of doubt, mountains of confusion. *What the hell?*

"Told me what?"

"Why didn't she . . ." *Why wouldn't she tell Amelia?* I'd taken for granted that Winnie would confide in her roommate, share the details of my clumsy confession the night of Lucy and Jeff's party.

Obviously, she hadn't.

"Now you're being a weirdo. I made you a promise once that I'd always tell you when you're being a weirdo."

Giving myself a quick shake, I sank into the chair and rolled it forward, needing to hover over my boring phone and stare at it as I asked, "Did Winnie tell you what happened between us, what I said, the night of Lucy and Jeff's dinner party?"

"No. What happened the night of Lucy and Jeff's dinner party?"

Winnie didn't wish Amelia to know? Why not? Potential motives marched in single file through my mind. Embarrassment, repulsion, continued disbelief—I discarded these three. Only *concern* remained as the primary suspect.

Winnie's principal motivator was, and always has been, compassion. If she thought, for even a second, revealing my confession would cause Amelia a moment of discomfort, she'd say nothing.

I, however, possessed no such compunction. Not about Amelia. Our friendship has persisted despite my aggressive bouts of honesty.

Would Winnie be upset if I told Amelia? That unknown gave me pause.

"Byron. What the hell?" Her voice teetered into shrill territory. I winced. "What happened with you and Winnie?"

"It's—it's nothing. Disregard—"

"Either you tell me, or I'll get it out of her. She'll tell me if I push hard enough, you know she will."

"Leave her alone," I bit out.

The worst thing about being friends with someone who is tough as nails is they often behave like a hammer.

"I'll hang up right now and get her on the phone and—"

"Don't."

"If you don't want me to badger it out of her, then you better tell me—"

"I have a thing for Winnie." My fingers tightened on the edge of the desk.

Dammit.

"A—oh! *Ooooooh*!" Amelia seemed to be working through several thoughts at once. A profusion of odd noises emanated from the speaker of the smart, boring rectangle before she blurted, "Oh my God! BYRON! OH MY GOD!!"

"Shh." I pressed my thumb against the button on the side of the phone, reducing the volume. "Calm down."

"I'm coming over. Right now. I want to know *everything*." She was squealing. *God help me.*

"I'm not telling you anything if you insist on making it a big deal."

"What are you talking about? It's a huge fucking deal, Bry. You've never—wait, and you told her? That night? You told her you like her?"

"I did." An echo of an ache in my chest had my fingers lifting to rub the spot, a phantom pain at the memory.

"I—huh. I had no idea. I've said it before and I'll say it again, you surprise the hell out of me, Visser."

"Why wouldn't she tell you? Doesn't she tell you everything?"

"I don't know. Sure, we pretty much tell each other everything—but Bry, I had no idea, you sly dog. Since when? Wait! Are you two seeing each other in secret? Is this a secret?"

"We're not seeing each other."

"Yikes." Her vocal grimace must've been paired with a facial one as it immediately conjured a vision of bared teeth and sympathetic eyes. "Okay. Awkward. I'm so sorry. So she let you down easy?"

"Not exactly." I pushed my fingers into my hair and scratched my scalp.

"Double yikes. Are you okay? Should I bring over ice cream?"

I shook my head at her nonsense. I didn't want sympathy, I wanted answers. "Why didn't she tell you?"

"Byron, bruh of mine, you do know you're my friend too. You could have told me, I could've helped you."

I leaned away from the rectangle, eyed the rounded corners of the device as I debated her surprising statement. "You would've helped me with Winnie?"

"Yes, absolutely! And don't give me that face."

"How do you know what face I'm making?"

"I can hear it in your breathing. I'm your oldest friend, of course I would've helped you."

Clasping, unclasping, and reclasping my hands over my lap, I asked, "Will you help me now?" before fully considering the ramifications of the request.

Did I want help with Winnie? Wouldn't it be better, in the long run, if Winnie and I remained friends? Then I'd know her forever.

Amelia laughed. "You're hopeless."

"Am I?"

I probably was. *I definitely am.*

"No. Actually. You're just . . . clueless."

"I accept that." Clueless was better than hopeless.

"Okay, I don't know if I can help, if you already told her how you feel and she doesn't reciprocate. If she said, 'No, Byron. I don't like you that way. We should be friends,' then you should respect that and move on. But this is a good thing. I can't believe you—"

"She didn't say anything like that." I stood, braced my hands on the edge of the desk, restless.

"Okay, what did she say?"

"She asked me if I was having a stroke."

Amelia paused, then busted out laughing. "Oh my God, no she didn't."

"Yeah. She did." Another phantom pain in my chest. "Then she refused to believe me. She thought I was joking. And then she thought I was messing with her."

"Oh, Winnie."

"I'm not sure she even believes me now."

"This was weeks ago. You two are still doing those videos, and you don't think she believes you were telling the truth about being interested in her?"

"Correct."

"Okay, something isn't adding up. Tell me *exactly* what happened. As much as you can, tell me precisely what was said, and by whom."

I recounted the story as close to word for word as possible, given my desire to forget the entire confrontation, beginning with her opening the door to my room while I'd changed and ending with Winnie's angry text messages later that evening.

When I finished, Amelia paused, then asked, "Is that it? Did anything else happen that night?"

"No."

"Okay. Stay there. I'm coming over right now. *Don't* leave."

Then she hung up.

* * *

Amelia enjoyed wine.

She often brought bottles with her, transporting them in a canvas bag stamped with Wine Time on one side. Even so, I always made available a few alternatives just in case she wished to try something new. But since it was barely past 4:00 p.m., I also arranged a selection of sparkling waters.

The front door opened, then closed. *That was fast.*

"I'm in the kitchen," I called out. "Are you hungry?"

"No. Hey."

I straightened from the wine fridge, my frown immediate. "What are you doing here?"

Jeff laughed. "I live here."

"You store your things here. You live at Lucy's. I didn't expect you."

"I wanted to talk." He sat at the kitchen island in the same stool Winnie had occupied two Thursdays ago when I'd made her dinner. "You keep leaving when I give you a heads-up that I'm stopping by, and we all know what happens when someone calls your phone."

I sighed silently, checking the time. "Talk."

Jeff leaned his elbows on the counter, making a show of inspecting me. "What's going on with you and Winnie?"

"None of your business."

"Have you thought it through? Do you think it's a good idea?"

I didn't even grunt.

"Does she know that you've been obsessed with her forever?" He smiled as he spoke, as though to convince me the question had been meant in jest. A joke.

I knew him too well. Concern simmered beneath the surface, and the lid he'd placed on top, the affable mask he wore, did nothing to conceal the truth of his opinions. He believed I was obsessed with Winnie. Denying it would only yield compounded suspicion. As with most people, discussing the matter reasonably, presenting facts and evidence when he'd already convinced himself of a lie, would be a waste of breath.

My eyelids lowered by half. I said nothing.

His grin widened. "Your secret is safe with me. If you hadn't told me years ago, I never would've guessed."

The one time I'd consumed too much alcohol in college, Jeff and Lucy had been present. I did not recall all the information I'd volunteered while intoxicated. However, I was aware—since Lucy never missed an opportunity to taunt me about it—that I'd confessed to my lack of experience and admiration for someone named Winnifred Gobaldi. Lucy had never forgotten, she thought Win's entire name was hilarious.

Jeff held his hands up, showing me his palms as though in surrender. "And I'm not telling anyone. But do you really want to ruin everything by talking to Win? She's great, don't get me wrong, but she's not going to live up to whatever idea you have in your head about her, I guarantee it. No one could at this point."

Unlike Winnie, who somehow—through magic, no doubt—managed to maintain an air of sincerity when diffusing tension, dealing with uncomfortable situations, or even while outright lying about her own well-being and comfort, Jeff's shoddy attempts at levity serrated my patience.

Regardless, he needn't worry.

I knew obsession. When I wrote, I obsessed. When I researched, I obsessed. I lost hours and days, sleeping whenever I passed out, eating when I grew light-headed.

Winnie was a reprieve, not an obsession. She wasn't air, she was a cool breeze. She wasn't sunshine, she was a rainbow. She wasn't water, she was rain.

Jeff's smile evaporated in the face of my persistent silence, his features sobering. "Right. Let's cut to the chase." His palms lowered to the countertop. "I wasn't going to say anything, but then I didn't like what I walked in on when Lucy and I stopped by. Winnie is a really good friend of mine, and she doesn't know you like I do, about your dating history."

"My dating history," I repeated, rolling the phrase around, examining it from different angles. "I have no history."

"Exactly. If you'd asked her out in college, or before you became this big, famous guy, that would've been one thing. But I'm concerned about what you have planned for her now that people see you as powerful and important, after obviously thinking about it and biding your time for so long."

I tried not to smirk at "biding my time." I'd never considered that he might think of me as a villain. When had I ever done anything but mind my own business?

"Why, precisely, are you concerned?" I asked, certain his reasons would be entertaining at the very least, and Jeff always needed to be heard.

If I didn't let him speak, if he didn't feel as though I'd listened, he'd cause drama. This habit of his was why he and Lucy would never work in the long term. She didn't listen to him. She wasn't a bad person, but she dismissed his fears, only paying attention when he lashed out, lost his temper, or when he stoked her jealousy and pride. He was too needy, and she viewed the emotional maintenance of their association as a chore.

Jeff didn't have enough self-awareness to realize this about himself or his relationship, but the pattern of behavior was impossible for me to miss as an impartial observer with a front-row ticket to their slow, arduous demise.

I pitied him. He was in love with someone who'd never felt as deeply for him as he did for her. His life a cautionary tale to anyone paying attention, the mistakes he made served as a warning to others.

"Waiting around for someone you've never talked to?" Jeff gave his head a sympathetic shake. "Carrying a torch with no fuel for six years? That's called being obsessed, man. Come on, you know you're weird." His smile returned, slathered in affection.

I didn't smile. I endured.

He'd called me weird many, many times during our acquaintance. It never bothered me. In this matter, I considered his perspective invalid given his personal failings. Likewise, his opinion about most topics mattered very little.

Admittedly, he was funny—sometimes. And not a terrible roommate. And good at *Super Mario Bros*.

But then he said, "You're not like other guys, Byron."

My back molars ground together, an instinctive tense and release, the statement hitting a raw nerve.

"You never have been. I get it, you're this literary genius, and geniuses get to be eccentric or whatever. No shade. It's cool. We're cool. But . . ." He paused here to take a deep breath, his body angling to one side, his expression bracing. "Do you think being a twenty-seven-year-old virgin is natural? Do you think only being interested in one girl is natural? It's not."

If we'd had this discussion two months ago, I would've responded with, *You, also, have only been interested in one girl, for eleven years. And do you think lying to yourself for those eleven years and staying with a woman who can barely stand you is natural?*

What the world considered normal never made much sense to me.

But Winnie and her goodness, her care for others, must've been contagious. I could be kind without being a liar.

Thus, I responded with a truth that should've been obvious. "What's natural for you isn't natural for me. I don't judge you for your choices. Maybe don't judge me for mine."

He heard me, but he wasn't listening.

"I didn't say anything before now because I figured—" Jeff tilted his head back and forth, contemplating his choice of words "—well, you'd always kept your distance. But Winnie is a nice girl."

"She's a woman, not a girl."

"You know what I mean, she's really nice. She's a good, decent person. Don't you think she deserves someone more like her?"

"More like her?" I glanced at the clock. Amelia should arrive any minute.

"Someone normal."

My eyes sliced to his.

The shape of his apologetic smile suddenly grated, specifically the arc of his bottom lip and how his mouth parted to display just the top half of his teeth. An abrupt urge to punch that mouth swept through me with a vehemence I hadn't experienced since I'd published my first book.

He wasn't finished. "Yes, you're an impressive dude now. You're the smartest guy I know. But do you think Winnie should have to put up with all your many, many idiosyncrasies? Put up with your weirdness? She's a social person and you can't stand to be in a room with more than three people! Would she go everywhere alone? You have a shit ton of money, sure. Some status to offer, but is that enough?"

Neither money nor status mattered to Winnie. He knew it, as did I.

"You forget, man. I know you, I know what you're like. I was there all through college. I was there when you got your PhDs. It's impressive to watch, but seriously think about how you work. Look at how you push yourself. There's no room for anyone but you. And you're never going to stop working."

About this, he was right. I needed the work. I needed an outlet for the voices and stories in my head, and I grew restless, unhappy when I didn't satisfy the need. Hobby writing wasn't an option for me, I wasn't built that way.

One side of his irritating smile fell, and he stood from the stool. "If you were together, you know she'd be ignored for weeks, sometimes months, while you're off writing. And when you're not writing, you'd cut her off from everyone. You don't like people. You think being with someone like that is fair to her?" He shrugged again, backing toward the front room. "All I'm saying is, think about it. You claim to like her so much. Don't you think she deserves better?"

CHAPTER 19
WINNIE

I came home early to find Amelia sitting at the kitchen table alone, drinking a glass of wine. *Oh no.*

"What's wrong?"

"What?" Amelia startled, her head whipping toward me. "You're home?"

"No after-school help hours. Next week is the last week of school, tests are over." Dumping my bags on the chair at the head of the table, I wiped a hand across my forehead. It had been hot today, almost eighty. "So what's going on? You're upset about something."

Amelia's eyebrows tugged together. "I'm taking a page out of Byron's book and drinking alone to drown my frustrations."

My eyes widened at that. "Byron drinks alone?"

"Not often. Maybe once a year, or every other year. But when he does, he gets totally shit-faced. He won't drink more than one glass in front of other people because—ack!" Amelia abruptly tensed, waving her hands around her head. "Forget I said any of that. Please. That was—Byron would kill me if he—"

"It's fine." I sought to relieve her anxiety, especially since this information didn't surprise me. From our time together, I'd surmised control was a big deal for him, he'd said as much. Of course he wouldn't want to get drunk in front of people and lose control. "I'm already forgetting. What were we talking about anyway?"

She crossed her arms and slumped low in her chair. "I'm frustrated."

"Why?"

"It's . . . Byron. That's right. Today's day drinking is brought to you by Byron Visser." She lifted her wine as though to make a toast, her forehead lined with consternation. "Yesterday, he asked me to help him with something, and he never asks for anything. I took off work early and was excited to help—you can't imagine how excited—but by the time I showed up, he'd changed his mind and wouldn't let me help. He *forbade* me from helping."

"Oh. That's too bad." I nibbled on my lip, debating, wondering if Byron would let me help. Probably not. If he hadn't let Amelia help, he wouldn't let anyone help.

She peered at me with what looked like hope. "Don't you want to ask me what it was?"

Sinking into the seat across from her, I placed my phone on the table and weighed my heavy heart. "I can guess."

"Really?" Now she looked even more hopeful.

"Yeah. I told him I thought maybe he . . ." I huffed. "Actually, that's not true. I told him I strongly suspected he had a sensory processing disorder and now, when I reflect on the conversation, I wonder if I'd blindsided him." I'd purposefully not called him this week, wanting to give him space. The last thing I wanted to do was make him suffer through an apology if he wasn't ready, or willing, to hear it.

I'd replayed the conversation a hundred times and felt worse and worse about it each time, even as I became more and more certain I was correct. But if he didn't know, if he had no idea, what right did I have to tell him of my suspicions?

Amelia sighed, the hope draining from her features. "Ah. I see."

Desperately wanting her opinion, I blurted, "But I think he does, and if he knew for sure, it might help him understand himself better, don't you think?"

"Byron understands himself pretty well already," she grumbled. "He's like one of the most self-aware people in the entire world. He's too self-aware. What he doesn't understand are other people."

"You don't think he has sensory issues?"

"Oh. He definitely does. He might've always known but never applied that kind of label to himself. And so what? If he's happy with who he is—which he is . . ." Amelia's gaze lost focus for a moment before she shook herself. "Anyway. I guess what I mean is, what difference does it make? He is who he is, and I'd be sad if he thought he had to change in order to be more normal."

"I would too. I feel like how he processes sensory information might be his superpower. When you read his books, how he describes details, it's so unusual and vivid and brilliant. I'd hate for him to try to change that about himself."

She perked up again. "Would you?"

"Yeah. I would." I eyed the bottle of wine next to her glass, debating whether to have some. It was barely past 3:30 p.m., but I had a lot I wanted to do tonight.

She sipped from her glass. "Then why try to diagnose him?"

I considered the question, mulling it over, then answered. "I think . . . I guess *I* want to understand him better."

"You do?" Amelia leaned forward.

"Yes. Absolutely. And knowing he has some sensory issues, I now understand that it's not him wanting to be rude or mean when he abruptly leaves a room. It's that he has to put up boundaries when he feels overwhelmed in order to be healthy." In retrospect, I had no idea how I could ever or would ever compare Byron to my uncle. They were *nothing* alike. "But before I realized what was actually going on with him, and we were spending time together, being with him was . . ."

"What?"

"Incredibly confusing." My shoulders slumped from the weight of the admission. "One minute he's cold and distant, and the next he's just freaking amazing, and then he's back to being frozen. But I *love* how he thinks, how he reasons through things when he shares that part of himself. I wish he'd talk more. I could listen to him talk for hours—days even. And he's funny. It's all the dry kind of humor, but I love his wittiness." I chuckled as I thought of those five pieces of steak and all the gluten-free scones. "And he's thoughtful."

"He can be thoughtless, like failing to communicate necessary information, or not giving people a heads-up about his plans But you're right, he can be thoughtful about certain things." Amelia's prim tone as she finished speaking brought my attention back to her face.

She wore a big—and I mean *big*—smile.

I straightened in my seat. "What?"

"You have the hots for him."

All the air left my lungs as we swapped stares. It was on the tip of my tongue to deny it, but I couldn't. Obviously, I couldn't. And I didn't want to. I was so tired of keeping everything bottled up inside.

Plopping my elbows on the kitchen table, I let my face fall to my hands and groaned. "Am I that obvious?"

"You were just now, yes. But prior to just now, I had no idea."

I peeked at her from between my fingers. "Do you think he knows?"

She barked a laugh. "Uh, no. Actually, I think he has absolutely no idea."

"Good."

"Good?"

"Yes. Good."

"Why good?"

"He's Byron Visser! That's why." I let my hands fall to the table. Eyeing the wine bottle again, I stood and walked to the kitchen to retrieve a glass.

I hadn't been seeking out any new stories about Byron and me on the internet, mostly because I didn't have time, but I also didn't want to further expose myself to the negative remarks. Toward the end of my time living with my aunt and uncle, I'd learned the value of tuning out negativity. I had to let my uncle bark at me, but I didn't have to listen to it. If I read the comments, it was no different from voluntarily listening to my uncle tell me how stupid I was.

But, unfortunately, I didn't need to seek the stories out. Strangers had started messaging me and leaving comments on my STEM videos, not just the videos with Byron, informing me that I wasn't pretty enough for him, that I didn't deserve him, demanding to know what he would want with someone like me.

I loved myself, absolutely. One hundred percent. But I defy anyone to be inundated with messages picking apart their looks, body, fashion choices, intelligence, and worthiness, and *not* be adversely impacted on some level. It had become so bad that I'd stopped reading all comments and turned off commenting during live videos.

"What are you talking about?" Amelia rolled her eyes at me. "He's just Byron."

"No. He's not, and you know it. He's not *just* anything. There's no one like him." I chose a stemless wineglass from the cabinet since I'd probably be drinking out of it all night.

"So? There's no one like you either. There's no one like me, or Elijah."

"You're being obtuse on purpose. I know you know what I mean." I poured myself a glass from the open bottle. It was a heavy pour, but then this was a heavy conversation.

"I don't know what you mean. He's just a person."

"He's not. He's—"

"What?"

I set the bottle down with a *thunk.* "He's perfect."

Something had fundamentally shifted over the last few weeks, even before it had occurred to me that he might be struggling with sensory issues, but especially since then. I now considered Byron's bluntness—what I used to think of as rudeness—to be perfect. In a world full of second-guessing and passive aggression, I appreciated his honesty so, so much. I loved that what he said was what he meant and, now that I knew that to be the case, I could just relax and trust the words out of his mouth.

Also, I didn't need nasty comments or direct messages telling me I was pathetic to highlight all the ways Byron was perfect. I'd spent the last several weeks with thoughts of him plaguing me day and night. I was well aware.

Amelia stared at me, visibly stunned. But then a warm, soft smile bloomed over her features and she reached across the table to grab my hand. "I am so happy to hear you say that."

"It's not a controversial statement. He is glorious. And his brain! I just want to—" I mimed grabbing motions with my fingers, unable to put into words how greedy I felt about his thoughts and words. "And his voice. God, I love his voice. And his hands."

Her eyes widened and she averted them to her wine, a secretive-looking smile on her lips, but remained silent.

Sipping my wine, I watched Amelia over the rim, kinda sorta just realizing I'd confessed to being infatuated with her oldest friend, and I felt a twinge of worry. "Does this make things weird for you? That I have a thing for him?"

"What? Are you kidding? I'm ecstatic."

"You are?" *Huh. I did not see that coming.* "But won't it be awkward? You won't be uncomfortable? Your roommate lusting after your oldest friend?"

"As you should." She winked and wagged her eyebrows.

"So this is what I can expect? You teasing me about it?" Instead of another sip, I drank a gulp.

"Absolutely. All the teasing. You two are the best people I know. And Elijah, of course." Amelia neatly sipped from her glass and then set it down in front of her. "Byron is just as amazing as you believe, but probably not nearly as tough as you or he thinks he is. And you are equally amazing, but much tougher than anyone gives you credit for, including yourself."

"Hey!" I frowned. "I think I'm tough."

"No, you don't. But that's a conversation for another time. My point is, I give you my blessing to lust after Byron, not that you need it. I'll let you two figure this out on your own." She nodded at her own assertion.

"What does that mean?"

"It means, if you like him, if you want his body, you should tell him."

Yeah right. "It's not that simple." I pulled up the short sleeve of my shirt, scratching my upper arm. Since I better understood Byron's bluntness, I had no doubt that if he'd wanted more than friendship with me, he would've already said something. "I don't think he's interested in me that way."

At my response, Amelia threw her head back and laughed, smacking the table with her palm. She laughed and laughed, hitting the table a few more times, as though she'd never heard anything so funny.

I crossed my arms and watched her, feeling left out of the joke even as growing suspicion and hope had me cracking a smile. "Are you going to tell me what's so funny? Do you know something I don't?"

"I have nothing to say." She wiped at her eyes.

"You won't give me a hint?" This time when my stomach fluttered, I let it.

This reaction from her, laughing at my statement that I didn't think Byron was interested in me *that way*, felt like less-than-subtle encouragement.

"No." She tossed her hands in the air. "As I said, I have nothing to say on the matter."

"Did he say something about me?" The tummy flutter became a storm.

"I couldn't tell ya." Amelia wrestled her smile into submission, almost managing to look innocent.

I stared at her, waiting, hoping she'd give me a hint. I really needed one. I'd played the night of Lucy and Jeff's dinner party over and over in my head, desperately searching for some sign that he considered his feelings something other than inconvenient. But each time, three key sentences jumped out and punctured all hope.

"It's not a big deal."

"I don't want or need anything from you."

"I like you, but I don't particularly want to."

Taking his statements at face value was imperative. He'd meant what he said, and precisely what he'd said. So . . . maybe he'd changed his mind since then? Maybe he'd spoken to Amelia about me and things were now different?

Really, Win? Doesn't this kind of make you pathetic? Hoping Byron will eventually like you enough to want something from you?

I covered my face again, rubbed it, and let my hands drop. I was so tired of the spin cycle in my brain.

Eyeing her, I tried a little reverse psychology, a tactic that often worked on my uncle. "I don't think you know anything."

She stared at me, a smile she was trying to hide pulled forcefully at her mouth.

"If you know something, if he said something to you, you would tell me."

"Would I?"

"Yes. Now you know how I feel. And if he feels the same way about me —or even half as much—then why wouldn't you tell me?" I shook my head. "Nah. You don't know anything. But maybe you suspect something."

"I do. I suspect you are smart, and lovely, and kind, and sexy as fuck, and it's ridiculous for you to think Byron—or anyone else—wouldn't think of you *that way*."

She had it wrong. I was well aware that despite how sexy I considered myself to be, it was not far-fetched at all to think others would not view me that way. This was not a reflection of my self-worth or confidence. This was simple logic.

I had proof of this phenomenon, using myself as the control group and several guys most people considered good-looking in college as the test cases. Though I was an extreme minority, I did not find those men sexy, or good-looking, or anything close to it.

Therefore, no matter how sexy a person might objectively be to most people, there existed at least one person in the world who thought that person was actually Skeletor-meets-Gritty-the-Mascot gross. Beauty, sexiness, and attractiveness were in the eye of the beholder, and that was a universal truth. No one is sexy to everyone, just like no one is unsexy to everyone either. Which was why whether or not a particular person found me attractive never impacted my self-confidence—strokes and folks and all that.

But rather than argue the point, I licked the tip of my finger and touched my shoulder, making a sizzling sound. "I am sexy."

"So sexy," she agreed, her eyes growing soft. "Don't let anyone ever, *ever* tell you otherwise."

I felt my grin go brittle as my gaze fell away. She'd read the most recent comments on my videos. I knew she would. We were best friends and nerdy soul mates. But I really, really didn't want to talk about it.

"Win—"

"I don't want to talk about it."

"Those people are assholes. Ignore them."

"I am." Yes, obviously, I wished people would stop messaging me and commenting on my videos, telling me how ugly my face looked, especially since Byron and I weren't even together. But they did, and I was doing my best not to be altered by any of it.

"When was the last time you talked to Byron?"

"About a week ago." I grimaced, then groaned. "When I told him I thought he had a sensory processing disorder."

"Have you told him yet? Have you spoken to him about the shitty comments? Does he know people are doing this to you?"

I shook my head.

"Winnie! What? Why? You need to tell him." She smacked the table.

I lifted an eyebrow at the sound. Amelia seemed to be hitting the table a lot tonight. "Why would I? I can deal with it. It's fine. I can ignore them."

Her glare told me she didn't believe me.

"It's a small price to pay if it means I get that community manager position, pay back my student loans, all while spreading the good word of STEM to hundreds of thousands of people I never would've had the opportunity to reach."

"Both are allowed to be true. You're allowed to be grateful for the followers and irritated by the trolls' mean, sucky behavior."

"I know," I said, unable to keep the hint of defensiveness from my voice. "I'm not saying I'm not upset, but I'm trying not to think about it. I'm grateful for the exposure, the followers, the new people I'm reaching, and trying to focus on the positive. I'm also ready for the weekend. Can we talk about something else?"

"Fine. But you have to promise me you'll come to me and rant if you need to."

"I promise. But for tonight, I'm looking forward to *Stardew* and chill."

"Oh!" She snapped her fingers, then pointed at me. "I know, call Byron. See if he wants to come over and play *Stardew Valley* tonight."

I glanced at my phone to check the time. "Are you serious?" She had to be joking.

"Maybe. Why? What's up?"

I gestured to the Rite Aid bag I'd placed on the chair earlier. "I was going to dye my hair tonight—for my series on the science of hair—but I guess I could do it tomorrow. Do you—what makes you think he'd want to play with me?"

Amelia's eyebrows jumped, her eyes growing comically wide.

I rolled my eyes, ignoring the blush caused by my poor phrasing. "I meant, play with *us*. Play *Stardew* with us. Does he play?"

She seemed to consider my question, tapping her chin while examining me. "Byron likes to . . ." Her eyes narrowed, like picking just the right words was a struggle. "Like you, he likes to play. But never with others, and definitely not with just anyone."

Frowning, I picked up my wineglass. "Then why do you think he'll play with us?"

She blew out a breath, puffing her cheeks. "Call it a hunch. Oh!" She snapped her fingers again. "Or—and just hear me out—you could have Byron come over and bleach your hair."

I scoffed, snorting. "He'd never do that."

"You don't know unless you ask." Once again trying to look innocent, Amelia took a dainty sip of wine.

Glancing at the ceiling, I shook my head. "I bet you a week's worth of dinners, Byron Visser will have no interest in dyeing my hair." I hoped that by baiting her she'd inadvertently reveal something (assuming there was anything to reveal). This was another tactic that had worked with Uncle Jacob.

But Amelia couldn't be manipulated into divulging anything. Grinning widely, she nudged my phone closer to my wineglass and lifted her chin toward it. "Go ahead. Call him. And put it on speaker."

"Why? What do you think he'll say?"

She nudged my phone again. "Do it."

"Now?"

"No time like the present."

I inspected her. "Fine. But I want sausage with my pancakes this week."

"Just call him," she sing-songed, wiggling gleefully in her seat.

Finding his contact information quickly, I ignored the escalating rhythm of my heart and hit the Call button, twisting my hands on my lap.

He answered on the second ring. "Fred."

My chest tightened, hot and spiky. "Hey."

"Hi."

I glanced at my roommate. She looked like the Cheshire Cat. "Amelia is also here. I have you on speaker."

"Hey Byron!" she said in her best Kristen Wiig Target Lady impression. "Long time no talk."

I squinted at her. She looked positively beside herself with excitement even as she returned my squint, her shoulders shaking with quiet laughter. *Was she . . . drunk?*

"What did you do, Amelia?" Tone dark and foreboding, Byron did not sound pleased with her.

"Nothing!" She giggled, shaking her head and clearing her throat as though to dispel the laughter and get control of herself. Then to me she whispered, "Ask him."

"How much wine have you had?" I whispered back.

"Ask me what?" Surprisingly, Byron no longer sounded irritated. He sounded interested.

"Uh," I split my attention between Amelia and the wine bottle, which I could now see was a quarter full. "Byron, do you want me to take you off speaker?"

"No, it's fine. Let Ames have her way. What do you want to ask?"

I leaned forward, looked at my cell's screen and realized I didn't have a picture assigned for him as a contact. When we spoke on the phone, he was represented by a gray circle with a capitol B. "It's not a big deal, but I wanted to ask you a favor."

"Anything," he said.

Amelia clamped a hand over her mouth, her big eyes dropping to the table. She must be drunk.

"You might regret saying that. Are you comfortable doing a video not included on my list? It's STEM related, not a challenge." I set my forearms on the table and pressed my palms together. *Was I really going to ask him this?* Suddenly, I felt foolish.

"Go on. What is it?"

I breathed through another bout of spiky lungs syndrome. *Goodness.* It was great to hear his voice. I hoped he'd come over, and this hope gave me bravery. "First, please say no if you don't want to do it."

"Fred. Ask."

"Fine. Okay. Here goes. I've already recorded several videos on the science of hair—this was a few weeks ago—but I haven't posted them yet."

"The science of hair?"

"Yes. I reviewed what hair color is, why people have the hair color they do—like redheads and Neanderthals—the origin of hair colors, the genetics involved in determining hair color and texture, that kind of stuff."

"Oh. Okay. Informative."

His praise pulled a smile from me, some of my nerves settling. "Then for the last video—and this is where I need your help—I want to record someone helping me dye my hair blond."

Silence. Then, "You want to bleach your hair?" He sounded a little winded.

"Yeah. I want to talk about the chemical process of coloring hair, what it does, and I've always wanted to go completely blond, like bright platinum blond, so I thought it'd be a good way to cap off the series and tie in to the chemical compounds video I did in April. I'll post the hair videos from now until August. And since next week is the last week of school, I'll have all summer to grow it out if I don't like it."

His side went quiet. After several seconds, I tapped on the screen to make sure the call hadn't dropped. According to my cell and the gray circle with the big B, he was still connected.

"Byron? Are you there?"

"I like your hair now."

"Okay. . .?" I glanced at Amelia. She still had her hand over her mouth, her eyes affixed to the table like she didn't trust herself to speak or look at me.

"Are you certain you want to bleach it?"

"Yes."

"I'll help."

I tried not to laugh. He sounded so resolved, like he'd just agreed to go into battle, not help me dye my hair blond.

"Oh! Okay. Great! Thanks—"

"But I have a stipulation."

The sigh I released probably sounded like a deflating tire, and yet I couldn't help but smile. "Why am I not surprised?"

"I want . . ."

"Yes?"

"You're not allowed to ask me why I want this particular stipulation."

Amelia rolled her eyes, finally dropping her hand from her mouth so she could take another sip of her wine.

"Okay. Fine. What is it?"

"I want a picture of you with your hair down, in your current color, like it was the night of Jeff and Lucy's dinner party."

My lashes fluttered. "You . . . what?" I asked breathlessly. He wanted a picture of me?

Flattered.

That's how I felt. Pleased and a little excited and a whole lot flattered. I was right, Amelia *had* been trying to give me encouragement earlier. My brain and heart were buoyant.

But then he said, grumpy and demanding, "No questions."

His tone didn't bother me or diminish my buoyancy one bit. "Well, I need to know more details. Can it be an old picture? I don't—I can look through my phone, but I don't think I have a recent picture with my hair like that."

"I want it to be recent. How about I take it when I come over?"

"I guess so." I touched the messy braid lying over my shoulder. "But then I'll have to wash and style it tonight, and that's—"

"Perfect. Agreed. Bye."

He hung up.

Smiling quizzically at my phone, I gave my head a little shake. "He wants to take a picture of me before I dye it blond."

"Yep. Typical Byron." Leaning forward, she refilled her glass. "He did something similar to me when I decided to cut my hair in eighth grade. And when our friend James in high school grew a beard, he wanted a photo of him without it. He doesn't always do well with change."

Ah. So maybe I shouldn't be flattered. Now I laughed at myself and my ping-ponging thoughts. Trying to keep track of what I was feeling for Byron compared to what I thought I should be feeling for Byron was absolutely exhausting.

I made a face to hide my disappointment, joking, "Or maybe he has a hair fetish?"

"Ha! No. It's any change. Like when my parents sold our old house to move into a bigger one, he took a video of the house before we sold it and took a few pictures of us out in front. You've probably seen them on his mantel at his house."

"Oh, yeah." I wondered when those pictures had been taken. Amelia was taller than Byron in the photos by about six inches. Now he had at least four inches on her five foot nine.

"When I move out of here," she continued, standing from the table, "he'll probably come over and insist we take pictures. Should I open another bottle?"

My heart stuttered, then stopped at her words. Plummeting distress sent my stomach to my toes.

"Win?"

"Yeah. Sounds good." I gulped the remainder of my glass. I'd been so busy and preoccupied over the last few weeks, I'd forgotten about the hints Amelia and Elijah had been dropping about moving in together. Or maybe I'd been purposefully ignoring them, pushing them from my mind. I thought I had more time. But the way she'd said it—

When I move out of here . . .

Not if. *When.*

They'd probably been waiting until the school year was over.

"I'll text Byron to bring some over too." Amelia pulled out her phone. "And maybe Serena can come over tonight."

Our mutual friend hadn't come over last week since I'd been so busy. She said she wanted to wait until we could all play together.

"What about Byron? Last week you said he wouldn't want to come if Serena were here."

Amelia blew a raspberry. "He can just deal with it. If he wants to see you, he'll have to suffer through Serena."

CHAPTER 20
WINNIE

I felt a little silly about it, but I took a shower and did my hair, blow-drying it straight even though it made the bathroom hot. I ended up opening the skylight to let fresh air in and took the forty-five minutes required to add the curls and waves. Since I fixed my hair, I figured I might as well do my makeup too. And while I was at it, I slipped on the black wraparound dress I'd worn the evening of Lucy and Jeff's party along with the knee-high boots.

While I got ready, I decided I would apologize to Byron for assuming he had a sensory processing disorder. I wasn't a medical professional. What looked like sensory issues to me might've been something completely different, or nothing at all. Even if Amelia, as his oldest friend, agreed with me, and even though I remained convinced I was right, going around armchair diagnosing people wasn't okay, and he deserved an apology.

When I walked out of my bedroom a full hour and a half after walking into it, my wineglass empty and Amelia nowhere to be seen, it was with determination and a repentant heart that I approached Byron. Sitting on the couch, he seemed to be reading a book.

His head came up, and his eyes went wide, moving over me. "Winnie."

"Hi." I tucked my hair behind my ears. "Sorry, I didn't know you were here. Have you been waiting long?"

"About fifteen minutes." He set his book to the side.

I backed up toward the kitchen. “Are you thirsty? Or hungry? Do you want anything?”

“No, thank you,” he replied, and stood to face me. “I ate.”

I nodded, my eyes moving over him. His hair, much longer on top than on the sides, had been arranged artfully away from his face, a style he seemed to be favoring these days. He wore a grayish greenish blue T-shirt instead of his typical black, and instead of dark jeans, he wore—wait for it—blue jeans.

“Feeling blue today?” I teased.

“Amelia told me to wear this. She texted after our call.”

“What? Why?” I strolled toward him.

“I’m guessing since I’m bleaching your hair, she didn’t want chemicals to get on my black clothes.”

I drew closer. My smiled slipped as the answer to my last question made itself clear. Suddenly, I was quite, quite hot. Amelia was super sneaky. Her outfit request had nothing to do with bleaching my hair. His eyes—so beautiful and unusual in his typical attire—were startlingly vivid now, the rings of his irises blending and matching the color of his shirt.

“What’s wrong?” he asked, inspecting me.

“Nothing. It’s . . . nothing.” I was going to drown in his eyes. I couldn’t redirect my gaze. They were ridiculously mesmerizing. A gradient of burning copper and barium, a new star being born, heat and vibrancy.

“Are you sure?” Standing directly in front of me now, his hand came to my elbow as though to steady me, the warmth of his skin bleeding through the thin fabric of my dress. “You look dizzy. How much wine did you have?”

“Just the one glass.” I was dizzy. Now. Now I was dizzy. I hadn’t been dizzy before now. *Think!* I spotted the empty wineglass in my hand. “Where’s Amelia?”

He grimaced. “She went to her room to rest. She had too much to drink.”

I made an O with my lips and nodded while reminding myself that staring into another person’s eyes for a prolonged period of time could be interpreted as aggression.

Byron’s gaze still felt assessing, which made me feel awkward, which helped me finally tear my attention away. “Uh, so.” I tucked my hair behind my ears again, spinning away, sobering as I remembered my determination to apologize, before I’d been distracted by his . . . face. “I wanted to apologize to you for last week, for what I said.”

“Be more specific.”

I smirked at his command. Placing my empty wineglass on the counter, I turned to face him and braced a hand against the kitchen peninsula. "I'm sorry I said, or heavily implied, you have a sensory processing disorder."

He lifted his chin as though absorbing this information.

"I'm really sorry. It was clear to me after that I blindsided you. It wasn't a possibility you'd considered or were receptive to consider. I didn't at all mean to imply there is anything wrong with you. I don't see sensory disorders as something *wrong*, per se. Just a different way of thinking and interacting with the world. But I am really sorry if it came out that way."

Byron's posture remained relaxed, but something about his eyes felt withdrawn and frosty, a quality echoed in his voice as he said, "Let's say, theoretically, for the sake of argument, I do have one or more sensory issues."

"Okay."

"What difference does it make?"

That's exactly what Amelia had said. They must've talked about it.

"Well, if you did and you were diagnosed, literature on the subject might help you understand yourself better. And you might be able to join a support group, meet people who experience the world in a similar way. It might help both you and them feel less alone, more—"

"Normal."

I felt my features flatten at his word choice and how he'd said it. "No."

"Would you like me if I were more normal? More like other guys?"

I flinched, the question making my heart ache. It sounded like an accusation. "Byron. No. What do you mean, 'like other guys'? It's not about me and what I want or think. It's about understanding yourself and—and—"

"I resist labels." He cut me off, obviously rejecting my logic.

"You resist labels?"

"Correct," he said with finality, as though that was that and the subject was now closed. The end.

I think I understood what he meant, but I didn't like how frustrated he looked, how withdrawn and determined and angry, like he'd been mentally arguing with me about this issue all week and wouldn't give me—or us—a chance to discuss it fully.

He could feel however he wanted. But I didn't want him to believe I considered him to be strange or was judging him. I needed to lighten the mood, make him laugh, so he'd be open to a real conversation with me.

Trying for teasing-skeptical, I turned my head to peer at him through the corners of my eyes. "What? Like food labels? You see the daily recommended sodium intake information and think to yourself, 'Screw you, label! You're not the boss of me. I'll drink sea water for breakfast. Resist!'"

He smiled as I spoke, his gaze growing hooded, much of his rigidity fracturing. *Reluctant amusement, but amusement nevertheless.*

"No, Fred," he drawled. "I'm referring to labels people apply to themselves. A diagnosis, an identity, an affiliation. Especially when they had no hand or say in defining the label."

I wrinkled my nose, not liking what he was implying. "But sometimes labels are really, really important. They help people—"

"I'm not talking about other people, I'm only talking about myself. If a label gives someone comfort, helps them understand themselves better, helps them feel like they belong and fit, whatever." He walked over to where I stood and leaned a hip against the counter, facing me and crossing his arms. "Good for them. But I resist applying labels to myself, or being asked to define who I am, what I think, how I feel by utilizing a label."

"Why?" I also crossed my arms.

He huffed, glaring over my head.

Reflexively, I reached out and gripped his arm. "Don't do that. Don't withdraw. I'm asking because I want to know."

"Why do you want to know?" he demanded, his voice hard. "Why do I have to explain myself?"

I briefly considered letting the matter drop, letting it go. We were friends now, of a sort, and if he didn't want to talk about himself, part of me didn't want to push.

But the part that liked him so darn much, the part that obsessed about him when we were apart, that part needed to understand.

I let my hand drop. "I want to know you better. I like you and . . ." I shrugged and gave him a half smile. "I want to know you. I'm not asking you to explain yourself. I'm asking you to help me understand so I don't misunderstand."

He blinked, giving me the sense my words surprised him. "You like me now?"

I laughed at his expression. "You nerd!" I pushed his immoveable shoulder with my fingertips. "You know I do. How could you think I don't?"

"You said you didn't." He said this like the answer was so obvious that he resented me asking the question.

"Weeks ago!" I shook my head at him. Did he think impressions never changed? "Admittedly, I didn't like you when your powers of brilliance and your intimidating persona made me feel foolish. But now that I know you better and you stopped offering unsolicited career advice, that doesn't happen anymore." *Now I just feel a lot of biological and heart-related urges. No biggie.*

"I wish I'd never given you a reason to dislike me." He sounded sorry, the words quiet and thoughtful, and his eyes dropped from mine.

"At this point, let's chalk it up to a misunderstanding, which is why I'm asking you about yourself. Are we okay?" I bent my knees to try to catch his eyes. "We're good? You forgive me?"

He nodded, not allowing me to make eye contact. "Would you, uh, say we're friends now?"

"What?" I pressed my hand to my chest in mock surprise, wanting to see his smile again. "Are we labeling this? I thought you didn't like labels."

The side of his mouth ticked up, making my heart flutter. "Some labels serve a valuable purpose."

"Like the label of *friend*?"

"And . . . others."

"Like what?"

"Like sugar. If it weren't labeled, I might think it's salt." He gave me his eyes again, full of purpose, their weight somehow heavier as they hooked into mine. "Are we friends?"

"I'd like to think so, but it's not just up to me. So I'll ask you the same, are we friends?"

"We are."

"Great—"

"But I have some stipulations."

Taken aback, I barked a laugh, shaking my head at him. "Are you serious?"

"Don't I look serious?"

He did look serious.

Still chuckling, I crossed my arms again, apparently needing to prepare for the negotiation of our friendship. "Fine. Go ahead. What are your terms?"

"If you're upset or unsatisfied with me, or I make you uncomfortable, you have to tell me." Byron shuffled closer, his hand coming to lean against the counter.

"Fine. And same."

His eyes narrowed, like my statement perplexed him. "I thought you said you didn't want my unsolicited advice."

"Yeah, I don't. Not about my life choices. But if I upset you, if I do something to you that makes you angry, I want you to tell me."

"Okay. I see the distinction."

"Other stipulations? Is this where you finally mandate I pick all the red M&M's out of your candy bag, and green towels only?"

His lips parted, but then his eyes sharpened with recollection. These were two of the ridiculous demands I'd postulated all those weeks ago when he'd initially offered to help me with the videos.

"I don't like M&M's of any color."

I tilted my head to the side. "You like See's candy, dark chocolate."

He flashed a quick, stunned smile, one with teeth. "How do you know that?"

"I have my sources, and I cannot divulge them."

"Fine. Then why do you know that?" His smile spread and his eyes did this wonderful thing, like they were eating me up, devouring every detail of my face.

It made breathing slightly more difficult, but—avoiding his question—I powered through. "What are your other stipulations?"

"Stipulations?"

"For cementing our friendship label."

"Right." His focus moved up and to the left. "I want to see you more often, more than just to film challenges."

This had me smiling in a big way. "What? Really?"

"Yes. Even after we're finished with the videos."

I was already nodding before he'd completed his thought. "Yes. Absolutely."

Maybe tomorrow, after sleeping on it, I'd feel a twinge of regret for my present exuberance, considering the fact that I now had a full-blown crush on this man. But that was something for me to worry about tomorrow, not now. Not when everything was going so swimmingly and the evening was filled with promise and he was talking to me without showing any signs of running from the room.

"One more thing," he said, leaning forward, his aftershave pounding on the door of my biology and saying, *Little Win, little Win, let me come in.*

I tried to breathe exclusively through my mouth. "What?"

"I want you to work only when you're being paid to do so."

Confoundedly amused, I tried to glare at him. "No. But nice try."

He shrugged, a tiny smile tugging at his lips. "It was worth a shot."

CHAPTER 21
WINNIE

He snapped my picture right where I stood, under the open skylights of our kitchen. It was quick and painless, and he used the phone Amelia had picked up at the behest of his agent.

With no reason to remain looking fancy, I changed into a baggy T-shirt and sweats. Byron then joined me in my bathroom, and I went over the instructions for how to dye my hair.

"I have a good idea what to do." He frowned at the paper that had come with the kit. "Prior to leaving my place, I watched YouTube tutorials."

"You did?" Of course he did. Byron did everything well. He knew everything. And if he didn't, he was a quick study.

"The steps here look similar to those in the videos." He nodded, scanning the directions.

Byron arranged everything while I filmed and narrated what he was doing. I then grabbed our least fancy apron from the kitchen, a glass of water for each of us, and gloves to protect his hands. I think we can all agree, Byron's hands must be protected at all costs.

He'd set up a folding chair in my bathroom. I filmed me helping him put on the apron, during which I made a point to wrap my arms around him to tie the back instead of having him turn around. This, of course, meant we spent a full minute with our fronts plastered together and his aftershave assaulting my mitochondria, but it was worth it.

Was I possibly taking advantage of the situation so I could be closer to him for a few short minutes? Maybe. *Yes*. But then I've never claimed to be a saint.

Meanwhile, he stood patiently with his arms up, frowning at the ceiling.

"What are you thinking about?" I asked, leaning back when I was finished.

"England."

I laughed—he was so witty, on and off camera—and ended the recording there just to set my phone to time-lapse and hit record again. Then, with Byron wearing a mask of determination and me making silly faces at the camera, we got started for real.

I paused the time-lapse at intervals to explain what we were doing next, and what we expected the results to be, and how the different chemicals acted on my hair.

Byron listened patiently as I spoke and worked meticulously when I sat. He couldn't have been more conscientious, and it was seriously the cutest thing. I made a mental note to add hearts to the finished video around his face, so adorably stern with concentration.

We chatted about mostly nothing—mainly the logistics of what would happen next or how he wanted me to sit—then suddenly, the first few notes of a song, all violins and harp, drifted in from the outer room.

Byron's head angled to the side. "What's that?"

Within seconds, Nat King Cole's voice joined the stringed instruments. I closed my eyes, grinding my teeth. *Amelia, the instigator.*

"That's one of Amelia's playlists," I said through my teeth. "Ignore it." *I'm going to get her back for this.*

It was her romantic songs playlist. Nat King Cole's "The Very Thought of You" was now playing, one of my favorite songs ever. The combination of his luscious voice plus the slow arrangement never failed to put me in a swoony mood. Swoony was not a mood I should be experiencing at present while Byron stood so close behind me, his hands working through my hair.

Really, there was no bad arrangement of this song. Nat King Cole, Billie Holiday, Ella Fitzgerald—all excellent.

Byron studied my reflection in the mirror, then returned his attention to his task. We sat in swoony-song wordlessness while the music continued. I tried not to appreciate the sight of him, the broad expanse of his shoulders rising over me, the wrinkle between his eyebrows and the way his tongue swept out and lingered on his bottom lip, illuminating the depth of his concentration. The curves of his biceps strained the cloth at his sleeves, his pecs a shelf for his T-shirt. Even his clavicles were sexy. And don't get me started on his forearms and the skill of his hands.

But when the piano intro of the next song began, Norah Jones's "Turn Me On," I lowered my gaze to the sink and rolled my lips between my teeth. *I'll strangle her. She's dead.*

Byron's hands stilled as soon as Nora sang the phrase associated with the song's title. I heard him clear his throat before turning and walking out of the bathroom while I suddenly wished I hadn't been so cheeky when tying his apron strings earlier. My arms buzzed with energy at the memory of being so close.

A second later, the sound of my bedroom door closing carried to me. When he reentered the bathroom, he closed that door too. We could still perceive the melody, but the words were now muffled—thank GOD—so I knew when Marvin Gaye's "Let's Get It On" started up, but at least I didn't have to hear him sing it.

"So . . ." I said, my mind casting about for something super boring to discuss so I would stop thinking about what it had been like to touch him. "Seen any good shows lately?"

"I don't watch TV."

"I didn't know that." My attention lifted to inspect his face. "Then why do you own one?"

"I should've been more precise. I watch movies, not television shows."

"Why do you watch movies instead of shows?"

He moved the section of my hair he'd just finished painting and picked up the bottle with the dye, squeezing out a bit more. "I like to be finished."

"Finished?"

"I like stories that have an ending. I dislike not knowing what happens next."

I smiled. Then I chuckled. "And you ended your first book on a massive cliffhanger, a brutal one."

Not looking up, Byron lifted an eyebrow, his mouth threatening to curve. "Are you complaining?"

"Not at all." I raised my hands. "But you are clearly a sadist." Even with the skylight open, the smell of the dye was making me light-headed. Or maybe it was being shut inside this tiny bathroom with the guy who occupied most of my waking thoughts. And many of my sleeping thoughts.

"I accept that," he said with a casual air, like he really did accept the label of sadist and wore it with pride.

"You like that label? You're okay being called a sadist?"

He smiled . . . kinda. His jaw slid to the side, and he flipped another section of my hair. "I don't mind it."

"I'm more of a masochist myself."

His hands stilled, his gaze cut to the mirror, met mine, held, and I struggled to breathe. So I didn't.

After a long moment, during which I felt certain the tension had taken on a corporeal form and if I lifted my hand I'd touch it, Byron blinked and dropped his eyes to the top of my head.

Whoa. What was that? Surely, I didn't imagine that. Surely not.

"I don't like to hurt people," he said, his voice gruff and rumbly. "But I don't mind . . . torturing them a little."

I expelled a laugh that felt hot in my lungs.

He wanted to torture people? *Well, mission accomplished, buddy.*

At the thought, I had to bite the inside of my cheek to keep from erupting in unhinged laughter. I said nothing as I struggled and wrestled with myself. Truly, it was myself that I struggled against, all of me. Not just my neurotransmitters or biology or body, but every atom of every cell. I had chosen the dark side. It had cookies and Byron.

Speaking of cookies, my stomach rumbled, the sound drawing me from my reverie, and I reflexively pressed a hand to it.

"Are you hungry?" He shifted behind me, sliding the pointy end of the brush through my hair to separate it.

"I didn't have dinner, but it's okay. I can wait."

"Do you want to order out? I could eat."

"I thought you said you already ate?"

His shoulders rose and fell. "I've been running a lot."

"Oh? Where do you run?"

"Through Interlaken Park."

"Really?" That got my attention. "I've always wanted to run there, but I don't want to go by myself."

"I'll go with you."

"Excellent. It's a d—" I bit off the word *date,* scratching my jaw, and finished clumsily, "—darn good idea."

His features told me he thought I was funny, or cute, or something like that.

My stomach rumbled again, louder this time.

"I'm almost finished. Do you already have something made? I can heat it up."

"Sadly, nothing fantastic. I need to go grocery shopping. But we could do peanut butter on almond crackers."

"If I ordered food, would you eat some?"

"Nah. It's fine."

"Because I'd pay for it? You don't want me to—"

"No. It's not like that." If he wanted to pay for takeout, fine. I wasn't proud in that way. Like Amelia, free food was my jam. If someone freely offered, I'd slather it on toast.

"Will you tell me why?"

My talkative stomach growled a third time. "I don't like to order from restaurants that aren't exclusively gluten-free. They say they have gluten-free options, but the kitchen is shared, and I get so sick if I have even a little bit."

Eyes on me, features thoughtful, he said, "So what you're saying is, I shouldn't take you to the National Festival of Breads."

I laughed, and he cracked a smile, and it was so nice.

"Hey, why don't we order from a gluten-free restaurant?" He gently pushed my head forward to access the area right above my neck.

"You'd be okay with that?"

"Yeah. Food is food. I don't care where we order from. While the dye sits, you call and order for both of us. It'll be a work-related meal. We'll talk about the trip to New York, and I'll expense it."

"You can do that?"

"I can do anything."

Glad he couldn't see my face, I gave into the urge to roll my eyes. "Of course you can. I bet you've never experienced a single embarrassing moment in your entire perfect life," I said, poking fun. "You probably didn't even go through puberty. You just woke up one morning looking like that"—I waved to his body—"birds making your bed and tying your hair in ribbons, mice sewing the holes in your socks."

"Everyone has embarrassing moments. Besides, you knew me in college. You know what I looked like."

"Yeah. Cute."

His movements seemed to slow. "You thought I was cute?"

Oh no. Change the subject!

"Story time. Tell me about your most embarrassing moment."

I heard him sigh. "No."

"No?"

"Fine. Tell me your most embarrassing moment and I'll think about it."

"Okay . . ." I pulled in a bracing breath, only giving myself two seconds for wisdom and good sense to raise alarms before shoving them away. My uncle had caused me mortification plenty of times, but none of his antics held the top spot in my memory. This was likely because I expected it of him. Surprise embarrassment, when you least expect it and can't prepare for it, is always so much worse.

I'd only told Amelia this story. But for some reason, I wanted to tell him too. "My freshman year of high school, when I was fourteen, I was wearing white shorts and I started my period—at school."

He said nothing, but I could sense him listening with interest.

"My cycle was so random then, I hadn't had it for two months before that, and I didn't know I'd started it, so I was walking around with these big blood stains on my butt."

"Damn."

"That's not the worst part."

"Oh no."

"Yeah." I was pleased he still couldn't see my face. It made reliving the memory easier. "So. This boy, this senior, came up to me in the hall between classes and was friendly. And he was really, really handsome, and seemed super nice and flirtatious. He asked me if he could walk me to my class. I was so starstruck by this upper classman who seemed to be interested in me, I was like, 'Yes! Absolutely.' So he walked me to class, asking me all these questions about myself. He pretended to hang on every word. By the time we made it to my class, I was completely infatuated with him. It was so sad, how quickly I fell and how a little positive attention made me feel."

"What happened next?"

"When we arrived at my classroom, he said goodbye, and that was it."

"That wasn't it." Byron's voice had deepened. He'd stopped brushing my hair with the dye.

"No. It wasn't. Only later—when I was tagged in a post on Instagram—did I realize that his friends, basically half of the varsity soccer team, were behind us filming my bloodstained shorts and he'd been surreptitiously turning to make gagging faces at the camera the whole time."

"What a—"

"Sheep-biting footlicker? Yeah." I chuckled, the sting of the memory so much duller than the last time I'd thought about it. All that hot embarrassment I used to feel—the discomfort and twisting in my stomach—it was all gone, replaced with a tepid mournfulness for the fourteen-year-old girl who'd been mortified.

"I was going to say what a bunch of trash humans, but sheep-biting footlicker also works."

"They called me Carrie in the video—you know, from the Steven King book—and that was my nickname my entire freshman year."

I felt the brush move over my scalp again, his movements not as fluid as before.

"And that's the most embarrassing thing that's ever happened to me."

"How do you do it?" he asked, his voice tight.

"What?"

"If I were you—no, that's not—what I'm trying to say is, if you were anyone else in the world, you'd never go on social media again. How do you keep doing it? Why do you do it to yourself? Why do you put yourself out there like that?" He sounded so upset, like the story had happened to him.

"Because I have to."

"No. You don't." Tossing the brush to the sink, he wrapped the plastic around my head. "You could delete all your accounts today, end all the feedback and noise."

"No, I couldn't." I watched him in the mirror as he yanked his gloves off. "I need to make my STEM videos, I need to—"

"But you don't." He threw the gloves in the trash, glaring at the interior of my bathroom and looking incredibly agitated. "Your audience doesn't need you. There are other resources for people, other accounts. You don't *need* to do this to yourself."

"You're not listening." I twisted in the seat before standing from the chair, lifting the back to fold it. "I didn't say that they need me. I said *I* need to make those videos. I need it. I need a place, a—a platform to share my love for physics and chemistry and biology and engineering and the beauty of how the world works in perfect harmony and disharmony and all of it. I get excited about articles I read, and I want to share what I've learned, what I know. I want to help."

While I was speaking, Byron took the chair from my grip and rested it against the wall. "Even when they don't want your help? Even when a video of a woman taking a literal shit on TikTok gets a thousand times more engagement than your videos on STEM?"

I reared back, my mind working. Either he'd been on TikTok recently or he'd just made an excellent guess. I doubted it was the latter. *Which meant he'd seen the comments saying how stupid, ugly, and unworthy I was.*

Gulping more air than saliva, I ignored the press of heat behind my eyes. "Yeah. Even then."

"I don't understand you." He moved as though to push his hands through his hair but stopped himself at the last minute, turning and opening the door.

"That's okay."

The music, still playing from the family room, was louder in my bedroom, and I could hear Billie Eilish's "Ocean Eyes" reverberating through the door.

"I mean it." He paced away. "You're so amazing. So incredibly clever and brave and good. And you just give away these gifts to undeserving people."

I placed my hands on my hips. "First of all, how do you know they're all undeserving? Statistically speaking, it's not possible for them *all* to be undeserving. It's just a small minority that leaves mean comments. And second, you give away your gifts too."

"Oh really?" He stopped pacing and shot daggers at me. "Pray tell, how so?" His question dripped with sarcasm, putting me on edge and making my heart race.

This is Byron. You can trust Byron. He'd never do anything to hurt you on purpose.

"Your books. Your words and thoughts, your imagination."

"I do not give my books away. I charge people for the work *I* do."

I straightened, my temper spiking. His unsubtle dig at me being a teacher made me see red. "Is that why you don't have social media? Because you can't make money off it? Charge people for access?"

"No," he ground out, his jaw ticking. "If people want a piece of me, then they're only getting what they pay for, and only what I want them to see. And that's it."

I shook my head at him. "You are one greedy, stingy b—" I caught myself before saying *bastard* and recovered "—Byron."

But he knew. He knew I'd almost called him a mean name, and his gaze flashed with hurt before it grew impossibly dark.

See? This is why you don't call people mean names!

"Yeah. I am a bastard. But I know my worth, Fred. And fuck those people who think they're entitled to any part of me I'm not willing to share."

My temper deflated, my shoulders slumping. "Byron—"

"No. Really. *Fuck* them. They want to slice me up into little pieces, discuss me and my history, my past, my origin, my worthiness like I'm a flavor of soda instead of a person, put me on a list and rank me." He shook his head, his eyes on me. "Fuck. Them."

The vulnerability and vehemence in his voice left me breathless with remorse. I'd struck a nerve, an extremely raw one if his restless, rigid posture—as though he were ready to beat the shit out of some hypothetical online trolls—was any indication.

Rushing forward, not wanting him to leave before I could apologize, I gripped his arms. "I'm sorry. I'm so sorry. I shouldn't have said that about being—about being greedy. I'm sorry."

He continued glaring at me, his breathing not labored, but not steady either. "Did Amelia tell you?"

"Tell me what?"

His hands came to my waist, his eyes searching. "About my family?"

"No. She's never talked about your family. Why?" Then a jolt of alarm had me blurting, "She didn't tell you about mine, did she?"

He shook his head.

Thank goodness.

The line of his shoulders eased, a tiny lowering of his guard, but I took it as a good sign. Hesitating for a second, I hugged him. Tightly. His posture told me I'd surprised him, how he held himself away, and I slammed my eyes shut, silently begging him to relax into the embrace.

His hands at my waist lingered, but then he opened his palms and slid them around my back, wrapping me in his arms as well.

"I'm sorry," I repeated.

His chest rose and fell with a sigh. "Don't be sorry."

"Don't tell me what to do."

His hand at the center of my back flexed and I felt his small laugh, the tension fully releasing from his bones. "Your hair smells terrible."

I smiled at that, my cheek curving against his chest. "It does, doesn't it?" Leaning back so I could see his face but keeping my arms locked around his torso, I peered up at him. "I am sorry."

"If you need me to say it, you are forgiven."

Holding his magnificent stare, I decided I needed to be honest with him. But since I couldn't fully escape my ingrained habits, I tightened my arms in mock punishment and tried to make my feelings sound like a joke. "You make me so mad when you say things like I don't know my own worth. I know my worth. See how strong I am?"

If I could ignore the comments, then so could he.

His eyelids lowered by half, telling me he was not impressed, not with my attempts to squeeze his muscular body into submission, nor with my assertion that I knew and appreciated my worth.

"If you say so."

I made a growling sound. "I do. You have to trust me. I don't let those comments get to me at all."

"You shouldn't have to deal with them in the first place." His hand lifted to my hairline and fiddled with the plastic.

"Don't worry about it. I'm sure they'll die down soon."

His body stiffened, his eyes cutting to mine. He blinked. "What?"

"The comments. They'll stop soon."

Byron's hands closed over my arms and gently guided me away. "Wait. What are we talking about? What will die down soon?"

"The—" I snapped my mouth shut. Apparently, Byron didn't know. He hadn't seen the comments, at least not the deluge of recent comments within the last two weeks. "Uh . . ."

His eyes narrowed with suspicion and his focus went blurry, giving me the sense he was replaying our conversation, searching for clues.

I twisted my fingers, shifting my weight between my feet. *Time to change the subject.* "We should rinse out the dye."

Sending me a quick, hard look, Byron turned and pulled out his phone in one smooth movement. His *smart*phone.

My heart jumped to my throat, and I reached around him to grab the phone. "Don't—"

He held me away. And when I made another grab for it, he stepped on top of my bed like it was a six-inch stair instead of a mattress three and a half feet off the ground. Soon we were playing king of the mountain, him gently shoving me off each time I tried to summit it.

"Byron. Don't." My throat tight with anxiety, I fought to put force into it. "Seriously, it's time to rinse my hair."

"Go ahead," he said, his attention on his phone. "You don't need me to . . ." His eyes widened. Then they narrowed. Then his lips parted, the veins in his forehead and neck suddenly in stark relief under his pale skin.

I covered my face with my hands. "Crap."

As diligent as I'd been about deleting the nasty comments and blocking the accounts, it was like playing whack-a-mole. I knew, without a doubt, what he found, what he currently read.

If haters and trolls applied their perseverance and determination to solving world hunger, we'd all be well-fed.

The springs on the bed made a sound, and I let my arms drop. He was now on the ground and had looked up from the phone. But his eyes weren't on me, and he seemed to be struggling to hold on to his composure.

"Hey. Hey. It's—"

"Don't say it's okay."

I balled my hands into fists, grimacing. "It's not okay. But it is what it is. And I'm not letting it bother me. You shouldn't either."

He pinched his lower lip with his thumb and forefinger over and over, squeezing and releasing.

"Byron. Please."

Glassy eyes sliced to mine, and beneath the fury I saw sorrow. "They're hurting you." His voice, low and quiet, shook.

I blinked against a rush of liquid emotion and covered his hand holding the phone with mine, gently prying it from his fingers. "They're not. I don't let them. Please don't let them hurt you either."

The contact spread warmth through my body and I had to resist the urge to touch him elsewhere, pull him close, pepper his face and neck with kisses.

He shook his head, refusing to look at me, and said nothing. I suspected he couldn't speak, not yet.

I took his phone. "Now I'm going to order a gluten-free feast and wash my hair. And you're going to open a bottle of Amelia's wine. And then we're going to drink and eat well. And do you know why?"

Throat working to swallow, he gave his head a quick shake.

"Some people are going to hate no matter what we do or who I try to be, so I might as well just be myself. Our job isn't to stress about them or please them, it's to ignore them and nullify their squeaky wheels by being awesome. Or—" Unable to stop myself from touching him this time, give him some comfort, I reached up and cupped his cheek. He immediately covered my hand with his, pressing it to his jaw and leaning into my touch "We drink champagne and watch their hater heads explode when our successes far outpace their poison. And then we let them choke on it."

CHAPTER 22
WINNIE

"Last day of school, baby!" I smacked Amelia on the butt as I ran into the kitchen from the front door. Then I did a lap of our tiny apartment, Rocky Balboa style.

"Woot!" She grabbed her phone and clicked through a few screens. Soon, the theme music to *Rocky* played over her cell's speaker. "And, *surprise*, you should be receiving a call next week about the community manager position interview."

"What?" I jumped up and down. "So soon? That's great!"

Finally.

Jeez. I felt such relief. After all the ups and downs with those videos and my social media accounts, the hard work was paying off.

She shimmied to the music. "You should celebrate!"

I felt so pumped, so ready for the summer. "I think I will!"

In addition to the awesome news about the upcoming community manager interview, my school's Parent-Teacher Organization had agreed to let me do a summer auction for the science fair materials as long as I secured all the items myself, wrapped it up before the start of the new school year, and didn't solicit any parents to donate anything or buy anything. I'd submitted a bunch of grants, but I didn't want to take for *granted* (Ha! Pun intended) that any of them would get funded.

Now I simply needed to find items for the auction. Over the summer. Without asking any parents for help. But I'd figure it out!

Amelia turned as I jogged past again and gave me a high five. "You should make a fancy dinner tonight."

"Wait, don't you have plans with Elijah?" I studied her attire: black dress, silk wrap, stockings.

Amelia walked to the kitchen table and grabbed her purse. "I'm about to go. But I don't need to be here for you to make fancy food."

"You're right. I think I will."

"And see if Byron can come over and share your fancy dinner."

I stopped running and instead danced in place, punching the air. "You know what? I think I will."

What the heck, why not? After dyeing my hair on Friday, Byron had left, not staying for a gluten-free feast. I'd let him go, not taking his need for space personally. Serena had come over and we'd roused a dozing Amelia for a game of *Stardew Valley* while they admired my new hair.

But Byron and I were officially friends now. We'd spent time together almost every night this week even though we hadn't recorded any new videos. Another fundamental shift had occurred in our interactions—a really good shift as far as I was concerned—and I attributed it not only to our honest conversations that night, but also to my physical avoidance of his body.

The notion had occurred to me last Saturday over breakfast while reading an article about imprinting via touch and smell. When Byron and I had met up later that day, I'd put my theory to the test and kept my distance. *Success!*

My heart still hammered out of my chest whenever he entered the room, my neck grew hot, and my stomach swirled. But something about erecting this boundary, promising myself I wouldn't touch him, and maintaining physical distance between us, significantly dulled the sting of both my biology and my feelings. It was as though moving him into an off-limits category made our interactions easier, and this mental shift was supported by the new physical boundary.

Tenable friendship boundaries for the Win!

"And then while he's here, you might as well film another challenge video." Amelia fiddled with the gold bracelet at her wrist. "You should try to amass as many followers as you can before the interview, get as close to 500k as possible."

I nodded in time to the music, liking this idea. "I think we will."

There were still six videos left to do, half of which gave me heart palpitations each time my thoughts strayed in their direction: the Toxic Dance

Challenge, the Leggings Challenge, and the Kiss Your Crush Challenge. How ironic that the last of these had gone from being 100 percent disingenuous to 100 percent accurate.

"And then hang out with him. Watch a movie. Whatever."

"I think we will." I raised my hands in the air.

"Maybe have some sex."

"I think we w—" My feet stilled as soon as I processed her words. Arms dropping, I glared at my friend. "Very funny."

As I'd predicted, Amelia had been teasing me all week about Byron, making suggestive remarks, placing a lingerie catalog on my nightstand. I loved her, but she was making me bonkers.

"That wasn't a joke." Amelia hiked her purse higher up her shoulder. "Seduce him. It's finally summer. Now is the time to get on it."

"If you have some information to share, some concrete insight into Byron's feelings that would inspire me to take action, please do share it."

"For God's sake, take a chance. What's the worst that could happen?"

Grunting, I turned away from her and paced over to the bags I'd left by the front door. She clearly didn't comprehend the situation.

Even before last week, even when I'd been flailing around, trying to put up boundaries that didn't work, Byron had started to feel like an essential person in my life, and so much more than just a good friend. He'd become a top-tier important friend, one I would mourn for a long time if I lost him. I refused to gamble with or do anything to jeopardize our friendship.

As much as I continued to crush on him every time he opened his brilliant mouth, I would not risk this relationship we'd built unless I was absolutely, 100 percent, without-a-single-doubt certain Byron wanted and craved and daydreamed about me just as much as I did about him.

But absent that? Nope.

"You are being a scaredy cat," Amelia called after me.

"MEOW."

She made a sound of pure frustration. "Sooner or later you're going to have to risk it all if you want to live a full life. I can't give you a shortcut. You need to learn how to trust all on your own, without being certain. Uncertainty in a relationship continues after the *I love yous*. You must learn how to operate on faith if you want it to last."

I hated how well she knew me, but—on this point—I was immovable.

"Are you listening to me? Take this first step blindly or you'll be paralyzed whenever you encounter a stumbling block. Nothing is ever certain. There is no concrete flooring in matters of the heart. It's all sand."

"You mean quicksand," I grumbled, lugging my belongings to the couch and removing the contents. It was weird to have this conversation while the theme to *Rocky* played in the background.

"I'm just saying"—her eyebrows arched and she shrugged—"there are condoms in my top drawer. Take as many as you need."

I exhaled a short laugh and waved her away. "All right, get out of here, funny lady."

"I won't be home tonight or tomorrow night, so please consider making some risky choices while you have the place to yourself," she said, and then she was gone, taking the *Rocky* music with her.

Knowing Amelia, she'd probably play it on repeat during the entire walk to Elijah's.

Bags now completely empty, I picked through the items I'd brought home, sorting and categorizing materials I hadn't gone through yet in my haste to clean out my classroom, and I debated what to make for dinner. I had chicken in the freezer that needed to be cooked, but tonight didn't feel like a chicken night. It felt like a king salmon night, with saffron butter sauce, braised asparagus, and a good bottle of pinot noir. *Yes.*

These were all things I could get from Pike Place while also visiting Serena at her tea booth.

Decision made, I grabbed two reusable shopping bags and started for the door. This wasn't a dinner that fit inside my budget, but if everything went as planned, the community manager position would not only allow me to pay back my student loans, but it would also enable me to actually save money. Maybe I'd be able to afford a place of my own in the city. Nothing fancy, a simple studio would suffice. But then Amelia could move out without worrying I'd be left in a lurch.

These were the thoughts running through my head when I opened my door and found Byron standing on the landing, his hand raised as though poised to knock.

"Oh!" I stepped back, grinning at this pleasant surprise. "Hey!"

He lifted two shopping bags. "I'm here to make you dinner."

"You are?" We hadn't made any plans. Last night, after leaving the art museum, I'd said I would call him this weekend, and that's where we'd left it.

His eyes moved over my shoulder before returning to mine. "May I come in?"

"Yes. Absolutely." At first I stepped to the side and out of his way, but then thought better of it. If he walked past, he might accidentally brush against me, or touch me, and I simply could not have that. So I held the door open with my fingertips until he crossed the threshold, and then I turned and walked ahead of him. "You must've been reading my brain waves. I was just about to text you to see if you wanted to come over for dinner. And then I was going to hop a bus to Pike Place."

"I just left there."

I stood on the family room side of the counter while Byron filled the kitchen side, removing items from bags, handing over a bottle of wine for me to open, and pulling ingredients from our pantry. We fell into easy conversation as he showed me what he'd brought for dinner, which included cod, asparagus, and a flourless, gluten-free chocolate cake from Nuflours.

"And scones for tomorrow." He lifted a white paper bag, showed it to me, and then placed it next to my teapot to the left of the range.

"You thought of everything." I removed the foil wrapping from the top of the wine bottle. "And this is eerily similar to the dinner I had planned. Except for cod, I was thinking salmon. But black cod is my favorite, so no complaints."

"Great minds think alike," he muttered, the entirety of his attention focused on prepping the garlic.

The wine open, I eyed the small space in the kitchen and how much of it his body—just by virtue of being himself—had claimed. "Hand me two wineglasses and I'll pour. What can I do to help? Do you want me to mince the garlic?"

"No. Sit. Relax. Talk to me." Byron spun while he spoke, retrieving pots and pans, knives and cutting boards, and finally two wineglasses for me to fill.

"Let me see. I have some good news."

He glanced at me, lifting an eyebrow. "Let's hear it."

"I don't know if I've told you about this, but I need to find a way to fund the science fair. I brought it back three years ago, and it's been so great. And the way I do it, the kids complete their entire project during class time, the parents don't have to buy any materials or get involved. You should see the students' faces when they present their posters." I clasped my hands over my chest, remembering their precious excitement. "It's like being back at a scientific conference, except every experiment is interesting and none of the presenters are blowhards."

He laughed, not looking up from the asparagus he cut. "Oh yeah?"

"Yes! One kid did this experiment on the amount of glucose in different kinds of apples, hypothesizing that the sweeter the apple, the more glucose. It was darling, and so relevant, and now we know the answer."

"I'd like to see his methods. How did he define sweetness?"

Pulling out a stool, I sat and leaned my elbows on the kitchen peninsula. "We did a survey in the class, all the kids sampled apple slices and rated the sweetness. It was double-blind."

He laughed again, lifting his eyes to mine this time. "No way."

"Yes way. I cut the skins off, so you couldn't tell what the outside looked like, placed the pieces in Petri dishes labeled A, B, C, and so forth. And I funded the whole thing—the apples, the Petri dishes, the posterboards, everything—using my Academic Olympics fundraiser." I heaved a sad sigh. "But the Parent-Teacher Organization wants to use that fundraiser to help buy new computers for the lab this year." My gaze returned to his and found him studying me.

"Please don't tell me you're paying for it yourself."

I mock-glared at him. "No. They gave me permission to do an auction over the summer."

"Nice. So the parents will pay for it."

Tilting my wine to the side, I studied its color. "Well, no. I can't ask parents to donate items or buy anything. But I'll figure it out."

"And that's good news?" He sounded skeptical, like he didn't understand why any of this would make me happy.

"Yes. Absolutely. Prior to today, I thought I'd have to rely on grants to pay for it or have to cancel it."

"What? No." He frowned. "You can't cancel it. And arranging an auction with the odds stacked against you is a complete waste of your time. I'll donate the money."

I scoffed. Loudly. "No, you won't. I didn't tell you about this so you would give me the money."

"Yes, I will. I'm not giving you money. I'm giving it to the science fair."

"No."

"You don't tell me what to do." He smirked, setting the asparagus aside, a lilting dare edging his voice and making sparkles twirl in my stomach.

I gripped my glass tighter, standing from the stool and pacing to the family room, putting distance between us. "I'm not taking your money and I don't want you offering it, not ever again. Okay?"

Byron leaned his hands on the counter, his lips pressed together in a line, and he considered me for a long moment beneath scowling eyebrows. "Listen, Fred. You have proven repeatedly that you are more than capable of taking care of everything yourself. Congratulations on never needing anyone. Just like I am more than happy living my life in complete seclusion, never needing anyone. But, given the option to change our situations, why wouldn't we?"

I opened my mouth, poised to ask a question, but I wasn't quite following his logic or what his point was.

He straightened, crossing his arms. "Look at it this way: is it difficult for you to spend time with me?"

"No."

"There you go."

"There I go? There I go what?"

"It's just as easy for me to donate money so the kids can have their science fair. I donate a percentage of my income every year anyway. I'll ask my manager to change the allocation so that some of it comes to your school. Same thing."

"It's really not." How could he not see the difference?

Byron stared at me over the rim of his glass as he took a sip, his eyes narrowing as he set it down. "Actually, you know what? You're right. Your time has more value than money. Money is money, one twenty-dollar bill is worth the same as any other. But your time is unique to you. It can't be exchanged for someone else's time. There is no substitute."

"So what you're saying is, my time is priceless?"

Taking up the knife again, Byron smashed the garlic clove with the flat side. "Whatever transcends pricelessness, your time is that."

"Nice try. The flattery is adorable and appreciated, but I'm still not going to allow you to—nay!—I *forbid* you from donating your money to the school."

"You forbid me?" Amusement behind his gaze, his voice dropped an octave.

"Yes," I said with forced stiffness. When he looked at me with this particular expression, it always felt like a caress, and it always got me hot. I didn't think the effect was purposeful—in fact, I knew it wasn't since he gave Amelia a similar look when he thought she was funny—but I couldn't help my body's reaction to the look any more than I could control its overall reaction to him.

He nodded once and turned. "Fine."

"Really?"

"Yep." Butter now in hand, he returned to the cutting board and concentrated on removing the wrapper.

I squinted at him. "What do you mean, *fine?*"

"I won't donate my money to the school."

"And you're not allowed to bid on any of the auction items either. Promise me."

"I promise I will not donate my money to the school, for the science fair or any other reason, nor will I bid on any of the auction items. Happy?"

I nodded, but . . . Was I? Was I happy? If I'd simply accepted his help, I'd be done. No need for an auction. No need for another project this summer. No need to run around, visiting local businesses, trying to convince them to donate items.

Despite my errant thoughts, I said, "Very."

His eyebrow ticked up, but he said nothing. I doubted I'd convinced him. I hadn't even convinced myself.

CHAPTER 23
WINNIE

"I take it you enjoyed the fish." Byron eyed my empty plate, wiped clean with a piece of gluten-free bread I'd retrieved from the cupboard.

I dusted my hands off. "Another sample might be required before I can definitively analyze the data." At one point, I'd been tempted to pick up the plate and lick his lemon butter caper sauce directly from the ceramic surface. The only thing that kept me from giving into the temptation was the fact that I liked the sweater I wore and I didn't want to get butter on it.

Byron's mouth curved. "There's none left. You ate it all."

"So I did. I guess you'll just have to make it again tomorrow. For science."

He laughed, and I loved his laugh, so rumbly and real. It gave me a moment to simply look at him, admire Byron without feeling like I was rudely staring or being inappropriate.

We were on our second bottle of wine—that's right, he'd had more than just one glass—and I was feeling good, full, satiated with delicious food and great company. We'd discussed all manner of things, from his theories on the Bronze Age Collapse to why we agreed dark chocolate was so much better than milk chocolate, and I'd asked a lot of questions just so I could hear his voice.

He'd given his brilliant thoughts freely and, if such a thing were possible, I would've soaked them up with a piece of bread, much like I'd done to the addictive lemon butter caper sauce.

"Now that you've spent a week with the color, how do you like your hair?"

"I like it," I said lightly, but it was a lie.

After a week of living with the blond, I decided I loved it. I loved it so much. The kit had come with toning colors, and the variation he'd added looked professional.

The epically awesome dye job plus this evening's supremely delicious dinner plus everything else I knew about him meant I was beginning to believe Byron when he'd said that he could do anything. If he wanted something, it would be his.

"Will you keep dyeing it?"

I pretended to think the question over and deflected. "Let me guess, you prefer my natural color."

"No." His attention moved to the top of my head, down to my shoulder, and then to my upper arm where my hair ended just above my elbow.

"No?"

"No." Byron looked away and rested his forearm on the table, his long fingers fiddling with the stem of his wineglass. "I like your natural color. But I also like it this way."

"Huh."

"You sound surprised."

"I guess I am. So, and I know I'm not supposed to, but I have to ask, why did you want a photo of me?"

His features grew contemplative, and I felt certain he wouldn't answer.

But then he said, "I like to capture the moment before things change. For most people, their life isn't like a book, they can't go back and read their favorite parts. I figured this out . . . too late for some memories. Now I take photos before things change and I write down my thoughts, memories associated with the present before the future comes to take them away."

I smiled as he spoke, falling deeper into my extreme crush, and I sighed dreamily when he finished with his explanation. See? His thought sauce was delicious.

"And you want to remember my hair?"

"I do." He inclined his head once.

"Can I ask why?"

Byron smirked, his eyes taunting. "No."

I mock-frowned, mock-glaring at him.

His smirk became a small smile. "But maybe one day, if you're really nice to me, I'll let you read what I wrote next to the picture."

"So, next week?"

He laughed, and his laugh made me feel like I was floating. I allowed the sound to flow over and around me, soaking that up too.

"How about . . ." he pressed his index finger to his bottom lip. "In ten years?"

"Deal. But you can't change what you were going to write because now you know I'll read it."

"I won't." He sounded so certain, so unconcerned, it filled me with disgruntlement. I supposed some part of me—a big part—had hoped what he wrote would be salacious enough that he'd want to keep it private.

And perhaps it was the disgruntlement that drove me to say, "You have too many rules about what I can and cannot ask you."

"Fine." Byron reached for the wine bottle and refilled his glass. Mine was still full. "Ask me anything and I'll answer it, but it can't be about the photo."

Oh! Well. This was an opportunity and a treat. And not one to be squandered.

"Just remember"—I raised a finger in warning— "you said *anything*."

Now saying nothing at all, he looked at me like he was completely unconcerned while I contemplated and ranked all the possible questions I wanted to ask. For some reason, his words from earlier played through my head juxtaposed against Amelia's rant before she'd left.

". . . given the option to change our situations, why wouldn't we?"

"Sooner or later you're going to have to risk it all if you want to live a full life."

Fueled by these remarks, I asked, "You claimed once that you liked me. A lot."

"Correct," he said, taking the question in stride, still appearing unconcerned.

"And then you claimed that you didn't particularly wish to."

"Also correct."

"Then when did you start liking me? And why did you always act like you couldn't stand me?"

His smile fell. Completely. "I'm not answering that."

"You said anything. You promised." I held up a finger between us, my eyes wide and serious.

He stared forward, the line of his mouth unhappy. "It's not as though I told you I love you, or asked for your hand in marriage, for Christ's sake. Is it so hard to believe that I have a preoccupation with you?"

"Me? Yes. Absolutely."

"Why?"

I didn't have to think about the question too hard before the answer came to me. "When we first met, you ignored me. You—"

"I didn't know you."

"So you didn't like me when we met?"

"I didn't like you, I didn't not like you. As I said, I didn't know you." He sounded so logical, so reasonable.

"Then what did you think? When we first met?"

"You seemed . . . fine." His hand on the table turned palm up.

"Fine?"

"Regular."

I absorbed the word like a punch, reflexively rubbing my sternum, and repeated, "Regular." *Ugh.*

"Yes."

Jeez. Now I wished I'd never asked. *But in for a penny, in for a metric ton.*

"Then all of the sudden, what? You had a *Dawson's Creek* or a *He's All That* moment where I showed up in a prom dress instead of overalls and wore contacts instead of glasses?"

His gaze swung to mine and told me that he found my question absurd. "There was no thunderstrike moment, Fred."

"Then tell me, when did I stop being 'regular'?"

"When you weren't," he said simply, like it was simple.

"Is that supposed to be a riddle? 'When is a person not average? When she isn't.'"

"No. It's a fact. Every time I saw you, you were consistently yourself. The glimpses added together until they multiplied exponentially."

"So what you're saying is, my personality is a logarithmic scale? I'm assuming base ten?" Yes, I was making jokes. No, they weren't for Byron's sake, he seemed fine. They were for mine.

"If you want to use that analogy, sure. You—taken as a whole person—are a Fibonacci sequence, the golden ratio, when you were unguarded and not actively gritting your teeth or rolling your eyes whenever I entered a room."

Oh yikes!

A twinge of guilt prodded just beneath my ribcage. "You noticed that?"

"The eye-rolling? The overt disdain? The seething rage and gnashing of teeth each time I spoke?" The right side of his mouth—the side that always seemed so poised to curl into a sneer—tugged upward in an amused, dare I say, teasing smile. "Why? Were you trying to hide it?"

"No," I answered, guilt ballooning. "I wasn't trying to—"

"Hurt me? I know. I. . ." His focus dimmed, the smile waning from his features. "I just have that effect on people. You aren't unusual in that regard."

Goodness, that hurt my heart, and I searched my brain for something to say that might contradict his self-assessment, something that also wasn't a lie or condescending or reeking of pity.

He held up a hand. "It doesn't matter. At the risk of telling you what to do, please, don't let it bother you. I'm content, and I'm incapable of being anyone other than myself."

"Byron—"

"My point is"— he spoke over me—"when you thought I wasn't watching, or present in the room, you were simply yourself. That's how I came to know you and . . . like you."

"By watching me?" I shifted in my seat, thinking back to all the times over six years that had added up to his current estimation of my character.

"Over time. It is possible to know a person by observing them."

"And what do you know about me? Through these powers of observation but no interaction." What made someone likable to Byron Visser?

"You are a thoughtful, wickedly intelligent, strong, brave, sweet, extremely funny woman with excellent taste in books, music, and art, and a determination to always do what is right and good, even when it's difficult."

"Oh." *Well.*

"You're also foolishly kindhearted."

I felt my expression wilt.

"And make choices that benefit others at the expense of yourself."

Now I held up a hand. "You can stop."

"Over and over, you do this. It's maddening, to be someone on the sidelines, watching this happen—"

"Thanks, like I said, you can stop."

He lifted his glass toward me in a careless gesture. "I doubt I'm the only person who thinks of you this way."

"What? As a pushover?"

"No. As extraordinary."

I gasped—short and sharp and silent—my lashes fluttering, and then found I had to chase my breath. There he went again, saying something wonderful right after being irritating. At times, talking to him was like riding a roller coaster.

"I'm probably one of several hundred thousand. Especially since you expose yourself to public comment," he muttered, obviously speaking to himself. "How much of a shock could my preoccupation have been? Why else would I seek you out so much?"

"You sought me out?" I sent him a side-eye, losing the battle against a disbelieving laugh. "Prior to spring break, I hadn't seen you in weeks."

"Ahh. But you did *see* me."

That made me laugh for real. More precisely, how he'd said it—the half smile, the crooked eyebrow, the deadpan delivery—made me laugh. He was right. I did see him every few weeks or months, which was more than any of our other college friends—except Amelia and Jeff—could claim.

He sipped his wine, and we fell into a friendly silence while I considered what my curiosity had gained me.

And what it cost me.

Staring unseeingly forward, I couldn't help but notice his recitation of my finer qualities neglected to mention my exterior, what I looked like. He'd said nothing about being attracted to my body, my face, or any other physical part of me. My mind drifted to our conversation at his house weeks ago when he'd made me steak and mushrooms, specifically when he'd talked about noticing a person's exterior—face, body, voice, and so forth. I knew he noticed exterior attractiveness.

However, he'd also just said, when he saw me for the first time, he'd thought of me as *regular.*

"What's going on over there?"

I blinked him back into focus. "Pardon?"

"What's on your mind?" He leaned back in his chair, setting his napkin on the table next to his plate while he openly examined me. "As I said, if you want to know something, just ask."

Hmm. . .

Was I going to be that person who fished for compliments on their exterior and asked *Hey, do you think I'm pretty?*

I grimaced, deciding that if I had to ask, I probably wouldn't like the answer, no matter what he said. If he said no, obviously I wouldn't like it. If he said yes, it would feel stale and forced since I'd had to ask.

Frustrated, I told myself it didn't matter, that I should value his words about me being extraordinary, and kind, and strong—attributes that were more or less an active choice on my part—more than a statement about the accident of my face and body, something genetics mostly dictated, and I only possessed slight influence over.

But it did matter.

As much as I admired and was attracted to Byron's kindness and strength and intelligence and thoughtfulness, and I wanted him for those attributes, I also wanted his body. I wanted to touch it, lick it, taste it, and have my way with it. And, thus far, he'd never given me any sign that he felt similarly for me.

Apart from that one time when we were on the couch and he looked at me like—wait. We'd been filming.

What about when he did the Opposites Attract—nope. Filming.

Oh! Or last week when he dyed my hair and—no. We'd also been filming then.

How about . . . I frowned.

I couldn't think of a single time he'd ever looked at me or behaved in any way but with platonic interest *except* when we were recording videos.

"Okay." I crossed my arms, deciding on a course of action that would settle the matter once and for all. "Let me ask you this. How much of the videos are pretend?"

He'd been reaching for his wineglass when I asked the question and froze mid-movement, his gaze growing cagey. "Be more specific."

Hmm . . .

"All right. When we're recording the video challenges—like the first one we did, where I sat on your lap, or the opposites attract one—were you acting?"

Wineglass in hand, his forehead wrinkled like my question confused him. "Yes, obviously."

I straightened my spine to counteract the plummeting of my stomach. "Yes?"

"Yes."

Grabbing my wine, I drank more than a sip, but not quite a mouthful. "You're a really good actor."

He'd been acting the whole time?

Byron, still looking at me like I perplexed him, set his glass down without drinking from it. "Isn't that what we agreed? Aren't we both acting in the videos?"

"Yes." The word came out scratchy, so I cleared my throat. "That's what we agreed."

Byron's gaze turned searching, which made me think something about my expression concerned him. I forced a smile, but that only made him frown.

"Fred. If we were not acting, we wouldn't record them at all. We act in the videos. We're not acting now."

"Mmm." I nodded noncommittally. I was definitely acting right now, or at least trying to. I was also blushing, I felt cold, and my stomach churned.

I got the sense he continued to address this subject because he could see I was having a difficult time with his responses. Maybe he wanted to make certain I understood him. Or maybe he wanted to be sure we were on the same page.

"Right. You are acting. We agreed we would be acting. The whole thing is an act. I get it." I nodded, twisting the hem of my napkin.

"Fred."

"Yes?" I gave him my eyes.

His eyes narrowed on me. "Aren't you acting in the videos?"

"Of course. I mean—" I scratched the back of my neck, not wanting to admit the truth but feeling compelled to since he'd been nothing but honest with me "—when we were at your place and we did the movie lap one, and then that other video that one time, I actually forgot we were filming." I gave him a self-deprecating smile, my cheeks burning hotter, and hoping he didn't call me out for being vague.

He leaned back in his chair, the intensity of his gaze, his interest, amplifying, like he found this information doubtful. "Did you? Really?"

"Yes. Toward the end, when you had your head on my lap and I was playing with your hair. It was relaxing. Nice. And I forgot."

"Huh." His eyes seemed to study me and then lost focus.

I didn't want him thinking too much about my admission, so I interrupted his thoughts. "Have you—uh—ever forgotten we were being filmed? For one of the videos?"

He didn't hesitate. "Never."

"I see," I croaked, lifting my glass to drink more of the wine but then thought better of it.

There you go, Win. There's your answer.

Byron wouldn't lie. He'd been acting. The whole time. Everything we'd recorded had been part of an act—the way he looked at me, when he'd dipped me, when he'd placed his head in my lap, when we'd shared that stare in the mirror of the bathroom. *Acting. Acting. Acting.*

I wasn't surprised, not really, and so I didn't know why I felt a sense of such brutal disappointment. But I did.

The silence between us started to shift from contemplative to awkward, so I shot up from my seat and grabbed my plate. Then I grabbed his. "Hey, so, speaking of the challenges, I do think we need to discuss New York."

New York was a safe topic, very safe. It was business instead of feelings. I would deal with these messy feelings later. Much, much later. *Or maybe never.*

And another thing, I was so glad—so enormously glad—I hadn't taken Amelia's advice and done something stupid tonight, like take a risk.

I walked the short distance to the sink and deposited the dishes, patting myself on the back for my caution. Caution for the win and the Win.

"What does New York have to do with the challenges?" Byron's grumpy tone helped me focus. He was clearly irritated about something, probably the idea of recording in New York when he was already apprehensive about the interviews.

"Well, one of the last challenges is me surprising you on a long-distance trip." Returning to the table to grab our utensils, I picked up his fork, then mine. "At first I thought we might do something camping related around here. But we already have New York on the calendar, so could we pretend I'm surprising you there? I doubt your part would be more than one minute, tops."

"I guess we could."

I wasn't looking at him, but he sounded distracted.

"I know you didn't want to talk about these ahead of time or stage them, but discussing this one makes sense." Loading my hands up with flatware and serving dishes, I walked back to the sink, slow and steady.

"It does makes sense." The sound of his chair scraping against the floor sent a shiver up my spine.

Instead of returning to the kitchen table, I detoured toward the family room and began to pace in front of the TV. "I'll be flying out by myself anyway, meeting you there, so I'll record some stuff during the flight. When I get to the hotel, I'll let you know and you can pretend to be surprised when I knock on your door. And then the rest of the trip will progress as normal. Speaking of which, do you have an agenda? Or a list of events?"

"I'll have my agent send it over."

"Do you think we could do a few of the other challenges while we're out there? It's not important to do them all, but Amelia was saying it would be good to post a few more before the interview. I'm supposed to be getting a call this week about the job, but the actual interview isn't until after our July trip." Talking about this—schedules and agendas and plans—definitely helped distract me from my distress and shake off the residue of disappointment.

"Which ones?"

"Let me see . . ." Not wanting to look for my planner with the original notes, I picked up my phone from the charging station and pulled up the Google doc that Amelia and I had worked on together.

~~*1- #BestfriendCheckIn / #OppositesAttract: Highlight how different you are from your bestfriend to prove that opposites attract and then dance in a circle while holding hands, camera facing up.*~~

~~*2- #VideoGameDistraction: Sitting on lap while playing video game challenge, bestfriend/crush.*~~

3- #ToxicDanceChallenge: Do the dance from "Toxic" (Britney Spears) to the music with your bestfriend.

~~*4- #AsleepChallenge: Pretend to be asleep when your bestfriend walks in, record what she/he does next.*~~

5- #BestfriendFashionChallenge / #MatchingOutfits: Change outfits, all match, jumping between each change.

~~*6- #MovieHeadRestChallenge: Lay your head in your partner's/crush's lap while watching a movie and record reaction.*~~

7- #TravelSurpriseChallenge: Surprise your bestfriend crush by traveling a long distance to visit her/him, record the reaction.

8- #KissYourCrush: Kiss your crush or secret crush / bestfriend and record the reaction.

9- #LeggingsChallenge: Wear the trending leggings for your partner/crush and record his/her reaction.

10- #WhisperASecret: Whisper a secret into your bestfriend's ear and record reaction.

Reading the list, I had difficulty swallowing. Making matters worse, Byron had come to stand next to me and currently read over my shoulder.

"We have—uh—three, five, and seven through ten left." Clearing my throat, I tried my best not to notice how great he smelled, or how lovely and warm his body felt pressed against my side. Nor did I turn my head to look at him. His face was too close.

As soon as I could, I would step out of his space. Enforcing my no-touching boundary seemed like the best thing I could do for my mental health.

"The Leggings Challenge," he said, sounding distracted. "Do you have the leggings?"

The question brought me up short. “What do you know about the Leggings Challenge?”

“You didn’t answer my question.” He stepped to the side and walked around me to the kitchen. Once there, he turned on the faucet and proceeded to wash the dishes.

My gaze followed the long line of him, the curve of his backside, the taper of his waist. “I have the leggings.” I knew we were just friends—and given what had just transpired during dinner, we’d only ever be just friends—but that didn’t mean I couldn’t engage in the consumption of eye candy from time to time.

Byron Visser was the Swiss chocolate of eye candy. I could be a good friend to him and still think he was sexy as Hades and twice as broody.

“Do you want to do that one tonight?”

“What?” My eyes jumped up just as he twisted his torso at the waist. I said a silent prayer of thanks that I hadn’t been caught admiring his butt.

“If you have the leggings, we could do that one tonight. I’ll do the dishes. You go change.”

“I thought you didn’t want to know when they were going to happen?”

He tilted his head back and forth, as though considering his response, facing the sink again. “With that one, it might be nice to have a heads-up.”

“The leggings video?” I wrinkled my nose.

“Yes.” He glanced over his shoulder.

I made a face and drifted a little closer to my bedroom. “What? Why?”

Now he made a face, and I suspected it was meant to be a teasing reflection of mine. But all he did was grunt.

“Oh? *Reeeeally*?” I pretended like I’d interpreted his grunt. “How fascinating. Now I see your point.”

He grunted again and turned his attention back to the dishes.

“Well then.” I walked to my bedroom. “How can I argue with that? I guess I’ll just get those bad boys on.”

CHAPTER 24
WINNIE

Shutting the door behind me, I exhaled a dry laugh and rubbed my sternum again. Now that I was alone, it hurt.

Don't think about it. I wouldn't think about it.

Focus on the positive. I would focus on the positive.

Be grateful you have such a great friend. I would . . .

I blinked against a rush of tears and scrunched my face. "No, no, no. You are not allowed to feel this way. You will not be upset that Byron Visser isn't besotted with the accident of your genetics. You will get over it."

Nodding several times and breathing in and out deeply, I walked to my closet and hunted through the pile on the floor. I found the leggings—still in plastic—and retrieved them. During the busy end of the school year, I hadn't found a spare minute to try them on. This would be the first moment I beheld myself in the magical leggings.

I tossed the package to the bed and pulled off my cargo pants. Then, on a whim, I also pulled off my sweater, which left me in a white tank top, sports bra, and white cotton undies. I turned to the mirror and inspected myself. The sports bra had a hole under the arm and didn't look great. I removed it and replaced it with a pink lace bra I never wore. It wasn't very supportive, and the texture of the lace seemed to show through everything. But, to me, my boobs sure did look fantastic.

I have fantastic boobs. I love myself and my body. And it's okay if Byr—I shook my head, trying again—*if other people don't find me attractive. Because I do.*

There. Sexy bra in place, the tank top went back on.

I then switched out my cotton undies with the pink lace underwear that matched the bra and returned to the bed for the leggings. Just as I was pushing my right leg through, there was a knock.

"Where is your phone?" Byron asked through the door.

I pulled the leggings up and stood from the bed. "Why?"

"I'll set up the shot."

"It's in my backpack, next to the couch. My password is 602214."

There was a pause, a low chuckle, and then, "Avogadro's number."

"It's easy to remember." Glancing in the mirror, I twisted at the waist and checked out my backside. My mouth dropped open. "Holy cow, these leggings are amazing!" I whispered. My butt had never looked better, and I liked my butt. But this was some next-level shapewear. "I look like a porn star."

Damn. I am HOT.

I laughed, loving how I looked, and lifted my eyes to my face. I was smiling. *Good.*

"What did you say?" he asked, sounding farther away.

"Nothing!" I called, breathing in deeply as I continued to admire my body in the leggings and mentally calculating how many I could buy and still afford food this week.

There is someone who will love every part of you, Win. I wrapped my arms around myself and gave me a hug. *And it's perfectly wonderful if it's only me, because I am awesome.*

"Are you recording?" I yelled through the closed door, feeling giddy for some reason.

Actually, I knew why I felt giddy. Byron was so good at these videos, I couldn't wait to see what he decided to do, how he decided to react. I was sure it would be perfect.

Walking over to the door, I opened it a crack. "I don't want to leave the room until I know you're recording."

"Here . . . now I'm recording. You can come out."

I hesitated, glancing down at my tank top, the pink bra, the magical leggings, and my bare feet. "Where are you?"

"Sitting on the couch."

"Okay."

I took a deep breath, pushed my hair behind my shoulders, and fully opened the door. I spotted his feet first as I came around the corner, crossed at the ankle. Then his calves, knees, and thighs before he came entirely into view.

His attention was focused on the TV, his arms along the back of the couch, and then he lifted his gaze as I said, "Ta-da!"

Byron's eyes widened, his lips parting. Then his eyes widened even further as they trailed down my body, starting at my chest where I held my arms away and continuing downward. I twisted to one side, then the other. "What do you think?"

He blinked slowly, comically, just once. When he opened his eyes, they were dazed. "Holy—"

"Don't say it!" I lifted a hand and rushed toward him. "Don't say it. Let's keep it PG."

"Too late," he rasped out, then snapped his mouth shut. That look of longing he wore when we filmed made its first appearance, causing sweet butterflies to awake low in my stomach.

Such a good actor.

At the very least, if I ever wanted to see this look again, I could always watch our videos.

"What's supposed to happen now?" he ground out, leaning forward and placing his elbows on his knees. His stare couldn't seem to settle. Meanwhile, I strolled across the room like I was on a catwalk.

"I'm not really sure. I suppose I walk around for a bit and then go take them off."

"Oh God." He covered his face.

"Byron." I stopped mid-stroll, a hand coming to my hip. I hadn't spotted my phone yet, but I trusted he'd set it somewhere that would capture all the action. "You're supposed to look. That's the entire point of the video."

Hands still covering his face, his words were muffled. "I'm not sure I can do that."

I laughed. Hard. Stumbling over to him—because I was laughing so hard—I grabbed his hand, pulled it away from his face and yanked, trying to get him to stand up. "Come on. Look! The whole point is for you to look."

"Not a good idea." His voice was so tight and raspy, he sounded distressed.

I turned so my butt was at his eye level and watched him over my shoulder. "Do they look bad?"

"No." He groaned and closed his eyes.

Through my giggles, I asked, "How can you tell? You have your eyes closed."

"I saw them when you walked in."

"So they look good?" I did a little dance, something like the Toxic Dance Challenge I'd been practicing.

His jaw ticked, eyes still closed. "Depends on your definition of good."

Even though I knew he was acting, I cracked up. "You are hilarious."

"I'm not."

I stepped back, spinning around in a circle. Then I danced a hearty jig. "Admire the magical leggings."

"We should do a different challenge."

I cracked up again, holding my stomach. "Now you're being ridiculous."

"I thought I could handle it." He leaned fully forward, burying his face in his hands again. "I can't. Please, make it stop."

I hoped we were both in the shot. I didn't think we'd be able to reenact the hilarity of this moment again. He may have been pretending, but my uncontrollable laughter was 100 percent solid-gold real. I laughed and laughed, enjoying myself and his performance so much more than I should have.

But as much fun as this was, I figured we were good. We'd recorded enough. Time to get back to real life and real Byron.

"Okay. Okay. Where did you put the phone? I'll put you out of your misery."

Byron motioned to our little TV stand. "It's over there." He leaned back suddenly, opened his eyes, and fastened them to the ceiling.

Giving him one more grin—which he didn't see since he wasn't looking at me—I turned to the phone and sashayed over. Bending at the waist, I lifted my thumb to end the video, but then my eyes caught on Byron on the phone screen.

He was watching me now, eyes zeroed in on my backside, and his expression made me pause. Desire that looked painful set the line of his jaw with a hard edge, his mouth an unhappy slant. In our previous videos, he'd looked at me like he adored me. But right now, he was looking at me like I was a meal. And he was starving.

My heart fluttered, and I swallowed past a sudden pang of sadness. I didn't need to remind myself that he was acting this time. I knew for a fact this was all for show. He'd just literally told me as much after dinner. I knew what was up, and I wouldn't mistake his mad acting skilz for anything but make believe.

But his excellent performance gave me an idea. Why not knock out two challenges tonight while I was still feeling brave and loose? We could complete the main one I'd been dreading and then I'd never have a reason to touch him again. It would be done, and we could move on to the rest of the videos on the list, none of which required my lips anywhere in the vicinity of his lips.

And that's how, instead of stopping the video as I'd planned, I ended up straightening and turning back around. His eyes lifted from where they'd been fastened to my bottom for the benefit of my audience, hooking into mine for a fraction of a second before going cold.

Now that I considered the matter, he always did this after our videos. His gaze dimmed, turned remote along with every aspect of his features.

"Did you get what you need?" he asked, voice rough, barely above a whisper. I doubted it would come through on the recording.

"Not quite." I shook my head, giving him an overexaggerated wink and then shifting my eyes meaningfully to the side toward the phone to let him know I was still filming.

Frowning, he tracked me as I sat on the couch next to him, tucking my legs under me and scooching close. I wondered if I should move the phone to get a better camera angle, but quickly dismissed the thought. This would be fine. Best to get it over with and continue on our friendship path without the ominous cloud of this kiss looming in the distance. What a relief that would be.

Rising to my knees, I smiled softly down at him, my attention fastened to his mouth. If I looked at his beautiful eyes, I'd chicken out. I knew I would.

"Winnie." I watched his Adam's apple rise and fall with a swallow. "What are you—"

"Shh." I pressed a finger to his lusciously full lips and leaned closer. Shifting my palm to his jaw, I cupped it, letting myself enjoy the omnipresent stubble, and angled his chin. *This is the last time I'll hold his face in my hand.*

His breath hitched as I lowered my head. Our lips touched, just a warm press. But within me, the warmth spiraled, became a raging need, a shock wave surging through my body, heady and addictive, and demanding that I believe this was a real kiss.

Or . . . maybe it could be real? Maybe he could eventually feel about me the way I felt about him. It was well researched that a person's opinion of another person's attractiveness could change over time and—

No. Do NOT go down that road.

All at once, I knew I needed to break contact before I experienced another of those embarrassing episodes where I forgot we were being filmed. He was acting, and this was all pretend.

Lifting my chin, the kiss box now checked, I managed to paste some semblance of a smile on my features as my eyes fluttered open and met his. I'd expected to feel relief. Instead, all I felt was unsteady, unsatisfied sorrow, and certain I'd made a huge mistake.

As I leaned back, Byron glared at me, his lips gently parted. Or I tried to lean back, but I couldn't. His hands had moved to my hips without me realizing and his fingers dug into the flesh of my backside, holding me in place.

A moment passed where we looked at each other, his gaze stormy, his breathing hard. I distracted myself from the sorrow I felt and the snare of his achingly believable performance by making mental notes about how to edit the video and what captions to include. This, right here, would be a good spot to end it, leave the audience wondering what happened next. I was about to say as much, but in the next breath, Byron surged forward.

Gripping my jaw and angling my chin, his mouth fastened to mine, seeking, starved, devastating, kissing without finesse. He moved us from vertical to horizonal as he laid me back on the couch, climbing over me and between my legs.

This is fake, this is fake, this is fake was the ineffectual chant inside my head timed to the rapid beat of my heart. I arched beneath him, genuinely hungry for the feel of his weight, his body. I widened my thighs to accommodate the hard press of hips. The fingers at my jaw moved to spear into my hair and closed around the strands, his movements jerky and unpracticed, tugging my head back, forcing me to open for him. I did, an involuntary moan slipping out as his tongue pushed inside.

A whole-body shiver had my arms convulsively pulling him closer, my feet searching for purchase so I could tilt and angle my hips to feel that exquisite hardne—

I gasped. He groaned. And my brain screamed *THIS IS FAKE!*

And yet it didn't feel fake. Nothing about it felt fake. The hardness rubbing between my legs didn't feel fake. His hands working to shove my tank higher didn't feel fake. His fingers pulling down the cup of my bra with shaking hands *certainly* didn't feel fake.

"Byron—" I choked. My breast was in his palm. He was touching me, massaging me, so greedy and grasping, and he was—and I—and—*ohmyfuckinggodthatfeelssogoooooood!*

"You want me to stop?" he asked darkly against my neck, his tone arrogant, like he didn't doubt the answer and only asked the question to mock me. How had his arrogance become so sexy? He rocked his hips forward again and I felt the entire, solid length of him.

That's how. Arrogance can be sexy. When it's reflective of reality, when it's deserved, it's sexy. *That big dick straining against his fly, that's why it's sexy.*

Byron did something illegal and sinful with his tongue in my ear, and I shuddered as he asked again, "Should I stop?"

"No, no. But—"

"Shh. No talking." He pulled away and whipped off his shirt, revealing the stunning expanse of his gorgeous body. My mouth went dry, and I'm sure I made a completely nonsensical sound of pure lust, my hands sculpting to his abdominals. He felt absolutely unreal, hot and hard and perfect, and I wondered how (or if) I'd ever be able to return to a normal life after this. His body made me want to kneel and pray. Touching him was, legit, a religious experience.

Meanwhile, his eyes trailed down to my skin he'd exposed, grew impossibly darker, hungrier, sending my racing heart straight to my throat.

But I managed to choke out, "Byron, what are you—"

"Shut the fuck up, Win. Please."

"The pho—oh God!" I threw my head back as his mouth closed over my nipple, sucking it between his lips like he'd been without sustenance his entire life, his tongue doing more illegal and sinful maneuvers while he grabbed the other bra cup, yanked it down, caught the center of my breast with his thumb and stroked, the touch nearly frantic.

His mouth continued giving my right breast the rough treatment while his searching hand slid down the side of my rib cage, my hip, to move between my legs and cup me over the magic leggings while I panted, trying to remember what important thing I needed to tell him. There was something, something critical, something about—

"The phone is still recording!"

CHAPTER 25
BYRON

There's this whiskey called Writers' Tears. My agent bought me a case upon my second book's release, the one that made her a millionaire. I opened the case when I arrived home from Winnie's.

Home. It sounded like *om*, the mystical syllable, an affirmation to something divine. I knew the origin of om, and I'd decided long ago that some cosmic force had been at play. The auditory similarity between home and om couldn't be a coincidence or a mistake.

Mistake. . .

Closing and rubbing my eyes, I battled another vicious swell of turbulence, my muscles tensing as I waited for the cresting wave to recede.

In Winnie's apartment, on the couch above her, the absence had found me first. The absence of sound and feeling after she'd screeched "The phone is still recording!" and broken the spell, my mind blanking when her meaning eclipsed the primitive, essential urgency to claim, to suffocate in sensation, to drown in it. I'd been anticipating the asphyxiation with wonder, hope, and so much foolish pride.

I'd thought she wanted me. Thus, I'd felt like the hero in every epic book and story I'd ever read. How foolish. What had I been thinking? I had been wholly and entirely unprepared.

Testing the memory for sharpness, I replayed the moment directly following her reveal: she'd said my name and I'd pushed myself upright; my skin had suddenly felt too hot; everything had been too loud—just too damn loud. I'd drowned in the truth instead of her touch.

Those fucking, goddamn challenges.

Presently, sitting on the floor with my back against the wall and my legs stretched out in front of me, I bent one of my knees to support my arm. Grimacing at the scraping sound made by the friction of my foot against the wood floor, I realized I still wore my shoes. Good.

If I couldn't drown the cacophony with Writers' Tears, I'd go for a walk. Or a run. Anything to escape the image cavalcade: Winnie's apartment coming sharply into focus, the white walls shaded gray in the fading summer sun, the smell of lemon and fish seasoning the air. And her perfume—gardenias. And sweat.

And Winnie beneath me, eyes wide, shocked, hair disheveled, hands bracing against the sofa, knees drawn up, lips swollen, her shirt—

"Fuck." The exhaled breath scored my lungs.

I'd never experienced anything like the bliss of kissing her, touching her, believing she craved me, wanted me. That greedy welcoming of the basest instincts, that brutal, seductive embrace. I'd wanted it to consume me. I'd wanted to surrender for the first time in my life, more than I'd wanted to know tomorrow.

But now it was tomorrow, albeit newly just, and here I sat, swallowing a mouthful of whiskey and contemplating these bare walls and this empty room lit only by shadows—as bare and empty as my experience with women—while I worried about her. Had I hurt her? Ferocious, biting anguish at the thought sent my eyes to seek the darkness behind my lids.

I'd had no idea what I was doing. I'd been acting on pure instinct. I didn't know what I didn't know, and I *hated* not knowing.

I'd thought the kiss had been real. I'd thought she'd been eager, welcoming. I'd asked her if she wanted me to stop. She'd said no. Had her response been for the benefit of the camera? She'd felt so right, luminous, silken perfection, her body's response the fulfillment and realization of my dreams. But dreams weren't life experience.

And weren't those recollections skewed? Biased? Could they be trusted if my memory had been rose-tinted? Colored by her false motivations and an absolute dearth of knowledge on the subject? All those moments of certainty and rightness had occurred before I knew the truth and before I'd reflected on how fumbling and unskilled I must've seemed to her.

Winnie's kiss had been a lie, but not a deception.

Not knowing what to think or believe or where to start—a novel experience, to be sure—I found I could not think at all, not even to assemble enough reason to postpone decisions until I calmed, until I could separate my visceral reaction, so loud in my brain, from my memory of the event.

Perhaps I should leave Seattle for a time. Would she want to see me again? Would she hate the sight of me? Or worse, would she immediately forgive my transgression? I wanted to do whatever made her life easiest. Perhaps I would leave for good. *But when I asked if I should stop, she told me no. Did she want me? Were her responses for the camera? Did she—*

Forcing my eyes open, I shook my head, the circular nature of my thoughts intensely frustrating. Perhaps she and I would be better served to forget. Perhaps Jeff had been right.

I would keep my distance but be available should she wish to discuss the incident. *Leave her alone. Leave.*

I winced, squeezing my eyes shut, struggling to inhale past the regret cinching my throat, fighting the urge to call her, to explain and apologize. Both actions would be entirely self-serving, a balm to ease my guilty conscience rather than give her the space she likely required, given what I'd done. And I needed to remain steadfast. Winnie would decide what happened next, and I would do whatever she wished.

Time moved over and around me while I searched for that suspended state of being, the absence of thought and sensation. What I required now was distance, darkness, and silence.

When I opened my eyes this time, the room had gone fuzzy. The liquor had finally, *finally* dulled the bite. I viewed the inferno of regret from a distance, through darkness, without the offensive presence of sound, rather than mindlessly losing myself to serpentine misery within the flames.

Floating in my lake of whiskey, my eyes on the stars of remoteness above instead of the shore of worry or tempest of doubt around me, I contended that no reason existed for me to submerge myself in the chaos of the unknowable. I should turn my quickly numbing thoughts elsewhere, to banal trivialities, to business and work, to subjects over which I had control.

Forget and move on.

I scanned the cavernous room once more, this time through the filter of self-imposed banishment. No part of this, the third floor, had yet been furnished. I loved my house, my home, my om, my mansion in the middle of Seattle. I loved its secret passages and doorways, allowing me to come and go without being seen or heard, like on the night of Jeff and Lucy's dinner party or any other night they'd gathered with their friends.

My house might've been the only tangible, material thing I loved other than the books on my shelves, though the books and the house were intrinsically linked. Ghosts of fictional people inhabited each dark room in this old mansion. When I'd first toured it with the real estate agent, I'd imagined it filled with literary figures, all characters, all friends. And so it was.

Some were mine. Some had been born from the minds and pages of others, now belonging to me since I treasured them, visited them, and loved them.

I stood, bracing a hand against the wall until I found my balance. Glass in hand, I walked the lonely halls like I imagined Miss Havisham might, lost to the madness of a nonsensical revenge plan. It was, I supposed, probably similar to being lost within an alternate reality of one's own design. Perhaps when those outside these walls were content to abandon me to whatever structure I eventually haunted, my mercurial existence no longer of interest, I too would wear the same outfit for decades.

"It'll be a suit." The words echoed and I nodded, gulping from the half-empty tumbler.

A three-piece suit with no tie. I'd be ready for my funeral when the time came. No change of clothes required, even in death.

I laughed at the thought, frivolous and indulgent, bringing the glass back to my lips for another swallow. It was empty.

Leaving the top floor, I held the banister as I descended the stairs, and I poured myself another helping of Writers' Tears when I stumbled into the salon. I believed, though I could've been mistaken, all writers identify to some degree with the abject horror of having to speak, to shower, to eat, to change anything, to even breathe when words are flowing like a river of magic, and the mind has entered the bliss of a preferred existence.

My previous experiences with being ripped from the perfection of the imaginary were similar to the moment I'd realized Winnie's kiss had been a lie. But with Winnie, exiting the fiction had felt like removing my head from my neck, or perhaps like removing a wedding dress that had become a second skin after thirty (or so) hateful years.

I lifted a glass to Miss Havisham, a villain I'd long admired, if only for her tenacious spite and the creativity of her self-indulgence. "To Miss Havisham."

Funny. I'd never experienced profound, bone-deep remorse from reading or writing a book, only from engaging in reality. I blamed myself. I'd already learned this lesson time and time again: nothing perfect exists outside of imagination.

Congratulations, Byron. You're officially a pretentious, philosophizing blowhard.

"I need to get out more," I said to no one, rubbing my forehead with aching fingers as I sank into a club chair. I could only shake my head at the reductive, absurd direction of my inebriated thoughts. But at least now, finally, I felt fully numb.

"I'll take you out. Where do you want to go?"

I stiffened, not even daring to breathe, and apparently not entirely numb as I'd hoped.

A moment later, her warm hand closed over mine, soft fingers curling around my knuckles. She pulled them from my face. My lungs expanded to bursting without me drawing a breath.

"Are you here?" I blinked, bleary-eyed, half expecting I'd conjured her.

But there she was, kneeling in front of me, her lovely features pinched with concern and illuminated by trespassing moonlight. The glass had been removed from my fingers. Only she and my accelerating heart remained.

"How much have you had?" Her voice was music. It serrated and soothed the very center of me, and I didn't realize how much I'd been anticipating, longing for the sound since I'd left her apartment.

"You shouldn't be here," I said, the words a slur.

"Why not?"

I gazed into her eyes, the color of cinnamon, so vivid. I could almost taste it on my tongue. "You need space."

"I don't want space. I want to see you, and you're just going to have to deal with it. Now, tell me. How much have you had?"

"I don't want your forgiveness," I said, my drowsy attention lowering to her lips. "You shouldn't forgive me."

I blinked, wishing I were sober. If this were to be the last time I saw her, I wanted to memorize her perfect, pink lips. They'd distracted me and disturbed my peace for years, how they curved to the right when her smiles first bloomed. I'd often traced the shape of them when I closed my eyes.

"Forgiveness for what? Leaving? You don't need to apologize for leaving." Her fingers pushed into my hair, the touch light and sweet.

My stomach churned with regret.

I caught her hand at my temple, removing it. "No, Fred. Not for leaving. For—" The thought bit off on its own, my voice breaking. I couldn't say it.

"For?" she prompted, sounding curious. At least, my liquor-soaked senses thought she sounded curious.

"I shouldn't have done that," I choked, refusing to close my eyes from the shame of it. "And I am sorry, but I don't want you to forgive me or make excuses for me. If you don't want to see me again, I understand."

"Byron, what are you talking about?" The hand I'd removed turned in mine, lacing our fingers. Her thumb swept against my knuckles. "The kissing? The couch? Don't you dare be sorry for that."

"I didn't know." *Dammit.* I hadn't meant to say that. It sounded like an excuse. There was no excuse.

"You didn't know we were still recording? Yes, I figured as much when my breast was in your mouth."

I winced. "Shit."

"You know what? We're not discussing this now. We'll talk about this in the morning, when you're not drunk." Her warm, capable hands used their leverage on mine to pull, presumably to make me stand.

I was too heavy for her, but I stood since she wanted me to do so. I would follow where she led. "Should I leave Seattle? I will. Just say the word."

Her eyes widened. "What? Why?"

"I don't wish to make you uncomfortable."

Winnie simply looked at me, her generous, pink lips curved, but her eyes were sad.

"Don't be sad." I lifted my hands to reach for her and discovered she still held them in her grip, we were still touching. "Don't ever be sad."

"I'm not sad. I just wish you were sober so I could tell you how much I loved—how much I love—what happened between us earlier and how much I hope it means you want something more than friendship with me."

I blinked and reared back—both were probably done in slow motion—and stared at her. "Why?"

"Because I want something more than just friendship with you."

I blinked again. "You do?"

Her gaze moved over my face and she laughed, apparently finding something about my features funny. "Come on. You need to hydrate."

"I—I need you," I said, my tongue made loose by her words and Writers' Tears and the new cacophony in my head, loud with anticipation and hope and ideas instead of worry and self-recrimination. "I'm going to improve. I've heard of classes, a coach who teaches without touching. And I'll learn to tolerate people. I'll learn how to tune out their idiomatic, scatological noises."

"I don't know what any of that means." Winnie breathed out a sweet, laughing sigh, disentangling one of her hands to bend and reach for something. A moment later, she pressed a cold glass into my hands. "Please drink this."

Was this real? Can I trust it? My brain felt slick, slow, tired. I held myself back from gathering her in my arms and crushing her, kissing her. I didn't want to misunderstand again. I wanted—needed—sobriety before taking action.

"Is it poison?" I teased, squinting at her, wanting to make her smile.

"Why would it be poison?" She did smile, and the smile both calmed and excited me. It was evidence that she wasn't angry or sad and that her words —her statements about what had happened—were true.

I can't believe this is happening. Could I trust it? *You're drunk. Trust nothing.*

I drank from the glass, my eyes on her the whole time. It tasted like Gatorade. I drained it.

"Good. I've also made toast." She took the empty glass. Food appeared from seemingly nowhere, but this could've been because my eyes were fastened to her face, everything beyond the pale of her glowing face outside the bounds of my vision.

When did she make toast? How long has she been here?

I wanted to kiss her. Right now. I wanted to pick up where we'd left off. Right now. I wanted to divest her of those offensive clothes, guide her to the club chair, and kneel before her spread legs.

Instead, when she lifted food to my lips, I took a bite.

"You need to stop looking at me like that," she said, sounding breathless to my inebriated ears.

"I can't."

"Try."

I was terrible at *trying* in the moment. I never tried unless I'd previously arranged things such that success was all but guaranteed. But currently, I did try. For her.

Between chewing and trying and swallowing and hoping she didn't disappear, I told her, "I had a dream about you."

"Oh?" She fed me more toast, but I wondered if maybe this bite was more of an effort to shut me up than help me sober up.

"Yes." I tried to catch her eyes but there were four sets of them. "You kissed me. But it was a lie."

"It wasn't a dream, and it wasn't a lie, and we should talk about something else."

I covered her hand when she tried to feed me more, holding it still. "Why talk about anything else?"

"Because, again, you are drunk, and we shouldn't talk about what happened until you're sober."

I nodded. My head felt like it was on a string and a puppeteer pulled it up, then down, then up and down. Her hand lifted, cupping my jaw. I leaned into the anchoring touch and asked, "What do you want to talk about?"

"Anything except what happened earlier tonight."

"All right." I gathered a deep breath and told her what was—and had been—foremost on my mind. "I want to fuck you."

She went still, the many versions of her merging into a single Winnie with wide eyes and a slack jaw.

Since she said nothing and her expression remained frozen, I clarified, "I'll take classes, read books, see that coach. I think about it all the time. I thought you should know. But I will never touch you again if it would ruin things between us."

She breathed out in a *whoosh*. "Okay, time for bed. I mean, for *you* to go to bed." Winnie left, returned, and grabbed my hand, pulling me somewhere while arranging my limbs.

My arm around her shoulders, I stared forward and tried to concentrate on helping her, but since we were on the subject, I wanted to know, "Do you know what a spreader bar is?"

Her steps seemed to falter. "I am familiar with the concept."

"I want to tie you up and cuff you to a spreader bar. And then I want to bend you over a table, holding your hands behind your back and—"

"Well, that certainly paints a picture," she spoke over me, her arm around my waist tightening as we reached the stairs. "Please hold on to the banister. I don't want you to fall."

I wasn't finished. "And then I want to make love to you."

"Oh? While I'm chained to a spreader bar?"

"Once I master the act, I want to love every single fucking perfect inch of you." I held on to the banister as instructed, my shoes full of lead. "Your neck. Your stomach. Your sides. Behind your knees. I want to count your ribs and your vertebrae using my tongue. I want to kiss your feet and fingertips and between your shoulder blades. I want to worship you, kneel and taste every inch of your pussy."

We stopped at the landing, and she set me away, pushing my back against the wall. Winnie's breathing had turned labored.

"If you were mine . . ." My eyes traced the gentle curve of her lips. I loved her lips. "I'd keep you handcuffed to my bed."

"Then I guess it's a good thing I'm not yours. I have that dentist appointment next week." She also leaned against the wall, but far away. Too far away.

"But more than that." I righted myself, reaching out to the banister for assistance, finding it, gripping it. "More than how much I want you, *need* you, I need you to be happy and well, safe and healthy. And that's why. . ."

"What?" She stood in front of me now, her hands at my arms to lend me balance.

"That's why I'll never tell you the truth."

She seemed to hesitate, or was quiet for a long time, then asked, "Which is?"

"I've loved you for years. You are the stars in the sky, the start and the finish. I'll die loving you, wanting you, and the torture of you is better than the bliss of anyone else. Last night, when you wore those leggings, your ass did look like a peach, and I've never wanted to bite something so much."

Her wide eyes had returned, as had her breathlessness. "You're very drunk."

"And you are all my sunrises and sunsets, rain on green leaves, fireworks reflected in a smooth lake, and a wood fire on the coldest winter day. You are sex and sin and a guardian angel. You are every beat of my heart and every moment of peace and every hour of pandemonium. You are the sweetest torture I've ever known. And you . . . will never feel one tenth for me what I feel for you. And that, also, is perfect."

Winnie bowed her head. "Are you trying to make me spontaneously combust, Byron?"

I shrugged. Or tried to. "The inferno inside me honors the spark within you, for however long it burns. Mine will persist, though yours may desist."

Turning, she placed my arm over her shoulders again and guided me to the next flight of stairs. "Now you're rhyming."

"I love you. Thus, I am a fool. For all who love as I do are fools. But if you are ready and willing, I will learn how to be the person you deserve. I'll learn how to cook all gluten-free meals and not hate the sound other people make when they chew. Or swallow. Or talk. Or breathe."

Winnie didn't respond, perhaps too busy focusing on our footing. We made it to the second landing, and then we were in my room, and then I was lying on my back.

"You need to get to sleep," she said, her voice somewhere nearby.

I heard a sound, a soft thud, and I lifted myself upright by bracing my hands against the mattress. Winnie, on her knees in front of me, had removed one of my shoes and now worked on untying the second.

Frowning at the sight of her laboring over my boot, I bent my knee and tugged it out of her grip. "I'll remove my own damn shoe."

She huffed and stood. "Fine. I'll get you more Gatorade and some pain relievers. Don't leave the bed." She issued this last command with a stern look and an index finger pointed at my chest.

I nodded, my lids drooping, and worked on the shoelace.

Ten years later, the shoe came off.

Ten years after that, Winnie returned. I tracked her as she entered the bedroom, placed items on my bedside table, a towel on the floor, and a bucket on top of the towel. "There," she muttered. "If you get sick and can't make it to the bathroom, use the bucket."

The sight of the stage she'd set irritated me. I should be taking care of her, not the other way around.

Clearing my throat of disgruntlement, I asked for what I wanted. "Will you stay with me?"

Her soft smile was immediate. "Of course."

Winnie stepped forward and threaded her fingers into my hair, her other hand at my shoulder. Guiding me to my side, she abandoned my hair to arrange the pillow.

"Can I . . . will you lay here?" I patted the bed behind me. "I won't touch you, if you don't want me to. But I'd fuck you senseless if you asked." Not that I had any experience fucking someone senseless. I was currently shit-faced, but if she asked, I'd figure it out. Starting tomorrow—Monday at the latest—I'd dedicate every waking hour to learning how to fuck her senseless, eventually becoming a world expert.

Winnie pressed her lips together firmly, but they twitched. "How about if I just hold you?"

"Would you?"

"Yes," she said quietly and left my field of vision. A moment later, I felt her behind me, her chest at my back, her arm draped over my middle.

Once she settled, I again asked for what I wanted. "When can I kiss you again?"

"When you're fully sober." She gave my body a squeeze. "Right now, I'm worried when you sober up, this is going to feel like a bunch of nonsense to you and you're going to wish you never said any of it."

"'If I had a world of my own, everything would be nonsense.'"

"Lewis Carroll."

"That's right."

"Go to sleep, Byron," she said, a smile in her voice.

I couldn't. Not yet. I had to tell her something. "I have to tell you one more thing."

"What is it?"

I turned to face her, needing to see her while she shifted back to the other side of the bed, putting space between our bodies.

"When we wake up, I don't want you to make a joke about this, or what happened yesterday. I don't want you to try to ease my discomfort. And if you want to be with me, if you're willing to give me a chance, you have to tell me. Tomorrow, when I'm sober and you're here, if you tell me my touch was—is—welcome, I will believe you."

"Good." She reached out as though to touch my hair again.

I caught her hand and placed it flat on the bed between us. "But if it's not, if I've hurt you, if I stepped over a boundary at your apartment, you have to tell me so I can make reparations. So I can do everything in my power to make things right for you. This isn't about me, except that I take full responsibility for my actions. This is about you and what you need. You will not upset me. I mean—" I shook my head, frustrated with the sleep and whiskey pulling at my eyes. "Rather, that is, I will be upset, but not at you. Your safety and peace of mind is more important than my comfort, or discomfort. Promise me."

Her eyes seemed to be shining, and I thought I heard her sniffle. Her hand beneath mine slipped from my hold and then returned to cover my fingers, clutching and bringing them to tuck against her chest.

"I promise," she whispered. "Now go to sleep."

On her command, my eyes closed. And I did.

CHAPTER 26
WINNIE

Heart full to bursting, but also heavy with trepidation, I had no plans to actually sleep. Nor did I believe sleep was possible given the varied and vast nature of Byron's drunken statements and declarations.

He loves me?!

He's loved me for years?!

. . . BUT WHY?

My instinct was to feel only happiness, and yet the sudden, drunken revelation of Byron's feelings while I'd helped him to his room had caught me completely off guard. I couldn't sort through the tangle between my head and heart, and the more I tried to dissect it, the more it twisted and spun and knotted.

I trusted him, I believed he'd meant the words he'd said while drunk, *at the time*. Would he say or mean them when sober?

It wasn't just the alcohol-soaked nature of his declarations that worried me. What if he really did love me? I'd never been loved by anyone before, definitely not the kind of love Byron claimed to have for me. I felt honored and humbled and overwhelmed, and also suspicious that there might be some mistake and he'd confused me with someone else.

My involuntary attraction and the intensity of my feelings had always been—up to this point—something to hide, contain, and suppress because I considered Byron to be one of the most impressive, intelligent, and talented people in the entire world.

How could I not find the idea of this man's love and eternal devotion completely intimidating? Especially since I'd spent the last month actively working to protect my heart from foolishly falling for him.

As I attempted to recall and catalog every moment we'd spent together and what signs I'd blatantly missed—I must've exhausted myself vacillating between giddy happiness and intimidated apprehension. I zonked out next to him in his big comfortable bed. The next thing I knew, the sound of someone singing roused me from a dream featuring Byron and me and his hot tub.

At first I thought I was at home in my room and Elijah was the source of the perfectly pitched rendition of "Cry Me A River." But then, after rubbing the sleep from my eyes, the enormity of the dark bedroom came into focus. I spotted Byron next to me, his arms sprawled out, one hand laying lightly on my stomach.

Memories from the previous evening rushed to the forefront and I blushed, smiling, wishing I could wake him up with kisses, wishing we could skip over the talking part and go straight to the undressing part. But if I wanted a lasting future with Byron as more than just friends—and I did—we needed to talk first, canoodle later.

Gently, I encircled his wrist and lifted his heavy arm up and away. Then I rolled off the bed, the sound of the song from beyond the door drawing closer, louder. It was just the refrain, over and over, like the singer didn't know any of the other words.

Is that . . . Jeff?

Picking up my phone from the otherwise empty nightstand on my side, I checked the time—8:42 a.m. *Whoa.* I'd had no idea it was so late. The blackout shades in Byron's room certainly were effective.

Rounding the bed, I cast a quick look at Byron, checking to ensure he was still fast asleep and Jeff's crooning hadn't woken him, then darted to the door. Once there, I cracked it open and peered out at the huge landing, squinting against the light overhead.

Sure enough, there sat Jeff on a Victorian-looking, blue velvet settee, a bottle of beer in one hand, his phone in the other, singing Justin Timberlake's infamous breakup song. By the looks of it, he was nearly as drunk as Byron had been last night.

Jeff spotted me as I slipped out of Byron's door and did a slow-motion double take, rubbing his eyes with the backs of his hands despite how full they were holding the bottle and his cell. Jeff ended up spilling a quantity of beer on the carpet in the process.

"What the fu—"

"Shh! Byron's sleeping." I ran forward and righted his hand to stop the waterfall. I then darted to the bathroom for a towel. Finding one on the rack, I ran back over to Jeff, dropped to my knees to sop up the wet spot on the ancient carpet, frustrated by his carelessness. This wasn't his house. It was Byron's house, and he was spilling beer on the carpet? "Should you be drinking up here?"

"Winnie?"

I glanced up at him and his incredulous tone. He now stared at me, apparently dumbfounded, his eyes bugging out of his head. I decided to swipe the bottle from his hand as it was lilting once again.

"Did Dionysus throw a party on Mercury last night, sending it into retrograde?" I grumbled, speaking to myself. "Is everyone drunk but me?"

"Winnie, what are you—did you just—are you—"

"Shh!" I shushed him again. Maybe it was because I'd just woken up, though I didn't think so, but Jeff's voice was very loud. Holding his beer hostage, I stood and stepped away, motioning him toward the back stairs. "Come on. We'll talk in the kitchen." I didn't want him to wake Byron. The big guy needed his sleep.

Or rather, I needed Byron to get his sleep so his liver would efficiently process that alcohol and he'd sober up and we could talk and get everything settled. Once and for all. *Then, canoodling.*

Not checking to see if Jeff would follow, I turned and tiptoed down the servant's small stairway which deposited me just off the kitchen. A few seconds later, I heard the door swing open with a soft squeak while I set his beer on the counter and scanned the tidy space for a laundry basket.

"What are you doing here, Winnie?" Jeff's demanding, unmodulated voice at my back made me glad we'd left the second floor.

"Where is the laundry basket?" I twisted around to question Jeff. "Do you keep one on this floor?"

"Put it down the laundry chute, it's in the butler's pantry," he slurred, shuffling around the diameter of the kitchen island. Making it to the other side, he noisily pulled out a stool and sank into it. "What the heck are you doing here?"

I frowned at his laundry chute suggestion. I didn't want to put a beer-soaked towel down the laundry chute. It would beer-soak everything beneath it.

"Hmm. . ." I eyed the sink. "I'll rinse it out first."

I felt Jeff's inebriated attention on me as I walked over to the kitchen sink and flipped on the faucet.

"Is there something going on with you two? Are you and Byron together?" The words seemed to burst out of him, making my hands pause beneath the running water.

Sneaking a look at Jeff, I found him watching me with a sullen expression. He looked like he'd had a hard night. And he was drinking beer before 9:00 a.m. *Hmm* . . .

Twisting the towel now that it was appropriately soaked, I shrugged and kept my tone light. "Something like that. Is Lucy here?"

He made a sound I couldn't interpret. "Uh, no. She's not here. In fact, we broke up. And this time I wouldn't take her back if she begged me." His voice had dropped an octave.

I felt my eyebrows jump of their own volition, but I said nothing. This explained his getting sloshed and the day drinking, but they'd broken up many times before. History told me the separation was merely temporary. Therefore, rather than say anything, I gave him a tight smile.

"Aren't you going to ask what happened?"

Shrugging again, my mind cast about for a subject change. I had no desire to discuss Jeff, or Lucy, or Jeff and Lucy. After weeks of distance from the dinner party as well as the subsequent and immediate snuffing out of my Jeff crush, witnessing their dynamic in retrospect made me feel like maybe I'd dodged a bullet.

"Winnie," he said, his hand moving over the counter, closer to the sink.

I glanced at him.

His bloodshot eyes searched mine. "I'm so sorry I left you hanging."

"What? Nah. It's fine." I waved away his apology and turned off the sink, wringing out the towel one more time before draping it over the edge to dry. "It actually worked out better."

"Getting a lot of followers, huh?"

"Yeah, and a lot of them are girls and women who read Byron's books, which is basically my target demographic. Funny how that works." I offered a smile around a yawn, distracted by thoughts of the beer still on the carpet upstairs. I wondered if I should roll the carpet back and check to see if any had soaked through to the wood floor beneath.

"But it's all fake?"

I shook myself, blinking at Jeff. "Pardon?"

"It's all fake?" he repeated.

"What do you mean?" I forgot what we were discussing.

"It's staged, the videos you two are doing. You're following a script, you're staging them like you wanted to do with me?"

Oh. "It's—no, we're not. But we're on the same page about it." I backed up until my bottom met the opposite counter. I leaned against it. "Why do you ask?"

"I was hoping that maybe you'd . . ." He bent his arm at the elbow and straightened from his hunched position over the counter. "Listen, I know I fucked up. I left when Lucy called, and I can't believe I was so stupid. We are not getting back together. Not this time, and never—"

"Jeff, you didn't eff up." *Don't cringe, don't cringe, don't cringe.*

"I didn't?"

"No. You love her. You two have been together for over a decade. If she calls, you're always going to answer."

His shoulders slumped. "It's such a relief to hear you say that."

"Please don't give it another thought. We're still friends."

"Well, about that." A slow smile pushed to the surface of his features. "How about that date?"

I flinched, certain I'd heard him wrong. "Excuse me?"

When he continued to stare at me, his gaze drifting lower over the front of my body, I did cringe. I also folded my arms over my chest. What the heck? Hadn't he just seen me coming out of Byron's room? Didn't he just ask if we were together?

"I asked you out before and you said yes," he said—like an agreement weeks ago lasted for the remainder of my life—and I recognized this voice. It sounded like the voice he'd used with Lucy the night of the dinner party, placating and pleading.

Yuck.

"No, Jeff. You just broke up with Lucy. You shouldn't be going on a date with me or with anyone else. Give yourself some time."

"I don't want time." Jeff sliced a hand through the air, his head moving in a sloppy but determined shake, his features twisting. "The last thing I want is time. Do you know what I gave up? How much I sacrificed by being loyal to Lucy for so long?"

"You should get some—"

"I could've had any girl in college. Anyone! Do you know how hard it was for me? Do you understand what it's like for someone like me to be faithful to just one girl?" He lifted a hand toward me. "I could've had you. But no. I was stupid. So fucking stupid. And blind." He shoved the base of his palms into his eyes.

Looks like everyone is revealing their true colors tonight. And Jeff's were skeevy celadon with a dash of conceited chartreuse.

Certain my face betrayed my thoughts, but unconcerned since he didn't seem to notice anything beyond his own gross pity party, I backed toward the stairway, deciding it was best to make a quiet exit. Maybe he wouldn't notice and—

"He's never had a girlfriend, you know." He hadn't looked up, his palms still covering his eyes.

I froze. "Who?"

"Byron."

I'd suspected as much, but having it confirmed made my stomach flip. "Oh? Well, I guess he never met the right person." *Before now.*

"He said, and this is a direct quote, 'Monogamy is for quitters.'"

That sounded like Byron's brand of dry humor, and I refused to read anything into it. That said, we would most definitely clarify the statement when he woke up and we talked through everything. I wasn't a person capable of accepting anything other than monogamy in a relationship.

"Maybe he was joking," I said.

"I don't think so. I think Byron doesn't commit to women because it inconveniences Byron to have people expect anything of him." Jeff chuckled, the sound devoid of humor. "Maybe he's right. Hell, maybe Lucy is right. Maybe she and I were too young." His hands fell away, smacking on the countertop as they landed. His stare dazed, he said desolately, "She cheated on me."

My weight shifted to my back foot, absorbing this information. I'd been cheated on once upon a time. It was why my high school boyfriend and I had broken up my sophomore year of college. I remembered the devastation being cheated on causes to one's self-esteem. "I'm so sorry, Jeff."

"She's been screwing this guy at her work. And before that, she'd been with a few guys in law school." His volume had lowered to a mumble, and he looked so forlorn. Broken. "She's been lying to me for years"—his voice cracked—"And like a total idiot, I fell for it."

Sighing, I sent him a compassionate look, my heart going out to him. Though I knew what it was like to be cheated on, my ex had told me the morning after it happened—via a phone call—and said he was sorry. He'd said he really liked me, but he didn't see things working out in the long term, that we were too young to be in a long-distance relationship and he was tired of waiting for me to be ready to have sex.

He'd cheated, but he hadn't lied about it. He hadn't led me on for years. I couldn't imagine what Jeff was feeling right now. I assumed anger must've been paramount.

No wonder he'd been singing "Cry Me A River" at the top of his lungs and had said all that stuff about staying loyal to her, wishing he'd slept around in college. I wasn't excusing his gross statements, but when people are hurt, they say and do things that aren't reflective of who they really are. *Poor guy.*

"She stole the best years of my life. I've wasted so much time." Jeff's elbows came to the counter, his forehead falling to his hands. "I'm so fucking stupid." He started to cry.

I tsked, muttering, "Oh no." Hesitating only a moment, I quickly walked around the kitchen island and came to stand at his side. Patting his back, I shushed him soothingly, murmuring nonsense I hoped would ease the sting. Or at the very least, I hoped a presence, someone simply being there for him so he didn't have to be alone, might help.

Jeff cried into his hands for several minutes while I waited, wondering what I could do or say to make it better. He was still my friend, and I wanted to be a good friend. Mentally, I thumbed through my joke database and came up empty, finding nothing relating to this subject that might make him laugh or cheer his spirits.

Then suddenly, he stood up, turned around, and pulled me into his arms.

I stiffened, surprised by the unexpected hug, and internally engaged in a quick, heated debate with myself.

On the one hand, this was Jeff, my friend, and he needed comfort, and it was just a hug. I hugged and cuddled with my friends all the time. On the other hand, he'd just asked me out, had made gross statements about "having me," and despite his turmoil and fragile state, I didn't particularly want him hugging me right now. It made me feel uncomfortable.

And in addition to all of the above, Byron and I were on the precipice—hopefully—of officially becoming more than friends. If the roles were reversed and Byron was consoling a female friend after she'd just asked him out and talked about easily having him, I'd side-eye an embrace, no matter how much she hurt and no matter how much I trusted Byron. Perhaps this was because I'd been cheated on in the past and I should've had more chill, but I wouldn't like it.

"Promise me you'll give me another chance." Jeff pressed his wet face into my neck, sniffling.

"Uh . . ."

My hands were still up, my arms held away from my sides. For the second time in my life, I decided my boundaries and comfort mattered more than potentially offending someone else. I both blamed and credited

Byron and his influence. Regardless, I wanted to extract myself, and so I would.

"Jeff, hey, let me go."

He held me tighter. "Winnie, I made a mistake. Let me, let me take you out. Just once. I'll show you. I know you still like me."

I grimaced, placing the flat of my palms against his shoulders and pushed. "I'd like you a whole lot better if you'd let me go. Jeff—let me—"

He kissed my neck, and I froze. A frigid wave of revulsion made my stomach drop. Then he kissed my neck again and again, his hands sliding over my back, grasping me.

I pushed in earnest, wrenching my neck and head away. "I said, let me go. Stop. Jeff—stop!"

Jeff lifted his head, then tried to fasten his mouth to mine, and I took the opportunity to slap him. Hard. He stumbled back, eyes wide, gripping his cheek.

Placing my hands on my hips, I drew myself up to my full height. "Now you listen. I know you're hurting, I know you're devastated. But I am your friend, not a convenient someone to be used, and you don't treat friends that way. Be better than that. Shame on you."

His face crumpled, and he nodded. "Oh God, Winnie. I'm so sorry. I'm so sorry. I thought you were into it."

"What? Why would you think that?" Just to be safe, I rounded the kitchen island again, putting some space between us and pressing a hand to my thumping heart.

Now that we were separated, I identified the surge of adrenaline for what it was. I'd never had anyone touch me like that, hold me against my will. Nor had I ever slapped or hit another person. I told my body to settle down, told myself it was over and I was okay.

His hand came to his forehead, hiding his eyes. "The way you were touching me, and you've always liked me and—sorry, I guess your signals confused me."

I mouthed the words *signals*, outraged because. . . what?

I wasn't giving him any signals. *Was I?*

"Never mind. Forget it." His hand fell to his side and his eyes lifted to the ceiling. "I guess you aren't interested in me anymore, now that you could have someone like Byron." The comment sounded offhanded, like he was talking to himself, but the words definitely weren't flattering.

Someone like Byron. What the heck did he mean by that? I didn't want someone like Byron, I wanted Byron. Besides, as far as I was concerned, there was no one like Byron. There was only Byron.

But since Jeff had said the words, I couldn't help but compare the two men as I backed up toward the stairs. They'd both made some shocking statements this evening, and both had obviously been hurting when I'd happened upon them. But Byron—who'd also been drunk, arguably even more so than Jeff—had kept his hands to himself. Even while intoxicated, he'd expressed concern over my well-being and comfort, and he hadn't touched me inappropriately. Not even once.

Whereas Jeff had made assumptions and tried to blame me and my nonexistent signals for his gross behavior. I guess I didn't dodge a bullet with Jeff, I'd dodged a nuclear warhead.

"Okay, well, you're drunk, and you're hurting. Maybe call someone so you don't have to be alone." I made it to the door and gripped the knob to disguise the slight tremor of my hand.

"You could stay with me," he said beseechingly, his eyes soft and sad. "I think I need you, Winnie. I think I need—"

"No, you do not need me." I cut him off before he could finish his thought, every cell of my body needing to leave this room. "I'm going to check on that beer spot on the carpet. I don't want it soaking through to the wood."

"Oh. I see. A wood floor is more important than a friend going through a hard time. Got it." His expression grew hard. Reclaiming his stool, he grabbed the beer I'd set on the counter and picked at the label. "I always thought you were such a nice girl, but I see now how it is, what you're really after. You and Byron deserve each other."

My chest tight with unease, disappointment, and the remainder of my adrenaline, I opened the door to the stairway and slipped inside, taking the stairs two at a time, wanting to be as far away from Jeff as possible.

I tried to remind myself that he was drunk and hurting. But this time, I simply couldn't conjure anything like the same sympathy as before, not after he'd grabbed me like that and wouldn't let me go. It would take a long time before I felt comfortable in his presence again—if ever.

There was a difference between making allowances for someone based on extenuating circumstances and allowing people to treat you like crap due to their extenuating circumstances. Until right this minute, I guess I'd done both. Worse, prior to now, I hadn't seen or understood the difference.

But from now on, no matter the extenuating circumstances, no one—and I mean *no one*—will treat me like crap.

With these thoughts forefront in my mind and while keeping an ear out for Jeff, I pushed back the velvet blue settee and rolled away the carpet, breathing a sigh of relief when I found a padded protector between the wood floor and rug. Just to be safe, I grabbed another towel from the bathroom and slid it directly beneath the rug to soak up any additional moisture. That done, I crept back to Byron's room. I didn't think I'd be able to sleep again, still feeling shaky from my run-in with Jeff downstairs, but I wanted to be there when Byron got up.

Slowly, I opened the door, not wanting to make any sound that might wake him prematurely. I needn't have worried. Byron was awake, pacing the room, his handsome features marred with a severe scowl. My heart leapt and I shut the door behind me as I inspected the nightstand on his side, pleased to find he'd drained the glass and taken the pain relievers I'd left out.

All at once, I became aware that he'd stopped moving, and my attention returned to him. Our eyes met, and the weight and intensity of his stare struck me like a gong.

This was the moment. This was THE moment.

This is it.

CHAPTER 27
WINNIE

"Hey there." I leaned against the door, a smile forcefully claiming my mouth, my heart in my throat. I'm sure I also had stars in my eyes. "How are you feeling?"

Byron stared at me, saying nothing, his gaze wary and watchful.

Huh.

I swallowed the abrupt, tight worry. I shouldn't be worried. Even if the worst were true and he didn't remember anything about what he'd said last night, all the declarations of undying love and devotion, he'd said them. I'd heard them. Now I knew the truth of his feelings which meant I was free to share the truth of mine.

Assuming he actually meant them, and they weren't drunken babble. . .

Blaming my exchange with Jeff for the slight tremor of my hands and odd bout of worry, I maintained my smile and my strategic spot blocking the door. "Are you happy to see me?" I asked lightly.

"I'm always happy to see you," he said. By all outward signs, he seemed to be telling the truth, his tone neither enthusiastic nor sarcastic, but it gave me pause.

If he's happy, why doesn't he look happy?

Twisting my lips to the side, I debated how best to initiate this conversation without embarrassing him if he didn't fully remember his inebriated proclamations. Perhaps that was the problem. The last thing I wanted him to be was embarrassed. I wanted him repeating those proclamations while sober so we could talk openly and figure things out together.

"So . . ." My mind quickly working to untangle how best to approach this plainly cautious Byron, I decided to start with the events he was most likely to remember. If I eased his concerns about what had happened at my apartment, maybe he'd relax. He was not currently relaxed. "Are we going to address the sex tape in the room?"

His eyelashes flickered, some emotion passing over his features, and then he turned, giving me his back and strolling over to one of the room's windows. Once there, he unhurriedly lifted the shade. "Go ahead."

Okay . . . I guess I could start. I could be brave with him even if every ingrained instinct told me to be cowardly.

"I don't know if you remember, but last night, before you went to sleep, you told me to let you know if I was upset about last night, what happened at my apartment." I balled my hands into fists, struggling to find courage, and said on a rush, "So this is me telling you, I am not even a little bit upset. I'm sorry you didn't realize I was still recording—"

"Don't apologize for that," he cut in, not turning around. "I'm the one who didn't want to know when you were recording."

"But I am sorry. I see now I should've given you more of an explicit heads-up, more than a wink and a nod. I could've just said something out loud and then edited that bit out later—"

"Winnie." Byron offered me the suggestion of his profile. "It's fine."

"Okay, if you say it's fine, it's fine. But I'm not sorry it happened. I'm *ecstatic* it happened. I'm very, very happy about it, and that's the truth."

Whoa. That felt good to say, the truth of it setting me free after so many weeks of fretting about my feelings. I waited for him to reply to my bravery in kind, maybe repeating one of his own confessions from last night.

Byron stared out the window for a long moment, then asked, "Do you still have the recording?"

I wouldn't lie and say I'd deleted it. I hadn't deleted it. Clearly, I was becoming a glutton for punishment and uncomfortable conversations.

"I do still have it."

"Are you going to post it?"

"What?! No!" I stepped away from the door. "I would never post it!"

"What are you going to do with it?" His tone sounded measured, carefully disinterested.

"I . . . I don't know." *Enjoy it?*

After he'd left in a rush, I'd watched it. A lot. Like, a lot a lot. Each time

I did, I was sure my brain had given me a massive dopamine hit, and the intensity of the hit had seemed constant, never fading, not even with repeated exposure.

I was basically addicted to that video.

And if that made me a weirdo pervert, then so be it. But it was *hot.* And it gave me lots of hot feelings. His hands had been all over me, and when he'd whipped off his shirt, revealing that chest and those shoulders and abs—OH THE ABS!—and all that skin, bending to pull down my bra cup and suck my nipple into his mouth—NEWTON TAKE THE WHEEL!

Byron turned his head, looking at me over his shoulder. I'm sure I was bright red. "Why did you keep it if you're not going to post it?"

His glare made me feel like a bug under a microscope. This isn't what I wanted to discuss. I needed to get the conversation back on track, but now my tongue wasn't working. I hated how shaky I still felt, and I wished I'd never tried to console Jeff. His behavior, when he'd grabbed me and kissed my neck, had set me off-kilter.

I needed to chill, calm down, get out of my own head. *Take a second and calm down.*

At my silence, Byron turned completely around to face me, his stare now searching. "Winnie."

"That's Fred to you," I quipped, hoping to lighten the mood and dispel my own nerves.

It somewhat worked. Byron's eyes narrowed, but his lips tugged to the side, and he drifted closer. I felt myself start to relax, to breathe through the remaining anxiousness.

"Why did you keep it?" he asked. Unfortunately, the question sounded demanding, and I tensed up all over again.

"I . . ." Frantically trying to read his mood and what he wanted me to say while battling the haze of my lingering adrenaline crash, I offered, "I can delete it. I can delete it right now if you want."

Glaring at me like I'd disappointed him, he grit out, "I don't care if you delete it, or if you post it. But I would like to know *why* you kept it."

Questions fueled by worry sped through my mind. *Wait . . . why the preoccupation with the video? Did he regret what he'd said while drunk? Did he not mean it? Did he not remember?*

Deciding this would be a better place to start, I asked, "How much of last night do you remember?"

"All of it."

A shock of heat warmed my cheeks, and I twisted my fingers. "Then you remember me coming over? Finding you in the salon? You remember what I said?"

He nodded, his expression inexplicably distrustful and tense. "I remember. You said you wanted more than friendship with me."

I breathed a sigh of relief. "Yes." Okay. Good. Now we were getting somewhere.

"And I told you I love you," he said, his voice a rasp.

I smiled nervously, my heart pinging with pleasure, along with a bit of obstinate trepidation. "Yes. You did."

"And you told me we'd talk today, when I'm sober," he continued evenly.

Licking my lips, I nodded, but my smile waned as I studied him. He still did not look happy. *Why doesn't he look happy?*

Before I could ask, he said, "So talk. Unless . . ." One of his eyebrows lifted a scant inch, his eyes trailing down my body in a blatantly suggestive examination. "Unless you don't want to talk."

A new burst of heat—this one radiating downward from the back of my skull to my stomach—made me lose my breath. "No, no. I want to talk. We need to talk." Maybe it was silly, but after being grabbed by Jeff a few moments ago, I didn't particularly want to be that kind of physical with anyone right now.

His gaze cut back to mine, seemed to grow impatient. "Then talk."

My heart jumping to my throat in the face of his annoyance, I scowled at him. "Hey! I already talked. I told you I'm not upset about what happened at my apartment, then I reiterated what I said last night, which is that I'm hoping we can be more than friends. Now it's your turn."

His eyes were a gathering storm cloud. "*My* turn? If anything, it's your turn. I told you I love you. I meant it. I love you. I'm in love with you. You said we'd discuss it when I'm sober. Now I'm sober. You want to talk? Talk. There's nothing left for me to say." He sounded demanding again, still impatient, and both continued to fluster me.

"I want—Byron." I frowned at him, tripping over my words. "What are we going to do about it?"

"Do about what?"

I gave him a hard look, my temper flaring unexpectedly. I was usually so good at staying calm, but I felt all twisted around. *And why is he being like this?*

Irritatingly, his lips curved, possibly against his will. His words sounded like an accusation as he said, "You are very beautiful when you try to be intimidating."

"I'd prefer to be intimidating when I try to be intimidating."

"You're that too."

Our gazes held, and I felt my own lips reluctantly curve, falling a little deeper into this magnetic field between us. But I couldn't fall, not yet. Not until we figured out what precisely our next steps would be. He loved me, was in love with me, but didn't seem particularly ready or willing to change our present friendship course.

I tore my eyes from his achingly handsome face and lifted them to the ceiling, then dropped them to the floor, then inspected the wall and window behind him, looking everywhere but at Byron as I searched for calm, focus, and the right words.

I can do this. Stop being distracted by what happened with Jeff. Concentrate on Byron. Be logical.

Finally, drawing sensibility around me like a blanket, I said, "Fine. I'll talk. Obviously, I'm attracted to you. And you've been quite up-front regarding your feelings for me. So, based on our mutual feelings, as I see it—"

"Mutual? Are they *mutual*?"

Trying not to dwell on his belligerent tone, I ignored his odd question and continued. "As I see it, we have a few options about what to do moving forward."

"Options," he echoed, sounding incredulous. I ignored that too. I would not react. Maybe he was feeling crappy due to his hangover, but I would be calm and rational.

"Yes. We have choices to make, and we should do so together, so we're on the same page." I snuck a quick glance at him, found his gorgeous gaze hooked on my face, his features stern. I unnecessarily tucked my hair between my ears and paced away. "Option one is that we date."

"Date." He said the word like it tasted bad.

I began to pace faster. "Yes. Date. That is the natural next step. I haven't dated anyone—seriously dated—in a really long time, and then just the one person, and I, uh, I'm not sure that I'm as experienced as you are."

"I've never dated anyone. If you've dated one person, you're significantly more experienced than me."

"Well, that's another thing." I snuck a second quick glance at him, Jeff's comment from earlier nagging and ringing between my ears. "I believe in monogamy. For me, if I date someone, it would have to be monogamous."

"Are we getting married?"

Stunned from my blanket of sensibility by his startling question, my attention cut to his face, the nonsensical words at odds with his forthright tone and the earnestness of his features. But it couldn't have been a serious question.

"I'm trying to talk this through with you and you're being sarcastic?"

"I'm not being sarcastic. I'm asking, are we getting married?"

"What? Why—what? Are you telling me the only circumstance under which you'll be monogamous is for us to get married? You can't be serious. We haven't—we—Byron, stop messing with me and be serious."

"I'm not messing with you," he said, his voice low and quiet and hinting at a boiling temper. "I'm in love with you, Winnie. Naturally, I'd want us to get married. If you don't feel the same, just say so."

I rocked back on my heels. "Marriage?"

"People who love each other get married. Either you love me, or you don't."

Something in the vicinity of my heart spasmed. "Are you being serious right now?"

"Do I not look serious?"

He does look serious.

Trapped in a sinkhole of bewilderment and weighed down by a renewed surge of the lingering anxiety I'd been trying to conceal, I spoke stream of consciousness clumsiness. "I'm—we—we're not getting married! Just because two people love each other doesn't mean they automatically get married."

"So you do?"

"Do what?" My voice was almost a screech, and I reminded myself to control my volume.

He gave me a grim look but said nothing.

I was all mixed up and turned around. Regardless, Byron was likely hungover and didn't need me yelling at him (even if he was driving me absolutely bonkers).

I closed my eyes briefly, doing my best to regather my composure. "Look, I don't even know if I want to get married, ever. And I'm definitely not getting married at twenty-six." This time, I endeavored to keep my tone gentle, but a note of frustration bled into my statements, and I grimaced at how shrill I continued to sound.

This wasn't a decision one made the morning of a hangover or after slapping a longtime friend for being a grabby asshole. This was a decision made after months—if not years—of a committed relationship, after knowing each other intimately, the good and bad and everything in between.

Byron was the most logical person I knew, the most well-reasoned. Perhaps he wasn't quite sober after all. I inspected him for signs of inebriation and found none other than his tired eyes and the dark scruff on his jaw. But while I inspected him, something behind his gaze seemed to harden, push me away, place me at a distance, and left me mentally scrambling to catch up.

Eventually, he nodded once, and said, "Fine."

"Fine? What's fine?"

His head moved in another subtle nod, his stare shuttering further. "Glad we cleared that up."

Cleared that up? Cleared what up?

I covered my face, no longer trying to or capable of hiding my frustration. "Look. This is—this isn't what I wanted."

"Then tell me. Tell me precisely, what do you want from me, Fred?"

Once again, I tried not to allow his tone—this time, sedate hostility—bother me, but it did. I felt even more unsteady, unable to think, and I studied him from between my fingers. Searching for some semblance of the spark, the inferno he'd displayed freely and spoke of last night, I found nothing but aloof indifference.

Needing a minute, I hid behind my hands and breathed deeply, gathering my thoughts, until at long last I focused on what I thought was the most important question. "Do you want to give things between us a try or not? Are you interested in being more than just friends?"

The answer was yes. Obviously, it was yes. If he was in love with me, then the answer had to be yes.

Byron was silent.

I dropped my hands and stared at him, trying to read him. I couldn't. "Byron. Answer the question."

"No," he drawled. "I don't want to give things between us *a try*."

I blinked. Sharp sadness swept through me, hard and fast and painful, making my lungs ache and my eyes sting. A new surge of adrenaline made my ears ring. I tried to swallow but couldn't. But I did nod, a reflexive, meaningless movement, and I turned away, stumbling toward the door.

Here I was again, confused. So darn confused. *I can't think.*

I wasn't going to try to be with someone who couldn't agree to monogamy. Maybe it wasn't the case for other people, but I considered it to be the most basic, for me, requirement of a committed relationship. And I wasn't going to casually date Byron either. I didn't need a period of getting to know him, I already knew him too well. I knew what I wanted from him, and if he couldn't commit right off the bat, then forget it.

I deserved more, and I shouldn't have to settle for less, and I wasn't going to let anyone—not even Byron—treat me like crap.

What the heck? No. Not what the heck. *What the FUCK?*

"I don't understand," I croaked, turning to face him on distressed autopilot, angry tears welling in my eyes. "I don't understand you at all!"

Byron's eyebrows pulled together, but his jaw was a hard, determined line.

He wanted to be silent? Fine. He could be silent. But I couldn't be, my nerves were too raw. "I don't understand why you won't even try. You claim you're in love with me, but you'd rather, what? Not try at all if we don't immediately get married?" I didn't care if I was screeching or shrill. I felt like I'd opened the cage around my heart just for him to reach inside and break it.

He blinked several times, striding forward and stopping directly in front of me. His hand lifted as though to cup my face. At the last second, he stopped himself.

Yet he did speak, his voice was as careful as it was agitated. "Win, if I tried right now, I would fail. And I do not want to fail with you."

"How can you say that you'd fail?"

"I don't know how to try. I don't even know where to start. I have no experience trying. I can't lose you because I'm a shitty boyfriend."

I felt like grabbing him and shaking him. "Because you believe monogamy is for quitters?"

He reared back. "What?"

"If you wanted to be a great boyfriend, you would be." I jabbed an accusing finger toward his stupid, gorgeous face. "And how is it logical to say you'd make a shitty boyfriend, but you want to marry me? If you'd make a shitty boyfriend, then one would think you'd make a reprehensible husband. And, for the record, I believe neither of those would be true if you actually wanted to be with someone, if they were important enough to you to —to—to be faithful!"

"No, I—I mean, I apologize for—I just need to know if—" He expelled a breath, his pale cheeks and forehead turning pink. His hands lifted as though to touch me, but he rubbed his forehead instead. "Forget about the marriage thing. That was cowardly of me. But please listen for a moment. I watch people, okay? I observe. And a phenomenon I've observed many, many times is that it's extremely rare for couples to remain friends after a breakup, not in any meaningful way. It happens, but it's rare. Once that line is crossed, if things don't work out, then the friendship is over. I won't try unless, or until, I'm guaranteed to succeed."

"But you just said you love me."

"Correct."

"Then what is happening?" Screeching for real, I tossed my hands up in exasperation. "You asked me what I want, but what do you want? It seems like you want everything immediately, on your terms, without risking anything in return." My voice pitched higher, and I combated the urge to punch something. "You know what? Why am I doing this to myself? I knew it. I knew this would happen. This always happens when I'm stupid enough to be brave or ask for what I want. Forget it. FORGET IT!" I turned to storm away from him and out of here. I'd officially lost my temper. I could feel myself teetering on the edge, about to say something I'd probably regret.

But he caught my elbow before I could go far, stopping me and crowding my back.

"Stop, stop. Just, listen," he said, his voice low and gravelly and sad. "I've already risked everything, Win. You don't love me. I accept that."

I closed my eyes as my senses were overwhelmed by his gentle closeness, my body instinctively listing toward his, my back pressing against his front.

"Please don't leave angry." His hand tightened on my arm, and he whispered roughly, "Please don't be angry with me. What can I do? I will do anything."

"Then try."

"Anything but that."

"Why?"

"I don't want to tell you, and I don't want to lie to you."

I shook my head. "You won't even try." My voice broke, but I didn't care. Even though I couldn't see him, this current quiet exchange felt like a gift compared to our angry words from seconds ago.

He lowered his chin and rested it on my shoulder, his cheek brushing against my temple. "I can't."

"You have to tell me why." Worried he'd move away, I reached behind me and gripped the material of his pant leg. "Why won't you try?"

His arm wrapped around my middle, hugging me to him, and I melted into his strength, such a relief after Jeff's unwanted grasping. "The only thing—the *only* thing—I can't risk is losing you completely." Byron's chest rose and fell with a momentous breath. "Better we continue as we have, keep the other part of our lives separate, and always remain friends."

. . . keep the other part of our lives separate.

A burst of jealousy seized me as hot, angry tears rolled down my cheeks. My eyes fastened to the door, I struggled to keep the resentment from my voice. "Better for whom? You? How do you see this working? We hang out all the time and then you sleep with people you don't care about while I wait for you to call?" I shook my head resolutely. "No, thank you."

"Have you not been listening?" His arm tightened and his whisper became harsh. "I'm not sleeping with or touching or fucking anyone! You asked for monogamy? Well, you had it before you even asked for it. I don't want anyone else. I'm in love with you. With *you*."

My mouth worked to no purpose as his words saturated my senses and wreaked havoc on my insides, my brain a disaster of disorder. Byron never lied, so I knew he was telling the truth. But this couldn't possibly be what he wanted, could it? To remain friends and also to remain celibate? And for how long? Years? He was being so unfair, not just to me but also to himself.

"I don't want our friendship ruined due to my inexperience," he went on. As he spoke, his mouth brushed back and forth against the sensitive skin of my neck as though he was purposefully sensing the softness there with his lips, his actions and the reaction in my body totally at odds with his words.

"Our friendship would not be ruined." I tried for a whisper, but the statement sounded more like a breathless pant. Desire pooled in my abdomen, the sensation verging on painful. What this man did to me with just a brush of his lips should not be legal.

However, despite the web of longing he spun, my brain tripped and then rewound to the first part of his statement.

I don't want our friendship ruined . . .

I blinked, stiffened, and held my breath. He'd said something similar last night.

I will never touch you again if it would ruin things between us.

"It would be, due to my lack of tolerance, skill, and lack of sophistication," he muttered, his arm around my middle growing lax. "I won't allow it."

Meanwhile, only half listening, I tightened my grip on his pants. "Wait—wait, don't move. Let me think."

Byron stilled his retreat, but his arm withdrew until just his hand on my hip remained, a light touch.

I was determined that he not leave me, determined we talk this through.

If we didn't discuss this now, he would run away every time I brought it up in the future. Forcing myself to concentrate, I considered all he'd said, everything taken together, removing my own hopes from the equation as well as the persistent unsteadiness I'd felt since leaving the kitchen. Focusing only on his message, his words, I scoured them, searching for his intent.

What did he want? What did he actually want? And was it so different from what I wanted that we couldn't find a way forward?

. . . it's extremely rare for couples to remain friends after a breakup.

You don't love me. I accept that.

I don't want our friendship ruined.

I sucked in a slow, deep breath, realizing we'd been having two entirely different conversations.

I'd been so focused on becoming more than friends, I hadn't realized how desperate he was to not lose what we'd already built. It had taken us six years to have an honest conversation, and another eight weeks before agreeing to officially become friends.

Byron couldn't shift his mental gears this quickly. A guy who took pictures of the present before accepting any change, everything for him was a prolonged internal deliberation, an analysis of right and wrong, of risk and benefit. We'd just kissed last night for the first time, and the circumstances had been disorienting, even for me.

I'd expected too much too soon and, knowing this, I now saw the path forward.

Reaching my other hand behind me, I grabbed a fistful of his other pant leg, just to be safe. "Okay. I think I get it now."

"You do?"

"First, let me ask, do you actually want to get married? If I'd said yes, would you want to marry me?"

I sensed his hesitation, the intensity of his reluctance, before he finally said, "I would marry you today if you loved me and that's what you wanted. But I might need some time to—to, uh, adjust."

AH HA!

Certainty dawned on me like the sun, and I wiped the tears from my cheeks. "Okay. I get it. I understand."

The answer was so obvious to me now, I couldn't believe I didn't see it before. I'd be embarrassed if I wasn't so relieved.

"What do you get?" he asked, his low voice laced with suspicion.

I smiled. "You need to take things slow." Why he couldn't just say this himself would go down as one of life's eternal mysteries. Maybe it was his hangover? Or maybe he didn't realize what he wanted? Hadn't he said once that people might claim they want one thing when in reality their subconscious wants another?

Byron's chest rose and fell, rose and fell, the rhythm of his heartbeat increasing between my shoulder blades. And yet he neither confirmed nor denied my statement, which usually meant he agreed. This was a quirk in his personality, maintaining silence when his thoughts either felt too unwieldy or too close to revealing desires he'd rather keep hidden.

I nodded, relief coursing through me. "So we will take things slow. We'll be snails. We'll start with holding hands, kisses on the cheek, cuddling on the couch—that kind of thing."

"Winnie." My name sounded like a strangled plea.

I turned—careful to keep one of his pant legs in my grip—and faced him. "What? Friends hold hands. Friends kiss each other on the cheek and cuddle."

His hooded stare burned, his lips undecided whether to frown or give in to an unwilling smile.

I shrugged. "You want to stay friends? Fine. We'll behave as friends do. And if, over time, our friendship becomes something more . . ." My smile grew, and I felt a renewed sense of giddiness as I leaned close to whisper, "So be it."

Byron's gaze dropped to my mouth and the hand he'd kept on my hip flexed. "In other words, you're going to torture me."

"I'd never do that to a *friend*," I said sweetly, feeling good about this, feeling certain this would work, *we* would work.

We'd get there. I just needed to be patient, not push, and go extremely slow.

Lifting my chin, I felt a joyful thrill as his eyes closed, his forehead wrinkling, his breath reducing to quick puffing pants when I grazed the corner of his mouth on my way to his cheek. Once there, I gave him a perfectly chaste, light peck.

He groaned as I took a step backward, his finger hooking into my belt loop. And I grinned.

Okay. Yes. YES!

I could definitely work with this. We would try and do and go *slow* until he was ready to try and do and go fast.

CHAPTER 28
WINNIE

Byron absconded to New York the very next day, sending me a text message while I shoveled a lunch of leftover salmon and quinoa into my hungry mouth.

Byron: I'm going to New York a few weeks early, boarding now. See you in July

On a whim, I'd made the salmon for myself last night after Byron had turned down my offer to cook for him. I didn't want to push, so I'd left him alone at his house after our conversation in his bedroom. I guess now I knew why he didn't want to have dinner with me, he'd been arranging travel. *EXTREMELY SAD FACE.*

Upon initially reading his message, I couldn't decide how I felt. The planned trip to New York was just under four weeks away, which meant I wouldn't see him or talk to him in person for four weeks . . .?! I made a sound of distress, my lungs constricting.

But at the same time, if he needed to leave, then weren't these feelings of distress selfish?

Several follow-up texts arrived in rapid succession, interrupting my conflicting thoughts.

Byron: Text or call anytime while I'm gone

Byron: Also send pictures

Byron: Let me know how the interview goes

Byron: Or if you need anything

Byron: I'll miss you

Ah . . . Okay.

My confusion dissipated and my sorrow was cut in half. Now I understood. He felt overwhelmed and needed space but didn't want all the space. *Got it.*

I supposed I was beginning to understand Byron-speak, which I further supposed made me a Byron-whisperer. If I wanted a future with him, I'd have to learn how to walk this tightrope.

Staring at the last few texts, I bit my thumbnail. It was also possible he believed leaving would benefit me in some way. Maybe he thought my feelings weren't lasting and would fade in four weeks, or that I'd forget all he'd confessed while drunk and while sober.

I shook my head, frowning. My lunch forgotten for now, I debated how to respond to set the tone for these next few weeks. I wanted to let him know I understood and respected his need for space, that I was in this for the long haul, and four weeks apart wouldn't make a difference to my feelings. And I didn't want to pressure him or push him outside of his comfort zone.

No! ASK HIM TO STAY!

I shook my head at the selfish thought, reprimanding myself. If he needed physical distance, I didn't want to encroach on that.

But my attention snagged on his request, "Also send pictures," and I blinked, a glorious and wicked idea hitting me upside the head. I sat up straight.

Should I?

Nibbling my bottom lip, I considered the merits and the wisdom of this glorious, wicked idea. I trusted Byron completely, so the danger of him sharing photos with others was a nonissue. He'd asked me to send pictures, so I wouldn't be swerving outside implicit or explicit boundaries. And friends sent each other pictures all the time.

That said, these pictures wouldn't necessarily be friend appropriate. Then again, I'd sent photos of me in a bathing suit to Amelia and Lauren before, asking their opinion on the fit, and this wouldn't be all that different. Friends did those kinds of things . . .

Am I really going to do this?

I slipped off the stool, marching to my bedroom before bravery could fail me, sending two quick texts on my way.

Winnie: I will miss you too. But if you need to go, I understand. Interview isn't until later in July, so you should be home for that

Winnie: Also, first picture incoming. I need your advice

Even though Amelia wasn't yet home from her weekend with Elijah, I shut the door to my bedroom, stripped, and quickly dressed in a matching red lace bra and panty set. Then I snapped several selfies, trying my best not to crack up at my imagination's depiction of Byron's reaction when he received them.

Picking the most flattering of the shots, I added it to our text message exchange, and then—taking a deep breath—I sent it.

No going back now.

Hurriedly, I typed out another message.

Winnie: So, friend, before you go, your opinion is needed. This is for the Jupiter Awards (under the dress). Do you like?

I tossed my phone to my bed like a hot potato and covered my face. I'd never done anything like this before and now I felt scorching and sweaty with uncertainty, but I refused to regret it. Worst-case scenario, I'd just made a fool of myself and he didn't want those kinds of pictures from me. If that were the case, I felt certain he'd say so. And then we'd both have four weeks of distance and space before seeing each other again, which should ease the sting of embarrassment on my side.

But I truly did not believe that would happen. Byron would be thousands of miles away. He'd have all the physical distance he needed. And even if it was selfish of me, I needed him to know I was committed and my feelings were lasting. This—sending sexy photos—would be a good compromise.

Yes. This was a safe plan.

Surrendering to my impulsive actions, I grabbed my bathrobe, slipped it on, grabbed my phone, and returned to my half-eaten salad. Keeping one eye on the cell's screen as I ate, my heart jumped when three dots appeared, then disappeared, then reappeared, warning me of an incoming message from Byron.

Eventually, after what felt like hours, though it couldn't have been more than five minutes, he responded.

Byron: I like.

The lovely swirl in my stomach sent heat to my cheeks, and I laughed my relief. And then I sighed.

Yeah . . . This was a good compromise. And this was going to be fun.

I scrolled back up to the photo I sent, smiling at my sultry expression paired with the sexy lingerie I wore. But then a seed of doubt had me squirming in my seat. I quickly texted him back.

Winnie: In all seriousness, if I send you something and you don't like it, or if you feel like I'm pushing, please let me know

I'd just turned off the screen when a chime announced his response.

Byron: You don't ever need to worry about that

Byron: You know how much I enjoy offering my opinions

The reply made me unaccountably hot and breathless, but the sound of keys in the front door ripped my attention away from obsessing about his answer.

"I'm home! Is everyone fully clothed?" Amelia shouted, distracting me from my mooning.

Setting my phone on the counter, I hopped up and met her at the door. "Hey! Did you have fun?"

She passed me her laundry bag. "Yes. Both the play and dinner on Friday were awesome, and Saturday was spent lazing around, doing all the laundry. How about you? Is Byron here?" Amelia craned her neck as though trying to peek around me.

"No. Byron is not here." I carried her laundry into her room while she juggled bags filled with groceries. I called over my shoulder, "I actually just got a text from him. He's heading to New York early."

"What?" Her question was sharp. "When?!"

"Today." Wandering back into the kitchen, I smiled at Amelia's grumpy expression and grabbed the grocery bag filled with perishables.

"Ugh! He is so infuriating!" She growled this at the ceiling.

Her overt display of frustration made me laugh, and I placed the sliced meats and cheeses in the deli drawer of the fridge.

"Why do you look so happy about it?" She inspected me. "Are you . . . glad he left?"

"Well, kinda." I thought back to our text exchange from moments ago. The back and forth made me certain communicating via text message was likely better for a few weeks, given the nature of our conversation yesterday and Byron's difficulty with sudden changes. And feelings. And trust.

I needed to be careful with him.

The written word was explicitly voluntary in a way face-to-face exchanges were not. Text messages required consent of both the sender and the receiver. With face-to-face, the person who talks has all the power, and the listener gives, at best, only implicit consent.

Byron never had to see my messages if he didn't wish to. He could block my number or ignore me until—if or when—he was ready. Or he could just ask me to stop. It was a fail-safe way to protect him.

"You're happy he left?" Amelia sounded disappointed and concerned. "Did you two have a fight?"

"Let me, um, tell you what happened this weekend." I tucked my hair behind my ears and launched into the story.

While we unpacked the food, I filled her in on the events of the weekend. I told her about the leggings video and the crush kiss video too, but without including the hot and heavy details—only that he'd kissed me back without realizing the phone recorded us. I also told her how he'd left suddenly.

She shook her head, her lips pressed in a firm line. "He's terrified of losing control, but at a certain point he's got to realize it's not just about him. Byron's hard shell might protect him in the moment, but it will ultimately hurt him and others."

I returned to my salad, planning to eat while we chatted and she fixed herself lunch. "No, let him have his hard shell if he needs it. I don't mind."

"But you should mind. He's not the only one in this relationship, his boundaries and needs don't count for more than yours. You should crack that shell! Get a sledgehammer and smash it wide open."

I couldn't help but laugh at Amelia's hammer-meet-nail approach to almost everything. "Just let me finish telling you what happened."

Her eyes widened. "There's more?"

I nodded. Reluctantly digressing from the current subject, I filled her in on all the sordid details about Jeff and his being gross, kissing my neck and hugging me. I didn't particularly wish to discuss it and had considered not telling Amelia at all, but I wanted to make sure I hadn't overreacted when I slapped him.

Once she'd ascertained that I was truly okay after the encounter, she called him many colorful names. None of them were skeevy celadon or conceited chartreuse, but they amounted to basically the same thing.

We then returned to the second half of what had happened with Byron. Instead of detailing how I'd found him drunk and all the particulars of his middle-of-the-night confessions, I provided a benign summary. Byron's privacy paramount in my mind, I told her I went over to his house without specifying when and that he'd admitted to having feelings for me without specifying he'd used the word *love*. As well, I explained that he was hesitant to jeopardize our friendship, which I understood.

Stabbing her newly made pasta with a fork, she grumped. "You understand? I don't understand. There's being cautious, there's being risk-averse, and then there's Byron Visser. This is a pattern with him, this self-denial. It's like he's so afraid of anything good, of wanting anything, hoping for anything. He sabotages it before it can start." Amelia eyed me as she chewed. "So. What are we going to do about it?"

"Glad you asked." I grinned, clasping my hands together. "I told him that we would remain friends—"

"What?! No!"

"—and behave as good friends do, by holding hands, giving each other kisses on the cheek, hugging, cuddling, and so forth."

Amelia's eyes narrowed and seemed to dance with giddy suspicion. "Oh, I get it. You're going to seduce him."

My expression flattened. "No. I'm not going to seduce him. I don't want to push him—"

"No, no. Hear me out. You told Byron about your plans? Of course you did! Now he's expecting it—which is good since he doesn't do well with sudden change—but now that he's expecting it, he's also anticipating it, which means he won't do anything to stop it. To stop it would mean a sudden change. Brilliant."

I laughed at her sinister summary. "Not really."

She gave me too much credit for being devious. My plan hadn't been to trap or manipulate him into anything but rather to ease him into the idea, proceed at a pace he found comfortable. I knew he didn't want to lose our friendship or jeopardize it. If we moved super slow, I hoped he'd trust our friendship would survive whatever came next. Or, if he wanted to pull the escape hatch and stop the deliberate march toward more than friends, we'd be going slow enough that he comfortably could.

And if he did pull the escape hatch, then I'd just have to settle for friendship and figure out how to be okay with that. Just like—if he didn't ever want to be more than friends—he'd have to be okay with the possibility of me moving on with someone new . . . *like that would be possible if Byron was still in your life.*

Shoving that errant thought away, I focused on being supportive and reasonable. I would take one day at a time. What I wanted was for Byron to feel good about the direction of our relationship, not terrified that he'd lose me—

HE WILL LOSE YOU! If he doesn't want more than friendship, there's no way you can go back to simply friendship.

I wanted that internal voice to shut the hell up. I refused to give Byron ultimatums, I refused to be unreasonable or—

Winnie! Wake up and smell the inevitability. It is not unreasonable to tell him how you feel. You cannot remain "just friends" with Byron Visser. You can't—

The clatter of Amelia's fork as it hit the counter pulled me from my misbehaving thoughts, and she rubbed her hands together. "Okay, so. What's the plan? How do we do this if he's all the way in New York?"

"Uh, well." I pulled back the collar of my bathrobe and showed her the strap of my red bra. "I was thinking pictures."

Her eyes bugged out and her mouth fell open. "You sneaky genius."

I giggled nervously. "There's nothing unusual about sending friends pictures of outfits and asking for their opinion."

"Nothing at all," she said primly, barely containing her glee. "And didn't you need a new bathing suit? I believe you were thinking about buying a string bikini, weren't you?"

"Oh yes. You're absolutely right." I was not thinking about buying a string bikini, but now I was definitely going to try one on.

"We'll need your friend Byron's opinion on those." Amelia put on a silly affected tone, beaming at me. "And the dress for the Jupiter Awards. He'll need to see all the options."

"Quite, quite," I said with a terrible British accent, lifting my pinkie finger as I ate another forkful of salad and smiled at my friend.

Between my plans with Byron and the call I should be receiving this week from Amelia's work, I couldn't remember the last time I'd felt so hopeful and excited about the future.

* * *

Amelia and I went bathing suit shopping on Wednesday. She met me at Westlake Center after work and snapped photos of me in various bikinis that I'd never, ever actually wear in public. I was a teacher, and if I was spotted on Alki Beach in a string bikini and skimpy thong by a school administrator —or worse, a parent and student—I'd have some 'splaining to do.

And I didn't particularly like thongs. Some of my friends loved them, but they'd never felt comfortable to me. I always felt like I walked funny when wearing them—both the underwear and the bikini bottoms. But they did serve a purpose for my current, specific aims.

"Which one should I send him?" I scrolled through the most recent photos as we left the swimsuit area in search of the formal wear section.

"Why only send one? Send them all. Oh! But send only one a day, at the same time every day. Then he'll be watching his phone like a hawk every night at 10:00 p.m. He'll be like Pavlov's dogs, but happier, with both saliva *and* a boner."

I snort-laughed at her vulgarity and opened the messenger app to my texts with Byron. Selecting a photo of me in a truly daring red bikini that was all tiny triangles and strings, I sent it through, and then added a message.

Winnie: Shopping for bathing suits. I would love your opinion about this one, friend

Over my shoulder, Amelia guffawed after she read what I'd written, wiping her eyes as we stepped off the escalator. "I swear, my entire friendship with Byron has been leading to this moment. This is the payoff, seeing him love every minute of being tortured by you. I can't tell you how happy this all makes me, for you both."

"You don't think the photos are a bit much?" I didn't think they were, and each time I checked in with Byron about it since Sunday, he'd voiced no complaints. But I wanted Amelia's critical, honest opinion. She'd known Byron longer than me. I'd stop if she advised me to stop.

"Are you kidding?" She wrinkled her nose. "Absolutely not! This is so good for him. He *needs* this. You are doing the Lord's work here. He needs someone who is persistent and trustworthy, someone he can count on to be honest and push him outside of his comfort zone, not make excuses for him or enable him to hunker down and keep avoiding life. But also someone who will stick in there for the long haul, get creative when faced with these walls he puts up."

Something about the way she said "stick in there for the long haul" made the fine hairs on the back of my neck stand at attention. I thought back to that night Byron dyed my hair, when he'd asked me if Amelia had ever discussed his family.

Amelia had mentioned in passing once that Byron's mother was some sort of engineering genius, a research professor at a big East Coast university, but she'd never mentioned anything about his father or—if he had them—his siblings. Now that I thought about it, Byron never mentioned his family either, except for that one time. And how could Byron be raised in Eastern Oregon if his mother had been a professor on the East Coast?

Before I could fully formulate or order my questions, my phone buzzed, announcing a text and sending my heart to my throat.

Since the photo of me in the red bra and undies, Byron and I had been texting back and forth. Nothing scandalous, just very normal chatter between good friends. We'd even talked briefly on Monday night, a quick ten-minute phone call about how loud New York traffic was. He'd said he wanted to hear my voice. *Sigh.* He was so sweet.

Narrowing my eyes on my friend to let her know I wanted privacy to read Byron's response, I peeked at his message.

Byron: More samples are needed. I require additional information before committing to an opinion on this subject. You'll need to send supplementary data points (i.e., pictures of various alternatives) ASAP

Trying not to squeal, I quickly responded.

Winnie: Fair enough. I'll send more data points this week.

I paused, swallowing around a bundle of nerves as I considered Amelia's statements from a few minutes ago. I wasn't sure I agreed with her assertion that Byron needed to be pushed out of his comfort zone. I didn't want to push him. More like, I hoped to leave a trail of breadcrumbs for him to follow should *he* want to step outside of his hard shell.

Maybe he wasn't ready to step outside his boundaries. Maybe he never would be ready. That was fine. I knew I had to protect my heart against that possibility—and I would, I would guard my heart, I would not allow myself to fall in love with him—but in an effort to provide that trail of optional breadcrumbs, I texted him again.

Winnie: Of note, I want to make sure you know that I am also here for you in a similar capacity, should you want my opinion on underwear, swimsuits, or even the sizes of hotel bath towels. But no pressure.

Grinning like a maniac—which seemed to be my baseline whenever texting with Byron these days—I lifted my gaze and found Amelia watching me, her eyes bright and her lips rolled between her teeth, clearly fighting the huge smile threatening to overpower her face.

"What?" I asked innocently.

"Nothing," she said, her voice equally innocent. Amelia looped our arms together and added, "I was just going to say—before we were interrupted by your very important message—that although Byron has me in his life, I'm like a sister from another mister, I irritate him just as much as I make him laugh. But he adores you. He's got banana pants for you. And he needs to know he's someone who can be adored, and that you have kiwi pants for him."

I cut her a sidelong look. "Kiwi pants?"

Amelia tilted her head as though considering my question. "You know what I mean. Fuzzy, juicy, fleshy, and tangy."

I scrunched my face, huffed a laugh, and sighed. I loved Amelia. She kept me on my toes, and I could always count on her, no matter what. But her brain certainly did work in mysterious ways.

"Come on." I tugged on her arm. "Let's go find the dresses."

We walked into the formal dress section of the department store just as my phone vibrated again. Amelia, content to dig through the racks, left me to check my phone without so much as a suggestive wink. Mentally preparing myself for another of his cute responses, my mouth fell open in shock, blood rushing to every sensitive part of me as I beheld his latest message.

Byron. Staring with his hooded, gorgeous eyes at the camera. A faint smirk on his face. A wee little towel wrapped around his narrow hips. And that's it.

I was still gaping, and probably drooling, when his next text arrived.

Byron: Opinion needed. Is this towel too small?

Certain I would pass out if I didn't remind myself to breathe, I heaved a shaky exhale and responded immediately.

Winnie: Really glad you asked. If anything, it's too big.

* * *

I was trying not to worry.

Three weeks had passed since the Friday night Amelia had mentioned I should expect to be contacted soon about the community manager interview. I hadn't received a call or email yet.

I'd triple checked the telephone number and email address I'd sent in with my resumé.

I'd circled back with Amelia last Friday, trying to be casual about my questions, asking if she'd heard anything about the interviews. She'd given me two thumbs up and said they were still working on scheduling everything and confirmed they would all take place after I returned from New York in mid-July, so I should relax and enjoy my summer. I tried to, but I couldn't shake the sense something was wrong, and it was definitely affecting my mood.

So when Jeff texted me after radio silence since his morning of drunken bad decisions—

Jeff: Can we please get together for lunch? I'm really sorry about what happened. I was drunk and not acting like myself. Are you going to tell Byron?

—I did not message him back. As much as I felt bad for him about Lucy, I did not believe my stomach could handle eating food while looking at his face. I hadn't told Byron what had happened, but not for any reason other than I simply didn't wish to rehash it. Or think about it. Or discuss it. So I didn't.

Unfortunately, I wasn't doing a great job of hiding my bad mood. During my live videos—which I'd started up again once the mean comments about my Byron worthiness mostly subsided—I'd get comments asking if I was sad or if something was wrong.

Even Byron, thousands of miles away, must've sensed my worry. He'd started calling me almost every night. We didn't talk about the sexy photos we'd been sending back and forth, and he never asked what was wrong, but he'd end each call with something like, "I hope you realize how extraordinary you are."

His sweet words would bolster my mood for a bit, but then I'd crash-land back into worry within an hour, toss and turn as I tried to sleep, and fret during my early morning jogs through Volunteer Park.

For the first time since surpassing one hundred thousand followers, I worried I wouldn't get the interview, and that made me sick to my stomach. I never should've taken for granted that I would. They didn't owe me the interview or the position, and it had been silly of me to pin all my hopes on the opportunity. Not wanting to count on grants that might never materialize, I'd pushed the Parent-Teacher Organization to let me have that auction for the science fair, hadn't I? I should've approached this community manager position with just as much skepticism.

Old fears resurfaced—about whether the additional content I'd been doing for my accounts had been wise, about whether the fashion, makeup, and romance challenges undermined my credibility as a scientist—and I found myself shoving them away repeatedly, making myself restless with anxiety.

Byron had helped me logic through these fears weeks ago, and I hadn't second-guessed my decision since. Until now. Until I was three weeks past a phone call, wondering what I did wrong—if I did anything wrong—and wishing there were something I could do to end this restless, listless discontent.

What I needed to do was formulate a backup plan. Counting on one person or one solution always spelled disaster. I knew this. I could only ever count on or expect things from myself. Over the course of my life, I'd learned this lesson too many times. Relying on anyone but yourself always led to disappointment.

Which was why, on the Friday that officially marked three weeks since Amelia said I should be expecting a call—the same Friday that Byron and I had shared our first kiss—I marched myself to the downtown Seattle Library with an iced tea, opened ten tabs in my internet browser full of potential leads on similar positions, and got to work.

I applied for anything and everything remote, STEM focused, part time with flexible hours, and social media based. Several hours later, finished with my job search for now, I rolled up my sleeves and got to work emailing local businesses about donating items for my science fair auction. I'd been so mired in sadness about the community manager job, I hadn't been as proactive with the auction as I should have been.

Starting tomorrow, I'd hit the pavement and go door to door in Downtown, First Hill, Capitol Hill, Madrona, and Montlake, asking businesses for donations. It would take me all week to cover every neighborhood, but so be it.

A new spring in my step, I decided to walk all the way home instead of taking the light rail but talked myself out of stopping into Phoenix Games to check out their new inventory. It had been well over a year since I'd bought a new board game, but I couldn't take for granted I'd get any job I'd applied for. I couldn't afford to waste money on something nonessential.

Instead, I contented myself with looking at the window display and blatantly ogling the box illustrations of a game called Everdell. The display version in the window had the 3-D tree. I'd been lusting after it for several months. *So pretty.*

"Winnie?"

My head turned at the sound of my name. I scanned the busy, sunny sidewalk and told myself for the hundredth time that I needed to buy some sunglasses. During the dark wet of winter, I always lost my drugstore sunglasses and spent the first half of summer squinting.

A woman I recognized walked toward me, her hand around a leash with an adorable-looking dog at the end of the lead.

"Oh, hey Christy. How are you?" I waved, kneeling to pet her dog as he arrived first.

Christy Burgess was my school's drama teacher and one of the most brilliant people I'd ever met. An expert on all things Shakespeare, she usually had a colorful quote for every occasion. One time, she'd had me in stitches with a list of her favorite Shakespearean insults. In order to help pay back her student loans, her side-hustle jobs included directing performances of Shakespeare in the Park, teaching drama summer camps for the performing arts center, and running a Saturday improv class for both adults and kids. I admired her so much.

"I'm good!" She smiled broadly. "Just stopping by Mud Bay to pick up a new brush for Iago here. How are you? Are you getting a chance to relax?"

I gave Iago my ear in order to avoid getting a tongue in my mouth, laughing at his slobbery friendliness. "A little bit. I'm just about to get started on the auction for the science fair, and—"

"Oh! Congratulations on funding the science fair. I was so happy when I heard. What a relief. I was worried it'd be canceled this year, and I know how much the kids going in to eighth grade were looking forward to it."

"Hey. Thanks." I stood, but I kept my fingers in Iago's fluffy mane. I'd always wanted a dog and had accepted it would be at least a decade before I'd be able to afford one. But I never passed up the chance to soak up some of their unconditional love. I also held out hope that—as a selfish upside to Amelia and Elijah eventually moving in together—I'd get to finally be a dog aunt. Amelia had always wanted a dog too. "It was a bit of a battle, talking the PTO into letting me do the auction, but it's going to be great. In fact, I sent out a bunch of emails today to local businesses and will be going around in person tomorrow to follow up."

Her eyebrows pulled together. "Why?"

"You know, for donations."

She gave me a confused smile. "Winnie, you don't need any donations. The science fair is fully funded."

"What?" Now I gave her a confused smile.

"Yeah."

"But how? And when?"

"Oh, sorry, sir." Christy wrapped the leash tighter around her hand as Iago tried to get fresh with an elderly man walking by and then turned back to me. "A few weeks ago. It was a line item in the budget planning meeting for next year and was marked as being funded by an outside source. I was at the meeting to lobby for three car washes this fall instead of just two. There's no way I can fund the sets needed with just two car washes."

"No, no. The science fair isn't funded. They must've meant it would be funded. I haven't—"

"No. It's fully funded for the next ten years." She patted Iago on the head when he didn't nosedive into the crotch of another passerby. "There was a note in the margin. I specifically remember Chen asking for clarification, and Bhavna said—oh shoot, what'd she say?" Christy covered her mouth with her fingertips, frowning at the pavement, clearly trying to remember what Bhavna, our school secretary, had said about the science fair. "Sorry." She let her hand drop. "It was something about a private donation, or a bulk donation for the wider school auction. Something like that. Anyway, you should email Bhavna." Her focus moved to some point behind me. "Listen, I have to go. But have a great summer, okay?"

Speechless, oscillating between hopeful confusion and pragmatic denial, I nodded and waved farewell as she and Iago continued on their way. As soon as she turned the corner, I pulled out my phone and emailed Bhavna.

Christy must've been mistaken. If the science fair had been funded, I would know about it.

CHAPTER 29
WINNIE

"Are you excited?" Amelia patted my leg, her grin enormous.

The pilot had just announced we were beginning our final descent, and I didn't know who was looking forward to seeing Byron more, me or Amelia. Or maybe she was excited to see me and Byron together in the same place after nearly a month of phone calls and text messages.

She's not the only one.

I pressed a hand to my stomach as I eyed New York City from my window seat. "I am excited," I offered faintly. I was nervous. In addition to the Byron-related butterflies I'd been combating—i.e., worrying I'd allowed my expectations of him and of this trip to get out of control—this had been my first time traveling via airplane. I hadn't enjoyed the takeoff, and the idea of going through the reverse with the landing made my palms damp with cold sweat.

"The landing is easier than the takeoff," Elijah said, obviously reading my mind. He leaned over Amelia to offer me a piece of gum. "For fresh breath and depressurized ears."

"Thanks." I accepted the gum, thankful to have something to do other than pray and swallow.

At the last minute, Amelia and Elijah had decided to fly with me to New York and tag along for the weekend. Amelia needed to get back to Seattle by Sunday night as her company's new grant monies had been distributed and activities were ramping up for a mid-August kickoff.

Meanwhile, no one from her company had called me about an interview. But that was perfectly fine, and I saw no reason to mention it to Amelia. It would be unfair of me to expect her to intervene on my behalf.

Determined to handle things myself, I'd spent the last week researching and filling out job applications. I wasn't counting on or hoping for the community manager job anymore and, as such, my mood had improved significantly.

However, I did hear from Bhavna. She'd returned my email last Saturday, the day after my conversation with Christy. To my complete shock and bewilderment, the school secretary had confirmed what Christy had told me. The science fair was funded and would be funded continuously for the next ten years. The school had received what Bhavna referred to as a "bulk item donation of one thousand samples" for the general school auction, earmarked specifically for the science fair, the new computer lab, and for new library books. She expected the money raised to fund all these initiatives in full.

I'd responded, requesting more details—what precisely was this bulk item donation, what kind of "samples," who donated it, and how did I express my gratitude—but Bhavna hadn't emailed me back by the time we'd boarded the flight to New York this morning.

"Okay! Byron said he's sending a car to pick us up. Elijah and I will drop you off at your hotel first and then head over to our rental in the Village. We'll meet you guys for dinner." Amelia turned to Elijah. "I can't believe Byron wants to go out to dinner. I've known him almost my whole life and we've never gone out to dinner. Not once. He hates crowds."

"Winnie knows the plan, Amelia." Elijah offered his lady love a stick of gum. "You've been talking about it nonstop. She's not going to forget about dinner."

"I know, I know. I'm just so excited about that apartment we got. Don't you think it's amazing that it wasn't booked for this weekend? It's like we were meant to fly out here with Winnie." She made a happy sound and turned back to me. "Are you sure you're going to be okay tomorrow? You feel good about everything?"

"Yep. Feel great."

Starting tomorrow and through Wednesday, I'd be accompanying Byron to his gauntlet of interviews, acting as his buffer. His manager together with his agent had sent me an agenda earlier this week with the finalized schedule. They would both be there. I'd made a point of researching each of the interviewers, scanning through their social media accounts for mentions of hobbies, tastes, previous jobs, where they went to college, etc. so I could engage with them and take the pressure off Byron.

With all my freedom this past week—since I no longer needed to go door to door asking for auction donations—I'd recorded several STEM and makeup tutorial videos for my social media channels and completed two continuing education courses. This was in addition to creating dossiers on the interviewers and applying for jobs. I'd also gone on a trail hike with Danielle and Olivia—the lovely ladies Amelia and I met at Lucy and Jeff's doomed dinner party—following it up with tubing down the Pilchuck River while wearing one of the more conservative bikinis I'd sent to Byron.

Yes, Byron and I were still sending photos, asking each other's opinions on everything from towels to bathing suits to gray sweatpants to more of those magical TikTok leggings. I still hadn't posted the leggings or the kiss your crush videos, even though Byron had told me both were fine to post whenever I wanted.

Obviously, if I did post the kiss your crush video, I'd edit the heck out of it, showing only the quick, chaste kiss instead of the makeout session that followed. But I hesitated, and the reason I hesitated struck me as painfully ironic. Since Byron and I were becoming more than friends, it now felt newly disingenuous to post videos of us pretending to be *just* friends.

Don't ask me why my brain is this way. I HAVE NO ANSWERS!

Worse, people were starting to comment on my videos and posts more and more, asking if or when Byron and I would do another challenge video. They continued to be, by far, my most viewed content, and I didn't know how to proceed.

So I'd deferred any decision-making until I saw Byron, counting on him to help me reason through the problem.

Closing my eyes as we plummeted toward the ground, I focused on chewing my gum, wondering if I could switch my return seat to an aisle instead of a window. *Or,* my brain offered, *next time just close the shade.*

Amelia gripped my hand and whispered words of encouragement while Elijah made small talk with a guy across the aisle. The plane touched down, my stomach rising when it bounced twice and as we decelerated.

And then it was over.

"See?" Amelia wiggled her hand, forcing me to loosen my grip. "Not so bad."

I huffed a laugh and nodded. *Indeed.*

Hopefully, the rest of the trip would be smooth sailing in comparison.

* * *

As expected, Byron's driver met us at baggage claim. Not as expected, there were two drivers. One held a sign with my last name and the other held a sign with Amelia's.

I'd checked a large suitcase to accommodate the dress and accoutrements needed for the Jupiter Awards. Since I needed the big bag anyway, I also added two boxes of See's dark chocolate for Byron, food therapy to help him get through the interviews.

Amelia and Elijah, however, had brought only backpacks and small carry-ons. They offered to hang out with me while I waited at baggage claim, but I waved them off, telling them to go check in to the temporary rental they were so excited about.

We said our goodbyes for now and they followed their driver out of the airport. About an hour later—during which my driver, Alvin, and I chatted about his life and where he was from and how he liked New York and how he met his wife—I also followed my driver out of the airport and to a waiting SUV parked in a section marked Private Transportation.

My sightseeing tour and friendly conversation with Alvin was interrupted about twenty minutes after walking out of the airport when my phone rang, Amelia's smiling face flashing on my screen.

"Hello?" I answered on speakerphone.

She heaved a sigh before she spoke. "Okay. I have some bad news."

"Oh no. What's wrong?" I sat forward in my seat.

"So, the apartment was a scam. It doesn't exist, and now I feel like a moron."

I could tell she was doing her best to remain calm, but I knew how excited she'd been about the apartment.

"I am so sorry."

"I don't know what we're going to do. I've been calling hotels for twenty minutes while Elijah has been looking online. Everything is booked. Even the airport hotels are booked." Her voice cracked, and I heard Elijah say something comforting in the background.

"Did your driver already leave?"

"Yes. He was awesome, but he's long gone. I didn't want him to have to wait around for our contact from the rental to meet us. I feel so stupid."

I met Alvin's gaze in the mirror, and he mouthed, "We'll go get them." I nodded.

"This is what we're going to do. Send me your current location. Alvin and I will come by and pick you up. We'll all go to the hotel where Byron and I are staying."

"I tried calling there already. It's *waaay* out of our price range, but even if we could afford it, it's totally full. That's where everyone seems to be staying for the awards."

"Text Byron, let him know what's happening. He might be able to wrangle a room even if they're telling you everything is booked. Worst case, you can stay with me. I have an entire hotel room all to myself."

"Win—"

"Don't worry about it! Besides, what am I going to do with a giant hotel room?" I asked cheerfully, sharing another look with Alvin.

He smirked but said nothing.

* * *

Apparently, New York hotel rooms are the size of closets.

"And I thought our apartment was small." I walked seven feet forward into the room and then stopped. That was as far as I could go. It had a small bathroom with a tiny shower, a full-sized bed, a sliver of a nightstand, and a TV hanging on the wall.

That said, it was tastefully decorated and the south-facing view from the window was gorgeous.

I turned and found Amelia and Elijah standing slack-jawed with dismay by the door. I couldn't help but laugh. There was no way we'd all be able to sleep in here. We barely fit standing.

Elijah and I traded a wide-eyed look and he also started to laugh, shuffling forward and pushing my big bag into the bathroom at his left. The hotel room door couldn't close, not yet, and it quickly became clear that Amelia would have to get on the bed along with their bags in order for it to shut.

At that moment, Byron appeared in the open doorway behind them and my spine stiffened, the small room forgotten as we locked eyes over Amelia's head.

I couldn't believe it. He was here. *He's right there!* My heart hammered. I shouldn't have been surprised, I knew Amelia had texted him, but the sight of him still took my breath away. He wore all black, as usual, and looked exactly the same. Well, almost the same. His hair seemed shorter than in his last photo.

At the thought of his last photo, my cheeks and chest ignited. He'd been shirtless and wearing gray boxer briefs and his . . . well, let's just say they were extremely tight and left very little to the imagination.

I wanted to cross the short distance to hug him, but Amelia, Elijah, and their bags formed a bottleneck in the doorway.

"Well. . ." Elijah—apparently not yet seeing or sensing Byron in the hall—guided a shell-shocked Amelia to the bed, encouraging her to sit and then loaded their bags on her lap. "I've always said that I wanted to get to know you better, Winnie. Now's our chance."

I watched as Byron frowned and removed his gaze from mine. He blinked at the back of Elijah's head and then his gaze shifted to the room—what there was of it—his eyes growing just as wide as Amelia's.

"What the hell is this?" Byron's voice had Elijah turning and Amelia peeking around the corner from where she sat.

"Byron!" Amelia tried to stand but couldn't. Instead, she waved. "This is all my fault."

Expression grim, Byron's attention hooked back into mine. "I had no idea your room was this small." He didn't sound sorry, he sounded pissed. "I told my manager to book you a suite. She will be hearing from me."

"Don't worry about it. I don't need a suite." I'm sure I sounded a little dazed. I didn't care where I slept, I was just so happy to see him.

"You can't stay here," he said, his voice gruff. "This isn't acceptable."

Elijah lifted his hand for Byron to shake. "Sorry about the trouble."

Byron glanced at Elijah's hand, his frown intensifying, and shook it. "Don't worry about it. But—uh—why don't you and Amelia leave your things here and head out. Winnie will come with me. We'll get this sorted and meet you for dinner."

Elijah, visibly relieved, thanked Byron and stepped out into the hall. Amelia pushed the bags from her lap and gave him a hug before joining Elijah. They both offered me silent waves over Byron's shoulder and then departed, leaving us alone in a room the size of my supply closet at school.

I shifted my weight from foot to foot as Byron stepped forward and allowed the door to close, his handsome features made severe with plain unhappiness.

"It's so good to see you." I found I needed to clear my throat before continuing. "In person, I mean."

Still hovering by the door, he slid his hands into his pockets. "I am so sorry about the room. I meant what I said, this isn't acceptable."

"It's fine."

"It's not. Don't say it is. And you're not going to—" Byron abruptly snapped his mouth shut, glanced at the ceiling, and inhaled deeply before continuing in a quieter, calmer voice. "If I can't get another room for you or for them, I would *prefer* if you didn't stay here with Amelia and Elijah."

"Okay . . .?" I glanced at the full-sized bed. "Then what should I do?"

He stared at me for a long moment, like I was a book he was trying to read. Then, eventually, Byron took a small step forward. "Would you stay with me?"

"With you?" I asked, my voice tight. My heart jumped around my chest and swooped down to give my stomach a high five.

The side of his mouth curved ever so slightly. "I have a suite with a couch and a full-sized bed. I'll sleep on the couch. You can have the bed."

"Oh." I nodded while my heart and stomach paused their celebration, not sure what to think. "But I should take the couch. I'm shorter."

"We'll figure it out." He drifted another step closer, dipping his head as he held my eyes. "Is that a yes?" he asked quietly, his gaze searching.

"Yes." I smiled. "Yes, that's a yes."

"Good." He returned my small smile, sounding pleased, then tilted his head toward the door. "Come on. Let's get this debacle sorted."

Smiling shyly, because—quite frankly—I felt a little shy, I followed Byron out of the room and into the hall. Hands still in his pockets, he stalled until I was beside him, then we walked toward the elevator side by side.

"How was your flight?"

"Good. Fine." I didn't feel like talking about turbulence right now. I wanted to know about him, so I changed the subject. "How has your time been here?"

Byron stared forward, his features growing cagey. "Uh, elucidating."

"Elucidating? Well, that sounds mysterious."

He sorta smirked but didn't look at me or say anything else as we neared the elevator. I was at a loss. We'd spent four weeks engaging in banter disguised as seeking each other's opinion via text without actually saying anything overtly suggestive, all the while trading photos of us wearing almost nothing. When we'd talked on the phone, our conversations had been both excessively friendly and platonic, neither of us mentioning the pictures.

I'd been patient for a month, and I was prepared to be patient indefinitely if that's what he needed. I told myself I didn't want to pressure him.

However, now that he was here and I was faced with the reality of Byron, some errant, irritating part of me did want to pressure him, did want to ask where we stood and what he was thinking and if he was ready to move beyond friendship, but I didn't know how to broach the topic.

I didn't understand this part of myself. This was not me. I didn't push, I left breadcrumbs.

Those breadcrumbs are stale. PUSH HIM!

Scrunching my face against the restless ache of my heart, I shoved down this bubbling urge to make demands, to want more than he might be willing to offer freely, and I decided to say nothing.

Yes, the answer was to not broach the topic at all. The answer was to simply relax and spend time being friendly with my friend, not expect too much, and let things come as they would.

Or, if he was never ready, so be it. I would be fine. I'd guarded my heart and had reinforced the walls since our talk in his room last month. The only way I would consider handing over the key to that lock was after months and months of us being more than friends. If we never made it that far, I would survive and thrive no matter what he ultimately decided.

Nodding and surrendering to the wisdom of this answer even if it made my heart feel like a suffocating, wild, caged animal, I reached forward to call the elevator.

"Where are we going? Down or up?"

"Down," he answered. "We'll go to the concierge first."

"Okay." I pressed the down button and stepped back, glancing at Byron and finding his watchful eyes on me.

"It's so good to see you, Fred." His stare drifted from mine to move over my face—hair, forehead, nose, cheeks, lips. "In person."

Even though I'd just decided to relax and approach our interactions as a friend would, my stupid heart staged a sneaky coup d'état. I gave his shoulder an impulsive, light shove. "What? You didn't like my pictures?"

Byron caught my hand and held it tightly. "I did. Very much. More than I'll ever allow you to know." His stare still fastened to my lips, he added, "But there's only so much one can do with pictures."

CHAPTER 30
WINNIE

Byron could not secure a different room for me or for Amelia and Elijah. No matter how much he made the concierge, the concierge's manager, and the hotel manager fret and sweat and apologize, there were simply no rooms to be had. All the area's hotels had been booked solid for months.

They made me a key for Byron's suite while he called Amelia and broke the news about the room. He also explained the plans for the evening's sleeping arrangements. I kept stealing glances at him, trying to hide my grin as he rolled his eyes at something Amelia said, his pale cheeks tinting pink after he told her how we'd be sharing his suite.

Despite my continued determination not to get my hopes up, I'd been grinning since he'd said that thing about pictures earlier, just before the elevator had arrived and cut the tense moment short.

Waiting for him to finish his call, I meandered around the VIP check-in area, cataloging the perks of being a VIP instead of a plebeian. They had a full-service bar in one corner with several big, comfy-looking leather chairs directly in front of it. A small business center with a copy machine, computer, and photo printer sat behind a wall of glass next to the desk where Byron stood, still talking on the phone. The big room also had one of those high tech, built-in coffee makers that brewed espresso, cappuccino, and drip coffee with the touch of a button.

"Ms. Gobaldi."

I turned at the sound of my name and found the concierge at my shoulder wearing a pained look.

"Hi." I gave her a little wave.

"Allow me to express again how very sorry I am that we could not accommodate Mr. Visser's request."

"It's fine."

She still seemed distraught as she gestured that I should follow her from the VIP area. "His representative booked Mr. Visser's suite back in December and only added your reservation in April. By then, all we had left were the standard rooms. But she did put you on the waiting list for a suite, should one open up. Unfortunately, we've had very few cancellations."

"Makes sense. Please don't stress about it." I glanced over my shoulder as we left the room, hoping to catch Byron's eye. He was still on the phone.

"Please allow us to move your bags to Mr. Visser's room. And here"—she gestured to an elevator I hadn't noticed when we'd walked in—"this will take you to the penthouse level." She scanned a key card, then pressed the up button, handing me the card once the light illuminated. "This card will allow you access to all the VIP areas. Mr. Visser asked that I send you up to his room so that you can relax before dinner."

The elevator doors slid open, and she motioned for me to step inside. Always one to follow directions, I did.

"We'll send up a tray of refreshments as well." She took one step inside the elevator and pressed the button labeled 35, then stepped back. "Mr. Visser informed us that you'll be eating elsewhere tonight?"

"Yes. That's right."

"Well then, when you return, let me know if there is anything I can do to make your stay more comfortable. Please don't hesitate."

"O-okay. Thank you."

"Anything you need, just say the word. If you're missing any toiletries or just want a midnight snack, do not hesitate to call. We are stocked like a drugstore and a grocery store. If we don't have what you want, I can send someone out, and I will personally make sure it happens. Nothing is out of the question."

"Uh . . . thanks." I tried to hide my discomfort in the face of her effusiveness.

Apparently, I hid it well considering how pleased her smile looked just before the doors closed.

* * *

Byron didn't come up to the room before dinner. He texted about a half hour after I left him in the VIP area, saying he had to meet his agent, publisher, and the producer who'd secured the movie rights for his book series. I remembered the meeting being on the agenda his manager had sent me last week. According to the schedule, it was supposed to last for several hours.

The suite wasn't one of those palatial penthouses you always see depicted in movies or TV shows, though the view was impressive. Central Park stretched directly beneath the floor-to-ceiling windows, allowing me to people-watch, figures as small as ants running and walking through the park. While I studied the little ant people, it occurred to me that today was the first time I'd ever seen Byron outside of my apartment, his house, or the dorms where we all used to live.

Obviously I knew he ventured into public places back in Seattle. He played rugby. He went to Nuflours and picked me up scones. He'd mentioned once that he went on runs in Interlaken Park.

But when I thought of Byron, I only ever thought of him being in a quiet, private space.

My bags arrived along with the tray of refreshments, none of which I ate just in case they were made with wheat or had traces of it. I leisurely changed into my black wrap dress and applied fresh makeup. I noted that none of Byron's things were scattered about. His suitcase was zipped and placed in a corner of the bedroom, as though he'd just arrived this afternoon as well.

Huh. I made a mental note to ask him about it.

Taking my time browsing the shops in the lobby, I met Amelia and Elijah at 7:00 p.m. in front of the hotel. We walked over to a restaurant Byron's agent had recommended called Le Chat. We were seated at a round table with four chairs in the center of the restaurant, menus handed over, and water glasses filled. When the maître d' left, Elijah and I nearly swallowed our tongues as we read the prices.

"I hear there's a good pizza stand in Times Square," Elijah whispered, shifting in his seat.

"Don't make things weird." Amelia chided her boyfriend. "Byron offered to take us out. Order whatever you want."

"That's easy for you two to say," he grumbled. "You're his best friend and Winnie is his girlfriend. I've only met the bloke three times before now, and I'm not used to being wined and dined by strange men."

His last comment made me laugh. But I didn't get a chance to correct his assumption about Byron and I dating. The man himself strolled into the restaurant, and this time I think I did swallow my tongue. Or I came dangerously close to choking on it.

Byron wore a delectable dark gray suit. Or rather, the dark gray suit wore a delectable him. Our gazes locked across the restaurant—his made even more vivid by the aquamarine color of his dress shirt—and I sucked in a slow, shaky breath.

"Huh," Amelia muttered, sounding thoughtful as he approached. "I haven't seen that one before. I wonder where he got it."

"Am I late?" Removing his eyes from mine just briefly, Byron nodded to Elijah, bent to give Amelia a quick kiss on the cheek, and then captured my hand, lifting the back of it to his lips for a kiss. "Have you been waiting long?" he asked me.

"Not long," I responded hoarsely, gazing up at him, and . . .

I'm sorry. What was I saying?

He squeezed my fingers, turning my palm to give the inside of my wrist a soft, slow kiss before releasing me fully. Byron claimed the seat next to mine, scooting our chairs close. "Have you ordered? White or red?"

"We haven't ordered," Amelia piped up, then I felt her eyes on me as she added, "Why don't you and I pick the wine, Byron? Elijah and Winnie would appreciate the reprieve. They both seem a little overwhelmed."

I stared unseeingly at my menu, suffering from a hot flash and memory issues as Amelia and Byron discussed the wine options. Was I actually surprised by my body's reaction to the sight of him in a suit? *No. No, I was not.*

I hadn't seen him in person for almost a month. Him, in person, in a suit after such a long 3-D Byron drought—and after all those pictures of him in very little clothes—obviously spelled disaster for my biology.

"Everything is gluten-free," Byron whispered, pulling me from my daze.

I glanced up and discovered he'd leaned in close. "Pardon?" I asked, succumbing to a heady hit of dopamine.

Just go with it, Winnie. Enjoy it. Enjoy him.

"Everything is gluten-free." His arm lifted and settled along the back of my chair, his hand splaying between my shoulder blades. "You don't need to worry. All the cocktails and drinks are also gluten-free."

"Oh. Thank you." I sent him a small, grateful smile.

He smiled in return, his eyes moving between mine. "You look very beautiful."

At his compliment, my gaze dropped, my cheeks flamed, my stomach twisted, and my smiled widened. Apparently, my body had a lot of feelings about his statement. "Uh, thank you. You look very beautiful too."

His hand slid up to my neck. "After dinner, is it okay if you and I head out? Or did you make plans with Amelia?"

"No, no. No plans. We can head out."

"Good."

His fingers threaded into my hair and administered a little tug to the strands, which forced me to turn my face more completely toward him and give him back my eyes. Don't ask me why, but the small action caused an ache in my abdomen, and I pressed my knees together, losing myself in his magnificent gaze.

I felt weak. And needy. And not at all hungry for food.

A sharp *bang* snapped us out of our staring contest. Byron's fingers fell away from my neck when I turned my head toward Amelia—the sound had been her smacking the table.

"Hey. Save it for later and help me decide on an appetizer." Amelia turned her menu toward me. "The bacon wrapped dates look really good, but so does the shrimp and crab."

"Uh, shrimp and crab," I said on autopilot, flustered and abruptly thirsty.

Byron's hand dropped from the back of my chair and, just as I was reaching for my water, settled boldly on my upper thigh. I stilled, releasing another shaky breath and needing a moment to regather my composure before taking a drink.

"Do you like bacon?" Byron asked Elijah.

Elijah tilted his head back and forth, as though considering the matter. "For breakfast. Or lunch. Dinner also."

Byron smirked at Amelia's boyfriend. It was a friendly smirk, but it wasn't a smile. "Then let's get both."

The discussion turned to main dishes and what everyone wanted to order. Byron pointed out to me that they had black cod, but then grew silent as Amelia and I reminisced about a fishing trip we took ages ago where I caught a small shark and freaked out. She'd had to unhook it and throw it back in.

As the evening progressed, I noticed that Elijah, Amelia, and I carried most of the conversation while Byron seemed more than content to simply listen. When he was asked a direct question—usually by Elijah—he gave short answers and redirected the dialogue with a question in return. It was, I realized, the first time I'd ever seen him interact with anyone in a friendly way other than me, Amelia, or Jeff.

But the longer the dinner wore on, the shorter his answers became. By the time our plates were cleared, he seemed mildly agitated. Nothing overt or rude, more like I got the sense that the sounds of the restaurant were distracting to him. He cringed whenever any table around us made more than a moderate amount of noise. He leaned closer and angled his body toward me. His hand on my leg flexed and relaxed at intervals and he began fiddling with his utensils with the other hand, arranging them in perfect parallel lines. At one point he failed to respond—or seemingly notice—when Elijah asked him a question, remaining silent with his attention on his fork.

I caught Amelia's eye and inclined my head toward the front of the restaurant, hoping she would read my mind and understand my intention to leave with Byron as soon as possible.

She nodded once, and I looked around for our server, planning to ask for the check.

But Amelia, being a genius, said, "Hey, so, I need your credit card again, Byron. Winnie needs a few more things for the awards ceremony outfit and I was hoping to pick them up tomorrow." Then to me, she said, "Why don't you two get out of here? I'll pay the check with his card. I know how tired you are after our full day of travel."

"Oh. Yeah." I yawned—actually yawning, I was tired—and covered my mouth with the back of my hand. I turned to Byron. "Do you mind? We got up really early."

He wore one of his barely there smiles, but his eyes, fastened to the tabletop, held no amusement. I thought he might argue or insist we all stay for dessert. He looked like he wanted to argue, but ultimately, he didn't.

Withdrawing his wallet, he wordlessly stood and handed the whole thing over to Amelia. He then helped me with my chair while Amelia withdrew his credit card. Reaching for my hand as soon as I was upright and he'd reclaimed his wallet, Byron threaded our fingers together.

"See you two later." I waved to Amelia and Elijah, then allowed Byron to steer us around the bustling tables and through the front door.

We turned left toward the hotel, and I couldn't help but notice how Byron winced when a car's horn sounded in the distance.

My heart pinging with the urgent need to do something useful, I released his hand to wrap my arm around his waist. "Is this okay?" I asked. I didn't know if more closeness would help or hurt.

Byron peered down at me, his features remote. It felt as though his gaze didn't belong to him, or like he studied me from a great distance. But his arm did come around my shoulders, and he allowed me to cuddle close to his side as we walked.

Despite all the noise on the street, Byron's body seemed almost relaxed by the time we arrived at the hotel. And when the doors of the private elevator slid shut behind us, he turned and slowly backed me against the cushioned wall, his eyes mostly vivid and clear.

"Hey," he whispered, his hand coming to my cheek.

"Hey," I whispered back, leaning into his touch. My heart didn't go haywire this time, but a lovely warmth bloomed in my chest.

"I know what you and Amelia were doing back there." He didn't sound mad, but the words did sound like an accusation.

"Oh yeah? What were we doing?"

Byron's attention moved to the hair at my temple, and he pushed his fingers into the loose strands. "Trying to rescue me from noise and people."

I shrugged, not quite sure what to say. Byron had needed rescuing, and wasn't that my job while I was here? To rescue him? Tomorrow I'd be rescuing him from having to interact with interviewers more than was absolutely necessary.

I opened my mouth to say as much, but he pressed the pad of his index finger tenderly against my lips, his eyes on the spot. "I'm working on being better. I will be better. But thank you," he said simply, his finger falling away. "Thank you for doing that."

"My pleasure."

He smiled, but it looked wry, cautious. "You don't mind?"

"Mind what?"

"That I'm someone who currently needs rescuing?"

I grinned. "Honestly? No."

"No?" He seemed surprised by my answer.

"No," I repeated, lifting to my tiptoes and brushing a light kiss against the corner of his mouth. "I don't think you should change who you are for anyone. You're perfect."

I don't know what I expected, but it wasn't him withdrawing, the unhappy expression he currently wore, or the scowl marring his features.

"What's wrong?" I asked.

Byron gave his head a little shake, stepping away from me and retreating to the other side of the elevator. "No one is perfect, Fred," he said gruffly, his attention lifting to the LED screen displaying our progress between floors. "Everyone has room for improvement."

CHAPTER 31
WINNIE

Byron's sudden temper shift persisted. He seemed deep in thought as we walked to our suite and remained quiet once we walked inside. We ended up taking turns in the bedroom, changing into our pajamas. This struck me as a little odd, the fact that we took turns, considering the photos we'd been sending back and forth to each other.

While I changed, Byron chose a movie which we watched from our separate corners on the small couch. But since it was so small, our legs touched, and the small contact plus not knowing why he was acting so distant made my biology go haywire.

Following the opening credits, I couldn't stand the mounting tension and blurted, "Will you lay your head on my lap?"

He glanced at me. "Pardon?"

My chest tight, I pulled my legs up so that I sat cross-legged. "No pressure, but will you lay your head on my lap? I like to play with your hair."

Byron stared at me for a long moment, and I grew antsy, wondering if I'd just made another mistake.

But then he scooched back as far as he could and placed his head on my lap, grumbling, "Would pressuring me be such a bad thing?"

I frowned at the side of his face. "You want me to pressure you?"

"I want you to expect more from me," he said flatly, like I frustrated him.

Staring at his profile, I felt my frown intensify along with my confusion, not realizing I'd been holding my hands curled against my chest until he reached up and planted them on his head.

"Play with my hair," he said, a demand. Then he crossed his arms and glared at the TV, our conversation now over, time to be quiet and watch the movie.

Unsurprisingly, I couldn't concentrate on the film. *He wants me to expect more from him . . .?*

What did that mean? More how? And how could I expect more from someone who left for a month to New York and didn't tell me of his plans until he was already on the plane? Irritation pressed against my ribs like fingernails clacking on a hard surface, impossible to ignore.

But then Byron shifted, making a grunting noise, and I noticed how awkwardly he was lying. The couch was simply too small for his big body.

As though reading my mind, he grunted again and said, "Do you mind if we move to the floor?"

I lifted my hands away. "No. Not at all. In fact, I was just going to suggest it."

We relocated to the carpet in front of the couch, Byron taking a moment to shove the coffee table out of the way before surprising me by laying his head in my lap and planting my fingers in his hair again.

"Much better." He sighed contentedly, snuggling his cheek against my thigh.

Smiling to myself at his catlike show of affection, I glanced behind us at the couch. It really was quite small.

"I should sleep on the couch. It's way too small for you."

"I'll sleep on the couch," he said, like the matter was settled.

"That's not possible. You'll never get to sleep. You won't fit."

"We'll discuss it later." He turned to peer up at me, his fingers rising to thread into the hair just above my neck. Then, once again surprising me, Byron's head lifted while he brought mine downward, our lips meeting in the middle with a firm caress.

My hands stilled in his hair, my breath caught in my lungs, he kissed me. It wasn't chaste and quick like when I'd kissed him for the camera, but it wasn't frantic and fast like those kisses that followed. It was slow and sensual, savoring, his lips soft and warm, his tongue teasing and tasting.

And then, with a sly little nibble, it was over. He let me go, his head falling back to my lap to snuggle against my thigh, his attention returning to the TV. And I . . . *Wait. What was I worried about?*

The film played on. I didn't absorb a single second of it, too stunned and too turned on to focus.

Hot flashes and memory issues.

Apparently, assuming Byron and I were to spend time together when he returned to Seattle, I should expect lots of hot flashes and memory issues in the future.

* * *

Playing with Byron's hair was, in a word, relaxing. So relaxing, I must've fallen asleep. I awoke to find myself in the bed with the covers drawn up, Byron nowhere in sight. Pushing myself upright, I glanced at the clock. It was just past 1:00 a.m. I glared at the untouched, empty side of the bed.

That couch is too small for him.

He was so darn stubborn!

Heaving a sigh, I pushed the covers back and climbed out, tiptoeing to the sitting room. If he was asleep, I would leave him alone and let him sleep. But if he wasn't, he would be relocating to the bed, and that was that.

The city lights streaming through the windows provided enough light that I could see the general arrangement of the sitting room and, to my frustration, Byron was nowhere near the couch. He was stretched out on the floor with just a pillow and a light blanket. He wasn't moving, and his eyes seemed to be closed.

I stared at his form for several seconds, trying to figure out whether or not he was actually asleep. It was impossible to tell without walking over and checking his breathing or saying his name and seeing if he responded.

Saying his name seemed like the least invasive test, so I whispered as softly as I could, "Byron?"

"Yeah?" he immediately responded, propping himself up on his elbows. "Are you okay?"

I sighed—loudly—and accused, "You are not asleep."

"Correct."

Shaking my head at his obstinacy, I walked over, bent, grabbed his hand, and yanked. "Come on. You're sleeping in the bed."

He didn't budge. "You're sleeping in the bed."

"This is not up for debate. I shouldn't have been the one in the bed. For one thing, you're a lot taller than me. For another, you're the one who is being interviewed in the morning. You need a good night's sleep more than I do."

He still didn't budge, and trying to tug him up to his feet was like trying to move a boulder. "I'll move to the couch."

Giving up, I let his hand drop and placed mine on my hips. "That isn't a full couch, it's a love seat. It'll fit half of your leg and the side of a foot and that's it."

Finally, he stood. I couldn't see his expression in the dim light. "I'll figure it out. Please go back to the bed."

Now that he was upright, I seized the opportunity to grab hold of his hand again and pull him toward the bedroom. "I will go back to the bed, I promise, as long as you go with me."

"I can't."

"Yes, you can."

"The couch is—"

"Don't be absurd." Our progress was slow as he'd dug in his heels. "Just, come on. We'll go to sleep. We'll both get rest. We'll be refreshed and ready for the morning."

His steps loosened and he allowed me to pull him almost to the bedroom before bringing us to a stop again. "Wait, wait."

I faced him, somewhat out of breath from all the effort to get him this far. "What?"

"If I sleep in the same bed as you, I will touch you," he said plainly. "Is that what you want?"

"It's okay." I shrugged. "It's not a huge bed."

He made a growling sound, something like his typical grunts but more frustrated. "That's not what I mean, and you know it."

Catching on, I ignored the flutter in my chest but did expel a hot breath. "You can't sleep on that tiny sofa, and you can't sleep on the floor out here. It'll be uncomfortable. And I won't be able to sleep thinking about you being uncomfortable."

He twisted at the waist and lifted an arm toward the sofa. "I'll use the pillows from the—"

"You're sleeping with me tonight, and that's final."

Byron grew very still, and I sensed a sudden shift in the air. That's when I realized what I'd said and how it sounded.

I grumbled, saying nothing of sense, but huffing past the surge of embarrassment. Reaching forward, I gently gripped his wrist, encouraging him to come with me without actually pulling.

This time he yielded. He allowed me to guide him all the way into the small bedroom without protest, but he did say, "Before I left Seattle, you suggested we take things slow. Do you still want to take things slow?" The dark, almost accusatory question made goose bumps erupt over my skin.

"Friends share beds." I tried to make my tone light and airy. "And it's just two nights, while Amelia and Elijah use the other room."

"But will we be friends if we sleep together?" His voice lowered to a near whisper, and he turned his wrist, threading our fingers together.

I tried to tell myself I didn't know what he was implying as a burst of nerves made me laugh. "I promise. I will face the wall and not touch you, okay?" I disentangled our hands and pulled back the covers to climb inside.

"I want you to touch me. And I will touch you." He said the words so simply, so earnestly. "If we're in the same bed, I will. So I'm asking, do you want this?"

Surrendering to the fact that I was presently incapable of catching my breath, I slipped beneath the blankets, gulping in air. "Fine. You know what? Fine. Touch me."

"Is that what you want?"

"Yes. You caught me. This is me trying to seduce you with my unicorn nightshirt and brown wool socks. Please, get in bed and get handsy." In my flustered agitation, my hands flailed around my head, and I struggled with conflicting hopes and pragmaticism while wrestling with the fact that my words—spoken sarcastically—were actually somewhat true.

That disobedient part of me that wanted to pressure him and push him was delighted that there was only one bed. It did want to seduce him in my unicorn nightshirt and brown wool socks. It wanted acceleration, not patience. It wanted to expect more from him than stale breadcrumbs.

The loud rushing of my blood between my ears made it nearly impossible to hear anything behind me as I punched and fluffed my pillow, which was why I almost didn't catch Byron's softly spoken, "I'm still in love with you, Win."

His quiet admission made my heart ache, the wild creature hurling itself against the guarding cage I'd placed it in to keep it safe.

I gulped in more air, and said on a rush, "We're both adults. If I don't like something, I'll tell you. And if you don't like something, you tell me. Now—" I sighed, the remainder of the thought caught in my throat.

What are you doing, Winnie? What are you doing? What are you doing? What are you doing?

For Hedy Lamarr's sake, what *was* I doing?

While I grappled with my actions, wondering if I should've stubbornly insisted that I take the couch instead of us both sleeping in the bed, he settled in. There was a brief lull, a moment of stillness and silence, and I told myself this was fine and I needed sleep. I was tired after all, sleeping shouldn't be—

The bed dipped and I sensed Byron resettle *right* behind me. The heat from his body cocooned mine, mirroring my position, extremely close without touching. A moment later, his hand came to my hip, and I almost jumped at the contact, the heat of it bleeding through my sleep shirt and underwear. I squeezed my eyes shut.

"Should I stop?" His whisper was a scrape, and his fingers flexed, then released.

"It's good. Fine." I said, trying for nonchalance.

The bed shook slightly as he smoothly shifted closer, his chest hitting my back. I drew in an unsteady breath. He exhaled. It sounded strange, tight somehow, but I couldn't see him even if I glanced over my shoulder. This room—unlike the sitting room—was pitch black.

A pause, then his hand slid lower and lower, over my pajama shirt, until his fingers met my bare thigh just as his groin pressed forward against my backside.

I ceased breathing. He was hard. So hard. So incredibly hard.

"How's that? Are you okay?" he asked, his roughened voice shaded with something I couldn't place. Not irritation precisely, but something like it. And a dare.

I gritted my teeth in irritation. Why did he keep asking me if I was okay? Did he think I'd kick him out of bed for being hard? Heck, I'd been damp in the pants since he'd dyed my hair (and several weeks before that). *Welcome to the club, buddy.*

That said, did I believe he'd actually allow things to progress further than this despite how much I desperately wanted him to? No. No I did not. This was Byron, and Byron never did anything in the spur of the moment.

Clearing my throat, I forced a smile on my face so it would be reflected in my voice rather than my frustration. "Great. Just great. But do me a favor and stop asking for status updates. Like I said, if I don't like something, I'll tell you. You don't have to treat me like a child that can't be trusted to know her own mind."

His chest rose and fell behind me, the scent of him pulled into my lungs. "You should take your own advice," he said darkly.

I frowned. "What does that mean?"

"I'm not a child either. I can be trusted to make my own decisions without you worrying about pushing me. And the last thing I want from you is to be coddled." Byron's lips brushed against the back of my neck while his hand on my leg skimmed the hem of my nightshirt higher up my thigh, over my underwear to my waist.

He stilled. "Do you want more? Do you want me?"

I nodded fervently, only capable of focusing on breathing and nothing else. Sensations and wants and *oh my god*s paraded loudly through my heart and head.

"Then stop asking for status updates, Winnie. Start trusting me by asking for what you really want."

Sharp longing that had nothing and everything to do with his words slithered from beneath my ribs, low in my stomach, tightening and twisting. Unbearable, delicious heat bloomed along my neck and chest, and it took every ounce of self-control not to arch my back to press my bottom against his groin.

He held perfectly still, giving me nothing except his hard body behind mine. I was too hot. And I was never going to be able to get to sleep tonight.

He wanted me to ask for what I wanted? Fine. "I want us to be more than friends."

"Done. You may now call me whatever you wish, and I will be that."

I exhaled my surprise and then my frustration. He didn't move.

"Byron—"

"What else? What else do you want?"

"Please," I moaned, squirming against him.

"Please what?"

I was tempted to ask him to marry me right this minute if it meant he'd touch me and we'd do something more than remain frozen in this limbo between nothing and everything.

Instead, I blurted, "Touch me!"

Immediately, his fingers skated along the waistband of my underwear, sliding to the front, his thumb grazing my belly button as he whispered, "Lift your leg and place it on mine."

I did. Immediately. My breath came fast, my heart thoroughly confused, and my brain frozen on IS THIS REALLY HAPPENING?

He wouldn't.

He did.

Between one breath and the next, his deft fingers slipped into my underwear and stroked me and—my God—that happened.

THAT HAPPENED! And I was so very into it.

Also happening? Me whimpering. Just a few small ones on a hitching breath followed by his name.

His hips pushed forward, his insistent erection rubbing against my bottom, his head lifting as he placed soft kisses along the side of my neck. His fingers dipped sinfully lower, and I knew what he'd find. Somehow, I couldn't bring myself to be embarrassed in the moment. I was too busy not thinking.

I knew the precise second he felt how wet I was. He groaned against my neck, his other arm snaking beneath my body to wrap tightly around my waist. He moved, circling a single finger around my clit, playing with me like he was learning me, his lips and teeth now at my ear, his hot breath fanning along my neck. I turned my head to give him better access, panting at the hot, slippery slide of his tongue playing with my earlobe while the hand in my panties played with my body.

But we were going so fast. Was it too fast? Would he regret this? Was he okay?

"Byron, are you o—"

"If you want me to do something, if you want something from me, please continue that thought. But no more careful check-ins, no more asking me if I'm okay." The arm around my waist relaxed and his free hand slipped under my shirt, up my stomach to my breast, brushing the backs of his knuckles back and forth in a supremely teasing motion. "I need this."

I couldn't tell if this last statement was for his benefit or for mine, if he was speaking to himself or to me, and I wasn't sure I cared.

My hips rocked against his fingers and I arched my back, searching for more than a light touch.

"More. Please." I whined. I was burning up. That twisting, delicious, disquieting sensation I felt whenever Byron and I shared the same space had entirely consumed me. I was on fire *everywhere*, from the top of my head to the base of my feet, a tangle of longing, a mindless pile of need and restlessness.

"You need this too, don't you?" He muttered the question, palming my breast, grabbing and massaging. "I'll do anything you want."

The words landed on my ears like a taunt, but I didn't care. In fact, I nodded. Frantically. *Yes.*

His hips surged forward, his dick digging into my backside, a desperate, growly sound rumbling out of him. "I'll give you anything you want."

Embarrassingly, at the offer, I was precariously close to coming. The hint of both vulnerability and smugness drove me wild. It was just so Byron. But I didn't know what I would do after I came, what I would say to him.

It wasn't supposed to happen this way, so suddenly, so fast. On some level I'd assumed he'd never want to take things this far, not without several discussions and stipulations and negotiations related to the location of the act, hand placement, areas off-limits, time allowed, and so forth.

You know. *Boundaries.*

But right now, there were no boundaries. There was only us. Raw and exposed. Honest and selfish and greedy for every inch of each other, for every light and dark place, for every secret ambition. And I gave in to it, to us. I surrendered and allowed myself to want all of him, to trust that he'd let me know if I crossed a line.

Gasping sharply, I reached behind me, my nails digging into his shoulder as I searched for purchase. The first shock waves made my muscles rigid, my mind ceding to my body, and all that seemed to matter in the moment was how much I wanted, *needed* this.

He'd been right.

I needed this. I needed him and his brutal focus. I needed his cherishing touch, his skillful hands, his impatient body. I wanted to crawl inside him and devour him and never leave, never breathe, never be separate from him as long as we both lived, and I needed that feeling even though it bruised my heart to contemplate it.

As I spiraled back down to earth, as his fingers continued to slide in and out of my body, my lungs greedy for the air I'd denied them, I trembled. Byron's teeth, lips, and tongue wreaked blissful havoc on my neck, and I became aware of how many layers of clothes were between us. The amount was unjust. Unfair. Unreasonable. My skin craved his skin, and in that moment, nothing less than everything was acceptable.

Licking my lips, I covered the hand that currently fondled my breast beneath my shirt. "Byron. Can we—"

"I don't have a condom."

I blinked, opening my eyes in the darkness. *Crap.* What had I been thinking?

Shaking my head of the lust cobwebs, I croaked, "Neither do I."

I felt him nod his acceptance of this simple, tragic fact, his stubble scraping against the back of my neck.

"I feel like I'm going to die," he said. The words were rushed, pained, tortured. "I'm going to die from wanting you." I doubted he realized he'd said them aloud.

As much as they made me smile—because I had a good idea how he felt—they also spurred me into action. I reached between us.

Byron sucked in a sharp breath, catching my hand. "Not without protection."

"No. I'm not—let me touch you, like you touched me. Let me make you feel good." I twisted my head and stole a quick kiss, echoing his sentiment from earlier. "I need this. *We* need this."

He shook with effort to hold me in place. He was panting. "I don't think you'll have to do much."

Slowly, I turned to face him, reaching for the front of his pants again. This time he let me, his whole body tense, his breath labored. He let me reach inside, my fingers encountering the springy, rough hair of his pelvis, but then he stopped me just before I could actually touch him.

"Wait."

I nodded. "Okay."

"Let me—" His hands moved to his waistband and, surprising the heck out of me, he tugged everything off and threw it. Somewhere.

My mouth went dry.

I wanted to ask if we could turn on a light. I desperately, *desperately* wanted to see every square inch of him with every single light in the world on. But before the request could make it past my lips, he fisted a hand in the hair at the back of my head and brought my mouth crashing forward, kissing me with urgency and hungry need while his other hand guided mine to his erection, both of us sucking in a breath when I tried to close my fingers around the hot, thick length of him.

"Fuck." Byron rolled away, his head pressed back against the pillow, his neck exposed, and I bent to lean over him and feast on his strong throat as I gave his smooth skin a rough stroke, then another, feeling the thrashing of his heart against my chest.

"I'm not—I can't—oh God—"

I tensed, startled, because . . . *oh my goodness.* He came. Byron came. He just . . . came.

Ten seconds, two strokes, and he erupted. I felt like laughing with delight but stomped down on that impulse. The few times I'd messed around with my high school boyfriend, he'd come really fast—not this fast, but fast—and I'd laughed in my surprise. That did not go over well.

His fingers still knotted in my hair, he urged my lips down to his again, inhaling and loving me with his tongue. Heedless to the mess of his release, he rolled me to my back and continued kissing me, his hands on either side of my face, his mouth starving but also cherishing, like I was his favorite wine, the most decadent dessert, and he was determined to taste and savor me from every angle. I loved it and everything that had happened between us, and I felt so joyful and hopeful.

The magnitude of my hope and joy scared the shit out of me.

But what could I do? Was I too far gone? Had he opened the cage? Was my heart in danger?

Bad news, Win. The answer is probably yes.

Swallowing convulsively, I didn't allow myself to contemplate it and I pretended all was well. I told myself that his leaving me a month ago possessed a bright side. He'd needed space, and now he was ready to try. Now we would try. It would be several months before I would consent to loving him. Maybe a year. Maybe never.

Meanwhile, that disobedient part of me rejected this notion and delivered a sucker punch to the cage around my heart, making it clatter and quake.

You're the one with the hard shell that needs cracking open.

I squeezed my eyes shut, but the disobedient thoughts roared through my head.

Maybe he'd needed to leave a month ago, maybe he is ready to try now, but you needed him then. And instead of telling him what you needed, you let him go.

And, sure, one could call my stubborn caution "patience," but that's not what it was. Not truly. I'd been afraid to ask for what I wanted. Afraid of this desperate feeling, of pinning my hopes on one person, of relying on someone and needing someone and wanting to count on someone. I'd been perfectly content to let him take the reins, take control, and set the pace.

And now, after tonight, after the unexpected and rapid acceleration of our relationship, I was even more terrified.

CHAPTER 32
WINNIE

I woke up shirtless, with chapped lips, and alone in bed.

Rubbing my forehead, I pushed back the mess my hair had become and peered around the room. It was also empty. My stomach dropped and I squeezed my eyes shut, frustrated with myself for being disappointed. See? This was why I shouldn't allow myself to believe the fantasy of last night or assume that everything would be wonderful this morning. I should've asked if he was okay. I knew Byron left when he felt overwhelmed and I—

"You're up."

My eyes flew open and my head whipped toward the sound of his voice. Every muscle in my body tensed at the glorious sight of him smiling softly, standing just inside the room, hands in his pockets, dressed for the day in a black suit, white shirt, and blue tie, and not looking overwhelmed. He looked. . . happy.

The threatening disappointment made a U-turn, leaving me with stars in my eyes and a sweet, hopeful kind of joy making everything feel and seem brighter and better.

And scarier.

Choking around the odd mixture of hope and terror, I tried to form the words to greet him.

He stopped me with a raised finger. "Hold that thought. I'll be right back." Byron disappeared through the door.

Clutching the sheet to my chest, I sat upright. A second later, before I could even begin to wonder where he'd gone, he returned, holding a tray of food.

"What's this?" I asked, my voice rough with sleep.

"Your breakfast." Leaning over me, he set it down on the bed and captured my mouth for a quick kiss. And then another, and another.

I didn't miss how his hand covered my shoulder and then caressed down my arm. His thumb hooked into the sheet I held loosely to my chest and tugged it down. Smoothly lowering himself to his knees beside the bed, he trailed kisses from my jaw to my neck to my chest, his hand now sliding around my torso as he revealed my breasts.

"You are so fucking beautiful," he said around a groan and closed his hot, wet mouth over one of my nipples, making me instantly hot and wet.

"So are—oh God—" My lungs were on fire. I glanced down to watch his tongue sweep out and circle the center of my breast, loving my skin. The fingers of one hand flexed and massaged my back while the other continued pushing down the sheet, revealing the rest of my body, and quite suddenly all my thoughts of terror simply evaporated.

Without speaking, or asking, or checking in, or requesting a status update, Byron cupped me over my underwear, the firm pressure of his hand a wonderful, terrible torture. Flopping back to the mattress, I stretched my too tight muscles and angled my hips. Grabbing his hand, I guided his long fingers inside my underwear, my skin shivery as I felt him smile against my breast.

He lifted his head to look at me, at my neck and arms, chest and stomach, thighs and calves, his irises growing impossibly dark as he watched his hand, hidden by my underwear, move inside me. My breasts bounced with my labored breaths and his gaze seemed riveted by my skin.

"I had a dream like this once," he mumbled, sounding distracted, his eyebrows pulling together thoughtfully. "Except you were tied to the bed."

A laugh burst out of me, a sheen of sweat misting my skin. I let go of his wrist and lifted my hands over my head, gripping the headboard mounted to the wall. "Like this?" I asked breathlessly, his fingers between my legs driving all reason from my mind.

"Exactly like that." His gaze, hooded and interested, looked approving. "And after, you tie me up."

I moaned at the image flashing behind my eyes and shut them, fighting the crisis, wanting to prolong the moment.

"You are so good at this." The words spilled out of me. "I—I've never —" I bit my lip to keep from admitting he was the first guy who'd ever made me orgasm. I'd been told—though I'd doubted—a man could bring a woman to such an intense peak with just his fingers.

Byron bent to my ear, his hot breath fanning against my neck, and whispered, "You've never what?"

I shook my head instead of answering. I didn't want him to know how inexperienced I was, not when he was clearly so freaking capable in the bedroom department.

"What have you never done, Winnie?" he said, his voice deep and masterful and coaxing. "Tell me so I can do it to you."

"Oh. Fuck," I said through gritted teeth, my back arching reflexively as I came, my center spasming and clenching his finger as wave after wave pierced me, my hands gripping the headboard, a single anchor in the tempest of this disorienting half pleasure, half pain.

Eventually, his strokes slowed to teasing, his tongue and teeth catching my earlobe, making me shiver and shake. As reality sharpened around me, I struggled to catch my breath and to comprehend the last few moments. Byron walking into a hotel bedroom with breakfast on a tray, removing the sheet covering me, and bringing me to orgasm with his fingers while licking and kissing my bare skin were now things he just simply did. This was apparently how things would be between us for the foreseeable future.

The pragmatic part of my brain told me to enjoy it while it lasted, and the anxious part of my brain grabbed me in a choke hold and demanded I not say or do anything to mess it up.

"I love your body. I love how sexy you are," he said, sounding a little grumpy. I understood why when he added, "I also hate it."

I laughed with amusement, but also as a way to dissipate a sense of lingering vulnerability. Pushing my fingers into his hair as he drifted lower to place more kisses on my bare body, I struggled to find comfort in my own skin and in this moment. "Why do you hate it?"

"You're distracting. And you wear too many clothes."

I laughed again, more genuine this time, dispelling some of the nervousness gathering in my stomach. I could relate to his frustrations. I felt the same way about him, and—now that my brain had caught up—it was quite nice to hear him say that he loved my body and thought I was sexy.

His kisses on my chest and stomach felt amazing, but a lingering twinge of vulnerability made me want to pull him closer. I needed him pressed against me, holding me. I thought about asking for what I wanted, but he was in a suit, his shirt perfectly ironed, his tie perfectly straight. I didn't want to mess him up.

But he said I should tell him what I want . . .

"What?" he asked, interrupting my debate.

I blinked, bringing him back into focus. He was still kneeling next to me beside the bed, hovering above me now, one hand between my back and the mattress, the other tracing my bare skin with his fingertips.

"You look fancy," I said, touching his tie. "And handsome in this suit."

"I know. That's why I wore it."

I pressed my lips together to keep from laughing in earnest. I loved that he never—or hardly ever—said thank you, but instead accepted compliments by agreeing with them.

"You have someone to impress today?" I lightly tugged on the bottom of the tie, delighted to find he hadn't secured it with a tie clip.

He gave me a quizzical look. "You're the only person I ever want to impress. Are you impressed?"

"I am." I slid my hand back up the tie and wrapped my fingers around it just below the knot, careful not to crush the blue silk. "You always impress me."

He grinned, his hand veering to my naked thigh, his palm smoothing over my knee. "I plan to keep impressing you, just so you know."

"Oh? For how long?"

"Forever," he said solemnly but with a smile, moving his hand to my opposite leg, sliding it upward to my hip and then pulling me toward him so I lay on my side. "But first, you need to eat." His fingers slipped inside my underwear again, but this time from the back, palming my bottom as he added dryly, "You need energy for the gauntlet."

Releasing his tie, I lifted an eyebrow. "Gauntlet?"

"The interviews," he said flatly. "They start in an hour."

"Ah . . ." I nodded, giving him a commiserating smile. "Don't worry. I'll be your buffer."

"I'm not worried." Giving my butt a rough squeeze, he closed his eyes and seemed to be gritting his teeth. "But I have to let you get dressed and stop touching you, otherwise we'll never leave this room." I got the sense he was talking to himself, issuing orders he didn't particularly like, but which made me grin like a maniac.

Byron released me then. He stood and stepped away. Eyes still closed, he tested the knot of his tie.

I smiled at his reluctance to let me go, feeling giddy and joyful again, his words and actions soothing my post orgasm apprehension. I also felt loose and relaxed, my body humming after his attentions, and my eyes reflexively dropped to the front of his pants.

Yikes.

"Do you want me to—"

"Yes. And no," he said tightly, walking away and to the bathroom door. A moment later, he called from within, "Can I take a rain check?"

I laughed at the strangled quality to his question and sat up, calling back, "Absolutely. Anytime."

Byron popped his head back in the room, his eyes dancing, a happy smile on his face. "Glad to hear it." He lifted his chin toward the tray of food. "Eat if you're hungry. And don't worry, I know the chef and saw the kitchen. It's safe."

* * *

The interviews took place in another hotel suite, only this one was massive. The sitting area was easily three times the size of Byron's entire suite, accommodating studio lights and cameras, two big couches, four chairs, a buffet table where drinks and food had been placed, and a dining table that sat twelve. The windows overlooked Central Park, just like our suite, but since the room was so large, it also had three times the view.

But as soon as Byron entered, two people broke away from the crowd of people milling about and pulled the drapes, covering the view and blocking the room from sunlight. This seemed counterintuitive to me. Wouldn't the cameras need the extra light?

Byron introduced me to his manager, agent, and the team responsible for editing and marketing his books at the publisher, distracting me from the newly concealed view. I made chitchat with them while he held my hand. Once again, similar to our dinner with Amelia and Elijah, he seemed content to listen and only speak when asked direct questions.

The first of the interviewers arrived right on time and quickly introduced herself to everyone gathered, taking her seat across from Byron without offering to shake hands, and then got right down to business without making any overtures or pleasantries. I was surprised by this. Based on my research, Jes Ekker was somewhat famous for developing a rapport with celebrities before launching into questions. She was one of the few I was looking forward to meeting as she had the ability to turn profile interviews into dynamic stories rather than just puff pieces. Ms. Ekker also seemed to be avoiding eye contact with Byron.

When she asked Byron her fourth question as though reading from a script, I leaned over to Byron's manager and whispered, "Does she not like Byron?"

She glanced at me, looking confused, and whispered back, "What do you mean?"

"It's just, this lady usually jokes around first, right? But she didn't even offer to shake Byron's hand or ask how he was."

"Oh." Byron's manager nodded in understanding. "It's all in Mr. Visser's rider. No chitchat, no conversation, only preapproved questions."

"I see." I rocked back on my heels, returning my attention to the scene before me, studying Ms. Ekker's posture. She seemed . . . bored, just as anxious to get this interview over with as Byron was, and that felt like a real shame, a loss of an opportunity for two talented people to form a connection and help each other.

Disheartened, but not sure what to do about it, I hovered at the edge of the room with the rest of the spectators and listened to the efficient, tedious interview until it reached its conclusion, at which point Ms. Ekker stood, said her polite thanks, and left.

The next interviewer was already waiting in the wings and the morning progressed in much the same fashion: dull exchanges; unimaginative questions; pragmatic, unsurprising answers. The longer I stood and listened the more dissatisfied I became with this lifeless version of Byron and the uninspiring interviews. It was all process, about as interesting and surprising as watching a wheel rotate on an axel over and over.

Tuning out, my mind drifted, debating this present situation and how at odds it seemed to be with Byron's request that he not be coddled. Every detail—from how they'd covered the view and blocked the sunlight to the list of preapproved questions—seemed to be specifically tailored to coddle him.

But there was a difference. He didn't know these interviewers. He worked well with his manager, agent, and the publishing team, but he didn't consider them close friends. They were colleagues, placed in their defined boxes and expectations of behavior. This wasn't a safe space for him.

But I was a safe place and person for him. Amelia was. He obviously didn't trust easily, but he trusted us. And maybe that was why he didn't want or need me to coddle him.

And you know what? I could relate to his perspective, though I—and I suspected, most people—approached the world so much differently.

Byron spelled out and enforced external boundaries to protect himself from untrustworthy people. This, his honesty, made most people uncomfortable around him, call him strange and eccentric; I'd witnessed this peculiarity firsthand and I'd done it myself, labeling his honesty as rudeness.

While I—and most people—approached the world with internal caution but with a mask of outward openness. Like Byron, we assumed most other people were untrustworthy, but our walls were inside our heads and around our hearts, not communicated openly for the world to see.

We all had just as many boundaries as Byron, but ours were internal. We didn't share them as he did, we pretended they didn't exist. The walls we built and the stipulations we clung to were hidden, and we expected other people to . . . read our minds?

I smirked at the thought, giving my head a little shake. Byron was honest and up-front with every person he encountered, and this made him eccentric. Whereas most people expected the world to read their minds, and *that* was perfectly normal. How ironic.

A gasp from Byron's manager cut through my reflections. I glanced at her and her stunned profile.

A second later, she charged forward. "Okay. This interview is over."

Byron's hands seemed to lay relaxed on his lap, but his eyes shot daggers at the man across from him on the other couch. He stared at Byron, affecting an innocent look, like he couldn't imagine what he'd done wrong. Unlike the other interviewers, he sat on the edge of the couch, leaning forward, almost crowding Byron's space.

"I thought we were allowed to ask about Dr. Visser." The interviewer glanced between Byron and Byron's manager. "No one told me his mother was off-limits."

"You didn't submit any questions related to Mr. Visser's mother. Any non-approved questions are off-limits, Harry. You know this."

Byron's eyes darted to mine, then fell away to his hands. He studied his fingertips as his manager and the interviewer named Harry debated about journalistic integrity and "entitled, spoiled creatives."

"All I asked is if Mr. Visser deleted all his social media accounts due to his mother's callous comments. That's it. It's a simple yes or no question. I'm on his side here."

Byron's manager lifted her hand and waved toward the publishing team I'd met earlier. "If you can't stick to the script, you leave."

"That video of her calling you a mistake, saying she didn't have a son. What went through your mind when she said that?" Harry was relentless, leaning around Byron's manager to keep questioning him. "Do you think she still feels that way now that you're so successful? Is the character of Subrah based on you? Has your mother read your—"

"Enough. Enough." The publishing team was there, tugging at Harry's jacket and placing insistent hands on his shoulders, and they pushed him out of the room.

All the while, Byron sat stone faced, still as a statue, eyes on his hands. I was already halfway to him before I realized I'd moved, and when I reached him, I impulsively sat on his lap, wrapping my arms around his neck and hugged him tightly.

I'd never heard any of that about Byron's mother. If it was true, I couldn't imagine what he must be feeling right now.

Even if he wasn't Byron, even if he wasn't a reclusive, taciturn, lovable grumpy pants, even if he was a random person on the street, those words would hurt deeply.

"Are you—" I cut myself off from asking if he was okay. Based on our discussions last night, I wasn't sure he wanted me asking him that.

"I will be okay. It's fine for you to ask," he mumbled quietly, the words monotone. He placed a kiss on my neck, holding me tight. "Thank you. I need . . ."

I waited for him to finish the thought. When he didn't, I prompted, "What do you need?"

"You."

My heart pinged, liking his response entirely too much. I leaned away as far as I could while he still held my waist. "You have me," I whispered to him even as that persistent, disobedient voice in my head screamed, *LIAR!*

Taking advantage of the scant distance I'd created, he turned his face and pressed it against my breasts, like he wanted to suffocate in their softness. "Thank God," came his muffled response.

I laughed, feeling my cheeks redden and trailing my fingers through his hair. He snuggled closer, turning his cheek to lay against my bosom.

"You feel like what I imagine bliss would if I could manifest the word as a tangible, touchable thing."

The cage around my heart cracked, the feeling stealing the air from my lungs, and I rested my chin on the top of his head while working to breathe past it. Cupping the side of his jaw not snuggled against my body, I held him while he listened to my heart. We sat in near silence for several moments—I sensed he needed the quiet, and honestly so did I—while my mind drifted again, this time to the statements made and the questions posed by the last interviewer.

Biting my lip to keep from asking about his mother—it was clear he didn't wish to discuss her, otherwise Harry would still be sitting on the other couch—I debated whether or when to raise the issue. Had she really said Byron wasn't her son? Had actually called him a mistake?

I think I hated her. *No, Win. You can't hate someone you've never met.*

In this case, I decided to make an exception.

CHAPTER 33
WINNIE

Byron's manager returned several minutes later and told us it was lunchtime, that Byron was free for the next hour and a half. We could grab food here in the big suite or go elsewhere if he needed a break. Unsurprisingly, he opted to go elsewhere.

Holding my hand, he steered us toward the exit, offering a quick and sincere thanks to his publishing team—which they seemed genuinely surprised by—and out of the room.

We made it about three steps down the hallway before someone behind us said, "Excuse me. Can I have a moment?"

I felt Byron's hand in mine go tense, his shoulders and neck visibly locking. "No," he said flatly, and picked up the pace.

I was just thinking, *Geez. These people are relentless,* when the speaker clarified, "Not you, Mr. Visser. I'd like to talk to the Chemistry Maven, if she'll give me a moment."

My feet stalled and, instinctively, I glanced over my shoulder, prepared to say, *No, thank you.* But I found the first interviewer—Jes Ekker—standing behind us, some distance away. She was leaning a shoulder against the wall and holding a copy of my favorite STEM projects for kids book, the one I always recommended in my videos.

I paused, bringing Byron to a stop with me, and asked, "Why do you wish to speak with me?"

She gave me a hopeful and sheepish half smile but made no move to come toward us. "It's actually for my kids. They're big fans. I was hoping you would sign this for them."

I frowned at the book. "I didn't write that book."

"I know, but we bought it because you recommended it and use it all the time. However, I don't want to impose, so if you prefer not to, that's totally fine."

I inspected her. She seemed wholly genuine. And she hadn't approached. And I'd never met one of my followers before. I was curious.

Tugging Byron along with me, I walked slowly back over to her. "I'm Winnie," I said, giving her a tentative smile. "How old are your kids?"

"My daughter is fourteen and my son is six. They both watch your STEM videos." She held the book out toward me along with a pen. "I've tabbed their favorite experiments with sticky notes, if you wouldn't mind making the first one out to Ryann—with two *n*'s—and the second one out to James."

"Sure," I grinned, glancing at Byron to make sure he wasn't in a rush. He lifted his chin toward Ms. Ekker while wearing one of his barely there smiles. This one looked proud.

Releasing Byron's hand to reach for the book, I beamed at Ms. Ekker. *How exciting!*

"When did they start watching?" I asked, flipping to the first page and carefully spelling Ryann with two *n*'s. "This last year?"

"No. It's been about two years now. My husband stumbled across your videos on YouTube and showed our daughter. She was going through this phase where—I don't know how to describe it—like she didn't want to be smart or be seen as smart."

"She was twelve? That's not unusual for girls," I muttered while signing. "There's all sorts of peer-reviewed research about that. Some girls who excelled at academics all through elementary school will purposefully start doing poorly around the age of twelve—especially with math, science, engineering, and technology since those have traditionally been considered male-dominated subjects—not wanting to be perceived as smart. It's a real problem, and actually why I decided to teach seventh and eighth grade STEM classes."

"I love that you're an actual teacher. It's very obvious in your videos that you know how to connect with kids. Also, we love the new content. Ryann is into makeup now, thanks to you."

"Really?" My question came out high pitched with disbelief, my heart soaring.

"Yes. We went out and bought her eye shadow. I was so surprised. The pendulum swung in the other direction when she started faithfully watching your videos and seeking out other engineering related stuff, TV shows and books. Instead of not wanting to be smart, it was like being smart—you know, nerdy—was all she wanted to be and there wasn't room for anything else. She didn't want to wear dresses, go with her friends to the mall. Which, fine. If that's what she wanted. But now she's been practicing makeup in the mirror."

I felt like hugging Ryann's mom. "That's so great."

"It is so great." She stepped forward, her eyes big and excited, looking like she wanted to hug me too. "I'm not a big pusher of makeup or anything, I don't usually have time to wear any. But, I guess, thank you. It was sad to me that she was either rejecting being smart or rejecting other parts of her, denying other interests. Like she thought she couldn't be both. We try to model better at home, but I don't know. She doesn't want to be a journalist or an art historian—that's what my husband does—she wants to be an electrical engineer. Maybe she needed someone to say 'Hey, it's okay. You can be everything you want to be, you're allowed to be interested in whatever you want. Nothing is off-limits.' You know what I mean?"

Finished signing both pages of the book, I handed it back to her and leaned a shoulder against the wall, settling in to talk. "Yeah. I do. Growing up, I was always looking for someone to do that for me, model that for me. And it was my friend Amelia who pointed out that I should model that for the girls who watch my videos."

"Well, you've modeled it for my son as well." She laughed, tucking the book and pen in her bag. "My son, James, also watches your videos and—get this—he asked me if boys can be engineers too or if it's only something girls get to do."

I laughed, shaking my head. "Well, if you need or want an account that shows male educators who also do live experiments and engineering projects, I have some suggestions."

She tilted her head back and forth, as though considering. "I might take you up on that. But you'll always be the first person that comes to mind when he thinks of his favorite engineers and scientists, and I love that. I love that he relates to you and it's perfectly normal. I don't think it's been encouraged for boys and men to relate to girls and females as personal heroes, until this latest generation. And it's just so beautiful to see it happen."

"I agree." I nodded exuberantly. *Oh my gosh.* I loved this woman. I wanted to put her in my pocket and keep her forever.

Her gaze drifted to the right, glancing at where Byron stood silent next to my shoulder, and her smile dimmed like she'd forgotten he was there. "Anyway." She shrugged, backing away, and offered her hand to me. I shook it. "Thank you so much for this."

"Anytime," I said, meaning it. "And if you're ever in Seattle, let me know. The science center there is awesome."

"I will. Take care." Giving Byron a tight, polite smile, she walked around us, down the hall, toward the elevator.

Meanwhile, I was grinning wildly, feeling amazing. So happy. So energized. My brain buzzing with new ideas, new experiments, new content possibilities.

"You know—" Byron came to stand in front of me, leaning his shoulder against the same spot Ms. Ekker had earlier "—you're extraordinary."

Bouncing on the balls of my feet, I gave him a quick kiss. "That was awesome! Wasn't that awesome? Wow. I just—I feel like everything I've been doing has been so worth it. I love this feeling, it's why I became a teacher, you know? The difference I can make in young peoples' lives at this critical time is worth so much more to me than all the money or fame in the world. All that stuff is so worthless in comparison to making a real difference. And I, uh, I . . ."

His warm smile had become an amused smirk, and one of his eyebrows arched.

Oh no. *ACK!* I didn't realize how those words sounded until they were out, and I clamped a hand over my mouth, saying through my fingers. "I'm sorry. I didn't mean, I didn't—"

"Don't apologize." He pulled my hand from my mouth and held it, giving my lips a light kiss. "I know you didn't mean to imply that what I do is worthless."

"I didn't. You do make a difference."

"Hmm . . ." His eyes narrowed, but it looked playful. "But maybe not as much as a difference as you?"

I shook my head. "Nah. No way. I'm not discussing this with you."

"Why not?" He tugged on my hand, leading us toward the elevator again.

"You used to bring up how underpaid I am for the work I do, and I don't want to talk about that."

Byron was quiet, his narrowed eyes growing thoughtful as we walked. When we reached the doors, he pressed the call button and faced me. "I'm not going to say you're underpaid, I know it bothers you."

"But?" I asked dryly, preparing myself for whatever he said next.

"But I was wrong about the fundamental issue, and I'm sorry."

My eyebrows jumped. "Excuse me? You don't think I'm underpaid anymore?"

"All teachers are underpaid by at least a factor of ten—in my opinion—but watching you with that woman, witnessing your happiness, your joy, I was wrong about why you accept the hefty workload for the paltry salary."

"And why do I accept the hefty workload?" Bracing myself, I sent him a side-eye.

"You measure success of a life in the difference made, not in the amount of money or fame earned, and not in terms of the freedom you're afforded." Byron's barely there smile returned, looking just as proud as it did before. "The work you do is important."

"I know."

"Good. And I'm sorry for all the times I was an asshole about it."

"You're forgiven."

"You're still underpaid—"

I rolled my eyes. "Byron."

"—but no matter how much they paid you, it would never be enough." He stepped closer and encouraged me to wrap my arms around his neck. "It's like trying to calculate the salary for a superhero."

I laughed. "I'm a superhero now?"

"You've always been a superhero." Byron slid his nose against mine, brushing our lips together and whispering, "You're a teacher, aren't you? The only difference is that teachers don't wear capes."

"Maybe you should get me one for my birthday." I nipped at his lip.

"Maybe I will."

"Maybe I'll wear it."

He leaned a few inches away, looking hopeful. "Maybe you'll wear it and nothing else?"

I tossed my head back and laughed.

* * *

We ate a quick lunch in our suite. It had to be quick. We'd spent most of the allotted time making out on the tiny sofa, me straddling his hips with my shirt unbuttoned, him biting and kissing, licking and touching every inch of skin I'd exposed.

Again I'd asked if he wanted me to ease his suffering, again he'd asked for a rain check, making me wonder if Amelia had been right, that Byron had a pattern of self-denial.

I should push him. I should . . . beg him, maybe? If I begged him, I wonder what he'd do? Would he give it to me?

These were my current thoughts as I stared at Byron from across the room during the second batch of interviews, which was probably why his eyes kept darting to me and he kept stumbling over his rehearsed answers.

"Did you two have a fight or something?" his manager leaned over and whispered from her spot next to me.

I shook my head, locking eyes with Byron again, my attention dropping to his mouth when he flicked his tongue out to wet his lips.

"Excuse me," he said to the interviewer. "I—I need a half hour break." Not waiting for the man to respond, Byron stood suddenly and made a beeline to where I leaned against the wall.

His manager stepped forward. "What is—"

"I need a half hour break," he repeated. But then he added in a quieter voice, "I will give you a twenty-thousand-dollar bonus if you clear everyone out of here in less than a minute."

Not waiting for her answer, Byron grabbed my hand and pulled me toward a closed door on the far side of the suite. He opened the door and walked us through. He closed the door and pressed me against it. And as his mouth crashed down to mine, I could just make out the urgent sound of his manager's voice telling everyone to leave.

"I can't concentrate," he said between frantic kisses, "when you're looking at me like that."

He grabbed handfuls of my skirt, lifting. But I hurriedly shoved his hands away, pushing him a step back to give me space to quickly survey our surroundings. We were in the suite's bedroom. The room was dark. The bed was king-sized. And I still didn't have a condom.

DARN. IT.

Byron reached for me again, but I dropped to my knees, my shaking fingers unfastening his belt.

"Winnie. What are you doing?" His voice shook and his fingertips fell to my shoulders, then jumped away, like he didn't know what to do with his hands.

"You asked me what I've never done before," I said on a rush of desire-fueled bravery. "I've never done this."

Maybe I wanted this so badly because every part of Byron was beautiful to me. Or maybe it was the primal, needy, clenching and twisting and demanding bit of me, the disobedient voice in my head that told me to ask for what I really wanted even if it might mean pushing him outside his comfort zone. The risk to my heart if he said yes was totally worth the possibility of him saying no.

"Fuck. Win, do you—are you—" The words were choked, a scrape of feeling and sound that reverberated through my body. I felt his restlessness, his uncertainty and reluctance, and—instinctively, somehow—I knew his reluctance and worry were for me. If he wanted me to stop, if he didn't want this, he would say no. I trusted him to tell me what he wanted.

So I used his statements from last night to cut him off. They were a perfect reflection of what I felt in the moment. "If you want me to do something, if you want something from me, please continue that thought. But no more careful check-ins, no more asking me if I'm okay."

I watched his hands ball into fists on either side of his hips, his mouth snap shut. A moment later, his head nodded with a jerk, and his eyes grew impossibly dark. And then I unbuttoned his pants, lowered his zipper, reached inside those gray boxer briefs that had driven me wild when he'd sent his last photo, and revealed his erection.

A primal, needy part of me clenched at the sight of him, my mouth filling with saliva, heat blooming across and beneath my skin. I couldn't remember thinking of a penis as beautiful before, but I did now. So incredibly stunning. I'd never wanted to have one in my mouth either, never felt like I might die if I didn't touch it to my tongue and taste it, suck on it, use my lips to elicit a reaction. I needed his reaction, his undoing, I needed his loss of control more than air.

Gripping his hips, I started at the base and licked upward along the shaft, watching with gleeful fascination as his erection jumped, the muscles of his lower abdomen—just visible between the parted front of his shirt—tensed, making them stand out in relief beneath his skin.

When I sucked the smooth, hot length of him into my mouth as far as I could, he groaned, a terrible, wonderful sound. In my peripheral vision, I saw his hands at his sides clench and unclench, like he still didn't know what to do with them. On a whim, as I pulled back, I grabbed one of his hands and brought it to the back of my head.

He immediately removed it like my hair burned him. "No. No—I'll—I don't want to do that. Not this time. You set the pace." Byron reached forward and gripped the doorframe, his eyes closing. "Please," he said, his voice cracking. "Please move. Please—I think—*fuck.* I need to be in your mouth, Win. Please."

I realized I'd been staring up at his face, greedy for all the expressions arresting his features, and hadn't taken him inside again. Giving myself a quick shake, I refocused my attention on his penis and opened my mouth wider, working to take more than before, then pulling back just to repeat the action again and again.

And I felt . . . like maybe I was doing it wrong? I couldn't get more than half of his length in my mouth without wanting to gag, his dick so freaking beautiful but also thick, the head of it pressing uncomfortably against the back of my throat. I tried licking him again, holding his erection in my fist as I studied the problem, mentally measuring his inches against the approximate distance between my lips and tonsils.

Licking my lips, I tried again. This time, I kept my hand at the base of his penis and tugged like I was jerking him off as I moved back, and a guttural sound shook out of him—half groan, half growl.

Eyes now scrunched closed, he pressed his forehead against the door, forcing me to lean backward on my knees to continue my ministrations.

Now trapped between his body and the door behind me, I hit the back of my head as I retreated.

"Oh, fuck. Sorry!" Byron straightened to give me more space, his face twisted in what looked like pain, his cheeks red. "Are you okay? I mean, *fuck*—" he covered his face with this hands. "Dammit. Sorry."

I wanted to preen and gloat when his apologies continued. More than how hard he was or the sounds he made or the expression he wore, more than anything, his fumbling statements betrayed how completely he'd lost control.

A surging sense of satisfaction roared through me, and I forced myself to go deeper, take more of him. Even if my movements were clumsy, and I was doing it wrong, and even if my eyes teared up and I made unattractive sounds as I gagged, I didn't care. Byron seemed to like everything I was doing very, very much. His unsteady sounds, curses, and complete loss of composure turned me on like a 500-watt halogen bulb. Soon, I was also groaning, my free hand gathering my skirt, reaching between my legs. I felt like I'd die if I wasn't touched.

"What are—are you—" He croaked the beginning of a thought and never finished it, his entire body going rigid. His hands coming to the part of my head he'd labeled forbidden, his fingers twisted in my hair and pulled. "Shit. I'm going to come. I'm—"

Abandoning my own need, I cupped his deliciously sculpted ass with both palms and yanked him forward, hungrily sucking his dick deep in my mouth. I wanted it. I wanted him. I wanted all of him. I was crazed with the idea of him spending anywhere but inside me.

And then he came and—holy scratched record, Batman—it tasted god-awful.

My friends had told me it didn't taste great, but nothing could've prepared me for the disgusting, gelatinous spoiled fish and mayonnaise flavored goop presently in my mouth, forcefully shoving me out of arousal town and thrusting me into repulsed town. I'd had no idea it was possible to flip off my sexy switch so incredibly fast.

Gagging around the texture and unexpected spunky tang, but being the champ that I was, I managed to regain control of my throat and swallowed it anyway—while also promising myself I would never swallow it again.

It was a promise I fully intended to keep until the moment I glanced up and saw the look of wonder on Byron's face. The look of complete devotion and longing and astonishment and desire. And love. So much love. I licked my lips, tasting him there, and his eyes were glued to the movement of my tongue, as though it held every answer to the universe and he planned to worship it, and me, always.

Then again, maybe sperm isn't that *bad.*

Byron gripped my shoulders and lifted me to standing with one strong, fluid motion, his attention still fastened to my lips. Pressing me against the door, he leaned forward as though to kiss me and on instinct I stiffened, my palms flat against his chest holding him at bay.

"Hold on. Let me go rinse out my mouth."

"I don't care about that. I need to kiss you."

I turned my head to the side and he still advanced, his mouth now against my cheek and neck, his tongue swirling just under my ear.

"I need to taste you. Will you let me taste your pussy?"

A hot spike of desire was immediately doused by the idea of Byron tasting me. No way was he going down on me. Yeah, I'd had fantasies about it—specifically about Byron doing it— I'd always wondered what it would be like, I'd heard it felt *amazing*, but no way was I asking him to do what I'd just done. Unlike with blow jobs, the liquid excretion would be constant. He'd have to taste me on his tongue the entire time, not just at the end. No way was I asking him to suffer through that grossness just so I could get off. His fingers were perfect, I did not need his mouth.

I grimaced. "Uh. No. No thank you."

At my refusal, Byron's kisses tapered, and I turned my head to find him frowning at my answer, his gaze questioning. "We have time."

"I know, but it's fine."

He blinked. "It's fine?"

"I mean, I'm good. You've already been more than generous."

The severity of his frown increased. "You realize that each time I've touched you has been an act of pure selfishness, not generosity, right?"

I laughed, kissing his jaw and chin.

Byron's hands came to my upper arms and held me slightly away, his narrowed eyes searching mine. "What's happening right now?"

"What do you mean?"

"I mean, what are you thinking? What's going through your head? Did you hate it?"

"Hate it?"

"Giving me a blow job."

"What? No! I loved it. I loved watching you. You are very sexy, you know."

The lust haze that had darkened his eyes earlier was now gone and the blue-green depths sparkled with intelligence and apprehension. "Fred. What did you dislike about it?"

"Byron—"

"You disliked something about it, and that something is why you don't want me to go down on you."

My jaw dropped open and a squeaky sound of surprise hissed out of me. "How—what—why would—" I didn't know how to respond to his mind reading, so I snapped my mouth shut. How could he possibly know that?

"Why won't you tell me the truth?"

"Why do we have to talk about it at all? If you enjoyed yourself, and I said I loved it—which I did—why are you pushing so hard for me to tell you what I didn't like? Wouldn't that ruin it for you?"

"No. If there's something I can do or change about you giving me a blow job that will make you more likely to do it in the future, I want to change that thing. But, more importantly, if that same something is holding you back from giving me the chance to go down on you, then I *most definitely* want to know."

My jaw dropped open again.

This time, he used my stunned surprise to gently tug me forward, slide his hands down to my hips, and start gathering my skirt in his hands. "I want to taste you, Winnie. I want you to come on my tongue."

I exhaled a shaky breath of longing but caught his hands. "I don't think that's a good idea."

His movements ceased and we stared at each other for a long moment, mine wary, his sharp with frustration.

"Why don't you trust me?" he whispered.

"I—I do."

"Are you not ready? Is that it?"

"Yes."

The intensity of his examination increased. "Do you think you'll ever be ready?"

I pressed my lips together, not wanting to answer. The answer was no. No, I would never be ready to have Byron taste me and find me gross. Nor would I ever be ready to tell him how much I'd hated the taste of his sperm. I couldn't imagine a scenario where that information wouldn't hurt his feelings, especially not after the way he'd looked at me moments ago when I'd swallowed.

He inspected me for a while longer, letting my skirt drop back into place and removing himself a step. "How about this, will you ever be ready to tell me why you don't want to do it?"

I shifted my attention to the room behind him, crossing my arms, and ignoring the panicky heat spreading from my chest to my neck. "I don't understand why you won't let this drop. Most guys would be relieved."

"Would they?" I felt his eyes move down my form. "Would they be relieved to never taste you? To have that pleasure? To never have your naked body spread before them like a banquet? I don't think so. On this subject, I believe I'm firmly in the camp of just like other guys."

Having nothing to say to that, as I was overheated and unfairly turned on and feeling trapped between the terror of honesty and the fear of hurting his feelings—both of which seemed to spell my doom and would ultimately make him angry—I turned and opened the door, needing to escape the confines of the bedroom, this suite, and Byron's relentless no-win questions. *That's me. I'm no-Win.*

"Where are you going?"

"I need some space." I sprinted to the suite's exit.

Byron's palm landed on the door just as my hand closed around the handle and he came around to stand at my side. "Wait, Win. Don't leave yet. If you don't wish to discuss this now, I understand. I will give you space, as much time and distance as you need. But may we discuss this later?"

"I don't wish to talk about this *ever.*" Keeping my eyes forward, I didn't look at him, and I had to stiffen my spine to keep from listing toward his addictive heat and strength.

"Then will you at least tell me where you're going? Please."

I shook my head. "I don't know. I haven't decided."

"Win—"

"Maybe I'll go down to the concierge and ask her to get me some condoms."

His exhale rustled my hair, fell along my cheek and ear. "Please don't do that."

I looked at him then and saw his request was serious. "Why not? Don't you want to have sex with me? Don't you think about it all the time? What's changed?"

"Yes. And yes. And nothing has changed, not for me." His expression grew pained. "But if you're not ready to tell me why you don't want oral sex with me, then I'm not ready for intercourse with you."

My jaw dropped open for the third time in three minutes and I reared back, my temper flaring quick and hot. "You—you're—you think—" I sucked in a breath as I labored to gather my flailing, incensed thoughts. "You're going to punish me now? Because I don't want oral sex?"

"That's not what's happening." His hand fell from the door and lifted to my arm.

I flinched away. "Do *not* touch me."

He made an exasperated, growly sound and pushed his hands through his hair, the strands standing in spiky chaos. "If you can't talk to me, if you don't trust me yet, then we should wait before doing anything else until you can and do." Despite his outward frustration, his tone was irritatingly measured and calm. "I don't want lies or half-truths between us. I want you to trust me like I trust you. I'm not fragile. I can handle the truth, no matter what it is."

I couldn't talk to him. All I wanted to do was scream. Here I was, trying to be kind, trying to spare his feelings. And there he was, punishing me for it.

Affixing my eyes forward, I said, "Move."

Unspoken words seemed to rise around us, and I felt his hesitation like a real, tangible thing, a hand on my back or fingers tugging in my hair. But eventually, he moved. He stepped to the side enough that I could open the door, which I did. Then I was out and walking down the hall to the elevator.

He didn't follow.

CHAPTER 34
BYRON

Concentration, thinking, and speaking about anything other than Winnifred Gobaldi were quickly becoming Herculean tasks.

Walter, the intimacy and sex coach from whom I'd been receiving theory instruction since arriving in New York, had warned me this would occur. He'd stated that if I loved Winnie as I claimed, when or if she and I breached the intimacy barrier with purposeful consent, my desire for her as well as my anxiousness for her good regard might multiply rather than attenuate.

At the time, unable to fathom how such a phenomenon could be possible, I'd doubted him. In Seattle, the intensity had already approached painful, well on the road to agonizing. How could it possibly get any worse?

Today, he'd been proven correct. Less than eighteen hours after succumbing, now that I'd touched her and held her in my arms as she'd broken into pieces while panting my name, now that I'd felt her come around my fingers, smelled her arousal and the sweet scent of her sweat heavy in the room, thoughts of recreating the experience—again and again, in a multitude of different ways, in a multitude of different places—consumed me. As did my anxiety at her hasty, angry departure.

I'd erred. I'd made her unhappy. I needed to make things right.

"We have one more interview. How're you doing?" Pamela, my manager, approached, halting approximately three feet from my shoulder.

Pamela had reconvened the interviews fifteen minutes after Winnie had left me alone in the big suite. I'd utilized the time by sitting in the dark bedroom and replaying every moment of our encounter on a loop.

I'd deduced Winnie's dissatisfaction, which she did not wish to communicate for unknown reasons, had been caused by the taste of sperm. She'd appeared earnestly eager every moment precluding my climax, even touching herself during the act. But when I'd tried to kiss her after, she'd wanted to rinse out her mouth first.

Fucking. Goddamn. Sperm.

I couldn't be certain, but I further hypothesized that since, by her own admission, she'd never given a blow job before today, Winnie had never been the recipient of oral sex either. Perhaps her initial (evidently repulsive) exposure to cum made her question whether her own body would be similarly distasteful? And this fear, this desire to spare me from discomfort, was —I assumed—why she didn't wish for me to go down on her.

My last several interviews had been spent working through this particular portion of the problem, reaching this particular conclusion, and wishing I could rewind time.

I didn't often entertain regret, but how I wished I'd gone down on her first. I doubted she'd ever let me now, and I could weep—or punch something, or run a marathon—at the unbearable tragedy of my lost opportunity.

The only mystery that remained was why she'd refused to tell me she disliked the taste. Why not tell me the truth? Did she believe me so fragile? Incapable of receiving feedback? And how could I change this perception? What could I do, change, say to prove I could be trusted? Whatever she needed.

"Byron?" Pamela shuffled a few inches closer. "Are you okay? Can we do the last interview?"

I'd forgotten my manager stood at my shoulder, forgotten she'd asked me about my current state of mind, forgotten where I was.

"Yes, sorry," I said, rubbing my eyes with the base of my palms. "Please proceed. Thank you for your patience."

I couldn't wait for this gauntlet to end. Every interview had been a different shade of beige except Harry Lorher, the asshole who'd questioned me about my biological mother. I should've been fine. I'd been preparing for today, for going to restaurants, for stepping out in public and engaging in conversations with strangers. I had confidence in my abilities. In addition to taking theory lessons in intimacy and sex from Walter, I'd used the remainder of the last month in New York wisely.

Intense, one-on-one therapy with a world-renowned expert in sensory processing disorders, applying myself to learning coping skills, had absorbed four days of each week since leaving Seattle. I'd also learned to prepare and cook gourmet gluten-free meals every Saturday. A one-day, six-hour class on living with someone with celiac spanned a full Saturday in the middle of the month. Additionally, I'd taken a short course on classroom management each Monday, which afforded me the opportunity of visiting several local middle schools to observe.

I wanted to understand Winnie. I wanted to be better equipped and experienced for her. And for myself, I needed to know we had a fighting chance at building a future. But all the preparation in the world wouldn't matter if she didn't trust me enough to tell me the truth.

Presently, and despite all the progress I'd made over the last twenty-seven days, the shirt I currently wore itched, the studio lights stung my eyes, and the murmuring conversation originating from my publishing team in the corner revolted my senses like cockroaches crawling behind my brain.

So, yes, I needed this gauntlet of interactions to end. I needed to find Winnie and convince her I could be trusted. I needed her to understand that I would do whatever was necessary to be the kind of partner she deserved, not just for her benefit, but also—and mainly, selfishly—for mine.

Pamela left my side.

The interviewer arrived.

I lifted my eyes and settled a soft focus over the person's head.

They asked their inane questions and I answered with inane responses, a paint-by-numbers conversation. Minutes stretched on and on, our rote exchange the equivalent of watching a tea kettle heat on the stove, until—at long last—it ended seconds before I boiled over.

Launching myself out of the chair, I strolled past the faces of people I should know but whose names I couldn't remember in the moment. Cell phone retrieved from my back pocket, I exited the suite, walked down the hall, and arrived at the elevator, all while texting Winnie.

Byron: I'm finally finished with my interviews. If you want to talk, I am ready. If not, I can wait. Either way, what I would greatly appreciate right now is you in my arms, on a bed, somewhere quiet and dark—assuming you wish to see me at all.

Rereading the words prior to sending, I stepped into the elevator without looking up. As the doors slid shut, I nodded at the clear, concise message. Trusting Winnie to tell me to fuck right off if she were still angry, I hit send.

Only then did I look up from my phone and realize I shared the elevator car with Harry Lorher, the asshole interviewer from this morning.

"Mr. Visser." He smirked, inclining his head, his unctuous stare slithering over me. "What a coincidence."

"Fuck off." I turned my glare to the "smart" phone that had just been responsible for making me stupid and careless. Checking the text I'd sent seconds ago, I saw Winnie hadn't yet read my message.

The man made a sound like a *tsk*. "You know everything you say to me is on the record. I'll have to print that. I owe it to my readership to let them know if you're the entitled, privileged, spoiled snowflake you pretend to be. On the other hand, you could change my mind."

"Quote me on this: Anyone who purposefully reads your sedimentary fecal residue is a leeching shit stain and can also fuck off." I glared at the panel of numbers, realizing I hadn't yet selected a floor and neither had he. Reaching forward, I chose the lobby. The last thing I needed was this asshole knowing where he could find me.

Harry Lorher chuckled, and I sensed him turn to face me. "So hostile, and for no reason. I'm giving you a chance to set the record straight and let people know your side. I just want to talk. I don't understand why you're so antagonistic when anyone tries to know you, understand you. Don't you owe your readership more than one honest interview every five years? Don't they deserve to know who you are?"

I said nothing and I tuned him out, counting the floors as we descended. Like throwing pebbles at a boulder, he repeated the same questions as before—about my mother, about her response to my success, about my feelings on being called a mistake. Thankfully, he only talked, he didn't approach or try to touch me. But by the time the elevator doors opened on the ground floor and I walked out, my nerves were shot. All I wanted was a tight, soft, heavy blanket and a dark room void of sound, light, and assholes.

Or, more precisely, a dark room void of everything but Winnie.

* * *

I escaped Harry Lorher by entering the room service kitchens where I'd cooked Winnie's breakfast earlier that morning. The walk-in freezer wasn't dark, but it was dim, and it provided relative quiet. Unfortunately, it also didn't have any cell reception. Putting the phone away, I waited.

I waited, leaning against shelves stacked with frozen hamburger, and closed my eyes to count my breaths, one number for every inhale and exhale until I reached ten. Then I began again. I waited, tucking my hands beneath my arms to keep them warmish, my shirt no longer itching but rather offering necessary insulation. I waited until nothing seemed loud, not even the inside of my brain or the hum of the freezer's compressor, and only then did I open my eyes and check my watch. The interviews had ended over forty minutes ago.

Time to leave.

Withdrawing a pair of small over-the-ear Bluetooth headphones from my shirt pocket, I set the app on my phone to a playlist of Seattle rain sounds. I then shoved my hands in my pant pockets and strolled through and out of the kitchens, my attention alert for Harry Lorher, or any of the other interviewers, or any person whose face sparked with recognition upon spotting mine.

Thankfully, I didn't see Harry Lorher, and no one approached by the time I made it to the private elevators by the VIP check-in. I thought about confirming with the concierge to ensure Winnie's gluten-free dinner had been sent up, but I decided against it. I didn't wish to speak at present.

Navigating to the suite proved equally uneventful, but—to be certain—I walked past my door twice, doubling back. Content and convinced no one followed me, or watched, or tracked, or traced, I tugged off my headphones, returned them to my shirt pocket, retrieved my key card, and opened the door to the suite.

The image of Winnie filled my vision upon entering, sitting on the little couch, her laptop balanced on her lap, a cup of tea in her hand. A peaceful oasis, everything kindness, tranquility, and beauty. Tension left my neck and lower back. I exhaled a silent breath, and she turned her head toward me, eyes the shade of sweet spice connecting with mine.

"Hey," she said softly, lifting her laptop and placing it on the coffee table, a frown pulling her eyebrows together. "Where have you been? Did you get my text?"

"I didn't get your text," I managed, my throat dry and rusty. I remained by the door, ready to leave if she wished. The mere idea of leaving her now made my lungs cramp in revolt and my bones brittle with exhaustion. Yet I would go if she still needed space.

Setting her tea down next to her laptop, she walked over to me, her fingers twisting in front of her. "Your manager called to check on you, said your number went straight to voice mail. I tried calling too. It's been forty-five minutes. Where have you been?"

"Sorry. I was. . . sorry." Too much had happened, the questions Mr. Lorher asked were not ones I'd ever willingly discussed with anyone. But I would tell her the story as soon as I could. Contemplating the events in this present moment felt too much like reliving them. I changed the subject. "May I stay?"

"What? Stay?" Her lovely gaze filled with confusion.

"Do you want me to go? Do you need space?"

"No. Stay. Please stay." Winnie reached for my hand with both of hers, her body stiffening as our skin made contact. "Byron, why are you so cold?"

At her touch, some fundamental aspect within me eased, a cellular shift. My throat loosened, breathing came easier, spoken words and internal thoughts were friends again. These same phenomena had occurred last night on the way home from the restaurant.

"May we discuss it later?" I asked, eternally grateful for this woman who wove both serene and chaotic magic into the tapestry of my life, seemingly without ever consciously trying. "I'll tell you, but not right now."

"Okay." She pulled me forward, toward the couch. Her phone buzzed and chimed on the coffee table. She didn't glance at it, but she did change direction, moving us toward the bedroom as though rethinking and then readjusting our destination. "Do you still want to cuddle on the bed?"

Oh God. Yes. Please. Fuck, yes, I thought.

But all I said was, "Please."

Judging by her grin, the single word must've sounded heavy with the entirety of my viewpoint on the subject.

"Hard day?" Her phone buzzed and chimed as she spoke. Then chimed and buzzed again.

I considered the question. I wanted to ask her about earlier, when she'd left me, but not now. Not yet. Not until I could figure out how to prove I was trustworthy.

Presently, she smiled just for me, beauty personified after so much ugliness. I wanted what she offered in this moment, and I couldn't think beyond it to my earlier concerns.

Thus, determined to keep things simple between us, I decided to answer her question with a double meaning. "Some parts were harder than others."

She laughed, her eyes dancing. Winnie opened her mouth, hopefully to respond in kind, but her phone rang, bringing us to a halt on our journey to the bedroom. Frowning, she leaned to the side and inspected the screen. Then, releasing me, she picked up the phone and rejected the call.

"It's Amelia. I'll call her later," she explained, reaching for my hand again.

My attention snagged on her computer screen. "Am I interrupting? Do you need to work?"

"No. Not at all." Her lips curved, her gaze seemed hazy as they continued to hold mine. "I'm just checking the status of some applications I submitted. No biggie."

"Applications?" I frowned at her computer, then at her. "Are you wanting to switch schools?"

"Oh, no. It's not for teaching jobs. It's for a side-hustle."

"Side-hustle? I thought you were going to work for Amelia's company?"

"Well, I didn't get an interview for that position." She tugged on my hand. "So I decided to apply for similar ones."

I didn't move.

Her phone rang again. Again, she glanced at the screen and rejected it.

"You didn't get an interview?" Floored by this news, I peered at her phone. "Does Amelia know? Is that why she's calling you?"

"No, Amelia doesn't know. But it's fine. Actually, it all worked out really well."

"It worked out well?" *What?* Why wasn't she upset?

"It did work out well, and now it's fine." She shrugged, like all the work she'd done, all the hateful comments she'd endured, like it was all just nothing. Like her feelings were *nothing.*

I blinked at her, endeavoring to bring her more sharply into focus. She'd wanted that job desperately enough to do those challenges when she couldn't stand breathing the same air as me. Her shrugging it off now couldn't have made less sense.

"You really wanted that job."

"I did, but—like I said—it's fine."

Fine?

"No. It's not fine. They didn't even call you for an interview? You need to talk to Amelia." A suspicion, a hunch if you will, held me in place. A sense that an imminently unraveling mystery lay just beyond the horizon of this conversation persisted, and it demanded I abandon my plans for simplicity.

She let my hand drop. "No, I don't. I don't want to bother her with it."

I couldn't believe my ears. "What are you talking about? How would it be a bother? She's your best friend, you've known her for years, you two—"

My building rant was cut off by the sound of Winnie's phone ringing again. She glared at the screen and answered via speakerphone. "Hi, Amelia. I have you on speaker. Byron had a hard day and—"

"I'm not calling about Byron. Winnie, we need to talk. It's important. Where are you?"

"We're in the suite, but—"

"I'll be right there."

Winnie spun away from me and paced over to the window. "Can it wait? We're kind of in the middle of something."

"I'm sorry, it can't. I just got an email from my work with the final list of candidate interviews, and you're not on the list. I don't understand what happened, but I wanted you to know, I'll take care of it. I'll figure it out and get you on that list."

Winnie peeked at me, her lips pressed in a line, and she took Amelia off speaker. "Don't worry about it. It's fine."

What the hell was wrong with her? Was she a robot? Did she not have feelings? Why wasn't she upset? Why hadn't she gone to Amelia?

I didn't hear what Amelia said in response, but I imagined it closely resembled what I'd been thinking. Winnie huffed and appeared flustered.

"No. No, stop. Honestly, don't worry about it. I'm not surprised. They never called, and—"

Amelia shrieked, saying *What,* or *What the hell,* or something similar, necessitating that Winnie hold the phone away from her ear. I didn't follow precisely what came after, but it sounded like a lament and a tirade, which elicited another loud exhale from Winnie.

"Calm down. I'm fine. It's totally okay. I—Amelia? Amelia?" She removed the phone from her ear again and looked at the screen. "She hung up!" Winnie turned to face me, her eyes wide with shock as they studied the phone. "I can't believe she hung up on me."

"She's angry," I gritted out, working to control my own rising temper. "Can you blame her?"

Her shocked gaze moved to me. "Why should she be angry with me? I didn't do anything."

Exactly. I paced over to her, reminding myself not to yell when all I wanted to do was erupt. "I know you asked me to cease giving you unsolicited advice, and I promised I would, but I'm breaking that promise. I was wrong. Never expecting anything from other people doesn't mean you have no self-worth, Winnie. It means you don't give other people enough credit, you don't believe *they* have worth."

"W—what?" She winced. "What are you talking about?"

I backed away rather than lean into her space. "Why didn't you ask Amelia for help?"

"Like I said, I didn't want to be a bother."

"Can you hear yourself? She's your best friend. It wouldn't have been a bother. Why can't you ask for help?"

Her mouth opened and closed to no purpose and I knew. I knew. I could see where before I'd been blind.

"All this time . . ." My stare grew unfocused. "I thought I needed to change and learn to deserve you, for you to trust me. But that's never been it, has it?"

"What are you talking about? I've never—"

"You once claimed that I treated you like an infant, but it's the other way around. You treat everyone like an infant. Everyone. Assuming they're going to let you down or aren't capable of functioning at your level. You think you're better."

Winnie gasped, and before my eyes I witnessed her temper catch up with mine. "I do not!"

"You do. And you know what? You are. You're fucking amazing. But you never expect anyone else to be anything but incapable of measuring up. Or you only expect them capable of letting you down." I turned and paced to the other side of the room, unable look at her. All the pieces were coming together too quickly.

She followed me, tripping over her words. "You—you are capable. You—"

"I think you even admitted it once. You said—that morning in my room—you said you never asked for what you wanted. You said something like you knew better than to be brave. Do you love me?" I asked, speaking stream of consciousness, unable to shut the hell up since it all made so much perfect, elegant, horrible sense. Her patience, her easygoing acceptance of everything and everyone, no matter how poorly they treated her.

"I—I love—"

"No, Win," I ground out. "Not like that. I know you *love* everyone. Are you in love with me? Are you invested? Would your heart be broken if we didn't work out? Would you be devastated?"

Her breathing changed again, grew labored, her eyebrows pulling together. "I'd understand if you decided—"

"That." I snapped my fingers, pointing at her, perhaps appearing a bit wild. "Right there. That's the problem."

"Problem?"

"I don't want you to understand if I let you down. I don't want you to understand if I'm an asshole. I want you to expect better. I want you to expect everything."

Crossing her arms, Winnie lifted her eyes to the ceiling, now glassy with unshed tears, her chin wobbling forcefully.

And just like that, all the anger and frustration evaporated, leaving behind only a sour flavor of misery. I had no way to fix this. She had to fix this.

"Okay. Byron, listen." She pressed her palms together, clearly fighting to keep her tone even. "You—you asked me yesterday if it would be so bad to push you out of your comfort zone. But I don't know how to do that. I don't want to pressure you. I don't want to hurt your feelings or make you—"

"Why the hell not? Pressure me, Winnie! Pressure me to be everything you deserve." I captured her hands between mine. "Expect me to exceed your expectations. When you don't, when you make excuses for me or assume I'm going to disappoint you—that disappointment is all I'm capable of—can't you see that makes it impossible for you to love me? If you're always guarding your heart, it's never open to me."

"I don't understand you." She turned her fingers, tangling them with mine. "How can you say you're a disappointment? You are hugely talented, and—and successful. Your books are—"

"I'm not referring to fame and money. We both know those are meaningless to you."

"Then what are you talking about?"

"You do not treat me or speak to me as though you believe I am capable." I extracted myself from her grip. "And if I hadn't just witnessed that phone call with Amelia, I would've taken it personally. But I see now, I understand now, it's not personal. If you—what did you say? You don't want to bother her? If you're not willing to bother Amelia, your closest friend of six years who has proven herself countless times, how can I ever trust you to bother me?"

She reached out and grabbed my arm, her grip like a vice. "That's completely unfair." Her voice wavered but she didn't cry. She was too stubborn to cry.

"Which part?" I asked softly, though I could guess her answer.

"All of it. I do not think I am better than anyone else. And coming from you, you who can't stand anyone, or give anyone the time of day, or—"

"I do not like people. I have never claimed to enjoy people. But you do. And why is that? Why do you like them when you believe people—all people, even me, even Amelia—will eventually disappoint you in some horrible, unforgivable way?"

Her mouth snapped shut, her eyes betraying uncertainty, and I could see I'd hit a nerve. I'd spoken a truth about her, one she'd taken as self-evident and never, or seldom, examined for veracity.

"You don't know this, but—" I had to clear my throat in order to speak around the cinching tightness. "I thought I was a problem. I thought I needed coaching and classes. I thought I could learn how to be what you need. I thought I could be better for both of us. I want to be. But can I? Will you ever trust me enough to be honest with me? Is there anyone you're honest with?"

Her breathing had quickened, and I could see her uncertainty persisted, yet she swallowed rather than spoke.

And what could she say? I was right.

Shaking my head as I shook her hand off, I placed essential distance between us, wanting to see her clearly before I left. I needed to leave. I needed to dissect this new problem that, quite possibly, had no answer. It wasn't something I could solve by myself. No classes or courses existed for me to take. I wasn't the one who needed to change.

"Byron, I—" She gulped, her fingers twisting. "I want to be honest with you."

"Do you?" I backed away toward the door.

"I do. But I don't . . ." she said, her tone croaky and cracking. "What if you don't want me anymore? What if I'm honest, and then you stop loving me? Or what if my expectations are too high? Or what if I push you when I shouldn't? What if I lose you?"

Her questions drove the air from my lungs. I found I needed a second or ten to find my voice before I could respond. "Before I left Seattle, when we were in my bedroom and we fought, you accused me of wanting everything immediately, on my terms, without risking anything in return. That's what you're doing to me right now."

Her face began to crumple, and the sight plucked at my internal strings of shame and remorse. I hated her tears. I loathed her sadness. I wanted only her happiness. But if there was one experience with which I had intimate familiarity, it was that love isn't love when it enables selfish, destructive behavior. Love isn't love when it makes excuses for abusive and hurtful choices. It becomes twisted, a perversion. It becomes cowardice.

Even so, the instinct to comfort her and apologize nearly overwhelmed the knowledge that coddling her now would only cause our ruin later.

Thankfully, she regained control over her features before I could lose control of myself.

"The thing is, Fred. Standing on this side of your fortified heart? It makes me feel like shit." I backed toward the door, not knowing where I'd go. Perhaps back to the numbing freezer. "So far, the way I see it, knowing what I know now, I'm the only one who has been taking any risks here. If you want me, if you want to be with me, you're going to have to risk more than your pride. It's not enough. Like you, I deserve more. I deserve everything."

CHAPTER 35
WINNIE

Amelia found me on the floor of the suite, crying. She took one look at me and walked into the bathroom, returning a short time later with a steaming hot towel.

"It's okay. We'll figure it out," she said, sounding almost cheerful as she pressed the towel to my sobbing face. "I'll email them back and demand they give you the interview. All will be well."

I felt her arm come around my back, encouraging me to lay my head on her shoulder. "Now, tell me why you didn't let me know that they never called you for the interview."

"Do we have to talk about this right now?" I asked through hiccupping sobs. I didn't care about that stupid job. I didn't care about anything. Nothing mattered. Not even climate change. And humanity was all destined to die from climate change. *That's* how upset I was.

"Yes! You were perfect for that job." She squeezed me. "We would be lucky to have you. Why didn't you tell me?"

I wiped my face with the hot towel. "You said to wait for a call. They never called. It's fine."

"It's not fine. You wouldn't be crying if it were fine. This last week, the whole flight over, you said nothing. Why didn't you—"

"I'm not crying about the stupid job!" I buried my face in the wet towel, a new bout of uncontrollable, excruciating sadness spinning through me like a cyclone. "It hurts," I wailed. "How can it hurt like this when it's not a physical wound. It makes no sense!"

Amelia was silent—silent and still—while I cried and cried. I could almost hear her pondering, thinking, debating.

And her debating was so loud, I felt compelled to blurt, "Byron told me he loves me and I am not worthy of him, that I'm an emotionally stunted scaredy cat who doesn't trust anyone or expect anything out of life except disappointment, and now he's gone, and I don't even care about climate change!"

I turned my head and cried against her neck, the towel forgotten as I clung to my friend and wept. He was gone and my heart felt like . . .

It felt like. . .

God, but it felt similar to the months after my mother had died and left me all alone in this world. I felt like the world was a yawning, cavernous, endless source of pain and misery, and I'd never wanted to feel like this again. How could I let this happen? How could I allow myself to want him so much, to fall for him when—

"No!" I said to myself, not caring if I was freaking out Amelia. "No! If I'd trusted him, if I'd been honest and asked for what I wanted, if I'd been brave, then I wouldn't feel like this."

"Ooo-*kay*." Amelia shifted next to me on the carpet, angling her body toward mine and wrapping me in a hug. "Why don't you start at the beginning? And this time, why don't you tell me everything."

Accepting the comfort she offered, I wrapped my arms around her neck and—through gasping sobs—I told her everything. My feelings and memories, worries and fears, concerns about wanting to bother her, anxieties about damaging her friendship with Byron, all spewed forth. I left out no detail, no conversation. I even offered to show her the video of us making out on my couch, still saved on my phone. I told her the whole damn story and, as I told it and as I listened to it, I realized what an absolute weasel I'd been.

The more I came to truly know and genuinely like him, the more afraid I'd been of embarrassment, of being rejected, of not having my growing feelings returned. I'd doomed everything. My greatest fear had been being a fool in his eyes, but hurting him was so much worse.

When I got to the argument we'd had in Byron's room before he left for New York, this time leaving nothing out, Amelia stood and began to pace. And when I told her about the blow job I'd given him this afternoon and how I didn't want him to go down on me because I worried I would taste bad, but how I didn't want to tell him that was the reason since it might hurt his feelings, she'd laughed hysterically. Then she apologized, raided the suite's fridge, and offered me a mini bottle of whiskey or gin. I chose whiskey. She brought me three of them.

I drank the first quickly, but then sipped the second, recounting our latest fight and everything he'd said and how right he'd been and how awful I felt and how I wasn't sure if I was good enough for him. I wasn't sure I knew how to ask for what I wanted.

"Sure you do," Amelia said, lifting her gin and tonic toward me. She'd turned hers into a mixed drink but not mine. "Repeat after me: Byron, your spunk tastes like junk. Now you say it."

I laughed, clutching the mini bottle to my chest, my head pounding, my nose stuffy, my lips dry and cracked. Crying was the worst, a bodily function that only served to compound misery. Are you miserable? Then you probably feel like crying. Don't worry, now you're not only going to be miserable, you're going to feel and look miserable too. Welcome to snot and tears!

"But don't you see? It's not just the sperm issue! My instincts are all wrong. I don't know how to ask for what I want without paralyzing fear. And doesn't he deserve better than someone who is always afraid to be honest? Doesn't he deserve someone as fearless as him? Someone as brave and wonderful?"

"Well . . . yeah. But that isn't really the point, is it?" Amelia returned to where I sat on the floor, my back pressed against the front of the couch, and she sat next to me. "He doesn't love that person. He loves you. And, ultimately, don't you think Byron wants love more than he wants bravery? Although, they're kind of the same thing when you think about it."

"Bravery is love?" I sent her a side-eye even though it hurt my brain.

She shrugged, a wry smile on her lips. "Only the brave love."

"So what am I supposed to do?" I placed my mini bottle of whiskey on the coffee table. "And please don't say 'Fake it till you make it.' What if he doesn't want me anymore? What if he never wants to see me again after this?"

Amelia made a face that told me she thought I was bonkers. "Okay, first of all, Byron's brain doesn't work like that. He's like one of those birds that's only capable of mating with one other bird. You know, the tall ones, with the feathers?"

"All birds have feathers. It's a defining characteristic."

"You know what I mean, Cheeky Charlie. Which bird mates for life? The tall birds with the long beaks and they live in Florida, but they're not flamingos. And then, if their partner dies, they wander around wailing and brooding until they die too."

I gave her a blank stare, having no idea which bird she was referring to.

She waved a hand at my expression. "Anyway, the name of the bird isn't important, it's the wailing and brooding part. That's Byron. And my point is, he's a one-bird kind of guy. If he's decided you're his bird, then God help you. You're stuck with him."

"How can he trust me to tell him the truth when the very idea terrifies me? He deserves so much more."

"Hmm. How about you practice on me then?" Amelia bumped my shoulder with hers. "Go ahead. Ask me for what you want."

Irritatingly, my chin wobbled. "I don't want to."

"Why not?"

"I'm afraid of making you mad."

"Is this about the job? I already said I'd email about getting you an interview. You should have come to me. I could have spoken to the team on your behalf."

"I know. In retrospect, I should've come to you."

"Yes. You should have." She bumped my shoulder again. "The community managers they're looking at hiring, I checked out their channels. None of them bring the same kind of energy you do, the fun, the openness. All of them are only STEM focused and so serious about everything. Not that there is anything wrong with that necessarily, but I believe we need more than just one type of influencer."

"Well, there you go. That's what they wanted, and now we know why they didn't call."

"Exactly, which—if I'd known—I would've argued passionately against. This is my point. When you don't tell people who love you the truth, and they're counting on you telling them the truth, you make everything harder for everyone. Case in point, by not telling me that they didn't call you, you've made my job harder."

"I did?"

"You did. We want the doors open wide to all women, with all interests, right? And now I'm back to square one. I was counting on you. *I* need you in that position. I could have advocated for you before now and things would've been simpler. But just like Byron, you have it in your head that you need to take care of everything yourself. You two are exactly the same."

"What? How can you say that? He's so much braver than me." As though to illustrate this point, I grabbed the bottle of whiskey and took another sip of liquid courage.

"Hear me out. He doesn't expect anything of anyone either. Well, he didn't. Until you. But the difference is, he goes out of his way to avoid people, wanting nothing from them, asking nothing without clear boundaries and expectations. Meanwhile, you go around giving everything to everyone and asking nothing in return. You're infuriating." Amelia clinked her gin and tonic against my mini bottle. "Need me, Winnie. Need. Me."

"I—I do—"

"I'm so glad we're finally talking about this, and that I'm drinking gin. I think this must've been bothering me for a while."

"What's that?" Taking my mini bottle with me, I stood and wobbled over to the fridge area in search of more tissues.

"I've been your best friend for the last six years, and you're still holding me at arm's length," she ranted behind me, her voice growing angrier. "What do I have to do? What more do I need to do or say to prove to you that I have your back?"

Trying my hardest not to be irritated with Amelia's claims to always have my back, I blew my nose, then tossed the used tissue in the trash bin. "I know you always want to have my back, but I can't expect you to always be there for me."

"Yes! You can!" She smacked her hand on the coffee table. "I will be there for you. I will always—"

"No, you won't! You're leaving."

Darn it! I hadn't meant to say that. But if we were doing this now, then I guess we were going to do this now. She wanted me to be honest? So be it.

Amelia straightened from the floor, wrinkling her nose as she crossed to me. "What are you—"

"You and Elijah." I pointed toward the door of the suite. "You're leaving. You two are moving in together. I can't count on you."

She reached for me. "Win—"

"No." I lifted my arms away from her grabbing hands and backed up. "I get it. You're in love, you want to move in together, your college roommate should not be a factor. I understand. I do not expect you to live with me indefinitely."

She eyed me. "You think I'm moving in with Elijah?"

"Obviously," I said. Then I took a sip of whiskey to keep from crying new tears. God, this hurt to talk about, which was why I didn't want to talk about it.

But Amelia was staring at me like I had three heads, and two of them belonged to demon goats. "No. Not obviously. We are not moving in together."

I stilled. "Wait, what? You're not?"

"Yes, he wants to, but I'm not ready." Amelia took a sip of her drink, watching me over the rim of the glass. "And even if I were, do you really think I'd just leave you? Do you really think I'd move out without considering you as well?"

"I—" I blinked, stunned.

"Yeah. That's what you thought. Well, thanks." She wagged a finger at me. "Thanks so much for thinking so little of me when I think the world of you."

"God, Amelia, I'm—I'm sorry."

"You really must believe everyone but you is a selfish asshole."

"I do not think you are a selfish asshole."

"You do." She threw her free hand into the air. "You won't let me advocate for you, for a position you'd be perfect for. You think I'm going to move out and leave you in a lurch. Either you think I'm a selfish asshole or your definition of a selfish asshole is completely different than mine."

I sat down heavily on the floor right where I'd been standing, leaned an elbow on my knee, and covered my face. "I'm sorry." *I am the asshole.*

"Why are you sorry?" she asked from above me.

"Because—" I shook my head. "I don't know. I'm sorry for not . . . trusting you."

Amelia didn't respond, but I didn't hear any sounds of her departure either. Swallowing for bravery, I let my hand drop and braced myself to meet either her gaze or an empty room. When I looked up, she was still there. Still standing in the same spot. Still peering at me.

"I love you, do you know that?" she asked, her voice more gentle than I deserved.

My chin wobbled. "I do."

"But do you trust it?"

I tried to swallow down the guilt and replace it with determination. I couldn't. So I nodded instead.

"Then you have to let me in." She sat down on the floor next to me again, covering my hand with hers. "You have to ask me for things. You have to have faith in me, like I have faith in you."

"Okay," I managed to croak.

"Come here." Sighing heavily, Amelia pulled me into an awkward hug given we still held drinks in our hands and were sitting cross-legged on the floor.

Immediately, my arms went around her, and I held on as tears freely fell down my face. Again.

Amelia petted my hair and said, “Winnie, I’m sorry your aunt and uncle taught you that no one can be trusted, that the only person you can count on to be good is you. But they were wrong.” She pulled back, holding my shoulder and capturing my eyes. “Don’t let them rob you of living a full life. Don’t let them rob you of believing in other people, thinking the best of them, and expecting them to be there to catch you. You’re not forcing me to do anything. You’re not taking advantage of me.”

“Okay. Okay.” I wiped away more tears.

“I love you, Win. I want to love you. It’s my choice. And I need you to finally let me.”

CHAPTER 36
WINNIE

Amelia left to meet Elijah for dinner, but only after I'd promised her three separate times that I really and truly and honestly wanted her to go. I also had to promise her I'd tell her what I wanted from now on, without her having to drag it out of me.

As I went to bed—alone—I resolved to voluntarily make requests of Byron, if he still wanted me, and of Amelia, to justify her belief in me. But also of myself. I deserved better than never expecting anything from anyone.

In the morning, after a long night of tossing and turning and checking my phone, I dragged myself from bed and stared at my list of text messages for the hundredth time. Still nothing from Byron. My heart sank even though I'd been certain it had nowhere left to sink. It must've been in the earth's core by now.

I wanted him to talk to me! I wanted him to come back and give me a chance to make everything right. I wanted him to—

. . . *wait a minute.*

Rubbing the sleep from my eyes with one hand, I began to type with the other.

Winnie: I want you to talk to me. I want you to come back to the suite and give me a chance to make everything right. And I want you to forgive me.

Rereading the message several times, I decided that about covered everything I could communicate without him being here in person. I hit send and I waited, checking the time at intervals. But when five minutes became seven and he still hadn't read the text, I placed my phone back on the nightstand. Instead of crying, I took a shower.

This was the dawn of a new Winnie, one who freely spoke her wants and needs instead of swallowing them and burying them under worry and fear.

It was an odd and fortuitous thing to have experienced basically identical conversations with both Byron and Amelia yesterday. Although, the discussion with Amelia had ended better than the one with Byron, a fact that made my heart hurt all over again and allowed that yawning, cavernous, endless source of pain and misery to surge to the forefront.

Scrubbing my face with hot water and face wash, I told myself that if he didn't listen to me, or refused to see me, or if my honesty was met with rejection, or if Byron stopped wanting and loving me because of it, then maybe we weren't right for each other. I supposed I would cross that bridge when the time came. Being brave enough to cross the bridge—despite whatever heartache that may await you—had to be so much better than this half life of never approaching the bridge at all.

Steam from the shower had fogged the mirror, and I wiped it with a hand towel in order to see my reflection for a pep talk. "If being yourself and asking for what makes you happy—not making demands or ultimatums, but asking in good faith—makes him stop loving you, then did he ever really love you? Or like you?" I pointed at myself, then wagged my finger. "No. He didn't. And no matter how much you feel for a person, you will not be with someone who doesn't appreciate you as you are, not even Byron."

This was a difficult possibility to face, especially since I knew my feelings for him were real. He'd always been honest with me and asked for what he wanted. Whereas I hid my wants and desires. How could he know me, trust his feelings for me, if I didn't fully share myself with him? My chin wobbled, but I firmed it.

No more crying.

Towel wrapped around my body and clutched to my chest, I exited the bathroom and crossed to my suitcase. While digging around for a bra and underwear, I heard the sound of the suite door opening and I straightened, my brain alert to the noises coming from the living room.

"Hello?" I drifted toward the open bedroom door. "Byron?"

"Yes. Byron."

Thoughtless of my current attire, I sucked in a steadying breath and forced my feet to march out and meet him, steam cloud of courage swirling around me. Right now, I felt brave enough to be honest. Who knew if this daring would last long enough for me to get dressed.

"Hi," I said as soon as he came into view, my voice less certain than I would've liked.

Do it. Do it now.

He was crouching next to the mini fridge, still wearing his suit from yesterday. It looked rumpled, the tie off, the shirt wrinkled. I noticed he hadn't yet shaved as he turned his head toward me when I entered the room. But his stern frown quickly evaporated, much like my steam cloud of courage, and I couldn't have that. I couldn't let my bravery evaporate.

So before it slipped away, I said, "I hated it when you left Seattle for New York without talking to me first. I hated it and I missed you and it made me sad. I don't want you to leave me anymore."

Eyebrows arched and eyes wide as they moved over me, Byron slowly stood and closed the mini fridge.

I wasn't finished. "I can appreciate that you need a bit of space from time to time, I do too, and that's fine. But leaving all night after an argument, or flying to New York or wherever, is unacceptable. You come back *the very moment* you can. You don't go flying off to different cities without talking to me first."

He drifted closer as I spoke, features open and slightly dazed. "Sounds good," he said, voice light.

"Also, I love it when you make me dinner, but I want to make you dinner too. You have to let me cook sometimes. And sending me home with five steaks is ridiculous. I had taco steak casserole in the freezer for three weeks. I'm not saying I don't appreciate it, but you have to admit, five steaks is excessive."

"Agree." His attention trailed from my lips to my legs.

Okay. Now for the harder ones.

"And please don't take this the wrong way—I honestly loved every part of going down on you today except this one little thing—but the taste of sperm does not agree with me. I do not like it. When, or if, we do that again, I'd prefer not to have it in my mouth."

"Great. Makes sense." Byron nodded, his gaze on my hands where they gripped the two ends of the towel to my chest.

This was going so much better than I'd anticipated. I should have told him what I wanted weeks ago!

"And I didn't want you to go down on me because I don't want you to have to taste gross bodily fluids."

This statement made his eyes jump to mine and narrow slightly, the first sign of resistance.

I rushed to add, "Listen, I've thought a lot about this, okay? When a man ejaculates, it's all at the end. There's a bit of pre-cum during, and that's actually not bad. It's watery and salty and the taste is a nonissue." Ignoring the instinct to feel embarrassed by discussing sexual bodily fluids with him so openly, I tightened my fists on the edge of the towel and forced the rest of the words out. "But a woman is, uh, making lubrication the whole time, not just at the end. It'll be spoiled fish and mayonnaise in your face for five minutes straight, and I'm not going to be able to relax knowing that."

Byron's lips pressed together, his eyes brightening with apparent amusement. Clearly, he was fighting either a giant grin or a laugh.

I would not be deterred from this frank and open discussion. He wanted honesty? Well, he was getting honesty. All of it.

"Maybe you don't hate the taste as much as me, but even if you hate it a little bit, I won't orgasm, and I won't enjoy myself. My brain needs to believe you love what you're doing, that you're just as turned on as me—even more turned on, in fact—in order for me to get there. I've been masturbating for a long time. I know how my brain and body works in this arena."

His amusement seemed to fade but a small, pleased-looking smile settled in its place, and he said, "Thank you."

I frowned, confused, skeptical of his sincerity.

I didn't think he was being sarcastic, but his expression of gratitude was unexpected. I wasn't sure what he was grateful for. And most everything he said was delivered deadpan. Even with my Byron-whisperer skills, I still had difficulty reading him.

He must've perceived my confusion and concern because he added with a hint of earnestness, "I am entirely serious. Thank you for those details—regarding your reasoning, the inner workings of your brain related to sexuality and arousal—thank you. I consider them a gift, one I intend to use wisely."

I would trust him, but my scowl remained. "Then, I guess, you're welcome."

Smile persisting, he shifted closer, entering my personal space. I had to tilt my head back a little to maintain eye contact.

"I understand your concern," he said haltingly, his tone sounding conversational yet careful. "But may I propose that you allow me to be the judge? Since I'll be the one with my head between your thighs, my tongue licking your pussy."

His words, and the imagery they conjured, knocked the wind from my lungs and made my body tighten deep inside. "Uh . . ."

"What if I love how you taste?" he asked, the question arriving with an air of logic and reason. Byron reached for one of my hands, gently prying it from the front of the towel and holding it, his thumb pressing against the center of my palm.

"You really think that's going to happen?" I croaked, reminding myself that this was just a discussion and we weren't about to test his theory.

Settle down, Win. You still have a lot to discuss.

"I will never know what you taste like if I'm not given the opportunity." Bending his head toward mine, he turned my hand and threaded our fingers together. "And you're assuming female arousal tastes like male sperm, which is a faulty assumption."

"That's—that's a good point." My mind felt muddled by his talk of tasting me, touching me, and I still had more honesty to share, unrelated to cunnilingus. "Well, what does it taste like then?"

"I have no idea. But I promise, if I don't like it, I'll tell you."

I blinked at him, my frown returning. "Wait, what? You've never. . .?"

He shook his head, dipping it to brush his lips against mine. "No."

"Oh." I was fighting a two-battle front, the butterflies and lovely twisting tightness low in my belly and a cloudy haze of lust behind my eyes. "I'm sorry, I just assumed you had."

"Why?" he asked on a whisper. "You think I have more experience because I'm a man?" One of Byron's eyebrows hitched, and the right side of his mouth—the side that always seemed poised to curl in distaste—curled instead into what looked like a sardonic, self-deprecating smirk. "As I've told you, you have a lot more experience than me."

"With relationships?" I couldn't seem to catch my breath with him so close. Narrowing my eyes, I stared at him, pondering his meaning.

"Correct," he said. "And everything related to them."

Everything related to them . . .

"Byron."

"Yes?" He kissed the inside of my wrist and then reached for my other hand. The realization of what he was about to do eclipsed my ability to process his statements.

I tightened my fingers on the terry cloth, trying to think.

He placed his palm over my fingers but made no move to remove my hand from the towel. "I'll ask you before I do anything. About this, now that I understand your reluctance, I'll check in."

"Wait." I closed my eyes, breathing deeply through my nose. And that was a mistake. He always smelled so darn good, even after twenty-four hours in the same suit. "Wait," I repeated, working to get my bearings. "You were so mad when you left."

"Yes. I was." His stubbly cheek brushed against mine, and a moment later, he placed a feather-light kiss on my neck.

I closed my eyes tighter, swaying toward him. "But now you're not angry with me?"

"I'm not sure." Still holding my hand hostage, he wrapped his arm around my waist such that mine—the one not holding the towel—was now behind my back.

"You're not sure?"

"I'm not sure I can be angry with you . . ." His softly spoken words just under my ear made goose bumps bloom over my skin. "When you're wearing nothing but a towel."

My eyes flew open, and I stiffened. "You're being agreeable because I'm basically naked?"

Tugging on the hand holding the towel in question to my chest, he tightened his arm around my waist, bringing me flush against him, saying between kisses placed on my shoulder, "That sounds like a trick question. I'm not answering it."

Lifting my eyes to the ceiling, I untangled my hand from behind my back and pressed it against his chest. "We need to talk until you're sure you're not angry with me."

"Okay." He began walking, backing me into the bedroom, still placing savoring kisses on my shoulder and neck, the swirl of his tongue making the muscles in my stomach clench. "You talk. I'll listen."

I huffed. He made me so incredibly hot. I told my unsteady legs to stop moving, but they disobediently allowed him to lead me to the bed. We paused at the edge of it.

"I don't want you to be angry with me," I reminded him and myself. "I don't want to do anything physical with you until everything between us is good again and you know I trust you, that I'll be honest with you."

I felt his body still, and he sighed. Then he released me and turned away, pushing his fingers into his hair. "You're right. We should talk. We should talk." He sounded like he was speaking to himself.

Apparently, I wasn't the only one who needed reminding.

"Okay. Yes. I will talk." I rubbed my forehead and tried desperately to regather my scattered thoughts. "Where were we?"

"Cunnilingus," he said, pacing, then added on a mumble, "Or, that's where I'm hoping we were."

His words flustered me, but after closing my eyes and taking a brief few seconds to find my bearings, I was able to remember the remainder of the issues we still needed to discuss.

"So. I've told you some of what I want. And there's more. But you're right. We were talking about why I don't want you to go down on me. I was—I am—trying to be honest about my concerns."

He stopped pacing while I spoke and shoved his hands in his pockets. "And I believe I said something about checking in with you, asking before I take action, and I will."

"Good." I gulped in a breath. My brain may have been ready to discuss serious issues, but my body was still confused as to why Byron stood way over there on the other side of the room and I stood over here by the bed, alone.

His gaze, still heated, turned wary, and the caution bleeding into it helped the lust cobwebs clear.

"What's wrong? What is it?"

"Win." Byron's chest rose and fell. "In all seriousness, I really want this. I don't know why, I can't articulate my reasoning, only that I do with you, and have for a very long time. But something about me you should know if you don't already, I will always tell you what I want. Even at the risk of you interpreting it as me pressuring you. I don't know how else to be other than either silent or honest."

I nodded, absorbing this information and all the ramifications of it. Given what I knew about him, and learned through our conversations, this all tracked as both true and unsurprising. Still, it was good that he'd stated it all so explicitly.

The heat behind his gaze dampened completely, his stare turning grave. "Which is why it's so critically important that you always be honest with me. Don't worry about injuring my feelings. I push when I don't know I'm pushing, which is one of the reasons I avoid people. I don't like hurting people, but I do when I speak, so I don't speak. I speak what I believe to be a benign request while others seem to consider it intimidation. If I could change, I would."

"Don't change." On instinct, I crossed over to him and grabbed his arm, my grip tight with urgency. "Please don't change."

His mouth curved with a wry smile. "I *should* change. It would do me well to learn how to live in this world—for me and for those I encounter—

but that's not my point." He pulled his hand from his pocket, his gaze studying the progress of our fingers as he twined them together again. "My point is, in our relationship, in and out of the bedroom, if you won't enjoy what I'm asking for or what I want to do, or if it's something you don't like, then—similar to your feelings on the subject—I won't enjoy it either. And then I'll hate myself for pushing you into it."

"I don't want you to hate yourself."

"And I don't want to railroad you into doing something you don't wish to."

Biting on my lip, I chewed on the problem, considering how we could move forward without either of us constantly fretting about the other person's wellbeing, and a thought occurred to me. "How about if we expand the check-ins? Not only before you want to do something new or different that's sex related. How about you ask in our day-to-day life—every once in a while—and I promise to tell you the truth."

Byron's forehead wrinkled. "So you want me to check in? While we're—"

"At first, yes. I think it would be a good idea, now that we've talked more about it. And I'll have something like the opposite of a safe word. If I say . . ." I searched my brain for something that sounded sexy or wouldn't pull us out of a good moment. But then I told myself not to overthink it. "If I say I love it, then trust me that I'm telling the truth. But if I say sheep-biting footlicker, then stop."

He looked at me like I was strange but also lovely. "Why not just say stop?"

"What if we're role-playing?"

He seemed to grow several inches taller at my question and his features brightened. Byron cleared his throat, then licked his lips, looking like a kid on Christmas. "Yeah, okay. Yes. I like this."

My Byron-whisperer skills told me what he was really thinking was something closer to, *hell yes*. His enthusiasm for the idea made me feel warm and giddy.

But we had a long way to go before we did anything like that, which reminded me of the main point of honesty I still needed to share.

"I have to tell you this last thing before we move on, before we call this good, okay?"

"Sure." He was leaning toward me, and I could sense his restlessness. "But I feel I must inform you, standing here and producing reasoned thoughts and coherent sentences while you're wearing only a towel might be the most challenging mental task of my life thus far."

Pulling the terry cloth tighter around my body, I internally rolled my eyes at the disobedient part of myself that found this information delightful and dared me to drop the subject, and the towel.

Instead, I backed up a step. "Should I go put on some clothes?"

"I'm never going to answer yes to that question."

"Byron—"

Grinning—which made my heart do somersaults—he brought his hands to my upper arms and said softly, "Go ahead. Say what you need to say. I'll listen, and I'll be good."

I shivered, disobedient Winnie wishing he'd be bad.

But I managed to focus. This was important. *Now for the most difficult part.*

Gathering a deep breath, I said the words I'd practiced after Amelia left yesterday, all night as I tossed and turned, and this morning in the shower. "I understand that you want me to push you outside of your comfort zone, but I'm not very good at that, and I don't think I ever will be. Pushing isn't a strength of mine, I don't enjoy doing it. I feel like I'm good at accepting and understanding people for who they are and providing encouragement and tools when they need help. That's my strength, that's fundamental to who I am. So, if you want me to be this person who is always pushing you to do or be something different, that will never be me."

His features grew pointed with contemplation, like I'd surprised him and he needed to quickly readjust his worldview. Or maybe he just needed to readjust his Winnie-view.

My heart seized with worry and fear—that this last revelation of honesty might make him love me less, see me as less, as weak—but I forced myself to push past the fear. I excelled at compassion, not confrontation, and surely that was okay. Surely the world needed both?

Setting aside this existential debate, I soldiered on with my last point. "But I've never, or I don't think I've ever, made excuses for you being an asshole. Before we started doing the challenges, I never made excuses for you. When I thought you were being mean, I would simply ignore you."

"Yes. I remember."

A shiver of unease chased down my spine to the back of my legs at his quiet, gravelly statement. But I couldn't get sidetracked by guilt for my previous actions when I was so close to finishing what needed to be said.

Straightening my spine, I did my best to ignore that my hair was wet, and I was cold. "Then you should also remember that since we started doing the challenges, I *have* spoken up. I have told you when you're being mean, or unreasonable—like during the first challenge when I told you to stop giving me unsolicited opinions, or before you left for New York when I yelled at you for your unwillingness to try."

He nodded, his features distracted, unfocused. "That's . . . true."

"And I believe it's unfair for you to say I'm never honest. I am honest when people treat me poorly. I do stand up for myself. Where I fail, where I need to do better, and where you were absolutely right, is actively asking for what I want instead of settling for what I'm given."

Byron lifted his chin slightly. I got the sense he was processing this information, the line of his lips looked contrite but not unhappy.

Eventually, he said, "You're right. I apologize."

My muscles, which had been tense as I waited for him to respond, relaxed; my shoulders sagged with relief. "You're forgiven. And thank you for apologizing. It's taken a lot for me to get to this point, to be able to call out people when they treat me poorly, and it's something about myself I take pride in." Something that had been hard fought and hard won.

Cocking his head to the side, he studied me. "Why is that? Why has it taken a lot?"

An unpleasant memory surfaced, one of many involving my uncle. "You have your first interview in about an hour. Do you want me to go get dressed and we'll talk about childhood trauma? Or do you want to make out and we'll save it for tomorrow?"

"Childhood trauma," he responded, no hesitation.

That surprised me. "Really? I thought—"

"I can't believe I'm saying this, and I know I'm contradicting myself, but yes. Please get dressed. We do need to talk." He swallowed thickly, his tone suddenly strained. "And when you're finished telling me about yours, I believe I may be ready to tell you about mine."

CHAPTER 37
WINNIE

Byron took a quick shower while I dressed in a hurry, mentally preparing myself for the uncomfortable, unpleasant conversation that was sure to follow. But, as it turned out, we didn't have time to talk before the first interview.

His manager called his cell. Then she called mine when he didn't answer, informing me that we had only fifteen minutes before the first appointment. When I'd expressed surprise, since the schedule had us starting at 8:00 a.m., not 7:30 a.m., she explained that they'd had to shift the schedule up to accommodate two more magazines. The magazines had sent their initial requests to the Jupiter Awards team instead of to Byron's publisher, hence the mix-up.

As he dressed, and while making our way to the elevator, Byron hurriedly filled me in on where he'd disappeared to after the interviews yesterday, and how the terrible interviewer, Harry Lorher, had harassed him.

"I'm sorry about last night, about our fight." He kissed the back of my hand once the elevator doors closed. "I'm embarrassed to admit, but I believe I may have been a tad dramatic."

I squeezed his fingers. "Don't be. Although it was difficult at the time, I'm glad you said what you did. I needed to hear it."

"Even so, I believe much of my anger stemmed from the interaction with Mr. Lorher, and I shouldn't have been so harsh. Please forgive me."

"Of course I do." I lifted to my tiptoes to give him a kiss, which he quickly deepened by wrapping his arms around me and holding me close.

He only pulled away when the doors opened and a ding sounded, announcing our arrival.

"Damn," he said, resting his forehead against mine for a brief second. He straightened, and then we walked out of the elevator together. "Okay. Let's go."

He looked so grim, and it made me sad. Even though we'd made up this morning, things still felt somewhat unsettled between us. I hated that he had to deal with the pressure of the interviews in addition to our fight. Not just that, but he looked exhausted.

"Did you get any sleep last night? Where did you go after you left?"

"I was able to grab a few hours, and I came here." Byron lifted his chin toward the door to the big suite, his feet slowing as we approached. "I took a chance that no one was using it at night, and I was right."

"If no one is using it, why didn't you just stay up here the whole time instead of the smaller one?"

"This one was booked by my publisher specifically for the interviews. I didn't like the idea of having people walking in and out of the room where I slept, so I asked Pamela to book me a different room." He pulled a key card from his pocket, waved it in front of the lock, and then we were back in the place Byron least wanted to be.

It was just as difficult to watch the second day as it had been the first. Each interview the same as all the others. But boring was definitely better than someone like Mr. Lorher going off script and harassing Byron about his mother.

Lunchtime came and went, but instead of being dismissed like yesterday, Byron had to work through it to accommodate the two new additions to the schedule. Each exchange might've been scripted, with the interviewers not allowed to deviate from the questions, but I marveled at how, even when exhausted, he was so incredibly polite with each person.

It might not seem like such a big thing, but on the sixth hour of the second day of interviews, the fact that he still said please and didn't allow himself to show any outward signs of impatience, felt significant.

So when the newspaper reporter finished ahead of schedule and hastily said their goodbyes, I jumped at the chance to walk over and put my arms around him, giving his shoulders a tight squeeze. We had ten glorious minutes, definitely enough for me to take his mind off the fact that he had another four hours left.

He grabbed my hips and sat me on his lap. "Sit here. I need it."

Smiling, I allowed him to rest his cheek against my breasts like he'd done yesterday. "What can I do?"

"You feel so fucking good," he said, the words almost a groan as he nuzzled closer. "Talk me out of paying Pamela another twenty-thousand-dollar bonus to clear everyone out of the room."

I laughed, trying to find a subject that might distract him and settled on a topic I'd always wanted to tease him about. "So, don't you think it's a little on the nose? Your name is Byron, you're tall, dark, and brooding, and you're a writer."

"It's a family name," came his terse reply. "My grandmother named me."

"If your name had been Albert, would you have become a theoretical astrophysicist?" Sifting my fingers through his hair, I let myself enjoy the soft texture of the silky strands. "Or if your birth certificate had listed Babe, would you have become a baseball player?"

He sat still for a moment, as though giving my questions serious thought, but then leaned away and angled his chin to look at me. "You're teasing me."

"I am."

He smiled, mostly with his eyes, apparently understanding my aim to distract him. "Thank you."

Returning his smile, I began playing with his hair again. "But really, why did you become a writer? You could've been anything."

"Not a baseball player."

"Okay, but a theoretical astrophysicist, yes."

His gaze moved to somewhere over my shoulder and lost focus. "It's . . . easy. To me. Writing fiction is much easier than anything else I've tried."

"So you wanted to do something easy?"

"I was tired of failing. So, yeah."

"What are you talking about?" I leaned back to catch his eye. "When have you failed?"

"Every day, when I was expected to interact."

"You mean with other people? You felt like you failed when you had to interact with other people?" I whispered, glancing around us to ensure we weren't being overheard. I was certain he wouldn't want anyone to hear this.

"I didn't feel like a failure, I was one."

"That's harsh."

"It's the truth."

"I don't—" I cut myself off before I could finish the thought. He was pretty terrible at interacting with people. But a failure?

"Fred. You don't have to always try to make people feel better. I'm okay with my failure. Everyone fails."

"You're okay with never interacting with other humans? You're fine just always being alone? Always? I don't believe that."

"Many writers I've talked to feel dissatisfied with themselves, their relationships, how they interact with the world, how the world interacts with them. Learning is easy, applying what I've learned is easy. But working in an office, in corporate or academia, would require me to interact with people—where people are shifting sands in a desert, impossible to predict—those interactions ultimately leave me feeling like a failure."

My lips parted as he spoke, and my heart gave a sad, sluggish beat as I absorbed his meaning. "Byron—"

"Writing a different reality, where I'm removed from the equation, and all the people are fictional, helps me feel less dissatisfied with this reality."

Narrowing my eyes, I shook my head. "So you're telling me you're dissatisfied with the world and everyone in it?"

"Not everyone, Jane Austen."

"Ha. You got that." Leaning forward, I gave his nose a quick kiss.

"Like a fly ball if my name were Rodney McCray."

"What obscure reference is that? Someone who caught a famous fly ball?"

"More like someone who caught a fly ball famously. Went right through a wall, had no regard for his safety." He frowned at me, his gaze thoughtful, and he gathered a deep breath before murmuring, "Reminds me of myself."

* * *

As soon as the interviews ended, we left. Thankfully, Byron's manager had arranged delivery from a gluten-free restaurant and we scarfed down our dinner in relative silence. I suspected we were both too tired to discuss the day, which was why I was surprised when he reminded me after dinner that we had a conversation to finish about childhood trauma.

Curled up and cuddling on the bed (fully clothed, sadly) we spoke late into the night, not caring about the hour since Byron had no appointments tomorrow until the late afternoon. I told him all about my mother's passing when I was ten, what it was like to grow up in my uncle's house, and how I suspected his treatment of me had exacerbated my propensity to go with the flow, turning it into fear of swimming against the current.

I thought it would be difficult to discuss my childhood with Byron, or with anyone, and it was at first, but not nearly as much as I'd anticipated.

He asked me so many questions, wanted specifics, requested that I describe the room, the time of day, add additional context, precise examples of what my uncle would say and how—specifically—I'd reacted. A few times, I wondered if this was what being cross-examined felt like. His questions did make me consider situations and people in a new light, my aunt and her complacency as well as my oldest cousin who was just one year younger than me.

But one thing Byron never did was make me feel like I was at fault, nor did he believe my uncle had been justified in his actions. He didn't ask what I'd said to set him off, what I could've or should've done differently to avoid being screamed at—questions my aunt and cousin would ask upon discovering me crying after an altercation with my uncle.

It was just after midnight when he said, "Unless a person is imminently in danger of catching on fire or of being hit by a motor vehicle, I'm not sure screaming is ever justified." Shifting to his side and a tad bit backward to catch my eye, Byron pushed a strand of my hair behind my ear. "Screaming might be understandable—given a particular set of circumstances—but not justified. There's a difference between understanding actions and finding them justifiable. I don't think you require me to say so, but your uncle's were neither understandable nor justified."

"I know." I yawned, then tucked my hands under my chin. My voice sounded tired from talking too much after a month of not teaching five days a week. "But I also know and have forgiven myself for the fact that habits formed as a child can become ingrained and eventually turn into instincts. I will ask you for what I want, but I'm not going to be perfect. You'll need to give me time to get better at it."

"So noted." His hand slid down my arm and plucked a hand from under my chin, placing my palm over his heart. "It's late. Do you want to go to sleep?"

"No." I smiled. "I don't *want* to go to sleep."

He smiled too. "Then what do you *want* to do?"

We'd already talked so much. I considered kissing him and letting our discussion of his childhood trauma wait until another time, when we both weren't exhausted from a day of upheaval and seismic shifts in our relationship. But there were things I'd wanted to know about him for a very long time, topics I'd never felt comfortable asking about, and I'd promised I would ask for what I wanted.

Choosing my words carefully, I said, "You don't have to tell me why, but I've always wanted to know, does the reason you deleted all your social media accounts have anything to do with that video of the girl at Comic-Con?"

He set his head back another inch, like he needed to see me more clearly. "Did you watch the video?"

"Maybe once, when it was being shared widely, not knowing you were in it at first. I never understood why it was bad enough to make you delete your accounts."

"It wasn't bad." He moved my hand from where it covered his heart and studied my fingers as he spoke. "A girl—thirteen or fourteen, I think—started crying when she got to the front of my line. She was distressed. Her distress concerned me. I walked around the table and hugged her until she stopped crying. Someone recorded the incident and uploaded it."

I waited for him to continue the story. When he didn't, I asked, "That's it?'

"Yes. That's it."

Maybe I was more tired than I thought, but I had to be missing something. "That's what made you delete your accounts?"

"No. Not at all. I . . ." Byron frowned at my fingers, placing my palm on the bed between us and covering my hand with his. "That's not why."

"Remember, I don't push. So if you don't want to discuss it, we don't have to."

"This isn't the reason, but . . ." He closed his eyes and frowned, breathing out through his nose. "My father isn't someone I can respect."

"Okay." What this had to do with his social media, I had no idea.

It took a few seconds, twenty maybe, before he opened his eyes again and said, "He and my biological mother got pregnant in high school, very young. She was fifteen, I think. She didn't want a baby, but my paternal grandparents, though they were older, had always wished for more children. She allowed them to adopt me. My grandparents were good people, but I do not have a high opinion of my father."

"I'm sorry." I scooched closer. "Was he abusive?"

"No," he said, but the word sounded loaded, unfinished. "No, not abusive. He never screamed at me or hit me or called me names. But he—I'm not even sure how to describe what he is. Amelia says he enjoys being pitied."

"Pitied? For what?"

"I'm not sure. Whatever he can be pitied for, I suppose. He likes to be pampered, fussed over. I didn't talk to anyone but myself until I was ten, and the people in the small town where I grew up always felt sorry for him because of me. My biological mother left, but he stayed, and the narrative he spun centered around the fiction that he'd given up his life and future to raise me."

"But I thought your paternal grandparents adopted you and raised you?"

"They did until they passed away within months of each other when I was eight. And then I lived in his house. For the most part, we ignored each other."

"Huh." I had several questions but didn't know quite where to start. Byron usually sounded so certain about everything—what he thought, how he felt, his opinions and beliefs—yet he seemed uncertain about his father, like he disliked the man on principal but also felt conflicted about it.

As I sorted through what to ask first, Byron lay quiet again for a long moment, picking at a loose thread on the quilted comforter, then he said, "He ignored me until it served his purpose to show me off, like a sideshow act, in order to elicit sympathy from others. That's what he did."

I flinched. "What?"

"For example, he enrolled me in sports without talking to me about it and would break down crying in front of the other kids and parents when I didn't speak to him at the baseball field or at the soccer pitch. He wasn't special. I didn't speak to anyone. But that's when I began to suspect he did it, the public displays of teeth-gnashing and hand-wringing, because of the sympathy of the spectators."

"He never, I mean, when it was just the two of you alone, he never tried to get you to speak then?"

"No. He didn't talk to me."

I flinched again. "Oh my God. I'm so sorry."

"It's okay. He never hit me, never yelled at me. He actually seemed pleased by my brokenness."

"Byron." I grabbed his shoulder, squeezing until he met my eyes. "No. You're not broken. You weren't then, and you aren't now."

"I wasn't a typical child," he said. "That's what I meant. I didn't necessarily want to play sports, but I did. I could."

"What did you want to do?"

He shrugged. "I wanted to read nonfiction and watch the news."

A disbelieving laugh burst out of me. "You wanted to watch the news? At eight?"

"Yes. And I read at a very early age. But now that I think things over, I believe he liked it, liked that I didn't speak or bother him." Byron said this lightly, like we were discussing something else, maybe the weather forecast. "When I did speak, around ten, he didn't seem particularly pleased."

"What did he do when you became such a success? Did it piss him off when he was proven wrong?"

One of Byron's bitter-looking smiles curled his lip. "He continues to paint me as a pitiful figure, as though I'm a modern Edgar Allan Poe, in danger daily of drinking myself to death in a ditch. He also claims I'm an ungrateful son who refuses to recognize all he sacrificed for my talent, and he takes credit for my success, giving interviews to anyone who will listen. Thankfully, after the initial wave of interest, and given that I haven't communicated with him in seven years, no one is asking him for his opinion these days."

I traced the line of his cheek and jaw, angry on his behalf. "Serves him right to be ignored when he ignored you."

"Actually, I didn't mind being ignored by him. What I hated was the attention he sought from other parents, but I never minded being left to my own devices. I did mind losing my grandparents, though."

"I'm so sorry. Losing them so close together."

"I loved them. My grandfather in particular, who was a man of few words and never thought it was strange that I didn't speak to him. But I never felt an affinity for my father, especially not after he married."

"He got married?"

"He married a woman who treated him—and who still treats him—like a child. She does everything for him. And he leans into it."

I hesitated before asking, "How does she treat you?"

"She treated me like I was something sad and disappointing."

And broken. He didn't say the words, but they were implied. His stepmother treated him like he was broken, and his father like a martyr. How messed up was that?

"Are they still married?"

He nodded, his tone remote. "They are."

"And your biological mom? What happened to her?"

"She left after high school and went to the East Coast for college." Byron didn't sound tired, but his voice remained at odds with the personal nature of our discussion.

"Have you ever spoken to her?"

"No. I only knew she'd gone to the East Coast as my stepmother would complain about how heartless she was, how selfish. She told me, without me asking, that my biological mother became a research professor in Boston and never married. Everything I know about the woman—all of it involuntary—came from my stepmom."

"You never wanted to know her? You never looked her up?"

He reached behind his head and fluffed the pillow. "I didn't."

"Why not?"

"She's a stranger," he said, like the answer was obvious.

"But you share DNA, you share some of her traits."

"I share DNA with every person on earth, and I don't want to know most of them either."

I gave his shoulder a little shove. "You know what I mean."

"I suppose I do, but no. I don't hate her, I just don't think about her. I have better things with which to fill my time than thinking about a person who has no time for me." With this statement, Byron launched himself off the mattress and paced to the window. "Is it hot in here? Do you think this window opens?"

"But how do you know she has no time for you unless you reach out?"

He fiddled with the blinds, holding them to one side. "I didn't know, but I do now. She said so."

"She. . . what?" I sat up and pushed my back against the headboard.

"After the video of me consoling the girl at Comic-Con went viral, a few students in my biological mother's class showed it to her—while filming her reaction, I'm assuming without permission—and asked what she thought about having me as a son." Byron turned from the window, which remained unopened.

"Oh no." I covered my mouth with my fingers. "How did they know she's your birth mother?"

"My adoption wasn't sealed or secret. Many people in my hometown are familiar with the story and happily shared my origins with any shady reporter who asked. Obtaining my birth certificate had likely been simple. By the time the Comic-Con video went viral, several papers and magazines had reported that she was my mother, including the *Boston Daily*."

I braced myself. "What did she say when they showed her the video?"

"She said . . ." His eyes lost focus and he smiled, laughing lightly, but his features held no amusement, only a tinge of bitterness and incredulity. "She said, 'I have no children.'"

"Ugh." My hands fell to my aching heart.

"And then, when they pushed her about it, since her name and social security number are on my birth certificate, she said, 'Everyone makes mistakes in high school. I'd appreciate if you didn't show me videos of mine.'"

"Oh my God." Now I covered my whole face, which had grown hot with secondhand feelings. "I'm so sorry."

"There is nothing to be sorry for. It saved me the embarrassment of reaching out one day and having her say those words to my face."

"But for it to be recorded and—oh shit." I pulled my hands away, gripping the fabric of my pajama pants anxiously. "How did you see the video? Did they send it to you?"

"No. They posted it on social media."

I groaned.

"It also went viral and was discussed widely. My biological mother is a bit of a big deal in the bioengineering space, and I believe her university issued a public statement on the video. I never read the statement, but that too was discussed widely online and in the media. By strangers. By people I've never met, will never meet, and who do not know me at all."

"Byron. I—I'm—" Not knowing what to say, I stood from the bed, crossed to him, grabbed his face, and kissed him. Hard. As I leaned away, I said, "They had no right."

"No, they didn't. But they do it anyway, don't they?" His smile was small and looked somehow sharp, his typically vivid gaze unusually dim. "The voyeurs, they lurk until they stumble across pain porn, and then they pick it apart, offer their unsolicited opinions about a situation and people they do not know or understand, ignoring context as though the bigger picture is a finger painting. They dissect the players, rate and make value statements about the subjects of their fascination, all in a public space for everyone to read and comment on."

"No wonder you don't like people."

He nodded. "No wonder I don't like people."

"But not all people are like that."

"Are you going to start a hashtag, notallpeople?"

I chuckled, but it was sad and mournful given the story he'd just shared. Smoothing my hands over his beautiful face, I pushed my fingers into his hair. "No, but I am going to advocate on behalf of those people who don't do this kind of thing. Not all people engage in the feeding frenzy of gossip and pain."

"You never saw the video of my mother? Truly?"

"No. I never did. It was my first year of teaching, and I wasn't on social media much. When Amelia told me you'd deleted all your accounts, I assumed it must've been the Comic-Con video because of the timing. But I didn't want to invade your privacy by asking. It wasn't any of my business."

"But you were curious?"

"Of course I was curious. It seemed like a big reaction to a fairly benign video of you and a fan."

"Huh."

"What?"

"Thank you for being you."

"You're welcome. But you know, there are more people like me out there. More people who actively avoid reading about the personal lives of others when there's no criminal activity or risk to public safety. It feels intrusive to me." Especially after what had happened to me in high school, whenever I witnessed or heard about a public-fail moment for a nonpolitician, I tuned it out.

Everyone made mistakes, stumbled and struggled and experienced embarrassment. In my opinion, what all people needed in these moments was time to process, grace to know they wouldn't be forever judged for a mistake or accident or a situation over which they had no control, and space to put the events into perspective so they could move forward.

Basically, the opposite of what had happened to Byron. I now understood why he hated social media and wouldn't give interviews. And though I didn't blame him for deleting his accounts and wanting to distance himself from public comment, I wished he'd be willing to explore a happy, healthy medium.

For better or worse, social media was now part of our daily lives. I saw the good it could do, the ways it could reach and connect people, help them feel less alone, more understood. They could easily find others like them, with shared niche interests, whereas before they'd been stranded on individual islands of one.

Sure, we didn't *need* social media, but we did need to live with it. Perhaps one day, Byron would be open to reassessing his options. He'd stranded himself on his island of one for so long. Maybe he'd been content. But he hadn't been happy.

CHAPTER 38
WINNIE

At first, I didn't understand why I couldn't move or why I was so hot. It wasn't until I opened my scratchy eyes, glanced down at my body, and spotted Byron's arms wrapped tightly around my torso that I realized where I was and whose body lay firmly against my back. Also, other than taking off my bra, I was still in my clothes from yesterday.

My memory felt fuzzy. Remembering precisely when we'd fallen asleep was impossible. Last night, I'd resisted getting up and changing into my pajamas or doing anything other than snuggling with Byron and talking and listening to every single one of his brilliant thoughts. I'd wanted time to stand still. It seemed unfair that the evening should ever come to an end.

"Winnie?" His rumbly words stirred my hair at the back of my neck. "Are you awake?"

"Yes. Just," I said, yawning around a sleepy smile. "How long have you been up?"

"A while. I've already taken a shower." The silence that followed this statement felt significant, and I was just about to ask him if anything was wrong when he added, "I'm supposed to check in and ask before I do anything, right? Before I touch you?"

Suddenly, my body was forcefully ready for . . . whatever he wanted. "What do you have in mind?"

Removing his arms from my torso, Byron climbed over me, his lips immediately coming to my throat, his hands lifting my shirt and roaming freely. He gave my nipple a punishing twist and pinch—the sharp pain reviving me fully from slumber—then lowered his head and soothed the spot with his tongue.

My fingers threaded into his hair, sifting through and petting the soft strands. "I love it," I moaned. I didn't want him to stop and check in. I wanted him to keep going.

I felt his wicked smile against my skin a second before he blew a stream of cold air on the wet spot left by his mouth, one hand caressing south as he helped me remove my shirt, his mouth returning to my neck, dotting a line of soft kisses on my jaw until he reached my ear.

"I want to taste you," he said, catching my earlobe with his teeth. "I want to lick your pussy. May I, please?"

I arched my back, panting, my forehead wrinkling as I tried to think. His fingers slid low and lifted my skirt to my waist, then delved into the waistband of my panties. A skillful middle finger circumvented my center, not touching me where I needed.

I whimpered, my nails digging into his bare back. And that's when I realized he'd returned to bed after his shower wearing nothing but loose gray sweatpants and—oh dear God—he was so beautiful, and sexy, his body making me lose my mind, making me want to say yes even though some distant, faraway part of myself still worried he wouldn't like it.

Byron bent again and trailed too soft kisses from the underside of my breast to my stomach, his tongue swirling, tasting my skin, his fingers hooking into my underwear and sliding them down my legs. As he returned, he settled himself between my knees and kissed the sensitive skin of my inner thigh, his fingers returning to tease my clit.

The rough friction of his stubble paired with his hot breath sent a cascading wave of pleasure from the tip of my head to the tips of my toes. His middle finger still a too light touch between my legs, I grabbed his wrist, trying to—literally—force his hand. He held firm.

"Winnie." He kissed higher on my thigh, spreading my legs wider. "You have to say yes or no. I will do whatever you want."

Exhaling an unsteady breath, I struggled to uncover my logic from beneath the mountain of arousal, but then he licked the interior of my thigh, just inches from my center, and my body shuddered, burying any and all worries under extreme *want.*

"Yes." I gasped, tilting my hips up in offering. "Please."

I heard him curse right before I felt his arms wrap beneath my legs and, holding me wide, he licked me. And then he groaned, a sound of pure, raw pleasure. Arms tightening, he delved right in, licking and sucking and grinding his lips against my sex.

Well, okay then. Mystery solved. I guess he likes the taste.

I huffed a laugh, relieved. But I was also perplexed by his technique (or lack thereof). The first lick—slow and soft, with the flat of his tongue—had nearly made me come. But what he possessed in enthusiasm, he lacked in finesse. His movements were too fast and chaotic.

But should I—

YES! Yes, I would tell him what I want. I should ask and trust him. He'd asked me to, but also, I deserved great oral sex.

I reached down, pushed my fingers into his hair, and tugged. "Wait—wait."

Immediately, he lifted his head, hair askew, eyes wide, lips wet, and the sight made my body tense low in my abdomen.

"What? Should I stop?"

I shook my head. "No. But can you go slower, softer, and with a consistent rhythm? The first, uh, lick was really good. Like that."

Listening with rapt attention, he nodded eagerly, then lowered himself again. This time, he did exactly as I asked. Using the flat of his tongue, he moved methodically, his head slowly bobbing up and down in a sensual rhythm. Damn, but he was a fast learner. And I loved that about him so, so much.

Soon—too soon—I was cursing, grabbing fistfuls of sheets and tugging. It felt so good. Too good. It felt like falling into an endless shadow, teetering over an abyss of too much pleasure, overwhelming and dangerous, and I needed to hold on to something.

And Byron, God bless him, slid a single finger from my clit to my entrance, and then slipped it inside, moving it in and out in tandem with his tongue.

I gasped, crying out, my thighs pressing against his ears as I lost control of my body. I know I said his name over and over, my voice pitched high and frantic, my lungs full to bursting. Darkness and stars filled my vision, and I was certain I'd die at the end of this. How could anything feel this perfect, this essential? How would I ever recover?

It did end. I didn't die. But I didn't quite recover. The retreating climax left me with a sensation of unguarded openness, and I caught myself just a fraction of a second before offering a breathless, *I love you.*

Eyes flying open, I bit my lip to keep the words inside, a shiver of awareness and shock coursing through me. Did I love him? Truly? Or was this biology?

This is not biology. You've loved him for a long time, dummy.

Oh my goodness, I have!

Then, should I tell him? Should I say it? Was now—

I glanced down, and my debate was violently shoved aside by the sight of poor Byron pulling my legs apart. I'd locked them around his head, and while I was lost to my thoughts about how and when I should tell him I loved him, I'd almost murdered him with my thighs.

"Oh my God. I'm so sorry!" I reached forward, still struggling to catch my breath.

"You're sorry?" he asked with a cocky edge to his usual, dry delivery, wiping his mouth with the back of his hand, sliding up my body and settling himself on top of me. "For what?" His voice was deeper than usual and sounded supremely satisfied.

I pushed my head back in order to see him better. "I'm sorry about squeezing your head." *And almost asphyxiating you with my vagina.*

"I didn't mind." He grinned, his eyes dark and liquid. "And anytime you want me to do that again, please know I am at your service."

"Really? You liked it that much?"

"Let me know when you're ready for round two."

"Hmm." I sent him a side-eye but couldn't control my smile.

"No matter what we're doing. Take Wednesday at the awards, for example. If the mood strikes, I'll find us somewhere to go. Or next week when we're back in Seattle and I'm making dinner—or you're making dinner—just say the word and I'll get right to it. Any room in the house. Or all the rooms. Nothing and nowhere is off-limits."

I laughed. "So what you're saying is, no pressure?"

Twisting his lips as though considering, he said, "Maybe a little bit of pressure? I would be exceedingly sad and disappointed, and it might take decades to recover should you decide against allowing me to do this daily, but I'll try my best not to hold it against you forever and lament it as my greatest regret on my deathbed."

I laughed harder. "That's what you call 'a little bit of pressure'?"

"That is my definition, yes." He grinned, and we stared at each other for several quickening beats of my heart.

"Winnie. I am serious. I loved it. I think we should do it every day. Twice or three times."

I regarded him, searching for any lies. No lies detected. "It doesn't taste bad?"

"No. It doesn't."

"It tastes good?" I found that hard to believe.

"No. You're not food, Winnie. You don't taste like strawberries and cream or anything like that. You don't taste good or bad, you taste like you. But the smell—" His eyes grew hazy, and I watched as he inhaled deeply, his tongue peeking out to lick his top lip. "Fuck, the smell is unreal."

"Huh." I stared at him, incredulous. A new kind of pleasure glided upward from my stomach to my chest, it felt like wonder and silly, giddy happiness. "You like the way I smell down there?"

"Yes." The single word sounded vehement, like he'd never believed in something so strongly before. Bending to my neck, he breathed in deeply again. "I love how you smell everywhere—your neck, your breasts, the heat of your skin, but especially. . ." He shifted to the side, his hand lowering between us to the apex of my thighs, and he cupped me firmly, his body going tense and his voice gruff as he said, "Especially here."

"Pheromones," I whispered, getting worked up all over again. I gulped in air and the scent of Byron's aftershave, my body abruptly restless even though he'd literally just given me the most intense orgasm of my life.

It's not pheromones. Maybe it's lust.

Soon, I had him on his back, my fingers unhooking my skirt, my mouth on his neck, breathing him in, my body warm and liquid and ready for more.

Lust was definitely a possibility, but lust didn't explain why I suddenly needed his cock in my mouth, why I couldn't wait to watch him go mindless, or why—even though I knew how much I disliked the taste of sperm—I started an internal negotiation, part of me wanting it just to watch his expression as I gulped it down.

I wondered at myself, at this anxious, urgent hunger within me. I'd never felt lust before. So maybe it was lust.

But maybe, at least part of it, was also love.

* * *

I thought about answering the phone when Amelia called, but I was just too busy in bed with my hot boyfriend.

And this was funny because, when Byron left to go take another shower and I listened to her voice mail, she'd said, "I know you're probably having sex with Byron right now, but when you two come up for air, call me. You have an interview for the community manager position, if you still want it. However, I also received a call from Byron's agent about a different opportunity, and I think—well, let me leave you on that cliff. Just give me a call."

"What'd she say? Did she mention the community manager position?"

I glanced toward the direction of his voice. He stood just outside the bathroom, one towel around his hips while he dried his hair with another. I sighed, wanting to make him sweaty and dirty again. Or maybe wanting to drag Byron into the shower and living out my very first fantasy of us together, the one that had discombobulated me so before our first video.

He needed to go to his appointment, and I needed to get dressed. But now I knew how he'd felt earlier, being forced to form coherent words when faced with the sight of him in just a towel felt impossible.

Instead of speaking, I handed him my phone and let him listen to Amelia's message. I couldn't think about anything but condoms and how much I needed them. At this rate, we weren't going to last past this New York trip, not that I wanted us to wait. If it were up to me, we'd get down to business ASAP.

But first, there was the tiny matter of him not knowing I'd never had vaginal intercourse.

I wasn't hiding it from him, but I wasn't sure how to bring it up. Was this appropriate dinner conversation? Or did I wait until we were making out again? Or at what point does one mention that one has never had vaginal sex? And, on that note, why did I have to bring it up at all? Why was it even a thing? Was it a thing?

Maybe it wasn't a thing. Maybe I was overthinking it. *Maybe it's Maybelline.*

Byron handed me back my phone and sat on the edge of the bed, his gaze trailing over the sheet covering my naked body. "That's good news about the job."

"It is."

"What are you going to do?"

"I'll call Amelia back, then take it from there." The job hunt, my loans, Seattle, school, the STEM fair, my social media—heck, those challenges we'd been doing and basically abandoned as well as all the public commentary on our "bestfriend" relationship—it all felt so far away.

Byron's expression turned thoughtful as he stared at me, and he settled a palm on my thigh, fisting the fabric. "Before I head out, I have to tell you something."

"Oh?"

"Yes. I have to tell you a few somethings." He tugged slowly on the sheet, revealing more of my skin.

I frowned. "Are they bad somethings?"

"No. I don't think so." Byron's attention lowered to my breasts and stomach as he continued the gradual removal of the white material, his eyes heating. "In the interest of specificity and exactness, I feel compelled to tell you that I did not come to New York last month for space."

"You didn't?" I caught the sheet at my hips, pulling it back to my chest and sitting up. I didn't want him or me to be distracted. This felt like an important conversation.

He released the fabric with obvious reluctance, resettling his gaze on mine. "No. I came here to deserve you."

"What? By leaving me?"

"I took some lessons and coaching here, to fill in potential deficiencies as a partner. Like cooking gluten-free cuisine, for example. There's a masters-level course at the culinary school for nonstudents. I did that, and now when we get home, I can cook you a different meal every day for six months. And I've been, uh, seeing an occupational therapist for my sensory processing issues. I've been learning how to better cope with crowds. You like people, for some reason, and if I want to be with you, I don't want you to have to choose between me and a party, or me and a concert. That's not fair."

I'm sure I looked shocked. But at the conclusion of his little speech, I'd regained enough of my own mind to launch forward and embrace him, holding him tight, loving that he did these things but also hating that he felt like they were necessary.

"I can't believe you did all that. Byron, you didn't need to. I want you just as you are. Please, please, please don't feel like you need to change for me."

"I don't feel like I need to change, I feel like I need to improve. There's a difference. And, uh, there's more."

Stiffening at the solemn note in his voice, I leaned back so I could see him. His temple ticked, the line of his mouth grim.

"More?"

He nodded.

"Should I be concerned? You look upset."

"I'm not. I'm embarrassed and therefore irritated." His tone held no trace of embarrassment but quite a lot of irritation. "I do not understand this embarrassment, which makes me irritated."

"That makes sense." I smiled, knowing exactly how he felt since being irritated by inexplicable embarrassment was basically what I used to feel whenever he entered a room.

Staring at me, expression stern, he unwound my arms from around his body and held both my hands in his. "Win, the real reason I came out here—there's, uh, services offered in New York that aren't offered in Seattle or most other major cities. Specifically, sex and intimacy coaches, otherwise known as pleasure coaches."

Uh . . . what?

"Excuse me?"

"It is and is not what you think."

I didn't know whether to laugh or . . . laugh. Or maybe laugh? So I did none of those and just stared, dumbfounded. "Did you get a sex tutor?"

"Yes and no."

A spike of jealousy made my spine stiffen. "Byron, did you—"

"I haven't touched anyone but you, nor do I wish to. And no one touched me. It was mostly talking, demonstrations on dummies, like anatomy 101. But absent me bringing a partner, there's nothing hands-on."

"No one has touched you?" My eyes narrowed, and the ferocity of feeling, of possessiveness, made me breathless. "I swear to God, if someone touched you, they're losing their hands."

His irritation seemed to dissolve in the face of my viciousness, and now he looked like he wanted to laugh. "Correct. No touching."

"Wearing gloves or over the clothes is still touching." Wresting a hand away, I lifted an accusing finger between us. "Don't give me any technically true BS."

"None of that. It was only Walter and me, no women were—"

"I don't care if it was a man or a woman or a nonbinary or anyone else. I don't care if it was sheep! No touching, no showing on anything breathing."

His shoulders shook with laugher he tried to conceal, like he couldn't help himself, while struggling to also speak. "Correct. It was all very scientific and theory based. Books, lectures, opportunities to ask questions. I had to do it."

"But why?! Why did you have to do it?" I pulled my hand from his and stood, yanking the sheet as I went. Sighing, he also stood so I could take the material with me and wrap it around my body. "I don't like this. I don't like that you did this. So what if you've never gone down on someone? Neither had I, and we figured it out. And so what if we need practice? We can practice on each other."

"I wanted to know what to expect. And it was important to me that I not be terrible at it."

"I don't understand why you think I would need you to know more than you already do. I don't understand—"

"I'm a virgin."

I reared backward, rocking on my heels, my mouth falling open again.

Byron's earlier amusement at my irrational jealousy disintegrated. His cheeks flared pink, then red. "And not just a virgin. When I told you back in Seattle that you had more experience than me, I meant it. I've watched porn, of course, but Winnie, our first kiss was *my* first kiss. And when we made out on the couch in your apartment, I'd never done anything like that before."

My brain felt stuck. I couldn't think. I was so confused.

But he'd told me before, hadn't he? Not just the morning after our first kiss, but here as well. He'd kept telling me I had more experience than him, and I couldn't fathom how that could be true. The world told me that men had sex, as soon as and as frequently as they could, with as many people as possible, and that was just the way it was, because *biology*.

"I wanted you and only you, so very much." His voice quieted, raspy with a vulnerability that echoed in his gaze. "I knew the situations and images depicted in pornography were unrealistic, I couldn't rely on that to be a guide. I definitely didn't want to practice with someone else so I'd be ready, if or when you ever looked at me. I'm not built that way. I couldn't."

I stepped forward and once more wrapped my arms around him, uncaring that my sheet slipped and caught awkwardly between us. I only knew that I needed to touch and feel him right now.

His body surrounded me, his strong arms coming around my back, his muscles relaxing beneath my cheek and chest. Then his hands grabbed my side and hip, and he whispered, "As much as I wanted to be good for you, I also didn't want to lose my chance with you if I were a complete disaster in bed."

This statement drove the shock from my brain, leaving me with wry delight and so much gratitude, but also concern for him and all he'd been through these last few weeks.

"You must be so tired. A month of constantly being around people, you have to be exhausted."

He grunted. "I've been in love with you for years, Fred. The only thing

I'm tired of is being without you. And the only thing that exhausts me is the idea of spending another six, or twenty, or fifty years knowing I could have lived my life by your side but was too fucking lazy to do what was required to make it happen."

I buried my smile against his chest. I loved his random grumpiness. "Thank you," I said, holding him tighter. "Thank you for being you, Byron. But also thank you for thinking about me, and anticipating what I might need, what might make me happy. Thank you."

"Fine. You're welcome," he said, kissing and nuzzling my neck. "But, as I said, my motives weren't altruistic."

Heaving a sigh at his determination to always be 100 percent precise, I gazed deeply into his gorgeous, unusual eyes, loving the unending wariness of his features, the slight curl of his right upper lip, the dark, judgmental-looking slash of his eyebrows, the angular line of his jaw. I loved his grumpiness, and I loved his face. And I loved him.

"I have something to tell you too." It was time. Not because I urgently needed to say the words, but because I urgently needed him to hear them.

His wariness turned to interest, his upper lip curving in a scant smile. "Did you take sex lessons too?"

"No." I laughed, feeling nervous but also oddly calm. "Actually, it's two things."

"Okay?"

"First, I'm a vaginal sex virgin too."

His eyebrows flew to his hairline and his lips parted. "What?"

"I've never had intercourse before. And, I guess, since I'm on birth control to regulate my periods, we don't have to hunt down those condoms anymore as I'm assuming we're both negative for STDs."

Eyes suddenly wild, he took a step back. "Are you fucking with me?"

I shook my head. "No. No I'm not."

His wild eyes grew unfocused. "But I thought you had a boyfriend. I thought you dated him for years?"

"I did, but I never had intercourse with him. We made out, messed around, but I never wanted to. I didn't feel ready."

Byron breathed out, his eyes blinking like he was having trouble absorbing this information. "That's . . ." He gave his head a small, subtle shake. "That's unbelievable."

"Well—"

"And a travesty."

Now I stepped back. "A travesty?"

"You haven't seen you come," he said by way of explanation. "We should record it so you can see it. But your body—Winnie, your body is made for sex, for having orgasms. I've never seen anything so beautiful. And so is your voice, and your mouth." His hand came to my jaw, his thumb tugging at my bottom lip while his other hand slid into my hair at my neck. "It's like if Mozart never picked up an instrument or LeBron James never picked up a basketball."

A sudden laugh burst out of me. Sometimes Byron was overly dramatic. And it was darn cute. And it drove me to give his shoulder a little shove and say unthinkingly, "Oh my God, I love you so much."

Except for catching my wrist as I retreated, Byron grew very still, his gaze acutely sharp and focused. "Sorry, what?" he croaked, his breath baited. "What are you saying?"

Feeling helpless beneath his increasingly forceful stare, and loving every second of it, I didn't fight my happy smile, nor did I second-guess what I felt and knew to be true. "I'm saying I cried my eyes out when you left, and it felt like the world was ending. I'm saying I was absolutely devastated when I thought of losing you. I'm saying if you were hoping I'd hand over my fortified heart at some point in the future, too bad. It's already yours. It's been yours for longer than I'd like to admit, but I'd buried my feelings under fear until you made it impossible for me to hide any longer. I'm saying I love you, I'm in love with you, and you are so freaking cute sometimes, it kills me."

Byron leaned toward me, eyes wide and searching. "Are you sure?"

"I'm sure." I stole a kiss, just a quick press of lips, and nodded firmly. "I'm sure."

He swallowed, hope battling doubt, his grip on my wrist growing lax. "This seems fast."

"How can you say that?" Now I shook my head, I laughed my denial as a rush of stinging tears flooded my eyes. "It doesn't feel fast to me."

"What does it feel like?" The question was a rough, halting whisper and his features told me he was greedy for my answer.

I cupped his jaw again, enjoying the sensation of his perpetually stubbly cheek against my palm. "It feels like you snuck past my defenses when I wasn't looking, Byron Visser. You were simply yourself, and I had no choice but to love you. That's what it feels like."

"This feels like fiction." His stare was absorbed, a little frantic, like I might disappear if he blinked. "This feels like something I've conjured from my imagination."

"Because I surprised you?"

"No." He pulled in a shaky breath, his eyelashes flickering. "Because it's perfect."

CHAPTER 39
WINNIE

"Sorry. I didn't mean to interrupt you and Lady Chatterley's Lover. I hope you're both staying hydrated."

I rolled my eyes at Amelia's teasing. I supposed Byron was my lover, even though we hadn't had home-run sex yet.

Amused against my will, I surrendered to a smile. "Ha. And yes, we're both staying hydrated. And you're not interrupting. Sorry I didn't call you back on Monday."

"It's fine. I knew you were busy. Everything okay with you two? I'm assuming you worked things out?"

Presently in the bathroom doing my makeup for the awards ceremony tonight, I picked up my concealer sponge and dabbed under my eyes, careful not to rub or pull. "Yes. Everything is wonderful. Thank you." Despite not yet handing over our V-cards to each other, everything was going swimmingly.

We'd been trading *I love yous* freely, doing a lot of gross, cute, coupley stuff, like staring at each other and smiling, or randomly kissing in the middle of a discussion, or trying to undress each other in a sneaky way, or forgetting we were in public while hanging out in Central Park and making out on a bench—not hot and heavy or anything, but definitely some serious necking.

We also filmed two more challenge videos. The Bestfriend Fashion Challenge, which had been fun since we'd had to go out and buy Byron clothes that closely matched mine, and the Travel Surprise Challenge. Both were discussed in detail prior to filming as neither made much sense to do off the cuff.

I posted the Travel Surprise Challenge right after filming and editing it, saved the other new video for later, and continued pondering what to do with the Leggings Challenge recording. Byron had told me he didn't care if I posted the leggings video but had admitted he didn't want to share our first kiss with the world. Therefore, the Kiss Your Crush video would remain a secret forevermore, to be enjoyed by just us two, and that was perfectly fine with me.

But every time we got close to having sex, and I thought I might lose my mind with wanting him, Byron would pull back, alter our course, or take a breather. I wasn't necessarily confused about it, and I wasn't upset. We had all the time in the world, there was no rush. Plus, I was certainly enjoying all the new and wonderful things I was learning about his body.

But I did tell him I would prefer we not turn it into a big deal by trying to make it perfect, or special, or a whole thing. I'd been told several times that a woman's first time having sexual intercourse wasn't a pleasant experience, no matter how many rose petals were strewn on a bed or how many candles were lit. I wanted it to feel natural, a healthy extension and progression of a relationship between two people who loved each other, and that's it.

"I'm glad to hear everything is wonderful." Amelia sounded like she was smiling. "But I'm not calling to tell you I was right about basically everything, I'm calling about the interview for the community manager position and about the auction."

Setting the concealer sponge down, I frowned at my array of eye shadow. "The auction?"

"Yeah, you know, your school's auction? All those books Byron's publisher is donating? Byron's agent wants a quote about what the funds will be used for."

I stared at the mirror, my brain working overtime to figure out what the heck she was talking about. When I couldn't, I said, "What the heck are you talking about?"

"I'm sure we talked about this. Or maybe—that's right. Pamela was supposed to give you an update when you were there for the interviews on Saturday."

"An update about what?"

"Byron's publisher is donating five hundred signed advanced copies for your school auction to fund your STEM fair, the new books for the library, and the computer lab. Isn't that nice?"

My stomach swooped, dropping and then lifting. Feeling dizzy, I leaned against the counter. "He . . ."

"Yes. He's signing the books when he gets back. You know how crazed people are for this last book in the trilogy, you'll probably raise more than you need. Smart of the school to make it an online auction."

"Yes. Smart." I shook my head to clear it, feeling overwhelmed with ***BETRAYAL***! But also, not betrayal.

Byron had promised. That night he'd made me dinner at my apartment and I'd told him about raising money for the STEM fair, he'd promised he wouldn't do this. He may've had more money than he knew how to spend, but taking care of my priorities and obligations, on my own, was important to me. ***HOW DARE HE!***

But also, why hadn't I wanted his help?

That's not the point. He promised and he broke his promise.

Except, hadn't it been silly of me not to accept his help?

Maybe, but that's still not the point.

But shouldn't it be a factor?

He went behind your back. How can you ever trust him again?

Eh. I still trusted him. But I was definitely annoyed.

"Winnie? Are you there?"

"Yes. Uh, Amelia, I didn't know about any of this. I'd heard from a teacher at my school that a bulk donation had occurred, but I didn't know Byron had been responsible."

"Oh. Sorry. Shoot! Maybe he wanted to surprise you. Did I ruin a surprise? But I thought for sure Pamela was supposed to talk to you about it at the interviews."

Tapping my fingers on the countertop, I considered what to do. "When did all this happen?"

"The first week of your summer break."

Hmm . . . *sneaky.* "And Byron was the one to offer the books?" I clicked the lid back on my concealer and picked up the brush for my eye shadow.

"I don't know. You should talk to him. But I do need that statement, the quote. I promised his agent I'd have it back along with whether or not you're interested in the cosmetics partnership opportunity—which is the real reason I'm calling."

"Cosmetics partnership?"

"Here, let me shut the door." Amelia's line went quiet for a few seconds, and I heard the sound of a door snicking shut. Then she was back. "So, I know I said you'd be perfect for the community manager position, and I still believe they would be lucky to have you, but Ethical Cosmetics reached out to Byron's agent to ask if you'd be interested in a remote, flexible, contract job where you highlight the technology, research, and engineering that goes into their products on your channels. Everything from the chemical engineering processes to the sustainable ecological practices they use, like the choice not to use palm oil because it leads to deforestation."

"Huh. That does sound interesting."

"It pays a lot more than the community manager job, and—not that you asked my opinion—but I think what you're doing with your social media is really unusual, and that makes you a commodity. Not many creators with your follower count and engagement are embracing STEM-focused content and traditional feminine interests at the same time, and doing both equally well, giving both equal focus. You've become this personality now, bigger than what you set out to do. As much as I think you'd be great here, with me, I think maybe the cosmetics partnership might be a better fit for you."

I valued Amelia's opinion and her honesty, but this was a lot to take in. "How long do I have to think about it?"

"Well, I need an answer about the community manager interview before you get back from New York. Those are being scheduled now."

"If I interview and they offer me the job, but I don't take it, will that make things difficult for you?"

"No. Not at all. In fact, I hope you do interview and you don't take it. I really want everyone here to meet you, feel the energy you bring, and try to find similar influencers. You already know how I feel, but it bears repeating: we can't keep thinking about women in STEM as us versus them, where girls are either good at engineering or good at quote, unquote *girly things*. That's changing in a big way—it's already shifted—and companies, nonprofits, advertisers need to catch up. I need the team here to be on the forefront of it."

"Then yes, I'll do the interview." I dabbed my eye shadow brush in the first shade and leaned forward toward the mirror. "But I am very interested in the cosmetics partnership. Do you have any materials? A job description?"

"Yes and yes. I'll email those to you. And, with your permission, I'll ask Byron's agent to reach out to you directly from now on. I love you, but I'm tired of his agency using me as a go-between all the time."

"Makes sense. And thank you so much. Thank you especially for helping me pull everything together for the awards ceremony tonight."

"Oh yeah! With everything else going on, I keep forgetting. How does the dress look?"

"I'm doing my makeup now. The dress goes on before the lipstick and powder, but after the eye shadow."

"Of course, of course. Everyone knows this." Amelia chuckled. "You should do an industrial engineering–focused video about the most efficient process for getting dressed for a fancy night on the town."

"Those industrial engineers love their processes." I grinned as I dusted my right lid with eye shadow. Her idea had merit, and I made a mental note to jot it down. It would also be fun to do a series of parody videos on how each type of engineer got ready for a fancy night on the town. Industrial engineers would of course be obsessed with the process and efficiency, where mechanical engineers might build a machine to store and retrieve each necessary item required to get ready, in order, via automation.

Grinning at the possibilities, I said my goodbyes to Amelia and turned the entirety of my outward focus to applying eye shadow while my brain worked on new ideas for my STEM tutorials and projects. These last few days with Byron had been wonderful and amazing and so precious to me. But I also couldn't wait to get back to my life in Seattle, all the work and plans I was excited about tackling there.

And now that Byron and I had figured things out, I hoped neither of us would think about the future in terms of my life, or his life, but *our* life. Together.

* * *

"That's not the point." My back to the door of the limo, I sat with my hands in my lap and regarded Byron's grumpy eyebrows. His grumpy eyebrows were adorable, even when they were also stubborn. "The point is that I specifically asked you not to donate anything, and you did."

"I promised I wouldn't donate money or items, and I didn't. My publisher did."

I laughed, frustrated, and shook my head. "You know it's the same thing."

"I promise you, it's not." Lip curling slightly with distaste or disgruntlement, he pulled at the cuffs of his suit jacket.

"I don't care if you're paying for it or if your publisher is paying for it, I asked you—I specifically told you—I wanted to do it myself."

He gritted his teeth, his eyelids drooping. My Byron-whisperer skills told me he was extremely frustrated. "These were books earmarked for destruction, two of the pages switched, they were going to throw them away. This is costing my publisher nothing. God, Winnie." His gaze cut to mine, his patience thin, but his tone remained calm and even. "We're on the same team here. If I pass you the ball, are you going to say no thank you because you didn't get it yourself? No. You're going to score a goal."

"Yes. You're right. We're on the same team. And, I admit, in retrospect, it was very silly of me to turn down your offer."

Byron blinked, straightening in his seat. "It was?"

"Yes. And in the future, I will not be so hasty to turn down offers from you that make my life easier, okay? But that's not really what I'm upset about."

"Then what are you upset about?" He leaned forward, looking curious instead of defensive.

"Like I said, you made a promise to me. Then you broke that promise. I don't care what the context was, or whether they were going to destroy the books. What I care about is being able to trust you when you make a promise."

His expression flattened and he stared at me, obviously contemplating and debating my words. After a few seconds, he nodded. "You're right. I'm sorry."

I smiled. I'd had no doubt we'd eventually get here, but I loved how willing he was to reassess his decisions when I took the time and energy to communicate my concerns. Maybe he wouldn't always come to see things from my perspective, but I trusted he'd always be willing to listen.

"You're forgiven. And I love you."

The curve of his mouth looked contrite, but also pleased. And this time, when his eyelids drooped, it wasn't due to of frustration.

"Hey. Come here. Kiss me."

Bracing my hands on the bench, I leaned forward and closed the distance between us, giving his luscious lips a soft kiss and whispering, "I can't give you anything more without jeopardizing my makeup."

"But I'm not wearing any makeup." I heard the intent in his voice just before I felt his hand on my thigh, just below the tulle of my fluffy skirt. "I could kiss you in other places."

I grinned, made breathless by his offer as my eyes darted to the raised privacy window. "I think that would jeopardize more than just my makeup."

He trailed his lips along the line of my jaw, to my neck, then along my collarbone to my shoulders, giving me soft, savoring kisses that had me wondering if it would really be so bad if we skipped the event entirely. My shoulders were bare as the dress was strapless, and he seemed to appreciate how much access this gave him to my skin. But he didn't bite, or suck, or do anything that might leave a telling mark.

Even so, the soft touches were making me dizzy, my pulse thrumming rapidly, my mind solely focused on his lips, which was probably why I didn't realize his hand had pushed up my skirt until he nudged my legs apart and pulled the lace of my underwear to one side.

"Are you wearing the red? The one from the photograph?" he demanded, his voice low, barely a grumble.

I nodded, meaning to say yes but all that came out was a high-pitched whimper. He was so good with his hands. His fingers were a miracle. I felt like I was melting, hot and unsteady and inured against everything but his touch.

"Do you love it? What I'm doing?"

"I love it. I do," I replied, panting.

His other hand slid up the back of my neck, tangled in my hair, and tugged sharply. "Don't come. Let me know when you're close."

"Don't come?" I squeaked. Was he serious?

"I want you wet all night. I want you to ache for me. I want to know, every time I look at you, that you're thinking about this moment. Do you know why?"

I shook my head mindlessly, tilting and rocking my hips, chasing my climax. But he must've realized how close I was, because his touch became light, teasing. He slid the tip of his tongue from my clavicle to my ear, and whispered, "Because it's all I'll be thinking about too."

With one more gentle kiss, he withdrew his hands completely, slowly and methodically righting the front of my skirt, and leaned back, leaving me hot and needy and incredibly frustrated.

My eyelashes fluttered open and I glared at him. "That wasn't very nice."

He brought his middle finger to his mouth, placed up to the first knuckle inside, and slowly sucked my arousal off his fingertip. "But you love it."

"I do."

He plucked my hand from my lap, bringing my wrist to his lips. "And you love me."

"I do."

"And so it wasn't very nice, but it was very good."

I nodded, unable to tear my eyes away from him, my heart beating like the wings of a hummingbird. Byron filled every space he entered in a way that had more to do with his intrinsic presence than with his height and size, he always had. I felt my breaths grow shallower the longer I stared.

This was what desire felt like—the pain, longing, frustration, the torture. I used to hate this feeling, but now I loved it, I wanted it, just as I loved and wanted him.

Our limo slowed while Byron was still pressing kisses along the thin skin on my wrist and the interior of my forearm and elbow. And when the limo came to a stop, he stilled and closed his eyes. His grip on my hand tightened, and I listened as he inhaled deeply.

"I don't want to do this," he said. "I won't be able to speak. I won't be able to think. I hate this."

"I know." Shifting the hand he held, I forced him to lift his chin. I wanted to press our foreheads together. "But I will be next to you. And I will be your voice and distract those who would seek to monopolize your attention. And I will kiss you and touch you."

"It's not fair that you have to rescue me again."

"I don't know about that." I played with the short strands of his hair at the back of his neck. "We're on the same team. If I pass you a ball, are you going to say no thank you? Or are you going to score a goal?"

He grunted, but I saw the beginnings of a reluctant smile eclipse his earlier misery.

"We will find a quiet, dark corner where we can be together, just the two of us."

"And what will we do there?" Byron angled his head back, his hands content to hold mine.

"Oh, I'm sure we'll figure something out." I winked at him just as the door on his side opened, noise and light and the smell of exhaust rushing in.

But Byron only had eyes for me, and his small smile didn't waver, not even when we left our bubble of contentment and the lights flashed and the crowd pressed forward. We were in this together, giving and receiving strength from the other, and it was so much more than I'd ever dared to dream, or ask for, or allowed myself to want.

EPILOGUE

BYRON

~Several Months Later~

"Did it bother you? When you read Mr. Lorher's article?"

I studied Ms. Ekker. She sat at the end of the rectangular table, Winnie at the corner on her left. I sat on Winnie's right. The woman's questions and manner continued to appear sincere and reasonable. Still, I debated how best to answer.

I'm terrible at predicting how people will react to my honesty because I don't believe I react normally to other people's honesty. It doesn't bother me, it doesn't typically hurt my feelings, it doesn't influence me one way or the other. It's a data point, and I don't feel pressured by it.

But what form of honesty would Ms. Ekker respond best to? This was the question Winnie had taught me to ask before replying to strangers.

"I didn't read the article," I replied honestly and accepted the hardcover book Winnie passed me.

"But your manager told you about it?" Ms. Ekker took notes and also used a transcription application on her phone. We were being recorded.

According to my manager and agent, Harry Lorher had managed to turn the three minutes we'd spent inside the elevator in New York into a ten-thousand-word article denouncing me as an entitled, no-talent hack.

"She did," I confirmed, glancing at my manager. Pamela stood by the door, ever the faithful guardian. She deserved a raise.

"What was your reaction to her description of the article?"

I shrugged, returning my attention to Ms. Ekker. "Why is it important?"

"I don't know that it is important," she said reasonably. "But if someone had printed that I utilized—and mistreated—ghostwriters for all my books, I'd be upset."

"He said, 'allegedly,'" I corrected. "He said I 'allegedly utilize and mistreat ghostwriters.' In reporter jargon, doesn't that make it acceptable? For example, I heard Mr. Lorher allegedly eats kittens for breakfast and spends his evenings as a bridge troll in Hampshire. Since I said allegedly, I do believe you can print that."

Ms. Ekker chuckled.

I gestured to Pamela by the door, letting her know I was ready for another reader to enter the room.

All of this—arranging the profile and interview with Jes Ekker, arranging to have me sign and inscribe the books my publisher had donated, arranging for the quiet room at the middle school so I could meet with each reader individually rather than being overwhelmed by hundreds of people all at once—had been Winnie's doing.

Weeks ago, Winnie had claimed that she did not excel at pushing people outside of their comfort zone. Either Winnie was ignorant to her own innate talent of encouraging others to try new experiences and be open to wonderful possibilities, or she was a liar.

Winnie was many things, but she was not a liar.

A man entered the room and I focused on smiling as he approached. Winnie had told me I looked handsome and more approachable when I smiled.

"Hello. I'm Byron."

"Hey. I'm David. Do you take credit card? Or—or cash?"

Glancing up from the book I'd been opening, I lifted an eyebrow at the odd question and responded with an equally odd answer. "Sorry, sir. I only accept items offered in trade—wheels of cheese, barrels of wine, livestock. No bushels of wheat or sacks of grain, though." I indicated to Winnie with a tilt of my head. "She's allergic."

"I—what?" The man gaped, his eyes revealing his panic. "You do?"

Despite my best efforts, my smile fell. "No. That was a joke." My delivery required work.

"Oh! Sorry. Ha ha." He laughed, visibly relieved, wiping his forehead. "Sorry. That's funny. I didn't expect you to be funny."

"No one does," I mumbled, flipping to the second of the title pages, poised to add my signature to it.

Win had talked me into the interview with Ms. Ekker during a moment of weakness (i.e. right after she'd given me a blow job and while she'd been naked) promising that I wouldn't be asked any questions about my parentage or my family, only about my life as a writer and the inspiration for my books.

She'd argued that giving an exclusive to a serious profile journalist—one who had a reputation for fairness and integrity—would satiate the public's curiosity about me, especially after the frenzy that had been the Jupiter Awards and Henry Lorher's unflattering account of our very special three-minute elevator ride of infamy.

Winnie nudged me with her elbow, a quiet rebuke. "You don't need to pay for the book, sir," she said, her customer service skills far superior to mine. "You already bought it via the auction."

Along with the purchase price of the signed book, the winners had been invited to a meet and greet, and for this opportunity they were more than happy to pay double. But to ensure I didn't feel overwhelmed, the winners who'd opted in waited in a separate area. Only one person at a time was allowed in this room for a chat and to have their book inscribed.

David gestured to me, but his eyes were on Winnie. "Oh. I don't need to pay for him to sign it?"

Like most people, I did quite enjoy being discussed in the third person.

"No. That was already included in the price." Winnie's hand came to my shoulder, likely sensing my irritation.

"Oh. Nice."

"Who should I make this out to? The same name as the purchaser?" I lifted the invoice, showing it to him.

He angled his head to read the paper. "No, that's my name. The book is for my son. S-T-E-P-H-E—"

"No." I stopped writing after the first letter. "My brain doesn't work like that."

"Like what?" Ms. Ekker asked.

"I cannot write letters or numbers as they're called out," I answered her question, then asked the gentleman, "What's your son's name?"

"Stephefen, with an 'F'."

I felt my eyes narrow along with the weight of Ms. Ekker's scrutiny. "Stefan?"

"No. Stephefen. But with an 'F'."

Acutely aware that I stared at the man with a face as blank as Mr. Lorhrer's list of accomplishments, and that Ms. Ekker watched the entire encounter, poised to capture it in all its ludicrous hilarity, I could do nothing. This man and his son's name had rendered me helpless.

After several harrowing seconds, I broke the awkward silence. "I surrender. I have no idea how to spell that name." It didn't sound like a human name. It sounded like the brand name of a pharmaceutical agent used to treat IBS. I didn't know what "step-a-pe-he-an" was or where an "F" might reside within it.

"Here, sir." Winnie's smiling voice cut in. "Could you write the name down on this piece of paper? Then Byron can use that."

"Sure," the man said, glancing between us.

I signed the book, I handed it over, I thanked the man for his support of Winnie's school, and he left.

As soon as the door closed behind him, Ms. Ekker asked, "Did you really tell Mr. Lohrer, quote, 'Anyone who purposefully reads your sedimentary fecal residue is a leeching shit stain and can also fuck off'?"

"I did." I accepted the next book from Winnie, turning to meet her gaze, and hoping she would read my mind and give me a kiss.

She gave me a wink instead.

I grunted.

"That seems harsh," the journalist said conversationally. "Do you usually tell people to fuck off?"

"No."

"Why is Mr. Lohrer so special? What did he do to earn your ire?"

"He is special because he harasses me with questions he has no right to ask." I sent the woman a meaningful look. "And, off the record, he's in love with his own self-importance and desperately longs for relevancy, which he's only ever achieved by representing delusions of grandeur and hysterics as truth. As well, given that he turned a three-minute elevator exchange—where thirty percent of my words were fuck and off—into a ten-thousand-word piece of electronic tripe, I suspect, like Victor Hugo, he gets paid by the word."

"Hmm," was Jes Ekker's only response besides her smile.

"What?" I glanced at Winnie, then back at the reporter. "Why are you smiling?"

"You're funny," she said. "I didn't expect you to be this funny."

"No one ever does," Winnie mumbled.

This time, when I looked at her, she did read my mind and gave me a kiss.

* * *

Friday nights were spent at Amelia and Winnie's apartment, playing a video game called *Stardew Valley* with a woman named Serena. She'd been a friend of theirs, and an acquaintance of mine, since undergrad. I enjoyed the game. Serena was fine. But I did grow weary of the three women comparing me to an NPC (non-player character) named Sebastian.

"Look! It's Byron! He's taking me out on his motorcycle," Serena called to us from the small kitchen table, her laptop open in front of her, as though we were three miles away instead of three meters. "This cutscene is so delightfully cheesy."

"You know, if you marry Byron—I mean, Sebastian—he makes you adopt a frog." Amelia sat on the other side of the kitchen table, across from Serena. "On the plus side, he'll sometimes make you coffee."

"Is this what I can expect if we marry?" Winnie rested her temple on my shoulder. "Frogs and coffee?"

Win and I sat next to each other on the floor of the family room, our laptops set on the coffee table. We'd decided as a group to move our weekly games to my house as soon as Jeff officially moved out.

Winnie hadn't told me about Jeff's actions the morning after our first kiss. Jeff had told me just last week, making a joke of it. He was now frantically searching for a new place to live as I'd threatened to place all his belongings in the road if he wasn't out by tomorrow.

It explained why Winnie had never wanted to spend any time at my awesome house. I'd been worried she didn't like my home and that I'd have to find someplace new, someplace she adored enough to consider, one day, sharing with me. Thus, I'd experienced both relief and anger when the real reason for her avoidance came to light. I could easily evict Jeff. But giving up my house would've pained me.

When I'd asked her why she hadn't told me about Jeff's actions, she could offer no explanation. I knew she did her best to communicate her wants and needs, but this revelation served as a good reminder that no lasting change occurs overnight.

She would probably always avoid difficult conversations; I would probably always avoid people; neither of us were perfect, but we were trying our utmost to be better.

Presently, I placed a kiss on her forehead and responded to her question about marrying me, I mean, Sebastian. “You know I want to move to the big city. People just don’t understand me in this small town.”

All three women laughed, and the conversation turned to how Amelia enjoyed giving trash to an NPC named Alex, the impressiveness of Winnie’s wine cellar, and Serena’s anxiety about iridium sprinklers.

I’d quickly learned with these three ladies, making fun of myself produced better results than broadcasting outward irritation at their antics. Oddly, after employing this approach over time, I found I rather enjoyed it too.

“Are you two done with all your challenge videos?” Amelia asked, turning in her chair to peer at us. “Or are you going to keep doing them now that Winnie has that hotshot job with Ethical Cosmetics?”

“There are three challenges we haven’t—uh—done, but we haven’t filmed any in months,” Winnie answered for both of us.

“Which three are left?” Amelia set her elbow on the back of the chair.

“Toxic Dance, Whisper A Secret, and Kiss Your Crush.” With the last, Winnie and I shared a glance.

I’d watched the video of our first kiss and what came after many times, especially on nights when she worked late, or days when her workload kept her from coming over at all. Any fears I’d possessed of my schedule and hyper focus on writing being a source of contention between us had evaporated at the initiation of the school year. Winnie was far, far busier than I.

“What about the leggings one? Didn’t you just post that?” Serena stood from the table, picking up her empty water glass and crossing to the sink.

“I’ve been posting the ones we have banked. The Leggings Challenge is the last one we have done, there are no others recorded.”

“You should do one tonight.” Amelia, still surveying us over the back of her chair, narrowed her eyes on me. “How about the Toxic Dance Challenge?”

I glared at my friend.

She smirked, standing from her chair. “Come on. We should probably end the game soon anyway. How about you two do the Toxic Dance Challenge and I’ll be the camerawoman?”

“Oh! I’ll play the song.” Abandoning her water glass on the kitchen counter, Serena pulled a phone from her back pocket.

Winnie glanced at me.

Tight smile on my face, I shrugged.

"Sure. I think I remember the steps," she said, standing and then offering me her hand. "Do you know what you're going to do?"

Nodding, I accepted her hand only so I could pull her forward for a kiss as soon as I was on my feet.

"Oh, don't worry about Byron." Amelia meandered into the family room, tapping through screens on her phone. "All those ballroom dancing classes? He's got moves."

Winnie laughed, obviously believing our mutual friend's words to be a joke. They were not a joke. I was an exceptional dancer.

When Winnie had given me the original list of challenges, I'd taken the time to research each one and watch several examples. Initially, I didn't know whether Win expected me to do the dance along with her, but I'd wanted to be prepared.

"I wish we had better light for this," Amelia said, lining up the shot while I pushed the coffee table out of the way.

The first notes of Britney Spear's song "Toxic" reverberated from Serena's cell phone and Winnie and I got into position, standing next to each other. I remembered most, if not all, of the steps and quickly scanned my memory, arranging them in order.

"Should we—should we do a practice one?" Win asked, pulling off her sweatshirt and tossing it to the couch, her question for Amelia.

Our friend shook her head. "No. I'm recording. It's almost time. And . . . go!"

And so I went.

Right arm over head. Lips. Touch. Body wave. Pull from waist. Heart hands. Drop. Cross hands. . .

In my peripheral vision, I could see that Winnie had stopped dancing the moment I did the drop, and I felt her shocked stare on me as I completed the steps. Meanwhile, in my forward vision, Serena's mouth had fallen open, her eyes widening to their maximum diameter.

Amelia, looking unsurprised and unperturbed, simply bobbed her head in time with the music until it was over. But when it was over, she punched her hand in the air and made a whooping noise.

"Damn, Byron. You need to try out for the next 'Magic Mike.'" Crossing the short distance, Amelia lifted her hand for a high five. I did not leave her hanging.

But Winnie's choking sounds soon had me glancing her way. Her mouth opened and closed, her gorgeous eyes round with surprise, but heating quickly. She grabbed the front of my shirt, her chest rising and falling with rapid breaths, and I read what was on her mind as though she'd spoken the words out loud.

"Amelia," she said, never taking her eyes from me. "I will give you a bonus of twenty thousand Chuck E. Cheese tokens if you clear everyone out of here in less than a minute."

I smiled at the memory even as my body hardened in response. The look in her eye, the intent, the need, were mirrors of mine. I never took for granted the moments I witnessed them reflected in her.

Not waiting for her roommate's response, Winnie dragged me by the shirtfront to her room, shoved me inside, and kicked the door closed with her foot. Then she attacked, leaping forward and jumping at my torso. I had no choice but to catch her and we both tumbled to her bed in a tangle of limbs and lips and grabbing hands.

Fuck. I loved this. I loved when she was hot for me. I loved when she became mindless in her pursuit of my submission, my loss of control. I loved how greedy she was when we touched, how she never seemed satisfied, her creativity, dedication, and curiosity.

So, fuck me, but right now, in this moment, I didn't know what I was waiting for.

"Byron—" she said between biting kisses. "Byron, *please.*" Straddling me, her hands shoved my shirt up and off, her nails scoring my chest. "I need you."

I groaned and fisted my hand in the hair at the back of her head, loving this spot and the control it gave me over the position of her head, how it forced her mouth open, how it pointed her eyes where I wanted them.

"What do you need, Win?" I pushed my hips up, wanting her to feel what she did to me.

She gasped in my mouth, her body tensing. "Where did you learn to dance like that?"

I didn't want to talk about dancing.

"Take your shirt off." I sat up and released her hair, my fingers moving to the front of her jeans, growling a curse when I encountered difficulty with the button. "And take these fucking things off."

"Yes, sir." I felt her shiver just before she stood, quickly moving to obey. "Anything else you want while I'm up?" she teased, yanking her tank top over her head and whipping off her jeans along with her underwear.

I watched her, my mouth watering at the sight of her body, my vision blurring everything in the room but her exquisite beauty, her cinnamon eyes, her vibrancy. She stole my breath each time our eyes met. She stole my thoughts with her laugh, rendered me unsophisticated and speechless with her touch.

So what THE FUCK are you waiting for?

My jeans off, my hands at the waistband of my boxer briefs, I paused, shaking my head to clear it. There must've been a reason. And it came to me as she unhooked her bra and threw it haphazardly behind her, rushing over again and tackling me once more.

We were always like this. Always frantic. Always mindless and starving for each other's bodies. I didn't want that for our first time. I wanted to make love to her.

Filling my hands with her breasts, I groaned, debating. "Win—"

"Me first," she said, biting kisses from my jaw to my neck to whisper, "Do you want me to sit on your face?"

I groaned again, a spike of pleasurable pain pressing along the base of my spine. "Wait, wait a minute."

"I don't want to wait," she whined, grinding herself against my cock, the fabric of my underwear the only barrier between us.

I need to gain control over the situation. I needed her to slow down. I was so fucking tired of waiting, of waking up in the middle of the night next to her, hard, desperate, the pain and ache of blinding desire, of wanting to be buried inside her sweet body but not yet trusting myself not to spend prematurely.

I wanted her to come. I *needed* her to come. Which meant I needed to be certain I would last.

"My face," I said through gritted teeth, reaching for her legs. "Come here."

I watched her breasts sway as she crawled up my body, spreading her legs over my mouth. Knowing exactly what to do, knowing precisely what she preferred, I made my tongue soft and flat and licked her like I was lapping up cream. And I enjoyed my view.

"Oh God—" she gasped, rolling her hips, tossing her head, arching her back.

She was already close, so close. I could feel it in her restlessness, the inelegance of her rhythm.

Now. Do it now. Make love to her now.

Wrapping my arms around her legs, I held her still and kissed the inside of her thigh. "Win."

"Yes?" She squirmed against my hold, wanting my lips and tongue.

I cleared my throat of all uncertainty and doubt, and said, "I'm checking in."

Her body stilled and she looked down at me, blinking. Then she blinked again, the unfocused quality of her gaze clearing, her lips parting with surprise.

I watched her chest rise and fall as realization dawned, quickly followed by a flicker of worry. "You want to . . .?"

She didn't finish her thought.

Keeping my eyes on hers, I gave the interior of her thigh another kiss, slower, softer than the first. "Yes," I said. "Do you?"

Winnie swallowed roughly, then nodded. Already shifting to the side, the movements were unhurried, her eyes wide and watchful. She reclined on her back, and I stood to remove my boxers, the gravity of the moment weighing me down.

She must've felt it too because she didn't reach for me like she usually did. She didn't tackle me or tease me. She simply lay there, her knees pressed together, arms draped over her breasts, eyes huge, and lips swollen from our earlier, frantic kisses. And when I pulled off my boxers, leaving them on the ground, her gaze lowered to my cock. Sucking in a silent breath, her body seemed to tremble as she released it.

I licked my lips, tasting her there, smelling her, my body pulsing, urging me to climb on top of her and between her legs, nestle myself in the wet heat of her pussy. And so I did. Studying her reactions carefully, I placed one knee on the bed and didn't miss how her lashes fluttered. She inhaled deeply again, this time holding the air in her lungs.

Using my arms to support my weight, I planked over her, watching her face. Her attention seemed to be fastened to the front of my body and I waited for her to open her legs, which she did upon releasing the breath she held. Lowering my hips to the cradle of hers, I felt her hitching breaths and watched her eyes close. She gritted her teeth.

Body rigid, breathing shallow, eyes squeezed shut—I frowned at her posture and expression. This didn't feel right. I found I needed to check in, and not because we'd agreed to do so. I *needed* it.

"Are you okay?" I whispered, holding still, waiting for her answer.

She gave her head a jerky nod.

My frown deepened. "Win. Open your eyes."

She swallowed, and then opened them. They were bracing.

"Win—"

"Just do it. Please."

Now I swallowed, my throat tight. "Are you dreading this?"

A little laugh burst out of her. "I am. But just this first time. I heard it's the worst, but it gets a lot better. I'm—I'm sorry."

"Don't be sorry. I'm dreading it too."

Winnie pressed her head back against the pillow, looking surprised. "You are?"

"Yes." I hadn't yet lowered myself fully between her legs and my arms began to shake with the effort of holding the plank position.

Her features seemed to relax at my confession, her gaze warming. "Why? Are you afraid I have teeth in my vagina?"

It was my turn to laugh. "No. You have teeth in your mouth and those don't scare me."

She made a biting movement, nipping at my lips. "Then why?"

"Because," I confessed hoarsely, "I can't predict how it'll end."

She stared at me, her expression warming, then heating, a small smile tilting her mouth up on one side. "It's not going to end," she whispered. "This isn't the end. This isn't the beginning either."

"Then what is it?"

Her hands lifted, touching me for the first time since I climbed over her. One palm settled on my ass while the other reached around to my front. She fisted me and my eyes rolled back, my arms bending by degrees as she guided me forward.

"It's the middle," she said, stroking me, spreading her legs wider and tilting her hips in offering. "Make love to me, Byron." Winnie kissed my eyelids, my nose. "Make love to me."

Swallowing thickly, I opened my eyes to find her watching me, grounding me, anchoring me, telling me that her love for me would be as constant and eternal as my admiration and love for her.

And so I said, "Make love to me too, Win."

"I will." Winnie's chin wobbled even as she smiled, and then she promised me, "Always."

The End

AUTHORS NOTE

STEM stands for: Science, technology, engineering, and mathematics.

While I follow the news closely regarding the subjects covered in this book, when I began my research in earnest, I refreshed my knowledge by immersing myself in peer-reviewed / published articles on the subject of women in STEM (under grad rates, post grad, positions held, senior positions held, faculty positions held, etc. etc.). The subsection / list of references is included below because: A) I found these articles particularly interesting, B) they're all fairly recent (within the last five years), and C) I like to bring receipts.

That said, if you want to skip over my receipts (i.e. you don't enjoy skimming through abstracts on pubmed), there's a nice summary from the US Census (Census.gov) on the status of Women in STEM fields within the USA entitled, *Women Are Nearly Half of U.S. Workforce but Only 27% of STEM Workers* by Anthony Martinez and Cheridan Christnacht (2021)

If you'd prefer a private research source rather than a publicly-funded one, check out Pew Research (not peer reviewed) on the current stats regarding women in STEM fields as of 2021, *STEM Jobs See Uneven Progress in Increasing Gender, Racial and Ethnic Diversity*. Of note, if you stop reading this article after the first few sentences, you'll walk away thinking all is well. Please don't. Dig deeper and read the actual percentages. Just because women make up 74% of the positions in Health Care doesn't mean it's okay that they account for only 15% of engineering jobs, or 25%

of technology jobs, or 40% of physical science jobs. On a positive note, life science jobs (such as biologists) are *almost* parity (at 47% female). However, a 74% overall stake in health care requires additional investigation to obtain the full picture. Higher profile positions are still (by a very large margin) filled by men. ". . . women are just 38% of physicians and surgeons, up 2 percentage points from 2016. They are 33% of dentists, up 3 percentage points from 2016. Among optometrists, 46% are women." (Pew, 2021)

If you're more interested in current numbers of women undergraduates in STEM, this article from United Nations Educational, Scientific and Cultural Organization (go to unesco.org) provides a short summary, *CRACKING THE CODE: Girls' and women's education in science, technology, engineering and mathematics (STEM)* which references the book on the subject with the same title (ISBN 978-92-3-100233-5).

Select list of references / articles of interest:

1. Bettina J Casad et. al. (2021) *Gender inequality in academia: Problems and solutions for women faculty in STEM*; J Neurosci Res
2. Brittany Bloodhart (2020) *Outperforming yet undervalued: Undergraduate women in STEM*; PLoS One
3. Ruth van Veelen et. al. (2019) *Double Trouble: How Being Outnumbered and Negatively Stereotyped Threatens Career Outcomes of Women in STEM*; Psychol; Feb 19;10:150;
4. Noonan, R. (2017). *Women in STEM: 2017 Update*. ESA Issue Brief# 06–17. Office of the Chief Economist, Economics and Statistics Administration, U.S. Department of Commerce
5. Riegle-Crumb C., & Morton K. (2017). *Gendered expectations: Examining how peers shape female students' intent to pursue STEM fields*. Frontiers in Psychology
6. Leaper C., & Starr C. R. (2019). *Helping and hindering undergraduate women's STEM motivation: experiences With STEM encouragement, STEM-related gender bias, and sexual harassment.* Psychology of Women Quarterly
7. (2018) Why Public Service Loan Forgiveness Is So Unforgiving; NPR
8. (2019) Broken Promises: Teachers Sue U.S. Over Student Loans That Weren't Forgiven; NPR

File under tragic: According to the National Education Association, the 2018-2019 average public teacher salary for the United States is $61,730. Teachers who have master's degrees have $50,000 in student loan debt, on average.

Moving on . . .

One random note, the word "fiduciary" in the context of the blurb ("… and his financial portfolio is the stuff of fiduciary wet dreams.") assumes the reader will understand that "fiduciary" in this context refers back to "financial portfolio" and therefore is a financial advisor in charge of Byron's investments. I thought "fiduciary's wet dreams" sounded better than "fiduciary financial investments manager's wet dreams."

As an author, I am always learning (and surprised by) where the line exists with readers regarding how much they are able / willing to read into a word that is nonspecific in nature. Fiduciary doesn't always refer to financial matters, but often does. Random aside, Registered Investment Advisors are legally required to follow the fiduciary standard, but not all investment advisors are fiduciaries. Do yourself a favor and ask if your financial advisor is a fiduciary (if or when you have one).

Anyway . . . let's talk about Winnie and Byron (but not Bruno).

Byron is based on several people. I never planned to write his point of view because he seemed like a real pain in the ass. But the moment I finished chapter 8, Byron showed up, loud and persistent in my brain, wanting to tell his side of the story. Curious where he'd take me, I let him have his chapter, believing it'd be a one-and-done situation, that I'd save it for bonus material but not include it in the book. Well, he didn't like that *AT ALL,* and so Ten Trends became a dual POV book. That being said, writing for him was an excruciating experience. He was incredibly exacting, all his words and thoughts had to be transcribed precisely, or else he'd brood and stare and sneer and make me uncomfortable.

Winnie is based on one person (not me), but her feelings and perceptions on women in STEM were based on more than just the one specific person she was inspired by. She was a damn delight to write, though often frustrated me with her fear of upsetting others. But this trait was true to the person who inspired her, one of the kindest, most understanding individuals on the planet, but also the least likely to rock a boat when they could just as easily row it to shore and get out themselves. Super capable people seem to be this way (is my opinion / in my experience). They're very, "Oh, I don't want to bother you. I'll just make seven hundred cupcakes myself, move an entire house of furniture, and learn brain surgery before tomorrow. Don't worry about it."

As always, I feel I must include the statement that no one person or fictional book character is a monolith. Each person's experience with life, a disorder, a disease, a struggle, a success, a career, etc. etc. will be as different and varied as the snowflakes that fall from the sky. If you or someone you know has been diagnosed with a sensory processing disorder and their path deviates from Byron's, I am not surprised. He is his own unique snowflake and gets to have his own unique snowflake experience.

OTHER THINGS!

This book was supposed to be 90k words. It is over 150k words. Though I do extensively plot my books, this was the first time I felt like I had no control regarding the word count and found myself constantly surprised by the journey between plot points. These two will forever go down as the most surprising and unexpected couple I've written. (At least, I hope they will. God save me if there are more surprises to come.)

Something else: A few short months after I was diagnosed as being on the autism spectrum, I was speaking with a teacher friend of mine who was in charge of a special education program at a public school (let's call her Rachel). I mentioned that I found the diagnosis "suspicious" (i.e. I was distrustful of the diagnosis) and Rachel chuckled and told me, "I knew you were on the spectrum since the first moment we met." And when I asked her why she never said anything (because I honestly had no idea) she said, "Sometimes, people aren't ready to know these kinds of things about themselves and I wouldn't be doing them—or our friendship—any favors by telling them."

I thought that was interesting in the context of Winnie telling Byron her suspicions, whether she was right or wrong to tell him she believed he had sensory difficulties, so I'm mentioning it.

Thank you Iveta. You're the best editor of all time. Fact.

Thank you also to my readers, Chelsea, Lee, and Amy. I appreciate your invaluable insight into the inner workings of the human brain.

Until next time,

--Penny

ABOUT THE AUTHOR

Penny Reid is the *New York Times*, *Wall Street Journal*, and *USA Today* bestselling author of the Winston Brothers and Knitting in the City series. She used to spend her days writing federal grant proposals as a biomedical researcher, but now she writes kissing books. Penny is an obsessive knitter and manages the #OwnVoices-focused mentorship incubator / publishing imprint, Smartypants Romance. She lives in Seattle Washington with her husband, three kids, and dog named Hazel.

Come find me -
Mailing List: http://pennyreid.ninja/newsletter/
Goodreads:http://www.goodreads.com/ReidRomance
Facebook: www.facebook.com/pennyreidwriter
Instagram: www.instagram.com/reidromance
Twitter: www.twitter.com/reidromance
Patreon: https://www.patreon.com/smartypantsromance
Email: pennreid@gmail.com …hey, you! Email me ;-)

OTHER BOOKS BY PENNY REID

Knitting in the City Series

(Interconnected Standalones, Adult Contemporary Romantic Comedy)

Neanderthal Seeks Human: A Smart Romance (#1)

Neanderthal Marries Human: A Smarter Romance (#1.5)

Friends without Benefits: An Unrequited Romance (#2)

Love Hacked: A Reluctant Romance (#3)

Beauty and the Mustache: A Philosophical Romance (#4)

Ninja at First Sight (#4.75)

Happily Ever Ninja: A Married Romance (#5)

Dating-ish: A Humanoid Romance (#6)

Marriage of Inconvenience: (#7)

Neanderthal Seeks Extra Yarns (#8)

Knitting in the City Coloring Book (#9)

Winston Brothers Series

(Interconnected Standalones, Adult Contemporary Romantic Comedy, spinoff of Beauty and the Mustache)

Beauty and the Mustache (#0.5)

Truth or Beard (#1)

Grin and Beard It (#2)

Beard Science (#3)

Beard in Mind (#4)

Beard In Hiding (#4.5)

Dr. Strange Beard (#5)

Beard with Me (#6)

Beard Necessities (#7)

Winston Brothers Paper Doll Book (#8)

Hypothesis Series

(New Adult Romantic Comedy Trilogies)

Elements of Chemistry: ATTRACTION, HEAT, and CAPTURE (#1)

Laws of Physics: MOTION, SPACE, and TIME (#2)

Irish Players (Rugby) Series – by L.H. Cosway and Penny Reid

(Interconnected Standalones, Adult Contemporary Sports Romance)

The Hooker and the Hermit (#1)

The Pixie and the Player (#2)

The Cad and the Co-ed (#3)

The Varlet and the Voyeur (#4)

Dear Professor Series

(New Adult Romantic Comedy)

Kissing Tolstoy (#1)

Kissing Galileo (#2)

Ideal Man Series

(Interconnected Standalones, Adult Contemporary Romance Series of Jane Austen Reimaginings)

Pride and Dad Jokes (#1, coming 2022)

Man Buns and Sensibility (#2, TBD)

Sense and Manscaping (#3, TBD)

Persuasion and Man Hands (#4, TBD)

Mantuary Abbey (#5, TBD)

Mancave Park (#6, TBD)

Emmanuel (#7, TBD)

Handcrafted Mysteries Series

(A Romantic Cozy Mystery Series, spinoff of *The Winston Brothers Series*)

Engagement and Espionage (#1)

Marriage and Murder (#2)

Home and Heist (#3, coming 2023)

Baby and Ballistics (TBD)

Pie Crimes and Misdemeanors (TBD)

Good Folks Series

(Interconnected Standalones, Adult Contemporary Romantic Comedy, spinoff of *The Winston Brothers Series*)

Totally Folked (#1)

Folk Around and Find Out (#2, coming 2022)

Three Kings Series

(Interconnected Standalones, Holiday-themed Adult Contemporary Romantic Comedies)

Homecoming King (#1)

Drama King (#2, coming Christmas 2022)

Prom King (#3, coming Christmas 2023)

Standalones

Ten Trends to Seduce Your Best Friend

Made in the USA
Columbia, SC
01 May 2022